Mary Ann,   *April 26/09*

Los Angeles Festival
of Books.
Chase the dream
not the competition.
Robert Preston Walker

Mr. Smoke is dedicated to my family.
For all that you have taught me, thank you.

W9-CYA-880

Mr. Smoke

by Robert Preston Walker

authorHOUSE®

AuthorHouse™
1663 Liberty Drive, Suite 200
Bloomington, IN 47403
www.authorhouse.com
Phone: 1-800-839-8640

First published by AuthorHouse   11/6/2008

ISBN: 978-1-4389-2248-5 (sc)
ISBN: 978-1-4389-2249-2 (hc)

Printed in the United States of America
Bloomington, Indiana

This book is printed on acid-free paper.

Acclaim for Mr. Smoke

I have read many fine books of fiction over the years, many with interesting plots and story lines. Few have come close to the story of **Mister Smoke**, as told by Robert Walker. It is a gripping tale of international intrigue, mystery and science fiction that will keep you glued to the pages. It was as if I were actually present in the vivid scenes, standing beside **Mr. Smoke** as his story unfolded before me. My hat is off to Robert for creating such an interesting character and placing him along with equally brilliant supporting characters into a plot as twisting as a mountain back road on a moonless night.

George Ethridge,
Golf Shores. Corydon, Indiana

I have read the manuscript of **Mr. Smoke** and would like to share, with all of you, some of my reactions.

Many feel that today's world suffers from overpopulation. All I can say is, "Move over world and make room for a new grand hero, **Mr. Smoke**! To say this story is 'smokin' (which it is!), is a gross understatement. Excellent characters, excellent plot, and I have to stop and remember that these are fictional!

Bravo, Mr. Walker, for supplying a wonderfully suspenseful and enchanting ride. I can not stop thinking and caring for these characters and am even imagining what is going on with them, even after the book has ended!

Robert, thank you so much for involving me in this project. I have the highest expectations for its success. It ranks with the best of the best.

Joe Peery
Joe Peery Group. Louisville, KY

In praise of Mr. Smoke by Wordsmith: Robert Preston Walker

I have often wondered what makes a novel a New York Times Best Seller. I think I know now. It is a novel that makes you think. That makes the people in it come alive and step outside the pages and into your heart and mind. That makes you relate to the people in the book, whether you like or agree with them or not.

A book that has a beginning, middle and an end that somehow comes together to bring closure to the story being spun by the tale spinner. A novel that makes you want to re-read and re-experience it again.

Mr. Smoke is such a story, told by master story teller, Robert Preston Walker. I *experienced* each Scene. I found I wanted to rush Mr. Smoke, but couldn't. I savored it, instead. You can't explain a taste. Each person has to experience it for themselves.

I call the author *Wordsmith*, because his words hammered into my brain. I laughed, I cried, I cheered and I raged. Robert left me satisfied, yet still wanting more.

Mark my words, world. Mr. Smoke by Mr. Walker is the next New York Times Best Seller in fiction. I look forward to a sequel.

John Isherwood
Calgary, Alberta Canada

Acknowledgements

My thanks to my test readers, John Isherwood, George Etheridge, Joe Peery, and a dear friend who wishes to remain anonymous. I would also like to thank Authorhouse, my publisher. I really don't know how to thank each and every one of them, except by thanking them in print. Special thanks to my beautiful wife, Karen, for her vital and impartial input. Well, not really impartial. A bigger fan, I've never had. Can you believe she wants an autographed copy of the first run? Now that's a fan! All three sons, Damon, Brandon and Tanner are expecting one also. The only one who hasn't asked for one, yet was beside me all the way, is Grace Catherine Walker. Also known as Thumper. Our cat. She would sit be me for hours as I worked on the story. Thank you, Thumper. I mean, Grace. I wish each and every one of you out there could have the kind of support that I have had with my labor of love, called Mr. Smoke.

Mr. Smoke

by Robert Preston Walker

Choices. Do you ever wonder about your choices in life? Are we *ever* in control of our destiny, or does destiny control us? These were the thoughts running through his mind as he looked out over the clouds, while the plane hurtled through the skies at over 600 miles per hour, on its way from New York City to London.

"Looks like you could get out and walk on them, doesn't it?" a soft musical female voice asked. He turned to find an exceptionally beautiful flight attendant bent over and looking out the window over his shoulder.

An old memory flashed across his mind's eye.

▲ ▲ ▲

The small young boy was looking out of the airplane window at the clouds below, as the plane sailed high above them across the open sky on an ocean of air. The flight attendant offered him refreshments.

"What is your name, young man?" she asked, when he respectfully declined.

"Damon Gray, ma'am."

He turned to his father.

"Dad, if I believe enough, could I step out of this plane and walk across those clouds?"

His father didn't smile or mock what he asked, as many parents would.

"No Damon, you couldn't." the flight attendant answered for the parent. "You would fall right through them!"

The child cast a surprised glance up at her and then returned to look at his sire.

After a slight pause, his father spoke. "In a small sense, she is accurate son." He spoke the words slowly, so that there would be no misunderstanding. He also looked straight at his son when he spoke. "Although with belief and knowledge, you could! Are you referring to what your mother said yesterday?"

"Yes, I was wondering if------" What he was about to say was interrupted by the flight attendant.

"Excuse me, but I am not *accurate in a small sense*, I'm *accurate* in a *very large sense*. I'll have you know that I have a Masters Degree in Quantum Physics at NYU. I don't think *sir,* that you should mislead your son!" The *'sir'* had a slight note rise in pitch, indicating derision.

Ignoring her, John continued, "What were you trying to say son, before the interruption?"

Before the boy could start to speak, the woman spoke again. "I wasn't trying to *interrupt*; I was just trying to *help*!" Her tone was that of exasperation, as if it was *obvious* what she was trying to do, what her *credentials* were, and that *he* should be more courteous.

Without a word, Nobel Prize winner Dr. John Gray, with doctorates in every major field including Quantum Physics, reached into his vest pocket, produced a business card and handed it to the woman and said firmly yet politely, "Please, Gertrude, *go away!*"

Gertrude, the flight attendant, opened her mouth to speak, looked at the card, and with her mouth still hanging open, walked away.

▲ ▲ ▲

Even after almost thirty years, the memory could almost make him smile. Something he didn't do enough, he admitted to himself.

"Yes it does." he responded. She straightened up.

"Would you like any refreshments, sir?"

"No thank you, but I could use an extra pillow."

"Right away, sir." A moment later, "Here you are, sir. Anything else, sir?"

"No, thank you."

She stood there. He looked up at her, quizzically.

She *still* stood there looking down at him with her dazzling turquoise eyes. *'A very unique eye shade.'* He thought to himself.

"Yes?" he asked.

"Aren't you Doctor Gray? Of course you're *a* Doctor Gray. I saw *that* on the passenger list. Your name and the other gentleman, Mr. Garret Hastings. What I meant to say is, are you Doctor Gray, the Gray Ghost?"

"And what Gray Ghost would that be?" he asked politely, with a blank expression.

She blushed, shaking her head, her heavy golden pony tail waving back and forth.

"What a *fool* I must seem." She laughed infectiously. "I'm sorry, I didn't mean to intrude. It's just that, if you *are* the famous Composer Pianist, the one who's performing tomorrow night with the London Philharmonic Orchestra, that I couldn't get tickets to because they are sold out, I wanted to ask you for your autograph. You see, I'm studying for and finishing off my Masters Degree in Music at NYU, and …." Her voice faded off in embarrassment. It rose again, "Of course you can't be *that* Doctor Gray, you're *much* too young! He's been around forever! I'm terribly sorry for bothering you, sir."

"No bother, Sylvia." He stated quietly, flatly. He opened his thick, chunky, outdated Mac PowerBook laptop computer and started typing.

△ △ △

3

"Could I have your attention, *please!* Would a *Sylvia Glockenhausen* please report to the Lost and Found! I repeat, would a Sy*lvia Glockenhausen* please report to the Lost and Found! Thank you."

Due to the inclement weather and heavy air traffic, the plane landed *late* at London's Heathrow International Airport, and Sylvia was in a hurry to meet her fiancé for a dinner engagement. Leaving the plane in a rush, she was surprised to hear her name paged over the intercom.

'*Damn!*' she thought. '*I must have forgotten something on board the plane.*' She undid her pony tail and shook out her hair as she hurried to the Lost and Found, and waited impatiently for someone to help her. Finally one of the personnel came up to her, asked her for her name and identification, and then handed her a small parcel with her name on it. Her full name: Ms. Sylvia Beatrice Glockenhausen!

Inside were two tickets to his concert the following night, with attached *back stage passes* and a signed copy of Doctor Gray's latest CD.

It read:

> *Thanks for the compliment Sylvia,*
> *Damon Gray*

▲ ▲ ▲

"After what you have described to me, he sounds like a bit of a *cold fish*. How in the world did he know your full name?" Michael Brighton asked his fiancé, over dinner that night, after she told him the story.

"You know, Mickey, I was so excited about getting the tickets and signed CD, I never really thought about it! That *is* strange! And you're absolutely right; he was a *cold fish*, as you so quisintly put it, with your wonderfully cute British accent."

"*Quisintly?*"

"You asked me not to say *ain't*, didn't you?" She smiled mischievously.

They pride themselves in their moral superiority. They claim that they are *Gods chosen instruments* in the war for racial purity.

As such, they piously consider *all* EH's Soulless.

Their stories matched what the EH Society had known for centuries.

Damon's Grandparents told him of their lives.

▲ ▲ ▲

David & Elizabeth Gray (not their names then) had escaped Germany to England just after Hitler had gained power.

They were the product of a long line of European *Enhanced Humans*. David and Elizabeth were the products of countless generations of *EH designed selective breeding*. They were born with and had *Abilities* and *Talents* beyond those of normal people. They were the result of, and part of, a centuries old Society of Others with *Gifts*.

One or more of the *EH Society* had been converted to Adolf Hitler's cause, and told him of their small *EH Society*. They gave him the idea of a super race. Hitler became obsessed with creating a super race, but he wanted *his* idea of a super race. Although they were *Gifted* with *Abilities and Talents*, the EH Society were not the physically perfect specimens Hitler had in mind. Therefore, they were a threat to his idea of the perfect human race that he wanted to create. The *EH* converts were taken, interrogated and then killed.

They gave all the *EH* names they knew. And, at the end, friends that weren't. They were not high in the *EH* Society, so were not privy to all the EH's in Europe.

It was enough for Hitler.

All known and suspect *EH* were to be exterminated. Adolf gave the order.

The German Secret Police had killed both David & Elizabeth's parents and were looking for them when the *Society* contacted them in their honeymoon hotel room and informed them. The *Society* assisted them in their escape. They provided them with the forged documents that they needed to flee the country. The young newlywed couple fled to England.

They met with Damons other grandparents, Eric and Irene McAllister (again, not their names then) in London, with whom they and their family had been in contact with for many years, through the *Society*.

David and Elizabeth's parents knew that Hitler was insane and were planning on fleeing Germany with their married children. They had been smuggling money and assets to Eric and Irene's parents for awhile. They had smuggled the bulk of their family wealth out of Germany, prior to David and Elizabeth's fleeing. They were killed by the SS, before they could flee with their children.

When David and Elizabeth fled Germany, the *Society* thought they were broke and had offered to advance them funds. They respectfully declined. They said that they would like to make it on their own.

In England, both Eric and Irene's parents had been killed in suspicious, supposedly random accidents. They were also a part of the Society. They, along with their offspring, Eric and Irene, also were highly *Gifted*. They jointly owned a large real estate company and owned many properties, which Eric and Irene inherited.

The four, the Gray's and McAllister's, decided to flee to America and disassociate themselves totally from the *EH Society*. It had been breached. To what extent, they didn't know. Both couples had been trained to be paranoid. Centuries of being hunted and killed had sharpened their survival instincts.

All *known EH's* were monitored by the *Society*. They were *known*. They had great *Abilities* and *Talents*. They could have *no* trails leading to them.

They could not afford to just disappear, so *they killed themselves*. It was a brilliantly simple plan. Find dead homeless people who closely matched them, dress them in their clothes with identification, then shoot and batter them, making it seem like a robbery, mugging, or

$Scene$ Six

S hortly after the plane crash that killed Damon's grandparents, in New York City, in a football stadium sized room in a monstrous high rise building, William Housteader sat in his hereditary chair as Head of Operations of the EHE Organization.

Today he sat in judgment.

The Two Hundred were present or represented. His position in the front and center of the room was elevated, so that everyone seated could see him clearly. His Chair and podium was situated in the middle and on top of an eight foot square, blood red, stone podium. Engraved into the front of it was a beautiful two handed engraved sword, overlaid with an engraved double bladed spear, in an X pattern.

The initials EHE were engraved before, over and after the X. The initials stood for Enhanced Human Exterminators. William knew that the initials were added only a few hundred years previously. The stone itself was from an unknown age, the engravings on the blades of a dead language, known only to *eleven* of the Two Hundred. The Head and his ten Cells. The markings meant the same thing as the initials.

He looked down at the man and woman standing in judgment before him. They stared back at him defiantly. They thought they knew him. They were wrong. Oh, *so* wrong.

His heart was heavy. He felt sick to his stomach. They thought they knew him, just like he thought he knew them. He was wrong also!

Though he knew who they were, William Housteader didn't know them anymore.

They were his son, Justin and his wife Nelly.

Where had he gone wrong? *How* had he messed up as a father? He had his son, Justin, trained by the *best of the best* to take over as the Head of Operations after William stepped down.

Looking down at them, he remembered fourteen years ago.

Scene Seven

Unbeknownst to Damon or his Grandparents, the bombing that killed Damon's parents was done by a young and extremist husband and wife team in the EHE.

Because the husband was the son of the Head of Operations of the EHE, they weren't killed, as normally would have been the case. Justin and Nelly were severely punished for it, because they had provided *no proof* that Damons parents were *EH*. Plus they killed *innocents!* The Gray's weren't even on the *EH* List. They had been investigated after their death and had come up *clean*.

The reason for coming up clean was that, years earlier, John and Mary Gray had saved the lives of the young New Head of the EHE, William Housteader, his pregnant wife, Samantha and unborn son, Justin.

Damon's father and mother had been on vacation, innocently driving behind the Housteader car, when an explosion blew the Housteader car off the road and over a cliff to land thirty meters below.

John Gray had immediately stopped the car, and he and Mary scrambled down the side the cliff and removed them from the blazing twisted wreckage. John provided immediate medical care and then he and Mary made the trip up the treacherous cliff, carrying and placing them in their car.

27

He then broke every speed limit driving them to the nearest Hospital. It was a small town Hospital in a small French town. The Hospital did not want to admit them, as they did not have a doctor on staff qualified to render the kind of immediate assistance the couple needed.

John took immediate charge and admitted them. He showed the Head of the Hospital his and his wife's credentials. The hospital head was satisfied. William Housteader and his wife Samantha were still unconscious when they were admitted. William had broken bones and medium to mild burns to most of his body. John set the bones. The hospital could handle the burns.

Samantha Housteader was a different story. Immediate action had to be taken.

Without either of the (then) unknown patients consent, and with his wife assisting, Doctor John Gray performed immediate life saving and reconstructive surgery on Samantha Housteader.

Dr. Gray had an intern doctor play camera man, from beginning to end, with John's vacation video camera. He talked briefly at the beginning about the condition of William's wife and what had to be done in order to save her life, and the life inside her. Neither William nor Sammi knew at that time that she was pregnant. Stills were taken before and after the surgery to show as proof why the operations were needed. After the immediate dangers were taken care of, Dr. Gray used Samantha's passport photograph as a guide to reconstruct her unrecognizable face. John's running commentary told of why it had to be done immediately and exactly what he was doing.

William regained consciousness shortly after the operation on his wife. He awoke to find John and Mary monitoring his vital signs. They introduced themselves and explained what had happened, why they were there, and what part they had played in the incident.

John told William that he and Mary had filled out a police report and that the Police were waiting to question him. William was also provided with John's business card with his private number hand written on it, in case he needed to be contacted. He was provided with and told about the video, and that transportation had been arranged to take both he and his wife to a major medical facility for the balance of their recovery. John also gave William a highly specific rehabilitation program, for each of them, for William to give the new hospital. John suggested strongly that it be followed to the letter. William agreed and made sure it was.

When William asked what he owed them, they both laughed and Mary just patted his hand and said, "Just get better and have a wonderful life." With that, they left.

At first with questions about the surgery and later just to talk, William and John became friends.

It was a *special* friendship that William Housteader kept private.

▲ ▲ ▲

Although police and the EHE organization investigations were inconclusive and no one claimed responsibility, William felt, inside himself, that *EH's* were behind the car bombing. William had been well trained from birth to hate *EH's* and he hated them with a passion that went well past the borders of *psychotic*. After years of investigations on the part of the *EHE*, the bombers were found and captured. They were not *EH!* They were assassins hired by someone in the *EHE* Organization, to take out the new Head of the *EHE*, so that he could take over. The assassins told all. It was William's right hand man Steven Johanson, the one who would take over the *power*, if something was to happen to William before his offspring were old enough to take over.

Steven was taken out of his home while eating dinner with his family one evening and taken to a waiting William. He plead innocence at first, but when he saw the instruments of torture, he confessed. William still had him tortured to find out if there were any co-conspirators. There were none.

Steven was tried and convicted by the Two Hundred and suffered a fate worse than death. He was kept alive, and was forced to watch, as all of his family was killed in front of him. He was totally insane when they mercifully killed him.

A message to all of the Two Hundred, *sanctioned by* the Two Hundred.

▲ ▲ ▲

Scene Eight

William Housteader came out of his reverie and looked down at his son and his wife. They had no children. She had wanted none. It would have interfered with her killing *EH's.*

By accident, Justin found out about the secret friendship shared between his father and John Gray. When he told his new young wife of it, she told Justin that it was a secret friendship *because* the Grays *must* be *EH.*

In full violation of *EHE* policy, they did the restaurant bombing on impulse, to impress William. Justin bragged to his father about it, as well as others in the *EHE.*

To protect himself and his wife, William had no choice but to call a disciplinary hearing before the *Two Hundred.* The Two Hundred only met when something of immense importance happened that affected the *EHE* Organization. The son of the Head of the EHE killing innocent people, *for no justifiable cause,* was just such a reason.

The disciplinary hearing was extremely intensive and had overwhelmingly proved the couples unstable characters. Even William was satisfied with the findings.

Without Justin and his wife present, William was told unanimously, by the *Two Hundred,* that they would *not* allow or entrust Justin to succeed him as Head of Operations of the *EHE.* William would have to choose another. They informed him that, if he had *not* been the son of William Housteader, Justin and his wife would have been put to death for what they did. William told none of this to his son.

Justin and his wife were put in minor positions in the organization. Fourteen years later, while they were out drinking, Justin found out from his cousin, Leroy Housteader, that when the time came for William Housteader to step down as Head of Operations of *EHE*, he would bequeath his position to his nephew, Leroy.

Justin and his wife Nelly went ballistic! They blamed Damon's whole family for their disgrace in the eyes of the *EHE* Organization. Had the family been proven *EH*, they would have been heroes!

On their way to celebrate his 28th Birthday, Damons Grandparents died in an oversea airplane explosion, orchestrated and conducted by Justin & Nelly Housteader. In their twisted minds, it was strictly a revenge killing, perfectly justifiable.

Because he was William Housteader's only child, Justin knew that he would get away with the bombing. He purposely leaked the information to the *EHE* Organization of what he had done, knowing it would embarrass his father. He also let it be known that they were going to wipe out the whole family line, by killing Damon also. That would help atone for the problems they had caused Justin and Nelly, by *not* being *EH*.

William had acted immediately. On their way to kill Damon after the brutal murder of Damon's Grandparents and all the other airline passengers and personnel, the pair were caught and brought before the *EHE* Board of Directors.

Again they had no proof of the Grandparents *EH* Status. When asked why they did it, Justin said, "Ask my father. I should be sitting where he is."

▲ ▲ ▲

Looking down with tears in his eyes, William said goodbye to his son from his chair. The couple was carried kicking and screaming from the room, uttering threats and pleas.

They were *exterminated*. A message to all *EHE,* that the wonton killing of *Normals* would *not* be tolerated.

All members were told, by William Housteader, that Damon Gray was *Off Limits.*

▲ ▲ ▲

William Housteader *knew* that Nobel Prize winners Dr. John and Dr. Mary Gray were on the suspect *EH* list. He had them thoroughly checked out after being released from the hospital after the car bombing. Nothing conclusive, just suspicions that anyone of notoriety would get. He was completely satisfied that they were *not EH.* He also would not let himself believe that the people who saved both his and his wife's lives, as well as their unborn son's, could be *EH.*

He personally, and secretly, removed their names from the list along with anyone related to them and destroyed all suspect and possibly potential incriminating evidence.

That was the reason he kept his friendship with John a secret. It would pose a danger to him and his family, if anyone found out about it. And it was also why he never mentioned it to John in any of their conversations.

As the years went by, William unconsciously hinted to John about his organization in their conversations. John listened and asked no questions.

▲ ▲ ▲

Because of this knowledge, Damon's parents and Grandparents studied laboriously, almost fanatically, to gain the knowledge they needed to manipulate their offspring's DNA to add and increase his abilities, thus his chances of survival.

With the input of their parents and supremely confident in their *own* extraordinary *Talents and Abilities,* John and Mary Gray altered, changed and added to Damon's DNA while still in the womb. They did not think they went radical in their manipulations. If anything, they felt that they were conservative.

They were initially shocked to find that the new *abilities* created additional *unknown abilities*, due to a crossover pathway effect. They were to find out that the new *unknown abilities* would bring them closer to Damon than either parent anticipated. John & Mary had a special psychic bond with Damon. Telepathic. Even in the womb.

▲ ▲ ▲

liability. Who the fuck could have done this to one of our coldest killers?') None of this showed on his face as he put on a smile.

"Now, now, Sean, don't get me wrong! I know that you're loyal. The reason that you've got to make one more drop is so that we can catch this Mr. Smoke character." (*'Before he can do any more morale damage.'* Frank thought.) "Now you can understand that, can't you?"

"Can't we use someone else, please? Why does it have to be me?" Again the fear and whine in his voice.

"Because, Sean, we don't know *where* he's getting his information. We can't afford *not* to have *you* make the drop. Don't you understand?"

Sean, looking confused, shook his head.

"We may have a leak in our *Cell*, Sean." Frank said slowly to the frightened boy. "Maybe even higher! We can't take *any* chances. Nothing *will* or *can* happen to you. This time, we will be waiting."

He paused, looked the young man in the eyes and said slowly, "Now, Sean, *will* you honor us and your mates by doing one more drop?"

Knowing he had no real choice in the matter, Sean answered. "Course I will, Frank. You know I will. For the cause! For the army! For me mates! Just promise that you'll get *that fucking bastard* before he gets me."

"Of course we will, Sean! I personally guarantee it! Not only that, I am going to be overseeing this operation *personally*." Slapping Sean on the back, he chuckled.

"Now go clean up your room. Maybe take a nap or something. Relax! We're not going to let anything happen to our *top* soldier!"

▲ ▲ ▲

Damon Gray now knew for certain that something was very different about his *'Gifts'*. All the years that they had been buried by his subconscious had not stunted them. They had matured in spite of everything! It was almost like they had never been gone. A strange feeling, to be sure! Almost!

He still had to test ... no – to explore them!

So much to do, and so little time.

▲ ▲ ▲

SCENE ELEVEN

It wasn't two weeks later that Sean Michael O'Brien planted the bomb that killed 232 passengers on Flight 432 from London. Even now, as he sat in his *'Safe House'* watching the tube, four days later, he didn't feel safe.

Frank had lived up to his word and had armed guards stationed in and surrounding the building, (well hidden, invisible even to the most astute observer), plus one outside his door. He'd even offered to put a bodyguard in the apartment with him, but Sean declined the offer. Felt it would make him look too weak in their eyes. Besides, the entire twenty one apartment complex was *wired*. Security systems were installed everywhere. There was *no way* that *anyone* could get into the building without tripping an alarm! No video, though. Frank told him there could be nothing the authorities could get their hands on that would show who came and went from the building. Too risky. Other than that, it was all *state of the art* equipment. The 'Best of the Best'!

He knew he should feel safe. He knew that twenty of the best of the 'Black Hand' soldiers were guarding him. He knew that Mr. Smoke was just one man. It was just that he was *sure* that Mr. Smoke could *not* be stopped.

He'd actually sent a package to a friend, with specific instructions on what to do with it, in the case of his sudden demise. No one in the Cell knew he had sent it. It would have been his death warrant if they had. The young man smiled, a little sadly. Damned if he did, damned if he didn't.

'I need another beer!' he thought to himself. Sean got up, turned to head for the kitchen, and froze in his tracks.

There, standing in the doorway to the kitchen, was a tall, slender looking figure, totally encased in dark gray. Even the silenced gun pointing at him was of dark gray non reflective metal. The only two things visible were the eyes. He remembered the eyes. Terror seized him, stark raving, mind numbing terror!

"Mr. Smoke, I can explain! I was made to do........." He never finished his sentence. He never heard the whisper soft puff of the silencer.

The terrorist, the killer of so many innocent men, women and children, was no more. All that was left was a young boy on the floor, with a bullet hole between his eyes.

▲ ▲ ▲

"Mister Smoke? Ahhh yes, I remember! 'I am mist or smoke'. Interesting....."

Damon Gray looked down at the body on the floor. He wondered at his emotions.

He had felt Sean die, experienced the fear and horror coursing through the young killers mind. The anguished pleading for life! The unfairness of it all! The candle flame of life snuffed out. Not a fire, not even a small blaze. Sean was just a candle.

Damon felt no horror, remorse or revulsion over what he had done. Or regret. It had to be done, and he was the only one who could do it. Now the only thing left to do was get out of the building without getting caught. He headed to the door, waited two minutes, eleven seconds, opened the door and walked out.

▲ ▲ ▲

Scene Twelve

….."exclusive to KXWY, Channel 66! Confessed terrorist, killed by a vigilante known as Mister Smoke! Here you have it folks! Right here on Channel 66! A KXWY exclusive! I'm Fred Conley, and have we got a scoop for you! The body of Sean Michael O'Brien, long suspected by authorities, but never proven, to be a soldier in the 'Black Hand' terrorist organization, was found dead, shot between the eyes, in a back alley, in heart of downtown London, two days ago.

"The authorities had put it down to a gangland slaying, but KXWY has exclusive proof, FROM SEAN MICHAEL O'BRIEN HIMSELF, that his death was the act of a hired assassin known only as 'Mister Smoke!' Delivered earlier today to KXWY, from an unknown source, we have a video recording of Sean O'Brien himself admitting to as many as thirty two personal killings, plus twenty two bombings. I have not seen the tape, nor has anyone in the newsroom. We are seeing it for the first time, just as you are. *Uncut! Unedited! Uncensored!* A copy of the tape has been sent to the proper authorities. This might not be appropriate for young viewers. Send them out of the room. Tell everybody …… you saw and heard it first on KXWY!!!"

Fred Conley smiled and his face faded as the face of the young terrorist appeared.

45

"My name is Sean Michael O'Brien. (Glances at paper on lap) I am a loyal soldier of the *Black Hand*. I believe in our cause, and have personally *offed* thirty two people and made over twenty two 'drops' for our glorious and just cause. 'Drops' is short for 'bomb drops', case' you was wonderin'. I think you know what *'offed'* means. (smug smile) If this tape is being played, *then...I...am...dead.* (dramatic pause)The reason I'm making this tape is (another dramatic pause) to let everyone know that I was *foully* murdered by a *paid assassin*, who told me his name was *Mister Smoke*. (Looking down at his self written script again) Now, I ain't no coward, but when a man in a dark gray ninja outfit appears in your 'so called' *SAFE room* in the middle of the night; paralyses you and promises to kill you if you ever do another 'drop' and puts you to sleep after .... well, it just plain scared the shit outa me. No guff! All I could see was his *freaky, scary eyes.* Said he was paid to give me a warning first, though. I told me 'Uppers' and they said they would *'andle* it. They set a trap for him, with me as the bait. Why me? 'Cause I'm the guy he threatened; that's what me Uppers told me! So I'm gunna make one more drop, but this one is not just for *the cause.* It's also for *MY* cause. This time it's personal! I'm doin' it 'cause they're gonna try to stop *him.* I personally don't believe that they can stop this *Mr. Smoke* creep, so that's why I'm making this tape. They ain't seen him, or felt the (glances at script again) *emptiness of life in his eyes, promising me a permanent death!* (Smug, satisfied look.) I ain't asking or beggin' for mercy, 'cause I ain't done *nuthin* I wasn't told to do. I *bin* a loyal soldier all me life. What I am askin' is for all me mates in the 'Black Hand' to find and *KILL* this bloke, and whoever the *sonofabitch is* who paid him. I guess that's all. Except to tell you all out there, that *I'm* the HERO, cause' I killed for a cause, not like this *'Mister Smoke' asshole*, who just kills for money! I don't deserve to die! *Mr. Smoke does!* Do not let my senseless death go *unavenged!*" (Solemn look at the camera and fade to black....)

"You're live, Fred."

"….just can't believe that goddamned, self righteous, pompous little *asshole!* I'm glad that *Mr. Smoke* popped his ass! God, this guy makes me sick!! Hero? What a *fuc…*"

"Fred, YOU'RE ON THE AIR!!"

"What? Oh damn! (Long pause) Wellll … what can I say; except that… what I said was *my opinion only* and not the opinion of this station or any of its sponsors. (Slight pause) More News on the hour. Remember you heard it first on KXWY, Cable 66. This is Fred Conley wishing you Good Night and Good News."

▲ ▲ ▲

The News Media went Crazy! All around the world, television, newspapers and even the internet ran stories about Mister Smoke. Talk show hosts were divided on whether this paid assassin was a good thing or bad, but one thing they all agreed on. To a person they applauded England's reporter Fred Conley's sentiments on Sean Michael O'Brien's taped message.

Copies of his outburst were everywhere on the internet. Tee shirts with his face and various renditions of his words sprouted up like magic. Fred Conley became an instant Media Superstar. Personal appearance and job offers from around the world were pouring in.

What started as a media blunder on his part to Superstardom nonplussed the News Anchorman.

First: getting his butt chewed out by his superiors at KXWY.

Then: a suspension and fine for his outburst.

Then: the owner of the station flying in personally and apologizing.

Then: the waiving of the suspension and fine.

Then: the station providing him with personal body guards, twenty four seven, (due to the very real threat of retribution by the Black Hand).

Then: increasing his salary by an unspecified amount with a *new ten year contract!*

Fred was overwhelmed! He knew he was a bit of a maverick as far as News Anchors were concerned. An Investigative News Reporter. Unheard of! Because of it, of going undercover, he had more exclusives than anybody on staff. He had been reprimanded on numerous occasions and warned to be more *'British'* or, as with his last warning, with only three months remaining, his contract *might not* be renewed. He was very popular in the ratings, but not enough to dismiss the threat of *not* having his contract renewed.

At fifty five, Fred Conley dyed his thinning hair chestnut brown to cover the advancing grey, had 'Show Business white teeth' and had a 'nip and tuck' smooth face to compete with the beautiful young sharks coming into the business. He knew that he tread a very thin line with KXWY. If he became more *'British'* in his style, he would be signing his career death warrant. If he went too far over the top, ditto.

Every year his agent tried to get a five year contract, but to no avail. James Lawson, the owner of KXWY and thirteen other stations, said that one year contracts kept his people 'hungry'. That was his favorite word – *'hungry'*.

Fred had always dreamed of being in a position like he was now, (except that in his dream, he was an *intentional* Hero, not an *accidental* one), and had written down, what to him was, the perfect ten year contract.

And they had signed it! Damned if they hadn't!

His Agent had told him he was crazy to 'demand' what he did, and advised him to 'ask' for less. Fred told him that if he didn't, or couldn't, get it signed without any changes, not to come back at all. Fred would get another agent.

The agent came back with the contract signed!

Fred Conley wasn't *'hungry'* anymore!

▲ ▲ ▲

Divorced for more than twenty five years and with no children, Fred had lots of spare time to pursue his passion. His passion, or 'Hobby' as he called it, was *crime and punishment*. He was a veritable encyclopedia of trivia when it came to that. His study of it, or *'obsession'* as his colleagues named it, came after being hospitalized from a mugging and beating he received when leaving a pub, when he was but twenty four years old.

He identified the perpetrator and had him arrested, only to have said mugger beat the system (and him), with a slick Barrister. In court, when Fred took the stand, the defendants' lawyer inferred that a drunken Fred had made untoward sexual advances to the defendant, and that the alleged mugging was nothing more than an argument perpetrated by non other than Fred himself. The defendant was just protecting himself!

Fred was outraged, and acted as such. Yes, he was drunk, but *no*, he had not made any *'homosexual'* advances to the defendant! The Defense played him like a fiddle, twisting and turning everything he said, until it fit into what the defendant was alleging!

His wife and a few of Fred's friends were at the trial to support him. None of them were with him six months later.

It cost him his marriage. Fred never forgot the pain of the mugging.

Or the two month hospital convalescence.

Or the pain and humiliation of the trial.

Or his loss of spouse and friends.

Thus his obsession with crime and punishment.

▲ ▲ ▲

Scene Thirteen

Damon Gray was unprepared for what happened when he got back to the hotel room the night he killed the 'Terrorist Bomber'. He walked into his hotel room, sat on his bed and started to shake. He started to heave, erupted on himself, staggered to the bathroom and continued to empty the remaining contents of his stomach. He continued to dry heave so much that his stomach muscles ached for days afterward. After what seemed an eternity, it finally stopped.

Damon stumbled his way into the bedroom, stripped of his strength. It was all he could do to put a 'Do Not Disturb Sign' on the door, peel off his clothes and crawl onto bed and under the covers. Then, *'Elseware'* took him.

▲ ▲ ▲

Knock! Knock! Knock!

An exhausted Damon became *'Aware'* two mornings later in a blind panic!

Was it all just a dream, a horrible nightmare? The strewn clothes, his guns on the floor assured him that it had all happened. Everything! The *'Knowing'*; the *'Rage'*; the *'Compulsion'*; and finally, the *'Killing'* of Sean Michael O'Brien (along with *experiencing his death*.)

He glanced at his watch, frowned, then looked at it again. He could hardly believe it! He had been *'Elseware'* for almost thirty six hours straight!

He didn't know where *'Elseware'* was, but he knew it could kill him if he didn't get a handle on it. Some kind of control, and fast.

The guns! He had to get rid of the evidence!

'Whoa, slow down!' he thought to himself. *'If I was under suspicion, someone would have been here by now.'*

"Hello?"

Damon sat stunned.

"Hello?" a female voice said again. "Room Service."

"Uh… come back later." Damon called from the bedroom. "I'm busy right now." The last said with authority.

"Yes sir." said a heavily accented melodic Irish voice. "I'm sorry sir, but I did knock. Twice, sir! You didn't have a 'Do Not Disturb' on your door. It was on yesterday but some kid must have taken it off. I'll inform maintenance to put another one on immediately. Sorry sir! I'll come back another time. Have a nice day."

Then the sound of a door closing and a lock being turned.

'Have a nice day! HAVE A NICE DAY?!' Damon started to laugh. *'Ouch! My stomach!'* But he couldn't stop. In the back of his mind he knew it was hysterical laughter, but he couldn't stop. Not that he wanted to anyway. It was releasing the tension, cleansing him, reviving him.

When he got it under control, Damon Gray stood up, ready to face the day.

▲ ▲ ▲

He was glad that his 'Tour' was over and he had the time off to try to understand what he was going through. His next 'Tour' didn't start for a few more weeks. And then it was only a short one, four weeks in Germany.

Reaction had set in. Not something he had counted on. As he left the *'target site'*, he was surprised that he hadn't initially reacted to

Sean's death, and so assumed that he wouldn't later on. Wrong! He was so used to *not* feeling that when he did, it took him by surprise and overwhelmed him. Intellectually he knew what *delayed reaction* was, but that did not prepare him for the reality of it!

On top of it, there was *'Elseware'*, whatever or wherever the hell that was.

What was happening to him? His small controlled world was shattered. Gone forever. His bubble had burst with the pinprick *knowledge* of the terrorist bombers identity.

Confusion, desperation and depression set in. He felt justified killing Sean the Bomber. That's not what bothered him. Not *'knowing'* who ordered the 'Drop' *did*.

It took him a couple of days of deep meditation and soul searching to come to grips with the whole thing. He knew, in his heart of hearts, that the killing of Sean Michael O'Brien was a buried rage at his parents' senseless death. *Misplaced Revenge.* No, not 'misplaced', *'transferred'*. O'Brien wasn't one of the two that killed his parents. He knew that. *'Hell'*, he thought, *'Sean hadn't even been born then.'* Not that it mattered one goddamned bit! It was as if every *'terrorist bomber'* in the world was responsible! To Damon Gray, it made perfect sense. To him, they *were*, and always *would be* the ones he held responsible for his family's deaths!

The Leaders, the ones who ordered the *drops,* would be powerless if no one made the *drops.* Unless *they* made them *personally*, and he thought that unlikely. *They* were the *Generals*, the *Leaders*! Not to be placed in danger. Who would lead *from behind,* if not them?

It was too bad he didn't know the identities of all of the *'Terrorist Bombers'* in the world, *so he could kill each and every one of them!*

▲ ▲ ▲

Scene Fourteen

It happened again! *'Elseware'*! This time it happened in a little Arab restaurant.

He became *'aware'* just as the ambulance arrived. The medics held him down until the convulsions subsided. Less this time than last, only a matter of minutes.

The restaurant owner said that he saw Damon, who was reading a newspaper, stiffen up. He thought that something was wrong with the food, came to inquire, immediately realized that something was wrong and called for the ambulance. Ten minutes, the owner said. Ten minutes Damon was frozen at the table! Scared him to death, he said. Thought he was dead. Couldn't see him breathing. Ten minutes, he kept saying, then the arrival of the paramedics, then the convulsions.

Damon assured the medics that he was alright and thanked the shaking owner for his concern, paid his bill (left a hefty tip for the hyperventilating waiter) and left the restaurant.

Still dealing with the aftermath of his reactions and emotions of killing a human being, and the return of his *'Gifts'*, Damon Gray was not prepared for the reaction to the second bombing when it jumped off the page at him during that breakfast, one month later, as he was reading the local newspaper.

'Fourteen Dead by Bomb Blast!' the headline read. He went on to read that thirty three were injured, three were in 'critical' condition, and not expected to recover.

Then, *Elseware*.

When he became *'aware'*, he knew who had planted the bomb! Who to kill!

Directly upon leaving the restaurant, Damon went straight back to his hotel room. The moment he entered his hotel room, Damon started shaking. He didn't try to control it.

Confusion was not something he was used to. And he was confused! The *'knowing'* of the bomber, was one thing. The rage and almost overpowering urge to rush forward and KILL that person was another entirely. Not wise! Not smart! Not rational!

The last one, the *rational* one, Damon had been for twenty one years.

'What is going on here' Damon thought. *'What the hell is happening to me?'*

▲ ▲ ▲

Damon was *feeling again* for the first time in twenty one years. Emotions were running rampant! Music was flowing from within again. The Magic was back.

Everything was new. It hurt that his family wasn't there, but not as much as before.

Father Time had done his job. Maybe part of the healing was the fact that he *now* felt somehow *still* connected to them. All of them, parents and grandparents.

That excited him! He would start delving into the Occult and Paranormal again. This time with a goal.

But First............

▲ ▲ ▲

Buried for twenty one years, the one emotion that time had not dulled was Damon's pure *hatred* for *'Terrorist Bombers'*, as he thought of them. If anything it had intensified.

This insane urge to kill, he had to control! And he was a man *out of control.*

For three days he struggled to understand the urge, *the burning hell fire need* to kill the *terrorist bombers*. On the fourth, he understood it. In its simplest form, its name was *revenge.*

On the fifth day, he controlled it! He *would not* be ruled by *blind rage and vengeance.*

▲ ▲ ▲

Scene Fifteen

Abduhl Jabhared was a skilled terrorist and explosives expert. A true *Legend* in his field. Law enforcement agencies, around the globe, had been chasing him for over thirty years.

At fifty one years of age, he should have been teaching the *young bloods* the art of terrorism *exclusively*, instead of doing some of the assignments himself.

Time and again his superiors had tried to sway him that way.

In his mind, he felt that he needed to stay *'in the loop.'* The world was changing too fast for him to become complacent.

His answer was always the same. *'Yes, yes. Someday .....* *someday.'*

▲ ▲ ▲

Abduhl Jabhared awakened in his tent, in the middle of an *Allah's Hammer* terrorist stronghold, to the sound of someone whispering his name.

Danger! Every instinct screamed! *Danger!*

Without moving, he tried to place where the voice was coming from. From behind his head!

His reflexes were legend in the camp, but when he tried to grab the gun under his pillow.....

He couldn't move!

That Mr. Smoke is a Lone Gunman, a Loose Cannon with a few bolts loose. An insane man with no fear. Sew fear and panic in all terrorist bombers. The benefit? Reap fear, panic *and* confusion.

Have *Terrorist Organizations* thinking that Mr. Smoke is one of them. That there are *Moles* in their midst reporting to his organization, thus creating panic *within the Terrorists' organizations*. And with panic … mistakes.

Have the Powers of the world *unwilling*, as well as *unable*, to stop him. Let them think that he may *not* be just *one* man, but *maybe* part of an organization. Thus, a man they could not afford to arrest, capture, or kill publicly.

The Global Powers must know which Hits, or '*Smokes*', as Damon preferred to think of them, are his, so that there would be no confusion, if Copy Cat killings occurred.

Use his computer skills to gain information. Top Secret Government information. Which meant getting into their systems without their being aware of it.

Damon smiled. First things first.

▲ ▲ ▲

Scene Seventeen

Saturday, mid–December:

Damon Gray, *aka Mr. Smoke*, arrived at Canterberry Cathedral, in the heart of Old Londontown, in a black security limousine (supplied by Lord Brighton, at Sylvia's request) at thirty minutes past the noon hour, exactly thirty minutes early.

The day was clear and sunny. The snow had been falling sporadically for days. The buildings and signposts had mantles of snow framing them, creating the perfect fairy tale setting for the wedding of Lord Michael Brighton to Ms. Sylvia Glockenhausen.

It was the talk of the town! Over one thousand guests, from all points of the globe, had been invited to the black tie event. If they didn't arrive in formal attire, they could not attend. They were politely but firmly turned away.

Even the attending media and crew were not exempt. Many who arrived and were turned away for lack of formal attire, rushed home and changed immediately and returned. It became the social event of the year.

Sixty percent were expected to respond that they were coming. Ninety eight percent had responded, many asking for additional invitations.

The News Media reported that it was rumored that over twelve hundred would attend. Resplendent in their traditional black and gold uniforms, the *'Royal Elite'* Guardians were at all the entrances, checking all Invitations and Identifications.

Damon was escorted through a side entrance, reserved for the VIP's and escorted to a private balcony. Both Michael and Sylvia respected Damon's wishes to avoid being photographed.

The wedding went off without a hitch. Twice decorated, by the Queen, for Bravery and Valor above and beyond the call of duty, Cardinal Lloyd Brown, ex-military Chaplin, and close personal friend of the Brighton family, flew in from the Vatican to perform the wedding ceremony.

Cardinal Lloyd Brown was also Two I C (Second in Command) in the A.T.C.U. (Anti-Terrorism Control Unit) directly under and reporting only to 'The Head', Lord Michael Brighton.

The Reception was held at one of the Brighton estates. Brighton Manner to be exact. It was the family's only residence with a parking lot large enough to accommodate all of the vehicles.

A handsome and fit couple in their early sixties, Lord Clayton and Lady Margaret Brighton, Michael's parents, being in the reception line, greeted each and every person that was invited.

When they met him again at the reception, they told Damon that they were big fans of his and that they owned his entire collection of music. That impressed Damon. He chatted with them briefly about which arrangements they liked. What he could, or should, change about any of them. Small talk. Then he joined the rest of the guests. He was the only one, under seventy, that came unaccompanied.

At one point, Michael had an opportunity to talk to Damon alone. Away from prying ears.

Just before dinner Damon entered the Men's Room and was washing his hands, when Sir Michael Brighton entered. Nodding to the attendant, (who nodded back, turned and immediately left the room to stand guard outside) Michael walked up to the sink beside Damon and started washing his hands.

With a casualness born from years of study and practice, Michael opened the conversation.

"Are you enjoying yourself Doctor Gray?"

"Call me Damon, and yes, absolutely! The appetizers were fantastic. A culinary delight. How about you? There has to be twelve hundred and forty two people here. How are you holding up?"

"Twelve hundred and forty two?"

"I didn't include the news media and staff, or your immediate family." Damon stated matter of factly.

Michael chuckled, "Oh, you didn't include the......." Lord Brighton's voice faded off as he noticed that Damon was *not* smiling. He had been serious!

Michael studied Damon for a moment, then said abruptly. "What are you doing for lunch three weeks from now?" He smiled at Damon to take away the sting of the way it sounded. "I'd really like to get to know you better, Damon. You're an amazing chap. What do you say? Three weeks from now, noon, at the Kings Court on Cheshire Street?" Impulsively, he put forth his hand.

Damon looked at the outstretched hand for a moment; then his liquid silver eyes moved up to meet Michael's.

For a split second, a jolt went through the body of the Lord, the instant those eyes met his. Then, Damon smiled, reached out and clasped his hand.

The smile transformed his face.

▲ ▲ ▲

As Michael told his bride later that evening.

"It was the damnedest thing. When our eyes first met, I mean really met, a bolt of pure terror shot through my body. As you know, Syl, I don't scare easily! And I can't ever remember feeling terror before, but I knew that's what it was. Damnedest sensation!" he closed his eyes at the memory.

"I don't ever want to feel that again. And the next second, he smiled and buried my hand in his. He seemed like another man altogether. Transformed! You know something, darling? I felt that he was accepting me into his 'Inner Circle'. Does that make sense?"

"Inner Circle?" Sylvia responded.

"Yes, 'Inner Circle'. Like he had made a decision ….. I don't know for sure, but I think I became his *friend* at that moment. And I don't think he has many friends in *this* world."

"What do you mean, in *this world?*" The new Mrs. Brighton asked.

"I really don't know what made me say it that way. It just seemed right, if you know what I mean?" She shook her head.

"No? Well, it really doesn't matter. One thing I *do* know. He did not choose me as *his* friend. He chose to be *my* friend. I'm glad. I would not like him as an enemy!"

"What a strange thing to say! Why in the world would he be your *enemy?*"

"I don't know. I'm just glad he isn't."

"Sometimes you men say the strangest things, Mickey! Forget about Damon Gray and get naked. It's our wedding night, and I'm your virgin bride! Take me! I'm yours!"

As she was saying it, Sylvia peeled off her *'Going Away Outfit'* and threw herself naked on the bed.

Michael laughed. "Virgin bride? Ohh …. Oh, yes. Virgin bride. That's right. Virgin bride! I've never seen you naked, or *any* woman naked, for that matter. Oh, my gosh, you're beautiful! Nakedly beautiful, that is. What are *those* things?"

With that, Michael stripped, posed and flexed, then jumped onto the bed beside her.

"I'll be happy to tell you what *these* are, after you tell me what *THAT* is!"

They both laughed and kissed ……………

▲ ▲ ▲

Scene Eighteen

"Why did you invite him for lunch, anyway?" Sylvia asked her husband the next morning over coffee.

"Because he knew who I am! Why can't you drink tea for breakfast, instead of that horrible coffee?"

She started to respond, then saw the twinkle in his eye. She laughed and sipped her coffee, making small moaning sounds.

"You sound like you did last night. Maybe I should have a cup as well. Gaston, a cup of espresso please."

When Gaston had left to get the coffee, Sylvia said, "Of course he knew who you are. We invited him to the wedding. Remember?"

"Yes, I *know* he knows *who I am*. What I meant to say is that he knows *what I do*."

"Don't tease me sweetheart. You told *me* what you do, *and* you *also* said that, outside A.T.C.U., only twelve other people in the world knew, and I'm pretty sure that Damon Gray was not one of them, seeing as we hadn't even met him yet. Right?" He nodded.

"Well then, how could he *possibly* know *what you do*?"

"I don't know," he said, a little desperately, "but I intend to find out! This could have catastrophic ramifications! Bye the bye, did I tell you he knew exactly how many guests were at the wedding, yesterday? Exactly, Syl. Twelve hundred and forty two. I had it checked three times. The first time, the total was different. I wasn't convinced. I had a strange feeling that he was right. The second and third totals were the same as his."

"How can that be? That's impossible … isn't it?"

"I wish I could answer that question, darling, but I can't. That is why I invited him to lunch. To get some, if not all, of my questions answered."

"Well, I think you'll find that Doctor Damon Gray wouldn't hurt a fly! Anyone who writes such soulful and beautiful music *couldn't!*"

"You're probably right, as always, my dear. If so, we will just have a fabulous lunch together. Pass the jelly, please."

▲ ▲ ▲

Scene Nineteen

Saturday, mid-January.

Sir Michael Brighton arrived at Kings Court on Cheshire Street at eleven thirty, to find Damon waiting for him inside the front door.

Michael noted that the pianist was dressed fashionably in a hand tailored, single breasted, solid flannel charcoal grey suit, dove grey french-cuffed dress shirt with a stand up collar, over sized custom made titanium cuff links, belt buckle and collar button cover (in a unique star design, each one slightly different), dark grey suede belt and matching shoes.

Michael was sure that the belt and soft soled shoes were custom made also. Over his left arm was draped a soft, charcoal grey, custom tailored, Armani cashmere overcoat. Non-belted, he noticed. Showing slightly from one of the coat pockets, he noticed grey gloves matching his belt and shoes. A dove grey cashmere scarf poked out of one of the coat sleeves. No rings and no watch that he could see.

'Tasteful, but a little drab.' he thought. 'He definitely wouldn't stand out in a crowd.' Then he remembered Damon's rumored paranoia.

"Good morning … Damon." Michael chuckled. "I keep wanting to call you Doctor Gray. Have you been waiting long?" He put forth his hand.

"Only a little while." responded Damon, as he reached out and shook hands.

'Not something that he has done often,' observed Michael.

Michael was impressed. The Kings Court did not let anybody in that did not adhere to their dress code. *Business attire or higher.* Damon must have researched the establishment before he came.

Michael was dressed in a navy blue suit, white shirt with thin gold stripes, gold and navy rep tie, black belt and shoes and finished off with a custom made wristwatch of an unpronounceable name. Topping the ensemble off was a navy cashmere overcoat, black gloves and scarf. (All custom made, of course)

"Are we too early to get our table Reeves?" Michael asked the Maitre de.

"Of course not, Lord Brighton. We are well aware of your habit of arriving early. Obviously, so is this gentleman." He nodded toward Damon and smiled. "He arrived just moments before you did. If you will please give your coats to the young lady at the Coat Check, I will escort you to your table."

After they had done so, the Maitre de said, "This way, please."

As the two men walked into the antechamber preceding the dining room, two men in black suits appeared, seemingly out of nowhere; stepped in front of Damon and Michael, and bowed slightly.

The taller of the two spoke softly, with a cultured British accent. "It seems that one of you gentlemen has forgotten to leave something with the young lady at the Coat Check."

"You mean *a tip?*" Damon said. "Maybe I'm way out of line here, but I thought that you left a tip *when you leave. After* you have received and evaluated what level of service you have received. If I am mistaken, please forgive me. Michael, I know that you invited me for lunch, but allow me ….."

"That is *not* what we meant, sir. *And I think you know it.* If you two gentlemen will *please* follow me." It was *not* a request. It was politely and quietly said, but it was most definitely *not* a request.

They were led to a small room off to the left side as you came into the antechamber. Inside the room were four more men dressed in black, positioned in the four corners, facing the center of the room, where a very attractive young lady sat behind a desk.

"Did one of you gentleman forget to leave something with the lady at the Coat Check? ..... Lord Brighton? *Again?*"

"Damn it Jane, you know I did! I keep forgetting. It's like it is a part of me. Please forgive me." With that said, Michael produced a custom made 9 MM Beretta from his shoulder holster and handed it to Jane.

"Sir Brighton, what *am* I going to do with you?" she gave him a dazzling smile to take away the sting of those words. "And you *do* know what must come next, don't you?"

Michael sighed, smiled and raised his arms as one of the men in black ran a security wand over him.

Satisfied the man in black turned to Damon. "You are next, sir. Please raise your arms to shoulder height please."

Damon looked at Michael quizzically.

Michael looked embarrassed. "I'm terribly sorry, old chap, but it's standard procedure. Whoever is *with* the culprit has to be security wanded also. Please forgive me."

Damon turned to the man in black, with the wand, lifted his arms and said quietly "Go ahead, Fred."

"Do I know you, sir?" Fred said as he ran the security wand over his body.

"You do now, Fred." Damon said with a smile.

"Yes sir, thank you, sir. All clear, Ms. Watson." Fred said stiffly.

"Have a nice lunch gentlemen." Jane Watson purred to the two, smiling sweetly.

They were escorted back to Reeves, who, acting as if nothing had happened, led the two to a table in the farthest corner, far from any eavesdropper.

"Again, my apologies Damon." Michael said after they had sat down, ordered and had their beverages delivered. Damon, a soda water with a twist of lime, and Michael, a double espresso.

"Hooked on the damned things." He muttered as he took a sip. "My wife's fault, actually."

Damon smiled. A real smile.

Michael smiled back. A real smile.

"Well," Damon said, "you found out one of the things that you wanted to know."

"Yes," Michael said, "Yes I did. Where are they?"

"In a locked vault, in the boot of my car. I knew that no guns were allowed here, so rather than risk someone messing with mine, I left them behind."

"Why did you leave on the shoulder holsters? They are beautiful, bye the bye."

"The suit was designed to fit with them on. And thank you, they were custom made to my specifications. I like yours also. Bensingtons?"

"*How in blazes* could you know *that?*" asked Michael.

"Like you, I watch … and notice the little things. It's the little things that make life interesting, wouldn't you agree?"

Michael nodded.

"Like your Beretta. A custom made piece of art. You lengthened the barrel, what, half an inch?' Again, the nod. "Made the grip slightly smaller and longer to fit you hand. I bet your score improved about, what, fifteen to eighteen percent?"

"Sixteen"

"Wow! That is a *great increase*, considering that you are a world class shooter. Would you consider giving me a few lessons sometime? I love to learn new techniques."

"Sure … sure." Michael mumbled as he tried to gather his thoughts. He was stunned!

Nobody was supposed to know of his shooting ability. Those awards were strictly hush-hush, with only a few people knowing of them. The Organization felt it was better to keep their *'Head Man'* a low profile character. A rich, fun loving playboy. Until recently. Now he was supposed to be a happily married, fun loving globe trotter.

If any terrorist group knew what he and his organization did, he and everybody associated with him, would be in *deadly* danger. Deadly as in *DEAD!*

He had to have answers from Damon and he had to have them *quickly*. But, how to do it?

He looked up and saw Damon looking at him intently. No, not *at* him, *through* him. As if he could read his thoughts!

"No, Michael, I'm not reading your mind." Michael jumped as if stung! "But I *can* read your body language, although not that well. You're good! What's on your mind? Why this lunch?"

Michael focused on his fingertips and calmed himself. Never had he met anyone like Damon. Making up his mind, he took the plunge.

Looking straight into Damons cold silver eyes, he said, "Damon, I've had my people checking into you."

"I know."

"Bull ... ah, I mean, that's impossible. You couldn't know."

"You didn't find much, did you?"

"No. How did you ..." He paused. "Alright, maybe you do. *How do you?* How do you seem to know all about me? Things that only a handful of people in the world are supposed to know? Will you tell me that?"

"Why?"

"*Why?* You ask me *Why?*"

"Yes."

"Because if word gets out, or is out, there are a lot of people that I know and love, that will die. One of them is my wife, Sylvia. Plus the *irreparable damage* to our organization and cause. It would take years to recover, if we ever could. Do you know what our *group* does?" Damon nodded.

"Our *group* was started under another government and god only knows if this one would sanction another one. I have to know *now*, before it's too late to salvage. *Does that satisfy you?*"

"Yes, it does." Damon paused, looked hard at Sir Brighton for a moment, as if considering something ... then said "I believe that you are a good man, Michael. I find that I am *seldom* wrong." Again, another pause, as if to gather his thoughts. Then, "I *will* answer all of your questions to the best of my abilities, Michael. But I must warn you. And I do mean *warn you! I am not a violent man!* I am a musician. If you believe the news media, *a very talented musician*, but still, just a musician. I make my living with my hands. For many years it has been the only thing that has kept me going. What you *have* found out about me is that, as you suspected, I don't have many friends. The reasons are unimportant. Suffice to say that I don't trust a whole lot of people. Also, and again I warn you, people close to me, friends and family that I loved, have *all* died horrible deaths."

'Who uses a word like suffice?*'* thought Michael.

"Does everything I say ring true?"

"Yes, Damon it does. How do *you know* what you know?"

"Computers."

"Computers? Garbage! …. I don't ..."

"That's right, Michael, computers. If you had time to check out my parents and grandparents, you would have found out that they were computer *Super Genius's*. They passed some of that talent on to me. They owned, *therefore* I *own*, a number of global computer and software companies, through shell corporations. The reason I met with you today is twofold. One is that I really like you and Sylvia."

Michael sensed that Damon really meant it. Friendship wasn't trivial to Damon.

"The second reason is selfish. Well, they're both selfish, I guess, but the first reason is a *good* selfish. The second is a, (pause) a *selfish* selfish. *I believe in your goals!* As you've probably guessed, I *hate* terrorism. Terrorism took my family from me. I want to help protect your *'Organization'*, and in doing so, myself. If I can break your system, others eventually will be able to. I have designed a system that even I can't break! I am offering it to you *free of charge*. As you already know, I don't need the money. My parents and grandparents left me wealthy beyond measure."

He paused, shook his head and continued, "I just want to keep on making music. In peace! If we agree, no one can know of my involvement! You're very lives would be in danger, and so would mine. There are people out there who want to kill me and all associated with me. And to answer your next question, yes, I have access to all types of top level government files." Michael did not react. "And no, you cannot have access to them. They are encrypted in a way that only I can access them. Remember that I am a computer genius. I only monitor to protect myself. I am strictly *nonviolent* in nature, but I *will* protect myself to the best of my abilities. That is why I carry two guns. They, also, are works of art, designed by me. I'll show them to you sometime. Have I answered your questions to your satisfaction Michael?"

"Will you let me use your system to protect our other government agencies?"

"No."

"No? That's it? No? How about, 'We'll talk about it?'"

"No."

"No."

"Deal?" Damon put out his hand.

Lord Michael Brighton hesitated. Damon trusted him! He was willing to put his life in Michael's hands on a handshake. Now it was *his* turn to trust Damon.

Could he do it? He looked long and hard into Damon's eyes.

"Deal." He said, as he reached forward and shook Damon's hand.

"Let's eat, shall we? The lobster here is just delicious."

▲ ▲ ▲

Scene Twenty

"All done, sir. All programs are active, as of right now."

"Thank you Mr. Kurten. Has everything been verified?"

"Yes sir, Lord Brighton. Everything has been checked at least a dozen times. No one has been able to breach our new system. Even the disk you gave us, that breached our old system, couldn't break it. And, if I might add, sir, *that disc* is a work of genius. It was designed to work *only* on our system! We tried it on others, and it wouldn't do a thing. Amazing! Our best boys can't break *it*, and they've been at it since they got it. In my opinion and that of my colleagues, nobody in the world, including the person that designed the *system*, can break it now. By that, I mean the *new system*, sir. I have never seen anything like it. In all of our opinions, we have the most secure operating system in the world!"

"Thank you, again, Mr. Kurten. Have all personnel been trained on the new system?"

"Yes sir!"

"Have you been able to decipher the new systems discs?"

"We'll keep working on them, sir!"

"I take it that means *no*. Ah, well! I was told by the person who created them that you wouldn't be able to. Don't spend a whole lot of manpower on it Mr. Kurten, just use it."

"Yes, sir. As you *say*, sir!"

▲ ▲ ▲

"Can you believe that Kurten called me at two thirty am to tell me that someone tried to break into our system, Syl?"

"We've been through all of this. More than once, if memory serves me. Tell me, are you angry or pleased? Pass the biscuits, dear." Sylvia smiled at her husband and continued. "And if memory serves, your *new system* tracked the culprits, and they are now in custody."

Michael sighed, passing her the biscuits. "Sorry dear. I haven't slept well in last few weeks, what with the installation deadline of the new system and all. It's just that we've only had the new system installed a few days and already someone tried to hack it. Thank God it was secure! I owe Damon a debt of gratitude."

"Damon (pause) *Damon Gray?* He designed your New Top Secret System?"

"Uh … well …… um ….."

"Damon Gray, the *pianist?* Our friend?"

Sir Brighton smiled.

"Why, you ……." sputtered Sylvia, "*Why* didn't you tell me!"

"I talked with Damon this morning, by secure phone, to inform him that his system worked flawlessly. As you know, no names were used. Initially, our agreement was that I would tell *no one* of his involvement. *No one* means *No One.* I gave him *my word* Syl." He paused and looked at his wife.

She sat quietly, waiting for him to continue.

"After we had finished our conversation and I was about to hang up, our friend, *Dr. Damon Gray,* said to me. 'I thank you for keeping your word to me. You may now tell your wife about me. But only *her,* and only if *she* agrees to our agreement also. Agreed?' *'Agreed',* I said. I knew I didn't have to ask you … did I?"

"Of course not, sweetheart! Wow! Damon Gray! The Gray Ghost! There is much more to him than meets the eye. Tell me more!"

He brought his beautiful wife up to date.

▲ ▲ ▲

"What did you mean when you called him the Gray Ghost?" Michael asked his wife over dinner that night.

"Oh that. Well now, let me think. Oh, yes! Now I remember. *Supposedly*, some disgruntled photographer who was unable to get his picture named him that. He has been referred to as the Gray Ghost a number of times since then. I always thought it was a publicity stunt by Damon's PR firm. I *still* think so."

She paused for a moment, then said quietly. "I know how important your word is to you Mickey. I respect that. Now I want you to give me *your* word on something and I will give you mine. If *ever* you can't tell me something, you need to make me aware of the fact. We need to have complete honesty between us. If you come home angry, I need to know why; if it's me; if it's someone else; if it's work related that you can discuss, or work related that you *can't* discuss. Am I making sense?"

"Yes, you are. And I agree. The only way our marriage will work is if we keep the lines of communication open."

"Deal?" she said extending her hand.

"Deal." They shook hands.

"Do you know what some of the husband's wives are calling the A.C.T.U?" Sylvia asked artlessly.

"What dear?"

"The *British Intelligence Group Control Unit Neutralizing Terrorism.* And you are the *Big Tomcat.*"

"The Brit….. Whoa! *No way!* That's just plain *rude*, Syl! Which wives?" he asked indignantly.

"All of us. We thought it was hysterical." She giggled infectiously.

Michael thought for a moment. Then smiled. Then laughed. "It *is* funny you know. *Bloody brilliant.* I'll bet it was you. Only *American* women think that way. You and I both know that if a *man* said that, his wife would neuter him, but if a *woman* says it, it's *hysterical.*"

He paused and then said. "If I'm the big tomcat, then that makes you the big ….."

Still holding his hand, Sylvia smiled, interrupted and said, "I think I have a craving for a *Mickey of English Liqueur.*"

Michael Brighton looked into his wife's large turquoise eyes. Sometimes blue, sometimes green.

"And I think I'll feel a *little Syllie* if I don't kiss your big beautiful lips and immediately produce your *English Liqueur.*"

"Oh? … Ohhhhh……"

▲ ▲ ▲

Scene Twenty One

Damon Gray sat at his custom laptop computer.

'I'm in!' he thought as he gazed at his screen.

To look at it, you would think that it was an old Mac PowerBook, thick, chunky and beefy looking. It needed to be. It was the most sophisticated and powerful computer in the world. He had exaggerated to Michael when he said that his parents had passed a small amount of computer programming talent on to him.

Under exaggerated!

He wanted *no one* wanting, or attempting, to steal his computer. It looked like a beat up, hard used (which it was!) old laptop. He had left it on purpose a number of times on benches to see what would happen. Only twice had anyone taken any interest in it. Both times, the culprits abandoned it when they realized that it was an old Mac, virtually worthless, even at a pawn shop. It also had a tracking beacon in it. He could find it anywhere in the world.

His hands flew over the key board like he was playing one of his symphonies, surfing the files of the A.T.C.U. He was virtually invisible to them.

Again, he had told Lord Brighton a bit of a falsehood when he said that even he couldn't hack their computer system. It *would* have been true had he *not* installed the *'Gateway'* when he installed 'ISPY' for the A.T.C.U. system. It was a flawlessly beautiful system.

Flawless *only* because he had created them with an entirely new, quantum physics design system. One that he had invented. Two limited, intelligent, thinking computer programs!

One, *'Gateway'*, that procreated in milliseconds, without leaving a trail.

Whenever ACTU's computer talked to another computer, a copy of *'Gateway'* was installed on their system. He named the A.T.C.U. security system 'ISPY', taken from the children's game 'I Spy With My Little Eye'. He created ISPY and *'Gateway'* on 'Mac'. *'Gateway'* did not interfere with any computer systems in any noticeable way. It was a key. An invisible key that allowed Damon total invisible access to everything in a computer with ISPY installed.

ISPY was, in almost all cases, able to track any who were trying to hack into ISPY's computer system.

In less than two weeks, Damon's *'Gateway'* was in every major computer system in the world. All it needed was ISPY installed to activate it. Without it *'Gateway'* would remain dormant, waiting. If Damon had his way, *'Gateway'* would not be waiting long.

He finished his information surfing and exited *'Gateway'*.

He looked down at the dozen plus passports, each in separate plastic baggies, lying on his desk. All genuine, if they were checked. All with different names and different faces than his, but all faces that he could change his into. All had a contact lens case included, each with three sets of identical contact lenses, matching the eye color of the picture in the passport.

He picked a passport package, a British one that said Jeremy Lionez, Travel Agent. He then clicked Mac to British Isle Airlines and booked a flight to Paris, France.

Abduhl Mohamed Jabhared of *Allah's Hammer* had planted another bomb. One that had killed *one too many* innocent people.

▲ ▲ ▲

Scene Twenty Two

To say the flight to Paris was *eventful* would be a gross understatement.

At the beginning of it, Damon closed his eyes to nap and went *Elseware*.

He stood in the center of a huge circular cave with a domed roof that receded into darkness. Tunnel entrances, or exits, honeycombed the cave walls and ceilings. The floor was of purest black. Light surrounded the area that he was standing in, but he could not see where it was originating from. Sensing someone or something, Damon spun around, dropping into a *TAONA* state and stance, senses alert and searching.

In the distance and off to his right, two figures approached. Both were dressed identically. Dark grey, flowing yet formfitting, hooded, *ninja* or *warrior monk* styled outfits. The eye opening was covered with dark, non reflective sunglasses. The one on his left was carrying a small package.

As they approached, they parted slightly, stopping just out of striking distance.

His striking distance, which was much further back than a normal persons.

Damon noticed that the three of them made a perfect triangle in the cave.

They all stood motionless for a few moments, in absolute silence.

Damon studied them. They, in turn, studied him.

They were the first to break silence.

The *almost monks*, as Damon thought of them, both bowed slightly, in unison and the one on Damons left spoke.

"So, the caterpillar has shed its cocoon." The sound of the voice was deep, melodious and disturbingly familiar.

The language was unknown to him, yet he understood it!

Damon bowed slightly in return. "Do I know you, sirs?" Damon asked politely in the same, unknown language. *Strange!*

"Should not the question be, *do we know you?*" said the second monk, the monk on his right. His voice was identical to the first monks.

Damon frowned. Something was naggingly familiar about them.

'Whoa ... wait a minute! Caterpillar? Cocoon?'

Damon glanced down at himself and suddenly realized that he was stark naked.

What the hell was going on! He knew he'd been here before, but those memories were somehow blocked, shrouded in a dreamlike mist that he'd only had glimpses of, since he'd regained his abilities. One thing he did remember. In the past, he'd always been clothed. Well, not exactly clothed, as in cloth, like the monks. More like clothed in *armor.*

Nudity had never bothered him before and it didn't now. He smiled and shrugged.

"Well, I don't know. Should it be?" Again, he asked politely.

"I think so." Said the *Right* Monk.

"Alright, do you know me?"

"Good question," said *Right* Monk. "The answer .... "

"Cut out the *bullshit*, Garnet." Said Left Monk. "We don't have time for this!"

"Yes we do, Gold. Time flows differently here."

"Yes, it does. *But it still flows and we have a time limit.* So, let's cut out the crap and get down to business." With that said, the monk called Gold tossed Damon the package he was holding. Damon caught it.

"Get dressed Damon." said *Gold*. "While you are doing that, I will try to answer some of your questions."

Damon opened the package to find an outfit identical to theirs.

As he dressed in the new clothes, Gold and Garnet dropped into Lotus positions on the ground.

"As to your questions, yes we know you. And yes, you know us." Gold then nodded to Garnet and both removed their hoods.

Damon was in the process of putting on his trousers when this happened and he almost fell down. With a supreme effort, he regained his balance.

Damon was stunned. To cover, he continued to dress. No wonder they seemed familiar.

They were *HIM*. Damon Gray. Exactly! The same hair color, the same small scar on the chin, even the same voice. He couldn't tell about the eyes. They were still wearing their eye coverings.

'*Hmmm* .....' he thought. Then he realized that one of them had asked a question.

"What? ... I mean, I beg you pardon?"

"I said, how much do you remember of our previous visitations here at *Elseware?*"

Damon folded and tucked his hood into one of his many pockets. His glasses, he tucked into another. He then shook his head slightly.

"I'm not sure. A lot of it is still hazy. I know that this place that we are in is called *Elseware*. How, I don't know."

"*You* named it. It was ....." said Garnet. A small, quick motion from Gold silenced him.

"Please continue." said Gold.

"I have misty memories of you both teaching me. My *Talents?*" They both nodded. "And vague memories of having me practice. They work a little differently here don't they?" They both nodded again. "It's harder here. I do remember that. A little is coming back, now. I remember practicing my abilities over and over again although, dammit, I don't remember what I practiced. I also remember sparring with the two of you. Again, not the actual sparring. On earth, I always won. Here, I feel, I never won. Oh I may have had some draws, but I don't feel I ever won."

Damon paused for a moment, concentrating, then continued. "Until the last time! Now I remember! Always before, you double teamed me, wore me out." Damon dropped back into the TAONA state. "The last time you almost killed me, didn't you? I don't remember much, just the pain, the fear and the helplessness." his voice harsh with anger. Again the nods. They didn't rise or answer. They just sat there.

More memories came, vague memories of them trying to help him. He relaxed his guard slightly. "I don't remember seeing your faces though. I'm sure I would have remembered. I don't. Why did you almost kill me and why have you waited until now to show yourselves?"

The two monks looked at each other. Garnet nodded to Gold to take center stage.

"Do you remember the first time we met?" Gold asked. Damon shook his head.

"Well, it's probably just as well. The reason that we didn't take off our hoods, until now, is for one simple reason. You couldn't have handled it. You had too many defenses up, too much armor. You had become inflexible. Your shell had almost become you. You said you felt you never won against us. Correct?" A nod. "Well, that is not exactly true. We were not trying to beat you. We were trying to break your armor, your shell, if you will, to set you free. When you saw that newscast about the bombing in London, it overloaded your mind and sent you to us in *Elseware*. It was the only time that we were here *before* you. You were going through your final *change*. You were disoriented. We tore your armor off before you knew what was happening. We held you down and then we healed you. Do you remember that?" Damon shook his head, not speaking. "When we had fully healed you, we tried to force a meld, blend, or bond with you. Healing you weakened us and strengthened you. You were stronger than us. You broke away and vanished back to your world. Until now, a world we have been denied."

Gold paused for a moment as if gathering his thoughts.

"This is to be our last meeting with you." Gold stated quietly.

Damon started to speak, but stopped when Gold raised his hand.

"Let me finish, please. There is not much time. Questions later, Okay?" Damon nodded.

"We are *real*, Damon. As real as you. We are you. Or should I say, two missing parts of *you*. No, not so much *missing*, as *extra*. Think of us as two additional parts. Two pieces that you desperately lack, in the jigsaw puzzle of your being. Maybe not pieces that *you* think you need, but pieces that *we* think you need. Pieces that *we think you need* in order to survive in your world, as well as in others. We ..."

"What are you? Who are you?" Damon asked bluntly, interrupting.

"We are *you* Damon, but we are not whole. Without us, you can exist. Without you, we *can't*." again, he paused, trying to find the words.

"This is difficult for me to explain to you, Damon, because I'm not the brains. I am a *prime instinctual*, and Garnet is a *prime emotional*."

Garnet spoke. "Damon, I apologize for trying to meld with you without your permission. I thought it was wrong! I told Gold that I thought it was. I know that we can't exist without you. I panicked! After we hurt you so badly tearing off your shell, Gold was convinced that you wouldn't trust us. He said that *he* wouldn't, and quite honestly, neither would I. I went along. We were wrong. No, *I* was wrong!" Tears were flowing down his face as he talked. His face didn't scrunch up as a lot of peoples did. His face didn't know how to cry, but his heart did.

He started to say more, then stopped and smiled at Damon. The smile was breathtaking to Damon. Pure joy, pure innocence, pure trust. And shame. Shame over something he had no right to be. Damon smiled back.

"As Garnet said," Gold continued, "we made the mistake by trying to overwhelm you and meld, or blend, if you will, with you. It will not happen again. It ends now. *Elseware* will always be here for you Damon, but not for us. When you go back this time, we will either be a part of you or gone forever." The last was said quietly, matter of factly, with no emotion. "The choice is yours."

Gold rose smoothly to his feet, as did Garnet.

"I can't make a choice like that without enough information. I *won't*."

"Maybe this will help." Nodding to Garnet, both took off their dark grey sun glasses at the same time.

Damon, who thought he was prepared, gaped.

Gold's eyes were purest liquid gold, with the pupils slanted like a lion, or cat, oversized with no whites showing. They glowed.

Garnet' eyes were a marbled deep blood red, again with no whites showing. His eyes had *no* pupils. Different colors of red kept swirling around slowly, sluggishly. They seemed to look everywhere at once.

Both looked like demons from hell. Damon shuddered involuntarily. How was this supposed to help?

Gold smiled. "Do you now understand why we didn't show you who we were at the beginning?"

Damon nodded. *'Dammit, all I seem to do is nod.'* he thought. He sighed.

"Alright now … how is seeing two demons from hell supposed to help me decide anything?"

Both demons looked mystified for a moment, not understanding the question.

Then Garnet laughed. "You tell him, you *golden eyed demon from hell.*"

Damon was getting angry. He was not a stupid man. What did he not understand?

"Read our auras," said Gold, "and *then* look into our eyes."

'Of course!' thought Damon. *'What is it about this place that confuses me? That makes me feel like an idiot?'*

Without answering, Damon turned up his aura vision and looked at Gold's aura intently. What he saw could not exist. Gold's aura was pure liquid gold, forever in motion.

Impossible! He couldn't exist.

No living beings aura was a pure color! He looked at Garnet and saw the same thing. Garnet's color was pure liquid swirling blood red, just like his eyes.

Damon got excited. Unbelievable! What an opportunity. He beckoned them closer. They came to within a few feet of him.

For what seemed like an eternity, he studied them, then he did as Gold had suggested but he added a twist. He reached out and took Gold's hands in his. Gold did not object. He looked into Gold's eyes with his aura vision. No matter how deep he probed, he saw no deceit. Damon also *felt* none.

He then took Garnet's hands in his and looked into *his* eyes. He saw and felt the same thing. Again, *no* deceit.

Something happened when he was in contact with them, but didn't realize until he withdrew his hands. He *knew* them in an extraordinary way.

What they said was true. Gold and Garnet could never exist in his world. They should not have been able to exist anywhere.

'Not anywhere, except Elseware.' He thought. *'In Elseware, they exist, and only for now, it seems.'*

"Talk to me Golden. Help me to understand."

"I'm, no, *we* are not sure how we were created." Gold looked at Garnet, who nodded in agreement. "We think that maybe you did, or your parents did, or that you and your parents did, when you all died.

That's when we *became ... aware*, when you first came to *Elseware*. You came and then we did. We don't think it was long after you came, but we don't know."

"How about the ninja warrior outfits? Whose idea was that?"

"Again we don't know. They were on us when we arrived, just as yours was with us this time after you arrived. We arrived knowing certain things. That is all we know. If we meld, you will know what we know. I have a feeling that we have almost run out of time. Don't ask how I know, I just do. I'm the *Prime Instinctual*. I'm not often wrong."

"How do we do this thing, Golden? Will *I* still be *me*?" Damon asked.

"Golden. That's twice you called me that. I *like* it. Yes, you will still be you, but more. It is hard to explain. You will know what we know when we bond. All three of us will do it. It will only take a few moments. I don't know how much time we have." He glanced around quickly. "If we're going to do it, we must do it *now*. Put this ring on the ring finger of your right hand." He handed Damon a silver colored ring. Damon looked at him quizzically. "Pure white Tarantium." said Golden. "Mine is pure yellow Tarantium and Garnet's is pure red Tarantium." They both held forth their right hands to show him their matching rings.

"Tarantium?" Damon asked.

"I know, it is a mythical substance with special properties that isn't supposed to exist, but it does here."

Damon looked at them closely. He noticed that all three were identical, except for the color. There were beautiful three dimensional triangles embedded all around the outside center of the rings. Not engraved, embedded. He ran his fingers over his and could feel no ridges, but you could see them. Amazing works of art! Masterpieces! He slipped his ring on the ring finger of his right hand. A perfect fit! Stranger and stranger!

"Let us join hands and create a triangle." intoned Golden. "Oh, and one more thing, Damon. I have a message for you." His voice changed to that of one whom Damon knew well.

"*Too many innocents are dying. Stop giving those damned terrorist bombers a warning, son.*"

Scene Twenty Three

"We are about to land, sir. Please raise your seat to the upright position. Sir?... Sir?"

A hand touched his shoulder.

Damon Gray (*Monsieur Lionez*) opened his eyes and smiled at the flight attendant. He raised his seat. She smiled in return and passed on.

Damon had awakened refreshed. He remembered! *They* remembered! Coming together as one. Holding hands, they recited the mantra that Golden had brought with him. '*We three are now one, never to be parted, each irrevocably bonded in essence, each bound by oath, each bound by trust, each bound by a Tarantium ring forged in the primal fires of creation. Beyond life. Beyond death. Forever. So be it! Ad Infinitum!*

The blending was beyond anything Damon could have imagined. Indescribable. It was the most painful and beautiful experience, intermingled in a way that went beyond words. *Forged, Blended and Melded by the Fires of the Universe,* he was now *'Three into One'*.

Damon Gray felt more alive than he had ever been, though still a child in many worldly ways, for all his thirty five years. Still with all the flaws of the human animal, but with a lot more passion for life than he'd ever felt before. There was still the *Void*, but *now* it was manageable. *Now* he had a *purpose*.

Just before they started the *Blend*, Garnet said to Damon. "Do you remember your mission statement? *The Bakers Dozen?*"

"No."

"You will."

▲ ▲ ▲

Scene Twenty Four

He now remembered it. No, not remembered it, *knew it.* He was fourteen when he made it in *Elseware.*

"I will always strive to:
- Put first things first.
- To myself, be true.
- Focus on the *solution*, not the *challenge*.
- Have the courage to do what must be done.
- Forgive myself when I need to.
- Welcome *fear* and ride it like a wild stallion.
- Laugh in the face of *Adversity*.
- Learn *when* to runaway, *then run as fast as I can.*
- Learn *when* to forgive, then forgive completely.
- Keep my weapons razor sharp and perfectly maintained.
- Continually grow, sharpen and control all my *gifts, talents and abilities*.
- Learn through observation, action and reaction, *each and every day*.
- Look at life as a wondrous journey, an adventure with only one final destination.

Damon smiled at the memory.

He had only been fourteen and had just lost both his parents. He had taken a long time to compose it, changing it countless times, (using many of his parents sayings), until at last, he was temporarily satisfied with it.

Other memories came. Like an avalanche. His mind sorted them easily.

At fourteen, when he became *aware* in the unknown place, he named it *Else Aware* because he was *unaware* of where he was. He then shortened it to *Elseware*. Not to be confused with 'elsewhere'. *Elseware* was a definite place. To a fourteen year old, it made perfect sense. Damon smiled at the memory.

One thing *had* worried him at the beginning of the meld. It shouldn't have. Both Golden and Garnet agreed with him totally.

Not one of them was averse to killing, when it *had* to be done.

He had become *Aware* just as the plane was to start it's descent into Paris International Airport, when the flight attendant had touched his arm to wake him.

When Damon deplaned, the flight attendant asked *"How was your first class service, Mr. Lionez?"*

Damon replied absentmindedly *"We had a great flight, thank you, Brigitte."*

'Careful', a voice seemed to whisper in his mind, *in the Elseware language*. 'We are *one* now.'

Scene Twenty Five

"*Do you have anything to declare, Monsieur Lionez?*"

"*No.*"

Clickedy, clickedy, click …

"*Your occupation?*"

"*Travel Agent.*"

Clickedy, clickedy, click …

"*Ahh! And the purpose of you visit?*"

"*Vacation.*"

Clickedy, clickedy, click …

"*How long will you be staying?*"

"*Two weeks, maybe longer.*"

Clickedy, clickedy, click …

"*Have a nice visit, monsieur Lionez.*"

Click

"*Thank you.*"

As Damon turned to leave, the Customs Agent smiled and said,

"*You're welcome. That is a beautiful ring you are wearing. I thought you might be a Jeweler.*"

Damon paused in his turn. Ring? What ring? He didn't wear jewelry.

The Customs Agent was looking at his right hand. He held it up.

There, on his ring finger, was a tri-color Tarantium ring with entwined triangles of all three colors circling it!

Impossible!

Smiling, Damon said, *"This? Yes, it is a pretty trinket, isn't it? A gift from a family member. A Coat Of Arms, if you will. Thank you for noticing."*

The word *trinket* did it. The Customs Agent promptly lost interest and turned to the next passenger.

"Do you have anything to declare ...."

Clickedy, clickedy, click ...

Damon continued his turn, pulled on his leather gloves and headed toward the Baggage Claim area.

▲ ▲ ▲

In the penthouse suite at the *Hotel Le Paris*, Damon removed his gloves and examined his new addition.

It was the most beautiful ring he had ever seen, and he was a collector of beautiful art! The three dimensional triangles of white, yellow and red Tarantium were impossibly intertwined. It gave him a sense of vertigo when he looked at it too closely, as if it was pulling him into it.

When he went to pull it off, the ring resisted. It resisted? *'How the hell could a ring resist?'*

He pulled harder and slowly the ring came off his finger. When it was fully off Damon placed it on the table and turned to the suitcase to get his tools.

The moment Damon's hand lost contact with the ring, he screamed as *something* slammed into his mind knocking him to his knees. The pain was almost unbearable. Almost!

Gritting his teeth, then relaxing them as his defenses kicked in, Damon slowly rose from the floor. He reached over and picked up the ring with his right hand.

Bang! The pain was gone! He let go of the ring. Wham! The pain was back. He picked up the ring again. Bang! The pain was gone.

He went to put it on the ring finger of his left hand and it wouldn't go on! No matter how much he tried he couldn't get it over his first knuckle.

Finally, he put it back on his right hand ring finger and stared at it. Suddenly, it hit him!

Slowly, ever so slowly, he slid the ring toward the end of his finger. As he moved it, he could feel the pressure building in his head. The instant his body lost contact with it, Wham! The pain! Sliding the ring on and off his finger a number of times confirmed what had hit him.

It was a Psychic Switch of sorts. The Melding had increased his Psychic *Abilities* exponentially. The Switch was his *control*, his buffer. Settling the ring back on his finger, Damon proceeded to open his mind and look at the ring. What he saw amazed him. He didn't even know he could do this!

The *Switch*, as he now thought of it, was a part of him! What was even *wilder* was that when he thought of the name '*Switch*', it pulsed, acknowledging its name.

'*Well, I'll be damned! Hello Switch!*' Damon thought. *Pulse!*

Knock! Knock!

"*Hotel Security! Is everything alright, monsieur?*"

'*Later, Switch.*' Pulse.

"*Everything is fine! I just tripped over my feet. Sorry!*"

"*Please open the door.*"

Damon opened the door, allowed the two detectives to enter and quickly tour the premises. He apologized again. He tipped them heavily. It's amazing how tipping soothes suspicious minds. On their way out, he thanked them for their concern and closed the door.

▲ ▲ ▲

Scene Twenty Six

It was evening.

In the top floor penthouse suite of *Le Hotel Meringue*, Abduhl Mohamed Jabhared looked out of his twenty sixth floor window, overlooking the valley of *Meringue*.

'What a beautiful, peaceful looking valley.' Abduhl thought, watching in awe as the suns final rays bathed the hills in golden splendor. *'It is strange how looks can be deceiving.'* He looked at himself in the full length mirror across the room. His reflection did not look like the man he once knew. *That man*, he knew, always looked confident, cool and prepared. That was *not* the bald person he saw in the mirror staring back at him with small scared eyes.

The last bombing felt *wrong* to Jabhared! That he was ordered to do it meant less than nothing. It was done to bring Mr. Smoke into the clutches of Allah's *Hammer*. Like a fine wine turned to vinegar, it did not taste right! He strove to find inner balance! He was *not* in balance!

Abduhl knew that Mr. Smoke was coming. Mr. Smoke *was Death* to him. He could feel it in his bones. He could feel *Death* coming. It was an eerie and debasing experience.

Gone was his noble self image. In its void was a terrified man, a man out of control. A lost man. A man no longer sure of his destination. One thing he felt strongly. No matter what happened with Mister Smoke, he was a man forever changed.

Despising what he saw, he looked away from the mirror. *He had to live!* He had to correct his image of himself before passing to the next world. To die as he was, was a fate that terrified him. He needed *time* to *prepare!* To fix what was broken. Inside.

Not as he and his superiors had *prepared*. The valley was riddled with terrorist militants, posing as tourists, awaiting Mr. Smoke to make his appearance. He was told to keep his head shaved. To taunt Mr. Smoke and give him a target that he could identify and seek. For the first time in his adult life, Abduhl was now relying on others to protect him.

He had personally hand picked his retinue. Each of them surpassed him in fighting skills, though he would never admit that to them. Twelve of them, nine men and three women. He had, at different times, bested each of them in personal combat. Not him, but his reputation had bested them. Some guessed, but most were unwilling to put their theory to the test. Neither was he! He could not beat them a second time. The couple of times he had been asked for a rematch, he had inferred that he didn't want to hurt them *anymore*, that they were too valuable for that. He also let it be known that *if* a rematch was to take place, only *one* would live.

Ten years earlier, two of his students challenged him in a way that he couldn't refuse. He told them that he would fight the winner of a fight between the two of them. They eagerly agreed. They didn't like each other and each thought that they were, in every way, superior in fighting skills to the other. Abduhl agreed to oversee the contest. The winner was to be given enough recovery time, then fight him. The two soldiers guarding the door were given instructions, by Abduhl, not to enter, no matter what they heard.

The battle was long, fast and furious. The victor could hardly stand when it was over. Abduhl glided across the room and killed the victor quickly, then walked over to the defeated man and snapped his neck with one blow. He then walked out of the room and told the guards that they had both attacked him at once and that he had no choice but to protect himself. Abduhl made sure the story got exaggerated over the years. It was now whispered that he had accepted the challenge of the two simultaneously and had killed both without breaking a sweat.

Now though, his students were looking at him differently. He was a mean, vicious instructor. He believed that *pain* was the quickest instructor. It had worked on him. The fact that he enjoyed inflicting it on subordinates alienated him from them. He had controlled them by fear. They had thought that he was invincible. Mr. Smoke had dispelled that myth.

Abduhl felt that his students looked at him with different eyes. Eyes that secretly smiled at his baldness. He could feel it as he walked by and among them. Nothing was said to his face, but it was there in their eyes. He could feel their cold, calculating eyes. They no longer feared him as they had. As *he* felt they *should have.*

"Once this Mr. Smoke threat has been dealt with, things will return to normal." the Control Squadron Commander had told him when they had talked about the plan.

"You are our best terrorist trainer. We will allow nothing to happen to you. Not one of your students will be allowed to challenge you again, and no more field work for you, after this next time. Is that understood?" Abduhl nodded. *"Good! As to our Mr. Smoke situation, we will move heaven and earth to see that he is caught and interrogated. Would you like to be in on the interrogation?"*

At this, Abduhl Mohamed Jabhared had smiled.

▲ ▲ ▲

Jabhared was *not* smiling any more!

He had made the *'Drop'* a month ago, and had been stuck in this hotel suite ever since. At first locked in, now locking himself in.

Surrounded by people who really didn't care if he lived or died. Not there to protect him, but to catch the terrorist killer, Mr. Smoke.

Abduhl found that he had no friends. He'd never realized it because he'd never needed them before.

Abduhl felt truly alone. Alone and scared.

Two things he had never experienced before.

The month had seemed like an eternity. At the beginning he was confident that Mr. Smoke would be dealt with quickly. But each day after that first leached away a little of his confidence and courage, until he was but a shell of his former self. The month had eaten away his manhood. He needed to get it back before it was too late.

He would never get into *Paradise* like this.

▲ ▲ ▲

There was a knock at the door!

"Abduhl, it is I, Sub Commander Karolin. May I come in?"

"Enter." Was the gruff reply.

With that, the door opened and in walked the Company Sub Commander. Sub Commander Karolin was short, fat and greasy looking. His navy business suit, although it fit beautifully, did not flatter him in any way.

He strode purposely across the room to stop directly in front of Abduhl.

"Our plans have changed. It seems that Mister Smoke is not going to appear. We are moving out ninety percent of our team today. Now! We can't afford to keep them here any longer. It is straining our budget."

Abduhl Mohamed Jabhared leaned slightly forward, toward Karolin.

"Budget? What, in Allah's name, do you mean Budget? I have done my job. You had better do yours." The last was said very softly, and with clear meaning.

Commander Karolin stepped back quickly. *"Are you threatening me? Do you know what will happen if I report you? Don't you dare threaten me! Don't you dare! I am leaving now. You will just have to adjust and adapt. That is your lot."*

With that said, he started to turn toward the door. He felt a hand grip his arm in a vice like grip that stopped his turn abruptly and slowly turned him around, even though his body was striving mightily not to.

"You will stand here worm, *until I give you permission to go."* Those soft words froze the sub Commander in his tracks. Perspiration popped out and turned his round face slick.

"You are not *pulling out ninety percent of our force. You may take thirty percent and that does not include my students. Of those, I will keep nine. I will keep six men and the three women. You can choose which students to take. I will choose the thirty percent."*

"That's impossible. I can't justify a thirty percent reduction, when I told command that I was taking ninety percent. How will I explain it to them?"

"You will just have to adjust and adapt. That is your *lot."*

"Do you really think you can make me? Do you know who my brother is?" Karolin sputtered. *"He's ..."*

"I know who he is. I also know that you are one of many brothers and he will miss you little. It is your choice though."

Jabhared let go of the Company Sub Commanders arm, turned around and looked out of his window. The building, *Le Hotel Meringue*, sat on top of a high hill overlooking the town. The sun had set, the stars shone brilliantly in a black sky and the lights of the town flickered in the distance, like the moon and stars were reflecting on the waves of a moonlit sea. Jabhared clasped his hands behind his back.

"It is a beautiful night to be alive, is it not Sub *Commander?"*

"Yes ... yes it is." Defeat was in his voice. He turned to leave.

As he put his hand on the door knob, Jabhareds voice stopped him.

"You may tell headquarters that you have re-evaluated the situation. You may also tell them that you will reduce the remaining force by fifty percent in one week if nothing has changed. Does that help?"

Commander Karolin smiled and breathed a sigh of relief. *"Yes, thank you, Abduhl. Have a pleasant evening."* He left the room and locked the door behind himself.

The terrorist smiled. Not *all* mocked him.

He now had a one week reprieve. He must make plans. Mr. Smoke could outwait them all!

He grabbed the phone and spoke into it. *"Room 317."* A pause. *"Bring me up some writing instruments and paper. Immediately."*

A few minutes later, there was another knock at the door. *"Who is it?"*

"Your writing instruments and paper sir!" came the reply in a woman's voice he recognized. It was Souad.

He unlocked the door and stood behind it. *"Come in, Souad."*

The door opened and a trim, well dressed, female entered the room.

She looked startled when she could not see him at once. She dropped her package and grabbed for the gun under her jacket.

Jabhared was upon her in an instant, pinning her arms to her side, disarming her. Quicker than a dessert snake, Souad slammed her head backwards, while stomping down on his instep and rabbit punching his crotch. She almost broke Abduhl's nose and came close to neutering him. He threw her away at the last second. She dropped, rolled and came up into a fighting crouch, seven inches of razor sharp steel, appearing as if by magic, in her right hand. Slowly she rose and replaced the knife back inside her clothing, as she saw Abduhl with *her* gun pointed at *her* head.

"Very good, Souad. Very good! You were caught unawares and still reacted beautifully. Pick up the writing equipment and take notes." Reversing the pistol, he handed it back to her. He smiled. She smiled back and bent to pick up what she had dropped. Bent in a way that kept *him* in her line of sight always.

Inside he was furious! He was almost taken out by one of his pupils! One of the best admittedly, but he had the element of surprise on his side. He should have been able to take her out easily. He was having a hard time maintaining his posture and composure, the pain in his groin was so severe. So much for the lesson he was going to teach her.

He forced himself to walk briskly back to his desk to sit down.

Once seated, he dictated what the new schedule for the remaining soldiers was to be, as well as their duties.

When she had left with her instructions, he closed the curtains and sat in the dark, locked room and brooded. He was past his prime. Time to admit it. His body did not react like that of a twenty year old anymore. He could smell the stale sweat on his body from the reaction to Souad's rabbit punch to his testicles. The stink. He hoped she hadn't smelled it while she was taking notes. He must get rid of it! He remembered the saying *'Cleanliness is next to Godliness.'*

'Dark!' Fear attacked him.

'Dark!' The word slammed into his mind *again!* *'Dark is* Mr. Smokes *friend!'*

Panic set in. Throbbing testicles temporarily forgotten, he jumped up and turned on all the lights. He was shivering.

'Stop it!' he yelled silently to his body.

He sat for a few moments and let the panic attack pass. He was sweating again. He could smell the stink of his fear.

He went into the bathroom, turned on the shower and stripped down. As he waited for the water to heat up, he posed in front of the full length mirror. He didn't like what he saw. He remembered, *vividly*, the soldiers laughing at him when he was dazed, shaved and naked in the desert.

In the mirror he *now* saw what *they* saw. His chest fat sagging over his pectoral muscles, his flat ass and wrinkled butt skin, as well as his loose stomach fat, his loose paunch hanging down and out, no matter how hard he tried to suck it in. He still had a tremendous amount of muscle but it was hidden underneath a middle aged layer of fat. He had gotten soft. How had that happened?

He didn't look like a *Legend* any more.

He stepped into the shower and closed the sliding door. He heard the phone in the other room ring. Stepping out of the shower, he wrapped a towel around himself and walked into the other room.

"What do you want?" Abduhl growled into the phone. He listened for a few moments, then interrupted, *"I'm taking a shower. I will call you back when I am done."*

Back in the shower, he smiled. The Sub Commander had informed him that his suggestions had been implemented. *Suggestions?* Oh well, might as well allow the little man an illusion or two.

He closed his eyes and put his head under the shower head to rinse off the soap. He felt a soft breeze!

'NO!' he silently screamed. *'I'm not ready!'*

Striving to maintain his footing on the slippery floor, he tried to clear his eyes and spin at the same time. He never saw the bullet coming. But he felt it.

▲ ▲ ▲

Scene Twenty Seven

Mr. Smoke looked down at the dead *terrorist bomber*. Abduhl was sprawled in a most ungracious position. Holstering his gun, Damon knelt and arranged the body to his liking. Without looking, he reached into one of his outfits many pockets; withdrew a tube of black lipstick and made a dark ring around the bullet entry point in the middle of Abduhl's forehead, smudging it to look like smoke. Then he reached into another of his pockets and took out a slim titanium case. From this he withdrew a slim cigar. He attached a miniature computer vacuum to one end of it and turned it on. He then lit the cigar and let the vacuum suck the smoke through until he was satisfied that it was burning right. Turning off and replacing the vacuum unit back into one of his pockets, he took the cigar and placed it securely in the bullet hole.

Stepping back, he produced a miniature camera and took pictures.

He then made a thorough search of the apartment, went back to the open window, hooked to the sill a grappling hook with a dull grey cord attached, looked down to make sure that there were no auras on the ground and jumped out of the window.

He dropped two of the twenty six floors before he slowed his descent, stopping on the twentieth floor. Using his body as a pendulum, he swung back and forth until he reached an open hotel room window at the far side of the hotel on the twenty first floor. Snagging the window sill, Damon flipped himself acrobat style through the opening; tucked and rolled to his feet in one fluid motion. During his last pendulum swing he saw an Aura come around the corner of the hotel on the ground floor! He carefully looked down from his window. Another Aura came around the corner. The two Auras came together and blended. Their colors changed. Damon smiled. Two lovers kissing. They turned and walked away together.

Damon then unhooked the grappling hook, pulled in his rope, and closed the window. After changing out of his newly designed Mr. Smoke outfit into his street clothes, he dismantled his gun, cleaned it, reassembled it with a minor variation and put it back in its case. He then put it, along with the rest of his things, including his Mr. Smoke outfit, into the open, partially packed suitcase laying on the bed, closed and locked it.

He sat down at his laptop, Mac, and sent off a pre-typed email message to the Surrette, France's Secret Service Police. Earlier that day, he had informed them that Allah's Hammer was in the *Meringue* valley, somewhere, with a bomb. He told them to be in downtown *Meringue* and await further instructions.

Mr. Smoke now sent off the exact coordinates to Abduhl's location.

Making sure there were no auras in the hall, Damon opened the door; left the hotel room and the hotel.

A few minutes later, directly across from *Le Hotel Meringue*, Jeremy Lionez, Travel Agent, was checking into the *LaGrange Hotel* when the Surrette arrived, in force, at *Le Hotel Meringue*.

Later in his penthouse hotel room, Jeremy ordered dinner through Room Service.

As he waited, he reviewed the day.

'All in all, a good Cigar!' was the thought that caused Damon to smile.

As an old time famous American actor had once said, 'A *broad* is always a *broad*, but a good cigar is a *Smoke!'*

The French Secret Police raided the villa where Abduhl was assassinated, and found the Abduhl's smoking body still warm in the shower. An anonymous tip, they told the hotel manager to gain access.

"No Comment" to the news media.

Scene Twenty Eight

The global news media were all over it. As reported on the French television station by François News' correspondent, Jacques Leoma:

"*Good evening everyone. We interrupt this program to bring you this important news flash. It cannot wait until eleven. My name is Jacques Leoma of François News at Eleven. Tonight we have news of the famous* international terrorist assassin, Mr. Smoke. *But first a prelude:*

"*A spokesperson from the Surrette neither confirmed nor denied that, earlier this evening, the Surrette entered a hotel room, shot and killed one known terrorist and arrested three others in, what is to be later verified,* international terrorist bomber *Abduhl Mohamed Jabhared's hotel room. The three arrested are confirmed members of the terrorist organization, 'Allah's Hammer'. Through information provided from an unidentified source, Abduhl Mohamed Jabhared himself was found dead in his shower shot once in the head. The three terrorists are being held without bail, for possession of illegal weapons, having false identification and illegal entry into the country with intent to commit an act of terrorism. They were not charged with the Jabhared killing. No other terrorists were arrested.*" Jacques paused for a moment.

"*And now for tonight's top story!*

"*The information about Abduhl's death came with pictures. If there are any children up at this hour, I would suggest that you* not *let them see these photographs. If you are offended by scenes of death, please change the channel now! They are extremely graphic in nature. I repeat: If there are any children up at this hour, I would suggest that you not let them see these photographs. They are extremely graphic in nature. If you are offended by scenes of death, please change the channel now! After you have seen the pictures, I think you will know who the unidentified source is. This newscast will be repeated on the eleven o'clock newscast, along with any further developments. Tune us in at François News at Eleven"*

The pictures were then shown. There were four pictures with four captions, one under each picture.

Below each of the pictures, in block letters, these words were printed:

FROM THIS MOMENT ON

ALL TERRORIST BOMBERS WILL BE KILLED

THERE WILL BE NO MORE WARNINGS

MISTER SMOKE

Every major television news station around the world received the same pictures at the same time, with the words written in the countries native tongue.

It was a shot that was seen and heard *around the world*.

Scene Twenty Nine

"*H*ow, in god's name, did the media get those photographs so quickly?" muttered Surrette Chief Jean Paul Perrier.

"*I don't know. It does seem like magic, doesn't it?*" enthused Inspector Pierre Benoit. "*They had them on the air before we left the hotel, and they were better quality than ours. They captured the smoke from the cigar beautifully. Mister Smoke must be a professional photographer. We probably didn't get a copy because our email is not listed.*"

"*Very astute, Inspector. Thank you for pointing out the obvious.*" The Surrette Chief snapped.

The look on Benoit's face stopped the Chief from going on. Taking a deep breath, he continued. "*I'm sorry Pierre. That was uncalled for. Sometimes the obvious is what we overlook.*" Suddenly his face brightened. "*You're right though! We didn't get those pictures because our email is not listed. Do we have a top security website that informants can reach us through? One that can't be 'hacked', I think the word is? One that we can track where it is being sent from and maybe by whom?*"

"*We don't sir, but the A.T.C.U. does. We had limited access into their system at one time but now they have a system in place that baffles all of our top computer genius's. They even sent us a letter asking us to let them know if we ever breached it. They knew what we were trying to do and they traced it to us. That should have been impossible! All our top techs*" *have told us it should be impossible, but it happened. Maybe we should contact them?"*

"Just like that? Contact them and ask for their security system? I do know about their system. It has everyone in the department talking." He paused for a moment, then smiled. *"What the bloody hell, as the English would say, why not? You are a genius Pierre. Set up a contact for me. And a meeting if you can. Use the Mr. Smoke situation as the reason. As Jean Luc Picard would say, 'Make it so'."*

"Excuse me, sir? Who is Jean Luc Picard?"

"It doesn't matter Pierre. It was just an actor on an old American TV series, Star Trek, the Next Generation."

Pierre nodded knowingly, but the Chief knew that, on this, he was clueless.

"I'll get on it right away sir. I'll 'Make it so'."

▲ ▲ ▲

Scene Thirty

Inside a room with a desk and one chair, in a nameless building whose address didn't exist on any data base in the world except one, two men were standing.

In response to a summons, a slender man was standing in front of another man, a monster of a man that dwarfed the smaller man. Although both men were the same height, the slender man looked wraithlike.

"Where the hell is that information I requested?" Taking a huge cigar from his mouth, United States General George Hammerdam, the Head of S.T.U.N.T. (Strategic Tactical Unit Neutralizing Terrorism), looked like his name. Huge and formidable.

"The men are working on it, sir. So far, no luck." responded Captain Roger Roy.

"Thought you told me they were the best in the *'universe'*, wasn't that the word you used, Sergeant?"

"Yes sir, and it's Captain, sir."

"Not if I don't get some results pretty damn quick."

"Then call me *Sergeant*, sir." Roy said quietly.

"What did you say, youngster?" thundered the General.

The slender man, still standing at attention, responded quietly again.

"What, are you hard of hearing, *sir*? I said 'call me *Sergeant*'. When you promote me to *Colonel*, I will talk to you again about the situation. I'm Volunteer Reserve and I *really really* don't have to take this abuse from a pompous, ignorant, self righteous, pig faced, loutish, asshole, who smokes a putrid smelling cigar," pause, "*sir*."

With that, he just stood there and calmly looked the general in the face.

The general clenched his fists. He saw Roy smile and remembered that the young man was a trained killer of the military's highest and finest caliber. Quickly relaxing his hands, he got control over his emotions. He had just gotten his ass chewed out from *his* boss at the White House, and was in a foul mood. He had made a big mistake coming down on Captain Roger Roy.

"What's that you say, son, you don't like my cigar. I'll have you know it's pure, one hundred percent Cuban!" he roared. "And who the hell says *putrid* anymore?"

Roy couldn't help it. He smiled. "Well, it may be Cuban, sir, probably, what, fifty dollars a pop?" the General nodded, "but it is the rankest smelling piece of shit that I have ever had the privilege of inhaling. Makes me want to puke, sir."

The General couldn't help himself either, he chuckled. Then his face sobered.

"It's a good thing no one was in the office to hear what transpired here, Colonel. I was wrong to handle the situation the way I did, and I apologize."

"It's Captain, sir, and your apology is accepted. I reacted badly also. My apologies for everything *except* that disgusting smelling leaf between your fingers. It has been a bad day for me also. I am as upset as you that my men can't find even a trace of where the email from Mr. Smoke came from. It just appeared in our system. That shouldn't be able to happen. I know. I am classified C12."

The general's body language gave nothing away, but he was impressed. C12 was the top accreditation for a Computer Super Genius. He took off his hat and rubbed his totally bald head.

"Have we been breached, son? What can I tell the Pentagon? They are demanding answers."

"Tell them, *we don't know,* sir. Tell them we are still working on it, but will probably never know for sure, unless we catch this Mr. Smoke character. They won't know what to do with the truth."

United States General George Hammerdam smiled, then chuckled. "Son, you have just earned your right to the Colonel's Eagle." Roy started to object. "Whoa, youngster. Now you have to keep earning it." Scribbling on a piece of paper, he handed it to the new Colonel. "Here is the Pentagon's number. The name is on there and the code number. Memorize and destroy. Let me know how it goes. I'll be in the cafeteria, feeding my loutish pig face." Colonel Roy's face reddened.

'*Shit!*' he thought, '*I'll never live that one down.*'

"Relax, Colonel. I accept your apology also. I like a man who speaks his mind. Just be careful who hears it," pause, "Understood?" Roy nodded. "Good! From now on you work directly under me, *full time* now. Man, am I hungry. I'll see you in the cafeteria."

He turned and headed for the door. Then he stopped, turned and walked back to the young soldier. He stuck his cigar in his mouth.

"Show me how fast you are youngster." talking around his stogie. "Take my cigar away from me."

Quicker than an angry viper, Colonel Roy's hand whipped out and took the cigar from the Generals mouth.

"Hmmm. You're fast Colonel, I'll give you that. Now throw your cigar in the garbage on the way out. And speaking of out, make sure you put it out."

As he started to turn he added, "Never mind. I'll do it myself."

Colonel Roy looked down at the hand that had been holding the cigar. His hand. It was empty.

He looked up at the General stone faced. The General looked at him hard and then gave a small smile.

The new Colonel stood and watched as the General, puffing on his cigar, left the room.

114

'Dammit, never *underestimate the opponent. I could have got my ass kicked!'* he thought. Then he smiled. *'No way!'* He had *let* the General take the cigar.

And he *knew* the General *knew.*

Looking at the paper, he walked over to the desk, sat down and picked up the phone.

▲ ▲ ▲

Scene Thirty One

Michael Brighton was sitting at his desk, reading reports on the Mr. Smoke situation, when there was a soft knock on the door.

"Enter."

John Sherwood entered. *He always reminds me of an old Rock and Roller.'* Michael thought as his eyes traveled over the trim form. He was wearing fashionably aged black designer jeans, a white heavy duty designer casual shirt, buttoned at the neck, no tie, chestnut brown loafers and belt, topped with a black Armani relaxed sweater sport coat. That, along with his long chestnut and grey streaked hair, tied in a ponytail, hanging halfway down his back, and his John Lennon glasses, created the old rocker impression. He certainly didn't look at all like the head of A.T.C.U. Security.

"Lord Brighton, we have received communication from the French Surrette. They would like to set up some kind of protected electronic satellite meeting with our top person, or decision maker, to discuss the Mr. Smoke situation. That would be you sir."

"John, do you even own a suit?"

"I may have one in storage, somewhere. Why do you ask sir?"

"Just curious, John. I can't, for the life of me, remember ever seeing you in one, that's all."

"I don't believe you have, sir. I'm sure I would remember it, if I had."

Michael smiled. John spoke in a very precise way. He likened it to a slightly inebriated man acting sober. An accident had caused it when he was but a child. He knew his Chief of Security never drank alcohol or used any mind or mood altering drugs. He would be very surprised if Sherwood even took aspirin. Michael enjoyed the way he talked. They had known each other for many years.

"How is the family, John?"

"Family, sir?"

"You have a cat, don't you? Oscar? He had an operation, didn't he?"

John smiled.

"Ahh … yes. The *operation*. It was successful, sir. He is now an *it*. Oscar won't be getting my neighbors angry any more by getting their purebred cats pregnant."

Michael laughed.

"The Surrette, sir?" his Chief of Security prodded.

"I did hear you, John. I wasn't ignoring the question. I was trying to figure out what to do. This is a first, isn't it? The Surrette trying to set up a meeting with *us*?"

"Yes sir, it is."

"Any thoughts or suggestions?"

"I think it's a ploy, sir."

"A ploy?"

"A ruse, sir."

"I know what a *ploy* is John." Michael smiled a small smile. "And a *ruse*. What I meant was, *what kind of ploy?*"

"I'm not sure, sir. I just don't think that Mr. Smoke warrants that kind of importance. Do you?"

"No, I don't. And that's what is bothering me. Let me think on it for a bit, and I'll get back to you. Assume that I'm going to do it, though, and take appropriate action."

"Very good, sir. Good morning to you, then." With that, John Sherwood turned and left the room.

▲ ▲ ▲

Scene Thirty Two

"Graystone Manor, Hastings here. (pause) I'll see if he'll take your call."

Damon Gray had just finished his morning exercise/training regimen, when Hastings walked through the door carrying a portable phone.

"A call on your private line, Dr. Gray. Line six. Asked to speak to you. Wouldn't give a name. The voice is electronically scrambled. I can't tell if it's a man or a woman, but the phrasings would suggest a man, sir."

"Thank you, Hastings." Damon said as he toweled his torso down.

"I'll call you if I need you." He reached for the phone.

"Very good, sir. I'll be in the kitchen, making breakfast. Would you like some?"

"What are you making? No, never mind. Yes, I'd love some Hastings. Whatever it is."

When Hastings had closed the door, Damon turned on the phone.

"Thank you for holding, how may I help you?"

"Is Damon there, please?"

"Whom shall I say is calling?"

"Listen, ma'am, I didn't tell the last person who I was, and I'm not about to tell you. Believe me, it is for your own protection. Please put me through to Damon."

Damon pushed a button on the phone handle.

"Good morning Michael, how are you this morning?" Silence. "I'm sorry for the false voice. It's an automatic voice scrambling system that I designed that helps me screen calls. I wasn't expecting a call from you. Please take off your voice scrambler."

He heard a small sound. Michael's voice came on.

"This bloody scrambler is supposed to be the best in the world. How in the world did you know it was me, Damon?"

"Elementary, my dear Michael. You are the *only one* I gave this number to."

"Well done, Mr. Holmes! It *is* Hemlock Holmes, isn't it? Sherlock's teacher? And please call me Mickey. All my *two* friends do."

They both laughed.

"Why are you calling, Mickey? I haven't talked to you since I gave you that computer program."

"That is why I'm calling. Someone has breached our system!"

Damon said nothing.

"I'm serious!"

Damon chuckled this time.

"Well, someone might have!" Michael grumbled.

"What in the world brought that on, Mickey? No one can break your system. It is break proof, even from me. I told you that."

"Just trying to keep you on your toes, old chap. Not often do I get to tease someone. Hope you didn't mind. I *was* hoping to fool you, though. Get even for looking like a fool on the scrambler thing."

"It might have worked if it had been anything else. *That*, you will never get me on. That system you have should be secure, conservatively, for at least twenty five years. Is this just a social call?"

"Is this *just* a social call? *Just* a social call? I'm wounded Damon. I never do *social calls*. They are frivolous. This is strictly business. You

120

told me that you used to fly fish as a young man. Would you be up for a fly fishing weekend getaway this weekend?"

"I thought you said you never made *frivolous* phone calls."

"Well, actually I do, all the time. But usually just to Syl." His voice lost its joking timber. "Damon?"

"Yes."

"Damon … I know you told me that you don't want to get involved in my work, but would you be prepared to listen to some of the issues that I'm facing? Issues that I think you are ideally suited to advise me on? Issues that need to be talked about on a fly fishing weekend and not on a phone line, no matter how secure?"

Damon was quiet for a moment.

"Is it that serious, Michael?"

Lord Brighton heard and recognized the name change. It was a *no go*. Oh, well… he'd tried. He told Syl he would and he did. She was the one who suggested it. He had presumed too much on their new friendship.

"Yes, I believe it is, Damon." He paused to think of a way to smooth things over.

"Well, if that's the case, I'd love to, Mickey. I must warn you though, I haven't fly fished in, at least, twenty one years. I may be a little rusty. I only hope I can find my rod, reel and fishing case."

"Pardon? I mean, *you're coming?* Great! Don't worry if you can't find your gear. I have a ton and I do mean a ton. I come from a fishing family. I've inherited at least a ton of equipment. Much of it over two hundred years old. I'll show it to you, if you like."

"I'd like that Mickey. Which of your residences do I come to?"

"It's called Blackstone, for some strange reason. Not Manor or Castle, just *Blackstone*, just minutes out of London, on top of a hill. I inherited it years ago. It's a little hard to find. Let me give you the directions." Michael provided him the address and directions.

"Oh, and another thing, Damon. I'd love to see your custom made shooters. I never did get the chance to see them. Bloody work pulled me away, as usual. Bring them if you like and we can get in a little target practice."

"Great, maybe you can give me some pointers?"

"I'd love to old son, but I hope you're not disappointed."

"I don't think I will. I feel I can always learn something from a master of his craft. Will Sylvia be joining us?"

"Little miss Annie Oakley? She'd love to. She loves to shoot. She used to do a lot of hunting as a child. Be warned though, she is competitive."

"Wonderful, although that's not what I meant. Will she be joining us on the fishing trip?"

"Would you mind?"

"I'd enjoy it."

"She'd *love* it. As you know, she has taken quite a shine to you."

"And I to her. I'll come to your house Thursday night, if that's alright, say, around seven oh four."

Michael started to laugh but stopped it before it started. Damon was not joking. *'Seven oh four? Who comes at seven oh four exactly?'* Then he thought, *'Damon Gray, who else?'*

"Fine, but why seven oh four, Damon."

"I can make it seven oh eight if that will be more convenient?"

"No, no, seven oh four is fine."

"Good, I'll see you when I get there."

"Fine, great. I'll tell Syl. She'll be ecstatic. Don't eat. We'll be serving dinner. Anything you don't like, or are allergic to?"

"Only poison, my dear Michael, only poison."

Michael chuckled.

"Would you and Sylvia like to see a magic trick when I get there?"

"I love magic and so does Sylvia. Absolutely."

"Until then." said Damon.

"Until then."

Damon hung up the phone. It was proceeding faster than he could have hoped.

He smiled and headed for the showers. He'd have to be quick if he wanted to get breakfast from Hastings and he didn't want to miss that. Hastings was by far the best chef he had ever known. He paused for a moment and then hit the intercom button on his phone.

"Hastings, do I have time for a quick shower?"

"Yes, sir. Take your time. I'm making something a little different today, so it will take a little longer. Be here when you get here."

"I'll be there in eight and a half minutes."

Scene Thirty Three

"Goodnight darling." Michael leaned over and kissed his wife.

"What do you mean *goodnight?*"

"I think *goodnight* means I'm going to sleep. Goodnight."

"You have nothing else to say?"

"I love you?" Michael responded innocently.

"No! Well ... yes, *that too*. But do you mean to tell me that you are *not* going to tell me *all* about your conversation with Damon?" Sylvia asked with pretended indignation.

"Which conversation would that be darling?" Again the naïve look.

"Ohhh ...! You know very well *what* conversation. Did you ask him to go fly fishing?"

"As a matter of fact I did, now that you mention it. I've had so much on my mind this past little while ...." His voice faded off to sleep, snoring softly.

Lying on her back, Sylvia turned her head towards her husband.

"You are not sleeping Mickey. You don't snore. Well, what did he say?"

Michael rolled over to face her and said solemnly. "He said he was busy."

"Michael!"

He laughed softly and nuzzled her neck.

"Oh, alright. Yes dear, your instincts were right on the money. He said he would be happy to come. He asked if we would like to see a magic trick. I said we'd love to."

"Great! See, I just knew he would. Did you mention anything about the reason for the weekend?"

"Yes and no."

"I hate it when you say that."

"Goodnight dear."

"Ohh …..! Goodnight sweetheart." She rolled over to face him. "But you had better give me the whole story in the morning."

"Yes dear."

"I hate it when you say that too!" she said nuzzling his neck.

"Yes dear. Goodnight dear."

"*I don't think so* …" Her hand reached down…

▲ ▲ ▲

Scene Thirty Four

The door bell rang.

Moments later Damon Gray was ushered into the living room of Michael and Sylvia Brighton.

Smiling, Sylvia rushed to greet him, giving him a hug. Michael and Damon shook hands.

"What is that?" asked Sylvia pointing to the gift wrapped package in his left hand. "I hope that's not for us Damon. You don't need to be bringing us any gifts."

"It is a little something for both of you. I make it a habit that when I visit a friends home for the first time, to bring a little gift." With that he presented it to her.

"Well, alright, but just this once, right?" He nodded.

"Sit down both of you. Mr. Whitner, bring us the refreshments please."

"Yes, Madam." The white haired butler that had shown Damon into the room, turned and left.

Reaching into the package Sylvia brought forth a small blue vase, beautifully decorated. She looked at Damon.

"Yes, it's a Ming vase." He acknowledged.

"We can't take this, Damon, it's far too expensive!"

"Of course you will. You did say *Alright, but just this once*, remember?"

"Michael!" She looked to her husband for support.

"That *is* what you said dear." Michael turned to Damon. "Thank you, as my beautiful wife *meant* to say. We will cherish it always and I agree with her, just this once, alright?"

"Alright."

Placing the vase on the table carefully, she then turned to Damon

"Where are your bags?"

"I left them in the entrance with Jackson. He said he would take care of them for me."

Sylvia frowned. "Jackson? Honey, do we have a Jackson working for us?"

"Yes we do, darling."

"Really? Hmmm, I don't seem to recall anyone with that name that works here." Looking up she saw her husband smiling at her. Her pretty face wrinkled in a mock frown.

"Alright … husband. What is so funny?"

"Jackson is our butler, dear heart."

"We don't have a butler named Jackson, I know that. What is with your silly grin? Tell me *now*, you hear?" With that, she stamped her small foot on the floor.

Michael could not contain himself, he burst into laughter.

"Sorry Syl. I couldn't help it. Now you know how I feel sometimes when I talk to Damon." Before she could respond to that statement, he continued, "Jackson is Whitner's first name."

A look of surprise replaced the gathering cloud on her face.

"I never new his first name. I was introduced to him as Mr. Whitner. I remember I asked him what his first name was, and he told me just to call him Whitner or Mr. Whitner, and that is what I've called him ever since. Silly of me isn't it?" She looked at Damon.

"How in the world did you know his first name?"

"Yes, Damon," smiled Michael, "how *did* you know his first name? My house staff names are not on any registry anywhere."

"*Magic.*"

"I told you he would be showing us a magic trick, remember?"

"Yes you did but I didn't expect it to be that. Come now Damon, please tell me how you did it. Please?"

"Oh, alright. A magician is not supposed to reveal his secrets. Do you both promise never to reveal my secret?" They both nodded.

"I picked his pocket while he was taking my coat. Took his wallet and looked at his identification. Don't worry, I replaced it. He will be compensated."

"You..." started Sylvia. She didn't have time to finish.

Whitner came into the room carrying a tray. He placed it on a table.

"Whitner, do you carry any identification on you?"

"Yes Madam."

"May I see it?"

"May I ask why?"

"I'm just curious as to what kind of wallet you carry. We have been talking about magic and how personal things can tell a lot about a person. Do you mind?"

"Not at all, but I really don't think it can tell you a lot about me madam. I replaced my old one just two days ago with this new one."

So saying, he reached inside his jacket, undid the button covering the flap, unzipped the inner lining and withdrew a thin, new, black zippered wallet.

Sylvia walked close and looked at his wallet. She then pulled opened his jacket and looked at his inside pocket. She let his lapel go, straightened his jacket, smiled at him and shook her head.

"Anything else, Madam?"

"As a matter of fact, yes. Let me guess. Inside the wallet is a clear plastic sleeve where you put your driver's license. Am I right Whitner?" she smiled at him.

"I'm afraid not. This magic thing you are trying isn't going very well, is it? On the inside of my wallet are slots that I put my identification in. I think four on each side if my old memory still serves me. It has a pocket on each side behind these, with zippers. Does that answer all your questions about my wallet?"

"Yes it does, Whitner, you can put it away now. That is unless Michael would like to look at it. Michael?"

Michael, who was standing close behind, shook his head.

"No dear. I saw what you saw."

Whitner started to put his wallet back when Damon spoke.

"Excuse me, but would you be so kind as to open your wallet and show Michael and Sylvia only, not me, the interior so that there can be no confusion. Please don't show any cards or identification, just the interior of your wallet, thank you."

Whitner smiled, turned away from Damon and opened his wallet to show the interior. When he spread it open a piece of paper fell out of it and fluttered to the ground. He bent down and picked it up, looked at it and gasped.

"What's wrong Whitner." asked a startled Sylvia.

Whitner just stood there, staring at the piece of paper in his hand, mouth ajar.

"What is it man, are you alright? You look like you've seen a ghost." Michael said grabbing him by the arm and startling him out of his shock.

"I think I have, sir. I think I have."

"I don't understand, Whitner. What are you talking about?" asked Michael in a concerned voice.

"It was you sir, wasn't it? You put it in here, didn't you? It wasn't here before. Thank you, sir!"

"What in blazes are you babbling about, Whitner? *I*, or *we*, didn't put anything in your wallet. What have you got there? I can't see it. Your hands are in the way."

"It's a stamp sir." Whitner whispered reverently, placing it on his palm. "One I've been trying to collect for over twenty years. Terribly expensive and very, very rare. I've had the money set aside for it for years but I have been unable to acquire one. This one is in mint condition. Look at it."

He held it up for the two of them to see it. Encased between two thin transparent sheets was a single stamp. "Where in the world did it come from?"

He straightened up sharply. "Is this some kind of joke, sir?" he asked a little sharply. "Is it? You want to sell it to me or something?" He looked at the two of them questioningly.

"Absolutely not, Whitner! My wife and I have never seen that stamp before, have we dear?" Syl shook her head. "I swear on my family's name."

"Then I ask again sir, where did it come from?"

"You're asking me?"

"No sir, I'm asking myself. If anybody inquires about it sir, I'll be glad to return it to its rightful owner. I'll just put it in here until after I serve the refreshments." Saying that, he unzipped one side on the back of his wallet and pulled it open to put the stamp in. It didn't want to go in. Pulling out the stamp Whitner looked into the opening.

"Something is in there. What in the world…" so saying, he withdrew a small folded piece of paper. He opened it and read the writing that was on it, then numbly handed the paper to Michael, who read it out loud.

In block type it read:

To Jackson Bernard Whitner. For services rendered, you are given this stamp as payment in full, thank you.

He went on to read that it had a verification number on the front of the cellophane panel and was registered under his name at the Global Stamp Institute.

"I don't understand sir. I haven't done anybody that kind of service."

"Jackson Bernard Whitner?" Sylvia asked, smiling.

The butlers face went dark. "It's just *Whitner* or *Mr. Whitner,* Madam." He said stiffly. "I beg you to remember that."

Handing him back his stamp, Michael said, "Take a break, Whitner. I know it's a shock but you must have done something to deserve it. Please take a little time to get yourself together man. We'll serve ourselves."

"Yes sir. Thank you, sir. Dinner will be served promptly at eight o'clock."

He turned to leave, stopped and turned around to face Michael. "Sir, about ..."

"No one in this room will tell anybody your given names, right Damon, right Sylvia?" Both nodded in agreement.

Whitner smiled and then bowed stiffly, turned again and left with his treasure.

▲ ▲ ▲

When the door closed, Michael spun on Damon, grabbed his hand, shaking it vigorously. He then let go and grabbed his wife and spun her in the air laughing like a madman all the while. Finally breathless, he put his astounded new wife on the floor gently.

Gasping with laughter, he turned again to Damon. "How in the world did you do that? No! No!" he said holding up his hand, "Don't tell me another one of your cock and bull stories. It's probably too easy. Don't tell me. Don't spoil it."

Pausing only a moment for a breath, he continued. "You know, that was the first time in my life that I have seen Whitner flustered. This has to be in the top four best experiences of my life." He broke into laughter again.

Sylvia couldn't help it. It was contagious. She started laughing as well. Damon just smiled. When they had settled down a bit, Sylvia said.

"In the *top four* best experiences of your life?"

"Well ... maybe top three." Michael said.

Sylvia burst into another bout of laughter, starting the whole cycle over.

When they finally sat down for dinner, Michael and Sylvia could hardly eat their meals, their face and jaw muscles were so sore from laughing, as well as their sides. It took longer than usual and everybody had a good time. Even Whitner's normally placid face smiled now and then. He kept looking at Lord and Lady Brighton in a strange way, and he took extra care to check all the dishes before they were served.

▲ ▲ ▲

After dinner they retired to the family library. Damon walked around the room looking at the books with Michael giving the tour.

"If there are any books that you would like to read, feel free to borrow them." Michael said after he was done.

"Really?" Michael nodded. Damon walked quickly around the room and picked out several books, seemingly at random and put them on the table. "Thank you, I'll borrow these. I'll return them before I leave. Is that acceptable?"

"*Is that acceptable*?" Sylvia intoned in a deep voice trying to imitate Damon. Then she smiled at him and said, "You have the cutest way of saying things Damon. Of course it's alright, and you should feel flattered. Michael won't let anyone borrow these books. All of them are first editions."

"I noticed, and I don't feel flattered, I feel honored. Thank you."

"You are going to read these, let me see," she said bending over, "five six, seven huge books in one weekend?"

Damon smiled. "I read fast."

▲ ▲ ▲

"Did you bring your *shooting irons* with you," Michael asked, "as you Americans would say?"

"My *shooting irons,* as we Americans would say, are in my suitcase. I'll go get them."

"No need to sir. With your permission, I will retrieve them for you." Whitner looked at Damon for approval. Damon nodded. Whitner then left the room and returned shortly with a well worn leather, brass and wooden case and handed it to Damon.

"Did you like them, Whitner?"

"Yes sir. They are beautiful sir, but how did you know I had looked?"

"Magic, Whitner." Damon smiled when Whitner jumped slightly. "Well, *no* not really, I have two cases. It would just make sense to check them both to make sure you had the right one."

"Ahhh, I see sir. Simple wasn't it? I love your grooming kit, very unique. Where in the world did you find it?"

"It was my fathers."

"It is a work of art. It looks well used also."

"It is. I'm on the road often."

"Very good sir. Will there be anything else, lady and gentlemen, or may I retire to my room to view my latest treasure?"

Michael and Sylvia smiled.

"That will be all for this evening Whitner, thank you." When Whitner had left, Michael turned to Damon.

"You are *good*. Had Whitner almost believing in magic. Now let's see what you have in there."

Damon opened the case and took out a set of handguns. He handed one each to Lord and Lady Brighton. Beautifully engraved guns with white pearl handles. One was of a bright shiny gold metal. The other was of a bright, blood red metal. The designs in them made them look liquid as they moved and turned them in their hands. Michael and Sylvia exchanged guns.

"My goodness, but they are beautiful! They feel a little strange in my hand though. Are they weighted differently than a normal gun? They don't look plated. They *look* like they are cast of a gold and ruby colored metal. Are they?"

"Very perceptive Sylvia. Yes to both questions. They are meant for show and tricks as much as shooting."

"I'm not sure I understand, do you mean you do tricks with them?"

"Well, I've practiced tricks with them but I haven't performed yet."

"Oh but you must!" She enthused. "This can be your first official performance as a gun magician."

"Whoa, I did not say I was a *gun magician*."

"No you didn't, *I did*. Now Michael, give me the gun and go sit down," She turned to Damon "and I'll introduce you."

"Wait a moment Sylvia. To do my routine I have to fire the guns. Don't you think that the shooting range would be more appropriate?"

"Yes, of course. Well, what are you all waiting for? We have a show to put on! If you all don't mind I'd like to change into something more appropriate. You might want to also. The powder, the smell… well, you know."

They agreed to meet in the foyer in ten minutes.

Ten minutes to the second, Sylvia appeared in the foyer stunningly dressed in a pale green and lavender designer hunting outfit that complimented her large turquoise eyes and accentuated her healthy feminine curves. Her thick golden blond hair was pulled up into a pony tail that she felt made her look years younger. It did.

Michael was waiting in a custom made hunting outfit of camouflage green that complimented his lithe athletic frame without binding or impeding him in any way. A matching colored peaked cap, on backwards over his black curly hair, made his dark brown eyes almost sinister.

Damon was waiting for both of them, wearing designer gold tinted shooting glasses and dressed in an outfit consisting of loose fitting red slacks, gold mock neck sweater completed by a silver three quarter length hunting jacket. It was finished off with a tan colored belt and rubber soled shoes. No hat, instead a silver, ruby and gold colored braided leather headband encircled his head.

▲ ▲ ▲

On the way to the shooting range, Michael asked him questions about his guns. Damon explained them. Michael was impressed. Damon told him that originally he and his father had designed and made them, just before his death.

Located three floors underground, the shooting range was incredible, with high domed ceilings, with sound baffles strategically placed throughout. It was now Damons turn to be impressed and like Michael, he did not impress easily. He took one look around and said to Michael, "Tell me everything you know about this place. It is phenomenal. This place is magical."

Michael told him that it originally had been a part of a large catacomb cave system which had been sealed off for centuries. Probably for safety reasons he said.

An unknown king or lord, in the long forgotten past, had man and beast carve and shape it into the chambers that stood to this day. The wooden beams, probably ironwood, were almost as they were the day they were installed. Mother earth had not bowed or broken their strength. Michael did not know how long ago the extra supporting metal beams had been installed. The castle had been in the Brighton family for countless generations, dating back to the days before its recorded history. The catacombs had been used over the centuries for countless functions.

Damon was fascinated and walked around touching the walls looking everywhere.

"Damon," called Sylvia "*Yoo-hoo... Damon!* Did you forget about us?"

"Sorry, but this place is a true discovery, more than both of you know. It used to be a dungeon or prison and a place to keep mentally unstable family members. But that's newer. This place dates back to prehistoric times. Rituals were carried on here. What, I don't know. I would love to explore this place sometime, if you don't mind, Michael?"

"Not at all. How did you know about the dungeon and mental institution? That has been a family secret *forever*. Nobody is supposed to know."

"It's just a feeling I have. Glad to know I was right. Ready to shoot?"

"Aren't you going to show us your gun magic?"

"How about after we shoot for a little bit, Sylvia? It has been awhile and I could sure use the practice. Besides, I came here to learn from you two. Michael called you Annie Oakley, didn't you Michael?"

Michael tried to look innocent.

"Who, me?" He frowned as if thinking. "Let me think ..."

"Oh don't try to deny it or look innocent Mickey. You've called me that before."

Michael grinned.

"Well dear, you do shoot beautifully. Let's do it. *Annie get your gun.*"

"Ohh ... groaner Michael ... groaner. Damon, do you want to use your guns or ours?"

"Yours please, Sylvia. I already know mine. I love new challenges and experiences. I love to learn. Teach me."

For the next hour they had a wonderful time shooting at targets and comparing scores. By mutual consent, they decided to call it a night. Damon thanked both of them and told them that he had learned a lot from them.

"I can't believe how good both of you are" he exclaimed "and you really are an *Annie Oakley.*" He said to Sylvia. She smiled and blushed.

As they were starting to pack up, Sylvia exclaimed, "Wait! We can't go yet, we haven't seen the gun magician! Michael, you sit over on the sofa, where I'll join you momentarily, after I introduce the *Gray Ghost; Gun Magician.* What do you need for props, Mister Gray Ghost?"

Damon smiled. "You've been reading too many tabloids, young lady." She grinned back. "As for props, I need to position your couch around so that you are off to the side but in front of me when I shoot at the targets behind you. Let's bring that high cartridge loading table over here."

When the couch and table had been moved, Damon placed his gun case on the table and backed off to the side to give Sylvia center stage.

"Ladieeeees and Gentaaaaaaaamen" she screamed, throwing her arms high and wide, fingers splayed, "can I have your attenshunn pulllleeeeese! Do we have a treat for youuuuuu tonight! Fresh frommmm centerrrrr stage of Caesars in downnnntownnn Lasssss Vegaaaaaas! We have spaaarrrrrrrrrred no expenssssse to bring youuuu an act of gun magic -- that's right folks -- GUUUNNNNN MMMAAAGICCCCCC from none otherrr thannnn the Grayyyyyyyyyyyyy Ghooooooostttttt. That's right! Right here in Brighton Asylum: theeeeeeeeeeeeeeee Grayyyyyyyyy Ghooooooostttttttt! Let's hear a big round of appalllllaussssse from all you idiots and morons, for the Grayyyyyyyyy Ghooostt! Yaaaaaaaaaaay!" clap clap clap.

She then bowed to Damon and ran to the couch and sat down by her husband who was pretending to be a moron, head back and waving back and forth, smiling and clapping and hollering "YAAAAAAAAY!" Sylvia joined him.

Doing a hop, skip and jump, Damon landed in front of them.

"Thank you --- thank you very much." said the voice of Elvis out of Damon. "It is truly an honor to be performing to a packed house." The voice now changed to a rumbling echolike ghostly voice. The type of voice used to tell scary stories around campfires.

"I'll need a volunteer from the audience." Both raised and waved their hands wildly. He looked over their heads ignoring them. The waving became frantic.

"Pick me!" they were both yelling at once.

"You miss, will you please come up here?" Grinning foolishly, like she had just won at bingo, Sylvia rose and skipped forward to stand in front of the gun magician.

Damon said "Now Miss …?" Sylvia stood very straight, then turned and looked out at the mythical audience.

"*Table Mable*, that's whut they call me. Yup, they allays holler at me…" She lifted her head and hollered, "*Get off the table Mabel, the money's for the BEER* -- like *I* (pronounced *ah*) was deef or sumthin."

Michael roared with genuine laughter and clapped. Damons face didn't change or flicker.

"Thank you for introducing yourself to the audience, miss Table Mabel. I won't ask *your occupation*. What I *will* ask you to do is to position these playing cards around the shooting area – in any position you like." He held forward his hand to her.

She hesitated. He smiled encouraging. He pushed his hand towards her again.

"Whut playing cards? I don't see no playing cards in your hand."

"What? Oh, they are magic playing cards. Don't be afraid – take them."

She reached out her hand hesitantly and closed her hand around the invisible playing cards. Just as her fingers were to touch together, playing cards suddenly appeared in her hand. Surprise almost made her drop them. She laughed involuntarily. "Where did they come from?"

Damon just smiled.

"*Magic?*" she whispered loudly, wide eyed.

Damon nodded. "Yes Miss Mabel – *magic*. Please tell the audience *exactly* what you have in your hand." She was already studying them, turning them over in her hand, flicking them with her finger.

"Yup, they're real. Let me see – eleven, twelve, thirteen."

Leaning toward Damon, she put the back of her free hand partially over her mouth and said in a loud stage whisper, "Betcha didn't know I could count that high, didja?" Looking out over the room she announced, "I have in my hands thirteen magic cards, all spades, from the ace to the king, or from the two to the ace, anyway -- all the spades." She turned them so that *all the audience* (consisting of one) could see.

Michael clapped again.

"Miss Mabel?"

"Oh yes, you want I should place these cards anywhere I want, any way I want in the shootin' area, right?"

"Correct."

"Huh?"

"Right."

"Well why dintja just say so?" Mumbling *"correct"* over and over under her breath she wandered around positioned the cards throughout the shooting area. When she was finished she came back to center stage, one arm crossed in front, one arm behind her back, spread her legs to shoulder width, bowed like a man, smiled and went and sat back down beside her clapping husband.

"Thank you, Miss Mabel. I noticed that three of the cards are turned with their edges facing out. Not very sporting if I want to shoot them is it?" Smiling she nodded her head in agreement. "Well, we'll just have to see won't we?"

Turning back to the table, he opened his case and withdrew the contents.

"Two unloaded hand guns, one for each hand" he said, holding them out for all to see, showing them the empty handles. *"Magic handguns!"* he said in his scary voice as he carefully placing them on the table. They seemed to glow under the lights. One Red. One Gold.

"Four loaded magazines, fifteen rounds in each." Again showing them to the room, two in each hand. Two of these he placed standing up on the table shoulder width apart. The others he expertly inserted into the handles of the two guns.

Holding the guns palm out he placed them back on the table carefully and said to his audience "Would somebody toss me a coin please."

"We didn't bring any." Michael said.

"Look between you on the couch."

There between them, on the couch, rested a brand new silver dollar. "Please put a mark on it with the pen knife in your pocket sir, one that you will be able to recognize again." Michael opened his mouth to speak.

"Magic, sir. Magic." Damon cut him off.

Lord Brighton closed his mouth, took out his small pen knife and scratched his initials on the shiny new coin.

"Show it to the people around you. Good -- good. Now toss it to me please."

Both Michael and Sylvia expected him to shoot it in the air.

The gun magician caught the coin that was flipped and placed it on the table. A table bare of any guns!

Damon jumped! His eyes widened in surprise.

"Where are my guns?" he whispered. He looked at the table, under the table and around the table. He waived his hands over the table and under the table to show that they were not there.

"I hate it when they do that! Oh well, I'll try it without them." Tossing the coin in the air, his hands flashed up and he said "Bang! Bang!"

The coin made a tinkling sound as it hit the ground unharmed.

"Where are you?" he called out to the room.

"Right here." said Sylvia.

"Not you, *my guns!* They are *magical* and have a mind of their own. Sometimes they make me look downright silly, like they did just now - vanishing on me. All right," he called out again, "I'm going to try it again. If you are not back to help me on time, I'm leaving you here. I'm serious this time, do you hear me. I'm tired of looking like a fool. This is it, your final warning. I mean it this time!"

Looking at Michael, he said "Would you be so kind as to pick up the coin, confirm that it is the one you gave me and hand it back to me? Thank you sir," he said when the coin had been handed back to him. "Have we ever met before? You are not part of the show are you?"

"No sir."

"Thank you and before you sit back down, please introduce yourself to the audience. What is your name?"

Turning to the audience he announced in a proud uncultured voice,

"*Dammit.*"

"Your name is *Dammit?*"

"Yes, sir."

"Who in the world would call a child *Dammit?*"

"Mostly it was my father, sir. Far back as I kin remember he would always say, *Dammit,* did you break my saw - or, *Dammit,* git your butt in here for supper - or, *Dammit,* you ain't got enough sense to come in outa the rain - or, *Dammit,* eat your greens like your fourth step-mamma says …"

"Alright, that's fine …" the Gray Ghost tried to interrupt.

"…or, *Dammit,* did you shoot another skunk under the house - or, *Dammit,* if I have to take my belt off…"

"Thank you -- thank you, we get the picture. You may return to your seat."

Sylvia was howling with laughter throughout the whole conversation.

Damon did not break character.

"Wonderful man, keen mind! I'll have to be careful with this audience. You're sharp as a tack. I don't think I can put anything over on you. I'll try the trick again and this time hopefully it will work, *dammit.*" he nodded to Michael. Sylvia and Michael howled with laughter. He waited until they had calmed down. In a louder voice he called into the air, "Remember *Gunnies,* this is your last chance!"

With that said, he put his hands together and juggled the silver dollar until it was between his thumbs, making quite a production out of it. When at last it was to his liking, he flipped the coin in the air with both thumbs at once, his arms and hands extended, following the arc.

Michael and Sylvia did not blink. They were not going to be distracted again. When the coin reached chest level on the way down, two things happened at once.

Michael and Sylvia could not agree on what happened next.

Sylvia said she heard a loud explosion that startled her into blinking, and the guns magically appeared in Damon's hands.

Michael said exactly the opposite. The guns magically appeared in Damon's hands and *then* the blast, making him blink.

Both agreed on the magical appearance of the guns.

"You're back! You're back! Thank you … Ah, what I mean is, *where have you two been?*" He paused for a moment looking at them, as if waiting for them to speak.

He then looked up. "I apologize. The only word I have been able to teach them is '*bang*.'"

Michael and Sylvia, who were sitting there stunned, burst into laughter and started clapping.

"Would someone from the audience go and pick up the coin that's leaning against the far wall and bring it back?"

Sylvia jumped up, ran and picked up the coin. She glanced at it and started to hurry back. Suddenly she stopped and looked at the coin again, turning it over and over again in her slender hands.

"Hello … HELLO?" Michael called.

"What? Oh, sorry dear, but you are not going to believe this. You are really not going to believe this." With that said she ran back to her husband and handed him the coin. His eyes widened.

Scratched on it were his identifying initials. That was not what caused his shock. Turning the coin over and over in his hands, he verified what Sylvia had seen.

It was badly warped and two half circle notches of metal were missing from opposing edges.

The coin had been struck by two bullets!

"What, didn't I hit it?" asked the gun magician looking concerned. Michael went to hand him the coin,

"No, no you can keep the coin. Think of it as a gift from the *Gray Ghost Gun Wizard.* I mean Magician, *dammit.*" Then he smiled, nodding at Michael. "I told you they were *magic guns.* Now sit back down Miss Mabel and be prepared to be *dazzled!*" the last word raising in pitch to set the stage.

"Come back here you two!" The two guns seemed to jump out of his hands. He grabbed at them awkwardly. They seemed to avoid his best efforts, making him look clumsy, firing off in all directions. The quicker he grabbed at them the more shots went off. He chased them around the room, climbing over furniture and fixtures.

Finally, just behind the cartridge loading table, he got his hands wrapped around them. Grinning, he held them out in front of him, over the cartridge loading table, to show his audience that he had everything under control. Suddenly the magazines shot out of the bottom of both guns and then they went crazy again. They jumped out of his hands, but he was able to grab onto them before they escaped again. Mightily and manfully he fought them and hung on. First one going up and the other going down, up and down, up and down making it look like he was dancing, then sideways, then they pulled his arms apart and behind his back till his hands touched. With a mighty effort he slowly pulled his arms to the front.

He grinned at the audience in triumph. It was short lived, however. Without warning the insane guns pulled him forward. Off balance he was unable to stop them as they slammed his hands down onto the table, driving the handles down and over the full standing magazines placed there earlier. Down so hard that the guns *again* flew out of his hands. This time they had him jumping, cartwheeling, tumbling, twisting and turning impossibly, until at last, Damon, grabbing at them frantically, stumbled and fell to his knees. The guns flew up and suddenly seemed to fly apart, the magazines popping out and all pieces flipping through the air to land back on the cartridge loading table.

Damon crawled over to the table and slowly raised his head and peeked over the top.

The Magic Guns were lying on the table, facing outward from each other, with two empty cartridge magazines nestled neatly on each side.

Standing up, he spoke to them, "Boy, are you two ever in trouble! You made me look like a fool. Just wait till we get home. Don't think I'm going to let you get away with this. I've a good mind to ..." glancing up at the audience, he stopped speaking.

Picking the guns up he carefully put them back in the case, followed by the cartridge magazines. Just before he zipped the case closed, he bent over and stage whispered into it, "Next time I'm going to load you both with *blanks!*"

Straightening and fixing himself, he turned to his audience.

"I guess they got mad when I said I would leave them here. *Dammit*, I sure won't say that again." Again the nod to Michael. Michael nodded back.

Making an elaborate and elegant bow, he finished by, "Thank you for coming. Tell all your friends. I'll be performing here for the next two weeks here at the Brighton Asylum in downtown *Las Vegas!* As a parting thought - Just because you *are* paranoid doesn't mean that they're *not* after you. Goodnight and goodbye."

Laughing, Michael and Sylvia broke into spontaneous applause.

Damon grabbed a chair, carried it over and sat down across from them.

Nobody spoke for a moment.

Sylvia was the first. "What in the world was that? I have never, *in my life,* seen anything like it. Are you sure you have never done this in front of a live audience? Can you duplicate it? Where did you learn those moves, a Charlie Chan movie?"

"That's Jackie Chan, darling." Michael corrected.

"I know sweetheart. I just like to keep you on your toes." Turning back, she continued. "Doctor Gray, thank you."

"Yes, I agree. Doctor Gray, thank you." Looking at his watch, he continued, "That was both the longest and the shortest fifteen minute -- whatever it was -- that I have ever had the privilege of participating in, or experiencing."

"Well, you are *both* very welcome. From what I observed, you both may very well be certifiably insane, and I say that as a great and sincere compliment. You both have a tremendous talent for improvisation. Thank you again and in response to your questions Sylvia; something that I have worked on over the years; no never; no; and no, at a dance class in Tibet."

"What are you talking about? Oh, my questions. What were they?"

"Never mind darling." Her husband laughed. "I remember and I'll tell you later."

"You both look exhausted. If you like, I can clean up here while you two go to bed?" Damon offered.

"No, no, my good chap." said Michael, "Whitner will do it in the morning. Just leave everything."

"I'd like to collect my shells, if you don't mind. I load them myself."

"We'll have Whitner bring them to you before you leave, if that's all right?"

"Of course it is. Thank you both very much. I have never had this much fun before. I will always cherish this memory." Standing up, he smiled and picked up his gun case. "Goodnight, and we will see you in the morning."

Michael and Sylvia arose as one.

"We?" asked Sylvia.

Damon hesitated for a fraction of a second.

"Why, the magic guns and I." he responded, smiling at her as he took off his shooting glasses and tucked them into one of his pockets. Sylvia smiled back.

At that moment, a beam of errant light caught his eyes and they instantly transformed.

Time stood still.

His right eye turned totally blood red and the left eye turned into a huge liquid golden cat eye.

Time returned. The beam passed and the eyes returned to normal. Sylvia gasped. Damon looked concerned.

"Is there anything wrong? Are you all right?" The words sounded far away.

'It was just the light.' she told herself. *'Silly girl.'* She chided herself.

"No I'm fine, just fine." Sylvia laughed shakily. "You two go on up to bed." Both men smiled at the same time.

She shook her head and smiled back sweetly. "Separate beds, you meerons! Separate rooms. I want to sit here for a few more moments and savor the experience. I'll be up shortly sweetheart." She bent into and gave her husband a kiss, then gave Damon a hug and promptly shooed both of them off. She heard them in the distance.

"Meerons?" Damon asked.

"Yes, it's a word she made up. She likes to do that."

"Oh."

The voices faded off.

After they had left, Sylvia sat for awhile, lost in thought and then got up and walked slowly around the room.

Every card that she had placed edge out was bullet sliced right through the middle. No bullet had been wasted. Every card had been hit multiple times and always through a spade. The face cards had their eyes shot out.

Later, much later, she crawled silently into bed, careful not to wake her husband.

▲ ▲ ▲

"Alright Syl, what is going on. You have been acting strangely all morning, ever since I told you about my conversation with Damon yesterday. Talk to me darling."

"Michael, have you ever had a dream *so real* that you thought it wasn't a dream?"

▲ ▲ ▲

After she had finished, Michael looked at his wife and said.

"Let me see if I understand this *real* dream of yours. You say that a gold, silver and ruby red dressed *color blind* Damon gave us a Ming vase, worth at least a million dollars, as a house warming gift?" Sylvia nodded.

"He gave Whitner a stamp worth many, many thousands of dollars because he stole and replaced his wallet out of a double or triple sealed pocket in a jacket that Whitner was wearing?" Sylvia nodded again.

"Color blind Damon had red and gold magic guns that flew in the air and shot playing cards in half edgewise?" a nod.

"Damon has one liquid golden cats eye and one swirling blood red one?" another nod.

"And you were *Table Mable* and I was *Dammit*?" Sylvia stopped nodding.

Michael noticed.

"Well, I *can see* how it would seem *so real!*" he said quickly.

Sylvia glared at her husband.

His eyes twinkled, but he kept his face straight.

Sylvia stopped glaring and a small giggle escaped her.

That started the laughter.

When the laughter died down, Sylvia said in all seriousness.

"I *know* it seemed ludicrous, unbelievable and silly, Mickey. I really *do* know that. But, in spite of that, it *did* seem *real*, sweetheart."

Michael went serious.

"I do believe you darling. I know that you have certain *abilities*. You told me about them and have proved them to my satisfaction on many occasions. I don't really doubt you. It just seemed so preposterous. But a few things did capture my attention. One was Whitner's first and middle name. Nobody but I knew that. *And* the fact that the catacombs were, in the distant past, used as an *Asylum* for the *insane.* Again, nobody knows that."

He thought for a moment. Finally he said. "What we have here is a conundrum."

"I am *not* going to look that up in the dictionary, Mister Smarty Pants!"

"Yes you will, Mrs. Smarty Dress."

Sylvia sighed. "Yes, I will."

▲ ▲ ▲

Scene Thirty Five

"Five, four, three, two, one ..." the door bell rang. "Well I'll be ... Seven oh four exactly."

Moments later Damon Gray was ushered into the living room of Michael and Sylvia Brighton.

Smiling, Sylvia rushed to greet him, giving him a hug. Michael and Damon shook hands.

"What is that?" asked Sylvia pointing to the package in his left hand. "I hope that's not for us Damon. You don't need to be bringing us any gifts."

"It is a little something for both of you. I make it a habit, that when I visit a friends home for the first time, to bring a little gift." With that, he presented it to her.

Sylvia looked at her husband. Michael raised his eyebrow slightly and smiled.

"Well, alright, but just this once, right?" Damon nodded.

"Sit down both of you. Whitner, bring us the refreshments please."

"Yes, Madam." The white haired butler that had shown Damon into the room, turned and left.

"I don't think I'll ever get used to being called a Madam. Do I look old enough to be called a Madam? No, don't *either* of you answer."

Reaching into the package, Sylvia brought forth a bottle of wine. A look of relief crossed her face. She looked at Damon and smiled.

"Why it's our favorite and very rare. We haven't been able to get it for awhile. How did you know?"

"A magician never tells his secrets."

Sylvia laughed. "That's the magic trick that you were going to show us?"

"No. That comes later."

"Do it now, I can't wait!"

"Suspense is half the trick, Sylvia. You don't want to spoil it do you?"

"No, of course not." Placing the bottle on the table, she then turned to Damon

"Where are your bags?"

"I left them in the entrance with Mr. Whitner. He said he would take care of them for me."

Whitner came into the room carrying a tray with a wine decanter and three glasses on it. He placed it on a table.

"You may take the decanter away Whitner. We are going to be drinking this Chateau de Roseau 1811." said Sylvia.

"A chalice of water for me, please. Alcohol and I are bitter, bitter enemies." Damon advised.

"And please bring us a chalice of water for Dr. Gray, along with a cork remover."

"Right away, Madam." Whitner turned to leave.

"Whitner?"

"Yes, Madam?"

"Could you please call me something other than *Madam*," she smiled a radiant smile at him, "please?"

"As you wish … my lady" (pronounced *m'lady*). He turned and left.

After he had left the room, Sylvia bent over slightly, bowed her legs and dropped one arm down like she was carrying a wash bucket. After wiping an imagined drip from her nose, she craned her head up to see them. Grinning impishly, she shook her finger at the two men and said in a very poor imitation of a cockney accent. "Oy'm a lady, oy am! An don't you two gentamin fergit it!"

Resuming her natural voice and stance she continued, "Bless his heart, Whitner is really a sweet man but I don't think he will ever change. At least *m'lady* has a certain youthful *royal* elegance to it, don't you think? That, I can handle."

Both men dutifully agreed and the evening continued.

With the exception of the gift upon entering and the library scene after dinner, the evening did not mirror her dream at all; and in the library scene, he borrowed *eight* books. Sylvia almost had to bite her lip to stop from repeating what she had said in her dream. She needn't have bothered; Michael did, almost word for word. Damon's answer was word for word what he said in her dream.

All of their attire was dress casual, with Damon in his usual charcoal gray. Sylvia did not feel the need to change, to go to the firing range, when, in fact, she dressed for it to begin with. She did not want to unconsciously sanction her dream.

Dinner was delightful, the dessert fabulous and the conversation stimulating.

When Damon's guns were brought down to the firing range, they were encased in an ordinary looking, dull black, non reflective, leather case with two traditional combination locks on either side of the double locks.

Taking them from Whitner, Damon placed them on the cartridge loading table and moved the combinations. When he was satisfied he stood back and looked at both of them.

"It is now time for the magic." He said in a stage voice. "Michael, would you like to open the case or would you like your new bride to?"

"I will ..."

"Michael Beauregard Brighton!"

"As I was saying before I was so *rudely* interrupted, I will ... let my beautiful wife have the honors." He grinned at Syl.

Ignoring the grin, she walked over to the gun case and reached for it.

"Don't touch it!" came the barked command from Damon.

She jumped. "W-Why not?" she stammered, surprised.

"Because it is a *magic* case and could whisk you off to a terrible dimension. You need to be introduced to it first." Damon intoned in a deep voice.

Sylvia couldn't help it. She tried to stifle it, but a giggle escaped her as she tried, and failed miserably, to keep a straight face. It went from a giggle to a laugh.

"Ahhh ... you laugh, but I just possibly saved you from being spirited to a world of *unfathomable horror.* A world filled exclusively with ...... *chocolate shops, flat shoes, control top panty hose and oversize paisley dresses!*"

Even Michael laughed at that one.

When the laughter had stopped, Damon introduced Sylvia and Michael to the gun case. When they both nodded at the case, it just sat there.

"You may open it now." Damon nodded to Sylvia.

Cautiously she reached over and opened the case lid slowly, standing off to the side, in case something shot out. Again nothing happened. When it was fully opened, she peeked in. She looked at Damon uncomprehendingly. Her husband came forward and looked in also. There was nothing in the case!

"Very cute Damon. You scare me half to death over and empty case?"

"What?" Damon looked in the case, then looked up at the two of them.

"You shouldn't have laughed at it." They both looked puzzled. He seemed serious.

"Please close the case *gently*, Sylvia." She did as he requested.

"What now, *oh mighty magician?*"

"An apology to it might help? No laughing this time."

"I'm *so* sorry *little black case*. There, did *that* do it?" she said with mock seriousness.

"I don't know, open the case again."

When she opened the gun case a second time, two hand guns, with four loaded magazines, were on display within it.

Both Brighton's clapped their hands. They checked and rechecked the case but could not figure out how it was done. They loved the trick. They then moved on to the guns.

At first glance, as both Michael and Sylvia agreed later, the guns themselves looked very ordinary. Like generic semi automatic hand guns, the standard kind that you would find in every new and used gun store. The bodies were of a dull non reflective dark grey metal, the handles of a black ribbed composite material.

They *were* extremely impressed with the modifications he had made, some of which they did not fully understand, but the guns themselves, to the two of them, were just ordinary looking extremely well made guns.

As Damon explained, looks can be deceiving. The guns were of the finest materials known to man. They were made to his exact specifications. Their simple lines made them look ordinary. They were jam proof, heat proof and almost indestructible.

Mickey and Syl both agreed with Damon that they did have clean lines.

The shooting range scene was nothing like the dream sequence. Michael did show him around and Damon did seem impressed, but that was the extent of it.

Damon did not shoot his guns, but Michael did. Being left handed, he shot with just one pistol and only one magazine.

Later he told his wife that it was the most accurate and perfectly balanced hand gun he had ever used.

Their scores were very close, and they had a great time. By the end of the evening Sylvia had dismissed the dream as nothing more than a dream with a few coincidences.

As Damon packed his gun case, he picked up all the cartridges that Lord Brighton had fired out of his gun. When he saw Sylvia looking at him questioningly, he said, "I try to keep all my shell casings. I load them myself. Well, really my automatic loader does, I just monitor it." He smiled.

She nodded thoughtfully and said "I see." And then she smiled back.

He took off his shooting glasses. As he was turning away, an errant beam of light struck his eyes and passed on. Time slowed for Sylvia as she focused. They did *not* change color. Time returned to normal.

"You boys go on up to the library and swap manly lies, while I tidy up a bit here."

"The staff will get it Syl."

"Oh hush, sweetheart. I'll only be a few minutes behind you. You know me."

"Yes, I do, darling. Well alright, but please don't be long."

Turning, he said to Damon, "Did I ever tell you the story about the fish that got away? No? Well now, let me think a moment. Ah, yes! It was two years ago..." The voice faded off into the distance. Sylvia picked up and straightened. When she was done she picked up the target sheets that Damon had shot and looked at them closely. Nodding, she folded and put them into an envelope and went upstairs and put them under their mattress. She then freshened her make up, checked her hair, and went down to meet her two men.

One she loved with all her heart. The other was her friend. And her husbands. *That* she knew.

▲ ▲ ▲

Scene Thirty Six

"Wake up darling. Time to get out of bed and put on your sexy pale pink spandex fishing micro mini skirt and tank top set. The one with the fishnet mesh down the side. The fish will love it. The sun is shining, birds are singing, a rare England morning."

Sylvia smiled lazily at her husband and stretched luxuriously, like a satisfied cat. Her thick golden hair was loose on the pillow framing her face like the rays of the morning sun.

"I'm supposed to wear the mesh part on the *side? What a novel concept!*"

Her husband smiled. "Only if you want to try something *different.* Come Syl, be like the sun, rise and shine."

"*I hear you talking, but you can't come in.*" she sang back at him. "*I hear you talking, go back where you've been.*" With that she patted the mattress beside her.

"That's not the way the song goes, and I'm already in. Plus, it doesn't make any sense except for the last line. And anyway, you couldn't handle it, after last night." he laughed, "Besides that, we have to meet Damon downstairs in forty five minutes." looking at his watch. "We just don't have the time."

"How about a quickie?" she purred.

"I don't do *quickies,* as you so quaintly put it, I only do *longies.* Now get up and get ready. We don't want to keep our guest waiting, do we?"

Sylvia slowly pulled back the covers and *very slowly* arched her naked body, spread her shapely legs and smiled at him.

"What the hell, I shouldn't knock something I haven't tried, should I?" He pulled off his boxer shorts and his slim muscular form jumped back into bed.

▲ ▲ ▲

Thirty minutes later Sylvia came out of the bedrooms master bathroom dressed to go fishing. She was wearing just what her husband had suggested.

"Wow, you look great!"

"Thank you sweetheart." But she said it in a preoccupied way.

"Is something bothering you Syl? Was the *quickie* too short?" She laughed.

"That is *not* what I meant!" he said indignantly, then smiled.

"Seriously darling, is something bothering you? You had a strange look on your face when you came out of the bathroom."

"As a matter of fact, yes. You remember the dream I had?" he nodded. "Well, I had pretty much dismissed it as just a dream, with coincidences, until Damon started picking up his cartridges. He said what he said in the dream but he changed it slightly. Well, not so much changed as added to, and it started me to thinking. From what you told me, Damon Gray is pretty much a zillionaire, right?"

"Trillionaire." he corrected nodding.

"Right, then why would a trillionaire need to keep his cartridge cases … yes, yes I know what he said. But it got me to thinking and after you two left, I tidied up a bit and then I looked at his targets. What do you think I found?"

"We know that he is a great shot, dear. His scores mirrored mine and I am considered one of the best marksmen in the world. Yours were also great, but I take it that that is not what you are getting at. I'm not sure *what* you found. What *did* you find?"

Sylvia walked around the bed, reached under the mattress and brought forth the envelope. Sitting on the edge of the bed, she opened it and took out the targets. She looked at them and frowned. She sorted through them quickly.

"What is the matter, dear?"

"Oh, nothing I guess." She said as she shuffled through them again. "I just thought that I had folded them the other way, but they are all here. The mind does like to play tricks, doesn't it? Come sit on the bed for a minute and look at these. These are Damon's targets. Tell me if you see what I saw."

Sitting on the bed beside her, he sorted through the targets slowly. Then he sorted through them quickly, putting certain ones together. Two of them he folded in half and held up to the window with the sunlight shining in. Looking at the wall he saw the two square shaped shadows. In the two shadows, there were sunbeams of five small circles of light. He picked up two more sheets, placed them face to face and did the same thing. On the wall, the shadows had six circles of light randomly around where the bulls-eye would be.

He looked at his wife.

"What do you make of it, Mickey?"

"Nobody can shoot like this. *Nobody!* I know. I've shot with the world's best!" He shook his head slightly. "I don't know what to make of it, Syl. I really don't know."

"Somebody *can* shoot like this sweetheart. These prove it." Suddenly she smiled.

"It's been stewing in my brain all night and I think I know the answer. It just came to me!" she said excitedly, clapping her hands like a child. Michael couldn't help it, he laughed.

After a moment of silence he nudged her with his elbow. "Are you going to share your insight with me, or should I assume that Damon is really the *Grey Ghost, Gun Magician and Wizard?*"

"Oh, I'm sorry dear. I was just checking my thought processes. I think I'm right. Damon doesn't fly on public airlines. That's where I first met him, on an airplane, that is. It was a charter flight that he had booked, just for himself and Hastings, I think his name is. Yes, I remember now! It was Garret Hastings. I remember thinking that it was a beautiful name. *Garret Hastings.* Doesn't that sound like a beautiful name?" Sylvia saw her husbands face. "Sorry sweetheart. Where was I? Oh yes. Damon once told me that he chartered planes when his private jet was unavailable. He was having his private jet overhauled and refitted. He is from the US but he spends a lot of time abroad, touring. To my knowledge, he always stays in expensive hotels. He could buy a number of nice homes, with servants, with what he spends. The only person I have ever seen with him is his chauffer, Hastings. I think he is a lonely man who has too much time and money and is maybe more than a little bit paranoid."

She nodded her head as if in conversation to a voice inside her head. She continued. "That would explain the eyes in the dream. His parents were killed in a terrorist bomb explosion. His grandparents were killed in a plane crash over the ocean, no survivors. He is the last of his family. I remember you saying that every one he loved got killed. I think that *he* thinks that there is a conspiracy, by people unknown, to kill him. I think he practices with guns far more than he is inferring. And computers. Ask him to work out with us tonight, okay?" He nodded again. "I think our pianist friend is a bag full of surprises."

She paused, then continued, "Or he could be a demon gunfighter from hell, like you said."

"That's not what I said ..."

"Just teasing dear, just teasing. I feel very comfortable around Damon. I really believe that he is our friend. Let him keep his secrets, alright? Good, now let's go. We don't want to keep our guest waiting, just because you got a little randy this morning."

"Me? Me? I wasn't the one who ... Yes dear."

"I hate it when you say that."

"Yes dear."

Laughing and holding hands they went downstairs to meet Damon.

▲ ▲ ▲

After they had breakfast, Damon asked for a tour of the estate. Michael was happy to oblige. The tour took several hours with Damon asking a lot of questions, most of which Lord Brighton could not answer. Damon didn't seem to care.

After the tour, they went fishing

They all had a wonderful time fishing the small lake nestled in the middle of a great forest at the rear of the castle. Damon was extremely proficient with a fly rod, but it was Sylvia who caught all of the biggest fish on the three day weekend.

When Michael had asked her secret to catching the whoppers, she replied demurely, "Fish have a keen sense of smell."

▲ ▲ ▲

It was during that time that Michael told Damon that through intermediaries, Mr. X, head of the French Secret Service, the Surrette, had contacted him concerning the Mr. Smoke terrorist assassination.

He told Damon everything that was said. Michael and Mr. X had talked at length about it and then Mr. X asked if A.T.C.U. would be willing to sell their computer protection program to them. He felt that this might have been a hidden invitation by the Surrette to network with them to eliminate terrorism.

He told their Leader that he would have to check with the powers that be and get back to him. For what was he, after all, but a servant of the people.

What a crock! He chuckled when he said that.

He told Damon that he was *'optimistically inclined'* toward the request.

Damon actually chuckled good naturedly at the usage of *'optimistically inclined'* and had agreed to think about designing a system, like theirs, for the Surrette.

Damon told Michael that as soon as he had an answer, he would tell him. His own safety was paramount to him, as well as Michael and Sylvia's. Michael said he understood, and he thought he did. *'But what does one really know of the workings of a paranoid mind?'* he asked himself.

Damon also accepted their invitation to work out with them in their private gymnasium, after each day of fishing.

Sylvia was right again. She continued to amaze Michael with her intuition and insights. They each did their separate workouts together in the gym and then did laps in the pool. Then he and Damon went into the men's locker room to shower.

Michael noticed his weight, when Damon weighed in before he showered. He was thirty three pounds heavier than Michael. He judged him to be his height, just over six feet. He was wider shouldered than Michael and stood military straight, perfectly balanced.

The pianist didn't look it, but was large boned. One would have thought that weighing in at the two hundred and eighteen pounds, he would look heavy. He didn't. Nude in the men's locker room after the workout, his muscles stood out like a medical anatomy picture, every muscle perfectly defined. Michael noticed that Damon carried most of his surplus muscle mass in the neck, shoulder and arm areas as well as the legs, extra heavy in the calves.

The perfectly proportioned gymnast body, he told Sylvia later that night.

Before the workouts, Damon's body looked like the Doberman Pinscher's that patrolled his Arrow Wood Estates.

With little or almost no body fat, he looked at least twenty pounds lighter than he actually was, leaning towards slender. But then, when Dr. Gray went through his training/exercise regimen his muscles seemed to come alive, twisting, writhing and seeming to swell to twice their size. Then, he didn't look slender at all. He looked like a juggernaut. Unstoppable. A force of nature. Beyond human.

It was a strange contrast, Lord Brighton thought, that clothed he looked quite the opposite, almost wraithlike slim. Damon had told him that all of his charcoal grey and black clothing was custom made for him by a personal tailor, to his personal specifications. That probably had a lot to do with it, he thought.

Damon gave Michael the tailor's name, Giovanni Bruno, and the tailor's phone number in Italy. Clothed, his body looked smooth and sleek, almost effeminate in the smooth feline graceful way he moved.

Lord Brighton was fascinated by Damon's hands. They, like the rest of him, were deceiving. They were large, long, seemingly slender pianist's hands. Big boned hands with long tapered fingers that made them look slender. Michael knew better. When he had shook Damon's hand, his was buried and Michael did not have a small hand. He had felt the controlled power in them.

Strong, powerful hands.

Damon's right hand had an incredibly beautiful tri-gold ring on the ring finger, with what looked like imbedded interwoven three dimensional triangles around it. He complimented Damon on it and asked where he might purchase one like it. Damon smiled, thanked him, and said it was a gift and did not know where it was made or even who had made it.

One thing stood out in Michael's mind. All the men that he worked out with in the past made a lot of noise when they worked out and had a lot of facial expressions. Even he and Sylvia were panting heavily when they were done. Not so with Damon. When Damon worked out, his face did not move. It was like he went into a trancelike state of concentration. He could see Damons chest expand and contract, but he could hear no sound. He would not have noticed it in a crowded gym, but here he did. Damon's movements were a controlled fluid motion, not jerky no matter what the weight.

And he swam like a dolphin.

During the Friday workout, Michael was envious of Damon's physique. Envious, not jealous. Michael had a fine muscular body and knew it. He'd worked hard to get it as a young man and he worked hard to maintain it.

During the Saturday workout, Michael admired and took note of Damon's movements and his routine.

During the Sunday workout, he mirrored Damon's routine.

He noticed that Damon changed his routine every workout and questioned him on it. Damon told him that he varied his routine constantly, because he put so much stress and pressure on his bones and muscles. If he repeated an exercise too consistently, he could cause damage to those muscles, tendons and joints. It also helped to keep him flexible, and it kept his muscles confused so they couldn't cheat.

▲ ▲ ▲

Scene Thirty Seven

As they were relaxing in the library Sunday night, the subject came around to France, in reference to the wine Michael and Sylvia were drinking. Sylvia mentioned that they had just returned from Versailles and had taken a tour of the rich and famous.

It was Sylvia's idea. She didn't want to miss anything and found that tours took them to places that most people would never find. She had booked a private tour with the city's top tour company. Sylvia had asked their *guide* if there were any fabulous places, that weren't on the tour, that they should see. Their *tour guide* had smiled and had taken them off course to a place that he described as *magical*. He said there was no other word to describe it. They came to an estate that was out of a fairy tale. She went on to describe it; the outside, the buildings, the grounds, the landscaping and everything else in between. They were not allowed inside the gates.

Sylvia *had* to see more, so she got the address, had Michael acquire the unlisted phone number and called to ask if she and her husband could view it. At first the man on the other end of the phone said no, no tours.

When Sylvia mentioned who she and her husband were and that they were interested in purchasing it, the whole atmosphere changed. The man on the phone asked *how* they had found out that it was for sale. Sylvia told Damon that she was astounded! Without missing a beat she told the man that she did not think it appropriate to give out that kind of information over the phone. Besides, she added, did it really matter? He, of course, said no. They set up a time to view it two days later.

When they arrived to view it, they had to provide identification documentation. Then they were searched, politely but thoroughly. Then they had to leave their transportation at the gate and were chauffeured in to meet their guide. The man they met was the *overseer*, as Sylvia called him. A round little man with a Napoleonic complex. His name was Napoleon.

Damon smiled.

Syl laughed. No, he did not have a Napoleonic complex, she said. He was a darling.

But what started out as a lark, turned serious. Both Michael and Sylvia fell totally in love with the estate.

Over dinner that night, Sylvia and Michael went on and on for hours describing things that they loved about it. To their mutual surprise they found that they both could find no fault with any of the estate!

It turned out that the owner of the estate died of extreme old age and had outlived his heirs. Land developers wanted the estate, but his will forbid it to be sold to developers or kin, and whoever bought it would agree, in a legal binding contract, that they must own it for a minimum of ten years, and that they could not sell it to a developer or family of a developer. They could build or add any improvements to existing structures and if by nature or accident any building was destroyed, it had to be rebuilt to the specifications of the architectural drawings on file at the local historical society. Any additional structures had to match the style of the existing buildings and be accepted by a local architectural firm that he had chosen or the local historical society. There was more, Sylvia said, but that was the gist of it. The previous owner did not want plastic and concrete to take over his estate.

It came completely furnished, except for the owners' personal belongings. It had an appraisal, inclusive of the furnishings, by the top appraisal firm in France. It was to be updated yearly. The appraisal price was the asking price. It was non negotiable. The proceeds were to be distributed according to the contents of the deceased owner's Last Will and Testament. Both Sylvia and Michael thought the appraisal was on the fair side of high.

A very private man, the deceased owner had asked Napoleon *not* to list the property on the real estate market. Maintaining a skeleton staff, his estate would pay expenses until it sold. It had been subtly advertised through word of mouth for almost a year. With Napoleon prescreening the prospects, it had been shown only a few times, but for one reason or another, none had made an offer.

Knowing of Lord and Lady Brighton and their recently publicized wedding, Napoleon felt comfortable inviting them without first prescreening them. Michael found out later that he screened them *immediately* after they hung up the phone.

"Good man." Michael told Damon, "Impressed the hell out of me."

It was due to be appraised in less than a month and both of them agreed that the price would go up substantially.

Damon asked questions, lots of questions. Not interrogative questions. He asked the kind of questions of someone who is genuinely interested in what is being said. Clarifying questions to some of Sylvia's extravagant descriptions and statements, as well as insightful ones.

He learned that they had not made an offer, because a conditional offer would not be considered. The simple fact was that Michael did not have that kind of money on hand and was not willing to borrow for its purchase, so soon after their wedding.

Both of them didn't want his relatives to think that she was a *gold digger.* They didn't want, or need, one word of scandal *in that regard.*

"Damon," said Sylvia, "it is so hard to describe to someone the way we feel about *Coutances*, that is what it is named. Isn't that a beautiful name, *Coutances*? Sounds like it should belong to a count and countess."

She smiled wistfully, dreamily. "Tell me Damon, have you ever felt like that? Have you ever seen a place or thing, that struck something inside you, like a chord or note and you knew that it was meant for you and only you? I think that only someone who has felt that can truly understand what we feel. Have you?"

"Yes."

"Awesome! Was it a place or a thing?"

"Like both of you, it was a place."

"Did you buy it?"

"No."

"Why not? It probably wasn't for sale, right?"

Damon laughed. "We'll talk about it later. Now, unless I'm terribly mistaken, I take it that there is *more* to the story?"

Michael laughed also. "Now what in the world would make you think that? That was a rhetorical question, bye the bye."

Damon smiled.

They went on to tell him that they had discussed the situation and decided to sell Blackstone. Michael had inherited it from his Granduncle, along with his *Lord of the Realm* title. The Granduncle had sired no children and had bequeathed his title as well as the property to Michael.

Michael and Sylvia liked it, but they had two residences in London and they liked Arrow Wood Estates better. This one was a little out of the way for them. And a little intimidating to Sylvia, she confessed. They had offered it to his family and relatives. None of them wanted it, for one reason or another.

Michael had even offered to get it classified as a historic landmark, by one of his friends in the government, so that the taxes would be next to nothing. He wouldn't do it for himself. It would, or could, cause too much of a scandal.

Word got out and they had some inquiries. The only serious one, they felt, was by a large residential apartment/condominium developer. There were problems though. Because of the catacombs underneath, the developers said that it would be atrociously expensive to correct, and they took that out of the asking price, plus they didn't want to purchase the contents, which is how they wanted to sell it.

Michael was miffed. He had the appraisal done by one of London's top appraisal firms Baker and Snively and all that was taken into account. Besides, he told Damon, like the deceased owner of Coutances, they didn't want to see Blackstone torn down, the forest destroyed or the small natural lake filled in.

The developer had made a verbal offer. They said to put it in writing and that after they had discussed it, they would get back to them.

"How much are you asking and how much did they offer?" Damon asked.

"We are asking the appraisal price minus five percent. That included all contents excluding the library. Full appraisal, if the library is included. The appraisal for the house was twenty six million pounds and the contents were conservatively appraised at ten million. I didn't ask them to appraise the library, as I was going to keep it. When Sylvia reminded me that we have copies of all of them at our main residence, I had them appraised. They appraised out at almost five million pounds." Michael shook his head in disbelief.

"It blew my mind! I had no idea that *books* could be worth so much money. The appraisal firm told me that the prices on contents could vary at auction depending on who was there, up to fifty percent one way or the other. I suspect the other, which is to say less, not more, which is why I dropped the price by five percent."

Michael saw Sylvia smiling slightly. His face reddened and he returned the smile. "Sorry! I do ramble on sometimes, don't I?"

"Sometimes?" Sylvia teased playfully.

Michael ignored her. "I guess the answer is that, we were asking thirty nine million five hundred thousand pounds, or forty one million with the library and they offered twenty one million pounds without the contents. Sylvia and I agree that we might be able to sell the contents at auction for close to the appraised price, but we may not be able to close on it until after the new appraisal of Coutances. We had it appraised to see what the new value would be. It will go up twenty five to thirty five percent. If we don't purchase it in time, I'm afraid we won't be able to get it."

While Michael was talking, Damon had taken out *Mac*, his laptop and his hands were flying over the keys.

When Michael had finished speaking, Damon stopped typing.

"Any suggestions, Damon?" Sylvia asked.

"No, no suggestions I'm afraid ..."

"That doesn't surprise me." said Michael, not noting the pause. "I've been wracking my brain for a week and have come up with nothing. What makes it worse, is that we have not received a written offer from the developer."

"May I use your printer over there with the Bluetooth wireless?" Damon asked, pointing towards the desk.

"Yes, of course you can. How did you know it was wireless?" Sylvia asked. Damon smiled. "I know, I know. Magic, right?" she laughed.

Damon laughed also and hit a button on Mac. A moment later the printer started printing.

"No, not this time, Sylvia. I noticed that there was no computer cable connected to it. But I do have one magic trick. I can read minds and multiple minds at once, in fact." He had their attention. "I know what both of you are thinking, *right now.*"

"What are we thinking?" Sylvia smiled. Michael did also.

"You both think that I don't know what you are thinking."

The smile dropped off their faces.

"What am I thinking now?" Sylvia said.

Michael and Damon laughed.

"What's so funny ... Oh, it's not magic but a joke, isn't it?" Suddenly she smiled.

"Damon, that is the *first* joke that you've told us, did you know that?"

"Well, it's a little of both. Feel free to use it."

The printer had stopped printing. Damon continued as he rose and retrieved the papers from the printer,

"I didn't finish what I was saying to you Michael. I don't have any *suggestions* but I do have a *solution* if you are interested?"

"Of course we are." He said looking at Syl. She nodded. He looked back at Damon.

"You have a *solution*, old chum?" Damon smiled and nodded. "My word! A man with a *solution* instead of empty words. By George, you might be a *wizard* after all, Damon! Was that what you were doing on your laptop, when I was giving you the numbers?"

"That is correct." Damon was writing on one of the papers. When he finished he handed them to Michael.

Michael started to read them, stopped and looked at Damon. Damon nodded.

He then looked at his wife. She looked puzzled. He started reading again, not looking up until he was done. He then took out his pen and wrote on the paper.

"Would someone please tell me what is going on?" demanded his wife in exasperation.

Without a word Michael handed her the papers. She repeated his scenario. When she was finished she took her husband's proffered pen and wrote on the paper.

She then reached out and shook Damons hand and accepted the check that he had just finished signing, handing it to her husband.

"Care to show us your new house, sir?" she laughed. Then she started to cry.

Laughing and crying she grabbed and hugged Damon, and gave him a huge kiss on the cheek. Then, jumping up and down like a woman possessed she turned and hugged and kissed her husband, all the time jumping up and down.

"II ddon'tt tthinnk I'lll eevverr bbuyy annotther hhoouse." Michael said while being hugged by his jumping wife. "II ddon'tt tthinkk II ccouldd surrviive tthiiss aaa seccconnd ttiime!"

That was how Doctor Damon Gray came into possession of Blackstone.

▲ ▲ ▲

Scene Thirty Eight

As Damon was leaving the next morning, Sylvia remembered to ask him about the property that he had fallen in love with, that he didn't buy.

"It was Blackstone."

Sylvia jumped up and down with excitement and impulsively clapped her hands.

"Yes! Yes! I knew it! I just *knew* it was Blackstone! I am *so* happy for you Damon! We're almost neighbors now. Thank you for coming for the weekend. Thank you for *everything!*" She gave Damon a big hug.

"Yes, thank you," Michael concurred, "although I feel that it is an inadequate response to a forty one million pound check."

"You are both very welcome Lord and Lady Brighton. It is the perfect response. And I thank you for allowing me to purchase it. Outside of the United States it is the only private residence that I own. Well, I should clarify that. That one of my corporations own. Please don't forget to contact your friend in the government, to have it declared an Historical Site. And please don't tell anyone that I own it. Tell whoever asks, that the Paladin Corporation bought it. That is the name on the corporate check that I gave you, so you won't be lying."

"We won't tell a soul." Michael assured him. Sylvia nodded. "As to the rezoning, it's already been done, old chap. I called my friend last night and he called back a half hour ago to confirm that it was done. Oh, and bye the bye, I did as you asked and talked to Whitner last night. He informed me early this morning that he had talked it over with all the staff, and that *he and they* would be *delighted* to stay on and work for you. It's strange in a way. I don't really know any of them all that well. I hardly ever came out here as a child or a man."

Damon smiled. "Thank you. I know *of* the house you two spoke of in France. In my opinion, it is a true work of art and genius. I know that it will be perfect for both of you. I *also* made a call last night. The *Coutances* is yours. *Guaranteed.* I look forward to visiting you there?"

"How in the world did you manage that? I mean ......" Michael's voice trailed off in astonished speechlessness.

"Of course! You don't need an invitation. And you never will, Damon." said Sylvia, filling in the void.

Michael nodded. "Why is it," he finally said, "that I always seem to be nodding when I'm around my wife? Could it be that I can't get a word in edgewise?"

"Oh, Michael!"

"Yes dear?"

"Michael!"

"Yes dear."

"You know I hate it when you say that!"

"Yes dear."

All three laughed.

When the laughter died, Damon looked at Michael.

"I've thought about it and it is a *go* on the Surrette matter."

"Great!" enthused Michael.

"Will you be staying the day?" asked Damon.

"No, we are leaving immediately. We both have a full plate today."

"Then I'll contact you on your cell phone with a time and a place for us to meet. Oh, I know you said that the *Surrette* probably used Mr. Smoke as an excuse to contact you. I don't think of it is an excuse at all, but a reason. Don't confuse the two. Both countries have had dealings with Mr. Smoke. I suggest that you compare the ballistics of the bullets found in the two terrorists."

"I'll try, but I doubt that they will prove to be a match. For one thing, a gun would never get through airport security. With today's electronic surveillance, security, detection and protection procedures, it would be virtually impossible. And talking about *impossible,* add trying to get other countries to *work together,* not only with us but with each other *also!*" Michael shook his head at the thought. "What a nightmare! Maybe you could come up with a *solution* for that, *Mr. Wizard?* Sometimes, new eyes see clearest."

"I'll see what I can *conjure up.*" Damon smiled.

Michael and Sylvia laughed.

"Until the next time." Damon said as he shook Michael's hand.

"Oh, wait a minute! I almost forgot." Michael reached into his coat pocket.

"It is my honor to present to you this *really* old black key. The key to Blackstone."

"Thank you, thank you very much." came the voice of Elvis out of Damon's mouth as he accepted the oversized key. Turning to Sylvia he smiled and offered his hand to shake. "And thank you also." She smiled, ignored his hand, and gave him a huge hug.

As he walked down the steps to his limo, he called over his shoulder, "Can I give you some words of advice that could possibly be of benefit to you, Sylvia?"

"Of course you can Damon. What is it?" she replied.

When he reached the vehicles open rear door, he turned. Hastings was sitting patiently in the driver's seat.

"Don't hide things under your mattress. It's the first place most professionals check. Someone like the Gray Ghost."

She stood there stunned, as he got into his limo, and Hastings drove away.

▲ ▲ ▲

Scene Thirty Nine

"Did you hear what he said? Did you?" Sylvia laughed. "He sauntered into our bedroom, took out the targets, turned them the other way, tucked them back in and then sauntered out. Without disturbing us. He did it for the fun of it. What a strange man. To him he did nothing wrong. It was a lark. What kind of man does that, dearheart?" She asked her husband that night.

They both had to leave for appointments, after Damon left that morning, and were not able to talk about it until now.

"I don't think he sauntered in or out darling, but I think you are right on the rest of it. I do think it was a lark to him. Call it intuition, but I think he was shocked and impressed by what you found, and I don't think he shocks or impresses easily. I've thought about it on and off all day, and I've come to the simple conclusion that *he trusts us*. He wanted us to know that he trusts us with his safety."

He looked at his wife thoughtfully. "That is also the reason that he bought Blackstone from us personally. He could have had the Paladin Corporation buy it and we would never have known. I know, I checked out the company today. No ties to him at all, but when I called the companies president, he informed me that Damon had given his permission to verify, *to me only*, that he owned the company. How did he know that I would do that? Because he knew that I would. He put himself in my shoes. He is an extremely simple man in some ways and unfathomable in others."

"*Unfathomable?* Who uses words like that? Does anybody but me understand a word you say?" She smiled impishly. "I just asked a simple question. What kind of man does that, Mickey? It's okay if you don't know the answer …. really sweetheart. I thought about it on and off all day also and I came to the same conclusions you did. (pause) *I* (pause) *don't* (pause) *know!*" Again *the grin.* "One thing I *do* know is that he is our friend and would not hurt us for the world. I guess right now that's all that counts." She paused, then said dramatically.

"I think he's gay."

Michael's jaw dropped open.

"My word, where in the world did that come from, and what makes you think that?"

"Simple. He didn't look at me at all in my hot pink fishing outfit. You did though, *a lot*, thank you sweetheart. Did he look at you, *that* way, in the men's room?"

"Although it highly offends me to say this; not at all, *dammit*. Not even a twitch and I thought I looked pretty darn good, top form and all that. Sorry darling. He is hairless from the head down and to be honest darling, he seems to be terribly under endowed."

"Under endowed? With all those muscles? Are you serious?"

Michael just smiled.

"He looked preadolescent to me, but what do I know, I didn't see him aroused. Sorry to dash your assumption darling."

"Not even once? With all your muscles pumped? Are you serious?"

Michael smiled that smile again.

"I guess I'm just not his type." Sighing, Michael pretended to flip his hair back. "I just didn't turn him on. Sorry darling…. Wait a minute! I *did* see him eyeing the grand piano a number of times, when he thought we weren't looking."

Michael Brighton looked at his wife knowingly. "Now it's *his* to do with *as he pleases*."

He shook his head sadly, "He does seem to be *unfathomable* doesn't he?"

"*Unfathomable?* Say that three times quickly right now and you will get lucky tonight. Under endowed? Really, who'd have thought?"

Lord Brighton couldn't do it. Because he was laughing, he claimed.

That night, she claimed that he didn't get lucky, he got *extremely* lucky.

Michael Brighton was a wise man. He was the *Head* of A.T.C.U.. He agreed.

▲ ▲ ▲

Scene Forty

One week later.

Fred Conley was working late in his new office. Security personnel were situated strategically throughout the building. He had just finished a story and was leaning back in his chair, feet on the desk, when his cell phone rang. He jumped slightly. It startled him. He looked at the clock on his desk. It was midnight. *'What the bloody hell!'* he thought. *'Who is ringing me at midnight? And on my private cell phone!'*

He looked to see who was calling. His private cell phone was a special one (part of his security package) that showed the names and numbers of all incoming calls, even blocked ones. No number came up on the screen. In fact, *nothing* came up on the screen. It was blank. It just rang.

'That's strange.' He thought as he answered it.

"Fred Conley speaking."

"Mr. Conley?" Asked a sexless voice. Fred's guard went up. He knew an electronically altered voice when he heard one.

"I just said that I was. Who's calling and how did you get this number?"

"You won't believe me, but I'll tell you anyway." The voice paused for effect. Fred smiled. He'd used that same psychological *acting tool* in the past himself.

He waited. Nothing. *Silence.* He stopped smiling.

"Well?" the Roving News Reporter finally prompted.

"I am *Mr. Smoke* and I got your number by breaking into, or *hacking* your mobile phone company's computer system. It took awhile, Fred. There are a lot of mobile phone providers. It is also *not* listed under your name. Does that answer your questions?" The phone went silent waiting for a response.

Fred was incredulous. He almost hung up, but something about the surety of the statements made him *not*. The silence continued. That *also* helped to convince him.

"How can you *prove* to me, that you *are* who you say you *are*?" Fred finally asked.

"That is exactly the reason I'm calling."

"Excuse me?"

"I said... 'That is exactly the reason I'm calling'." Responded the sexless voice.

"I heard you the first time. What I meant was, I don't understand your response."

"I see. Let me rephrase it in a way that you will. I am calling to prove to you that I am Mr. Smoke. Does that make sense to you?"

"The words make a coherent sentence but the meaning eludes me. How can your phoning me prove that you are Mr. Smoke? I have people who call me all the time with that claim."

"Really? Wow! On your private cell phone number?"

"No."

"With electronically altered voices?"

"No."

"With no number showing on your special phone?"

"No."

"Knowing that you are in your office, *right now*?"

Pause, then, "No."

"Well?"

"You *do* have valid points, but I wouldn't consider them conclusive."

"Really?" there was another long pause. Fred didn't prompt him this time.

The voice continued, "What *would* you consider *conclusive*, Fred?"

"How would I know? I'm not Mr. Smoke."

"But if you *were*, how would you?"

Fred thought for a moment. "If I was you, I'd come see me *personally*."

"Good! That was my thought also. How about your office in, say, one hour?"

"There are highly trained security throughout the building! You *will* be caught!" Fred said quickly, uneasily. His feet came off the desk and slammed to the floor as he stood up in alarm!

"That's a chance I'll take, Fred. You might want to inform the Head of Security that I'm coming. I would suggest that you make your office *off limits,* after Sam or his men initially search it. I don't want to have to hurt anyone if I can avoid it …… *but I will.* I'll leave that up to you. I'll see you in one hour."

"Wait! I …" too late. The phone had gone dead.

Fred Conley sat down for a minute and collected his thoughts. He looked at his special cell phone. He checked the incoming calls. His last call didn't exist! *'Damn!'* he thought in frustration. *'I've no proof to show anybody.'* He had a feeling that it *was* Mr. Smoke that he had been talking to. If that was the case, he *didn't* want him stopped *or* caught! If it wasn't Mr. Smoke, but a terrorist out for revenge, he *did* want him stopped *and* caught. What was he to do?

Finally, he shrugged. He had made up his mind. *'I guess I'll just do as he suggested.'*

Fred called Mr. Ellis, the Head of Security and told him to come to his office. He did. Fred asked his first name. All he had ever called him was Mr. Ellis, that's how he had been introduced to him. He said his first name was Samuel, but his friends called him Sam. It did not surprise the Roving Reporter. He *should* have known. Mr. Smoke did.

Fred asked Sam to check and search his office. He did. Fred then told Sam that Mr. Smoke had called and said he would be coming over to see him. It might be a hoax and it might be a threat. They were to stop anybody from entering his office for the next two hours, and that his office was *not* to be entered for two hours. *Not for* any *reason.* He needed to be alone for those two hours, was that understood? The Head of Security said yes, it was absolutely clear. Fred had him repeat the instructions. Sam gave the office a final once over and then left to deploy his staff.

Satisfied, Fred sat down to wait.

Mr. Smoke watched as Sam left Fred's office. He watched on a small screen as the security team was apprised of the situation and positioned throughout the building, via his remote miniaturized cameras that he had positioned yesterday morning. He had monitored and recorded all the security teams' movements for the past forty hours. He knew their patterns.

He had also been in the building all day waiting for Fred to finish his work. He was known for his late work habits. Mr. Smoke monitored the security team's movements for fifty five minutes and just before the hour was up, he made his move. When the nearest auras were turned away from him, he passed, unseen by them, to Fred's office door.

Scene Forty One

Fred was seated behind his desk with a gun in his hand when his special cell phone rang. He jumped up and almost fired his gun. Still standing, he reached down and picked up his phone with his left hand. He looked at the display. It read *Mr. Smoke* with 666 as a phone number.

Fred laughed and answered it. "I like your phone number. Decided not to stop by did you?"

Silence answered him.

"Hello? .... Hello?" Nothing. Frustrated, Fred Conley disconnected the phone.

"Damn it." he mumbled to himself.

"Put your gun on the desk, please." Instructed a deep melodious cultured English voice directly behind him.

Fred froze. Then he started to turn slowly so as not to startle the man behind him. He felt a cold gun barrel press into the base of his neck, where his vertebrae and skull met. He froze again.

"Please place your gun on the desk in front of you, *now*." The words were spoken slowly and clearly.

Fred cursed himself soundly. He had forgotten that he still had his gun in his hand! Slowly he placed his gun on his desk and then flicked it out of reach. The coldness against his neck receded.

"Please sit back down in your chair." Fred obeyed.

Suddenly a large puff of smoke billowed from the floor in front of him and when it dissipated, a figure was standing before him.

A man, dressed in a dark grey ninja outfit, complete with tinted eye coverings.

Scene Forty Two

One week later.

"Good evening viewers! This is Fred Conley with KXWY Channel 66 News at six. Tonight we are deviating from our regular format to bring you an hour long program about the International Terrorist Bomber's *Assassin*, Mr. Smoke! *I have been in contact with, and have talked to Mr. Smoke personally!* Phone your neighbors, phone your friends. You don't want to miss what's coming up! We are going to take a *five minute commercial break* for you to call all your friends, families, co-workers and neighbors to tune in. After the commercials there will be no more commercial interruptions for the balance of the hour. Pop your popcorn, take your bathroom break, make your calls, set the video recorder, then sit down and prepare yourself for, what might very well be, the news story of the *decade*, if not the *century*! Make sure you ask whoever is watching with you *not to speak until it's over*, so that you won't miss a single word. This is Fred Conley with KXWY Channel 66 News at six. *I'll see you in five minutes!*"

▲ ▲ ▲

Eleven thirty that night.

Fred Conley was sitting in his office, sipping a cognac and unwinding. He had never experienced anything like it in his life!

Tonight, he had not only *reported* the news, he *was* the news! He had followed Mr. Smokes outline and script *to the letter.*

When he had come back on the air five minutes later, at least sixty six percent of the world's television viewing audience was watching! It was the largest viewed show in the history of television. Billions of people all over the world watched Fred Conley with KXWY Channel 66 News at six.

Fred smiled as he reviewed the highlights in his mind.

He told the audience exactly how he had been contacted by the famous international terrorist bomber assassin, known as Mr. Smoke and how Mr. Smoke had appeared before him.

When he described how Mr. Smoke had magically appeared, behind and beside him, a cloud of smoke exploded on the blue screen. When it had dissipated, Mr. Smoke was standing there!

Pretending to be unaware, Fred described him in detail. The loose, non-restricting, yet formfitting Ninja outfit. The unique, non reflective, dark grey molded metal face mask, the collapsing and expanding scaled neck guard and the matching tinted sunglasses, or *eye coverings*, as he liked to think of them. He could not see Mr. Smoke's eyes through them. They were connected to the oval ear guards attached under the hood. No weapons were showing.

When he saw the control room waving frantically at him, he smiled his signature smile, and told the audience that he had an animated three dimensional likeness of Mr. Smoke created by the top computer 3D animator, Valkyrie Blipinstein.

He then turned and nodded to the life sized 3D Mr. Smoke standing just behind and to the right of Fred's chair. The 3D head of Mr. Smoke turned, seemed to look down at him and then nodded back, showing how the scaled neck guard worked. His head then returned to its original position. He just stood there, relaxed, breathing, fabric moving ever so slightly, as would a normal persons, making him look *so* real that, for a moment, you would think that Mr. Smoke was actually standing *in* the News Room. Mr. Smoke's height

Fred estimated at six foot two, because he was sitting throughout the entire meeting. Fred knew he was close.

Fred twirled his right index finger at the control room. Slowly the figure of Mr. Smoke rotated three hundred and sixty degrees and continued to do so, every ten minutes or so, to dispel the notion that he *was* in the room.

Looking at the monitor, even Fred thought that Mr. Smoke was behind and beside him.

Every time Fred made a statement that sounded unbelievable, he would look back over his shoulder at Mr. Smoke. Mr. Smoke would repeat his nod as if confirming his statement.

He had the Vice President of his cell phone company and his lawyer come onto the set, to discuss what had happened with his cell phone. Fred and the station expected some mild smoke screens and *'We'll have to look very seriously into this.'* discussion. Nothing of the sort happened.

It turned out that the cell phone company didn't want to come, and the person calling from the TV Station inferred that, without representation, their company could suffer *irreparable damage.* That changed their minds. They sent in their best and most aggressive mediator, Vice President Anthony Knowling and their top staff attorney and litigator, Miss Angela Granger.

Fred explained to the two of them what happened. *Nobody was prepared for what happened next.*

Mr. Knowling immediately went on the attack and arrogantly stated that what Fred said about the phone calls could *not* happen. Angela warned of lawsuits.

Fred showed the VP the 666 number. Anthony Knowling lost some of his bluster. How the 666 number appeared, he could not explain. To divert attention away from that, he vehemently denied the *alleged* (Fred smiled at the use of the word *alleged*) blank screen on Fred's *alleged* first call, stating emphatically that it *could not be done!* He challenged anyone in the television audience to do it. He said he would personally pay ten thousand dollars to the first person that could do it before the show was over. The VP then turned and asked Fred for his cell phone number. Before he could answer, Fred's cell phone rang.

Fred actually jumped up and out of his seat. He stood and looked at the Caller ID and nothing showed. The screen was blank. He showed the viewing audience. He showed it to the VP. He answered it.

"Fred Conley, here. You are on the air."

He held the earpiece up to his microphone.

A sexless *altered* voice came on and said "It *can* be done." then disconnected.

White faced, the cell phone company's Vice President sat there stunned and speechless for a few seconds, then got up and stormed off the set. A red faced Angela Granger scurried after him.

Fred had not expected Mr. Smoke to do that! The phone call was not scripted. It gave Fred Conley *instant credibility!*

Looking back he realized that it also protected his station from any potential lawsuits from the cell phone company.

He had Sam Ellis come on and verify his part and his teams as to the night of the meeting. He verified the Mr. Smoke and the 666 number on the cell phone two hours later. He said that no one to his knowledge, during those two hours, went into or left Fred's office. There was a camera in the outer office that monitored the room. It was a rotating camera. He admitted that someone extremely fast could cross the room and enter Fred's office before the camera could pick him up, but not anyone that he knew. Fred then showed footage of his office door closing, less than half an inch, on a return sweep. It was almost unnoticeable. If Fred hadn't known the exact time that Mr. Smoke was to appear *and did*, it was doubtful that anyone would have caught it.

Fred then had Liam Flaherty, a Police Ballistics Expert from Ireland, come on with his equipment and describe how bullets were matched to guns by the rifling of the barrels. Like fingerprints, no two guns had the same rifling. Fred asked Liam if he had brought with him the ballistics of the bullet that had killed Sean Michael O'Brien, soldier of the 'Black Hand'. He had. He was asked if Fred produced a bullet fired from a gun, could he tell if it was a match. Liam assured him that if the bullet was in good shape, he should have no problem determining if it was a match. Fred produced a bullet.

Fred Conley smiled at the astonishment of the ballistics expert, when he was handed the bullet. Liam said nothing at first. He tested it and weighed it to make sure and then announced, "Fred, it is a perfect specimen, but do you realize that this bullet is *solid gold?*"

Fred said he thought so, but wasn't sure. A buzz went through the news room as camera men and technicians talked excitedly. Then quiet descended as Liam proceeded with his tests. Liam didn't take long to produce the results.

He confirmed what Fred knew. The golden bullet was a perfect match with the one that killed Sean Michael O'Brien, the *terrorist bomber* that had been assassinated by Mr. Smoke.

The Roving Reporter announced to the world that the golden bullet had been given to him by none other than *Mr. Smoke!*

Fred stunned the world with the news that he had been given a *limited supply* of the *golden bullets* to sell to *certain Police Agencies* around the world, that were on a list provided by Mr. Smoke, to him. They were to be used as a ballistic check, to confirm a Mr. Smoke *Terrorist Bomber Assassination,* and also to be used to refute all of the *copy cat* killings.

The price was five thousand dollars!

Or a five thousand dollar receipt of payment to a recognized charity of the police forces choice!

Under no circumstances were any golden bullets to be offered to the public. *For any price!*

Fred said that Mr. Smoke had also promised that if he ever switched guns, he would send replacement bullets to all police forces that had purchased the first ones.

Fred then took prescreened calls from around the world.

The rest of the program was all downhill. To Fred Conley:

It was bedlam!

It was pandemonium!

It … was … fabulous!

Privately, Fred Conley was under instructions, by Mr. Smoke, to send every police force on his list *a golden bullet*, even if they didn't pay.

In the heat of the moment, Fred announced to the world that KXWY Channel 66 News would match the price in a donation *to the charity* of the global police departments *produced receipt*.

The Golden Bullet would be verified, by Liam, as a match before it was sent.

They all paid! Everyone on the list! Damned if they didn't! Fred was overjoyed.

One *Golden Bullet* was left for the news anchorman. He had it made into a necklace. He watched the entire process to make sure that it was not copied.

The KXWY Channel 66 News *President* was not pleased that Fred had offered to match the police donations to charities, without consulting him first. When they got together after the broadcast, Fred immediately told him it had been a whim and that he would pay for it himself. That took the wind out of the president's sails and calmed him immediately. He said that it *was* a great tactic and that the Station would pay gladly. He advised Fred to try to curb his impulses in the future and consult with him first. He slapped the news Anchor on the back heartily and gave Fred his private cell number.

For a long time, KXWY Channel 66 News at six became the most watched news show in the world.

Fred got another contract. Bigger and better! Without his asking!

Scene Forty Three

Damon Gray watched the television intently. He had just finished an expedition exploring the catacombs underneath Blackstone, his new home. Fresh from a workout and shower, he was watching the news.

The world news media were in heaven and in a whirlwind of frenzy. According to them, in the last six months, twenty two suspected and known terrorist bombers in seven countries had been killed by Mr. Smoke, even though they had only received eighteen sets of pictures. News ratings globally went through the roof.

Damon knew that only nine would match the ballistics check. The nine that were his.

He was delighted when Fred Conley had announced on the news that *all the police agencies on his list* had purchased his golden bullets. He was relieved that Fred didn't name any of them.

His mind switched back to the program.

In the United States a roving news reporter was interviewing people on the street about their thoughts on Mr. Smoke's assassinations of known terrorist bombers when one young man said that Mr. Smoke had to be an *American*, and that he was glad the bombers had been 'Smoked'. The world news media jumped all over it. The internet was alive with it. Instead of calling them assassinations as they had earlier, they were referred to as; *Smoked by Mr. Smoke*.

Anti-smoking campaigners jumped on the band wagon; 'Terrorist bombers would tell you if they could, *Smoke will kill you dead*' and 'Ask any Terrorist Bomber and they will tell you, *Smoke kills, Guaranteed*' and '*Smoke Kills*, as *Abduhl Mohamed Jabhared* found out' and '*Smoke Kills you Dead, just ask* Sean Michael O'Brien', along with a slew of other names. T-shirts with *Smoke Kills,* with a picture of the famous cigar beneath the words, were a very popular item.

"They come in every color imaginable" a young, well endowed, bra-less, anti-smoking activist/starlet told television reporters, posing and modeling the pink one she was wearing. She went from starlet to superstar with that interview.

Late night talk show hosts joked about the media waves he was causing around the world.

Daytime talk show hosts had doctors of every kind on to talk about the Mr. Smoke phenomena. One even had what he called a mini-series on '*The Mind of the Man behind the Mask of Smoke*'. It was a hit. His ratings skyrocketed.

Some religious leaders condemned, others praised. Most were wise enough to keep their mouths shut!

After the street interview, every country claimed ownership of Mr. Smoke.

The governments of the world were rumored to be in a panic, talking behind closed doors about the situation. Some were rumored to be collaborating with other governments to bring about Mr. Smokes demise. Or, as one informant was reported to have quoted to a news reporter: "Bring about the demise of the Bomber Terrorist's *Terrorist*, Mister Smoke."

Just recently, there had been another global news flash. An undisclosed reliable source claimed that the gun with the golden bullets, killed *every one* of the terrorist bombers! *Ballistics proved it.* No government would comment on that. Rumors again ran rampant.

One night, a late night TV host, tired of all the hoopla, paused during his monolog and looked out at his studio audience.

Quiet descended in the room.

Looking very serious he said, "I have something very serious to say. (pause) My writers have been complaining to me for some time and I'm tired of it! Every week they complain more. (pause) Rather than fire them I'm going to try to stop their insipid whining and sniveling about the same thing over and over."

Turning to look directly into the camera he continued with a deadpan look, "Mr. Smoke. Please! Please! Just kill off all the damn terrorist bombers in the world, so that my writers can write some *other* jokes. Please?"

The audience howled with laughter. "They are getting writers block. They want to go back to writing about *politicians*."

The audience went into hysterics.

▲ ▲ ▲

Damon switched channels.

Nothing of value there, he thought. No, not *nothing of value*, he corrected himself. All the publicity had slowed down terrorist bombings tremendously. What he meant were no reports of *new* terrorist bombings.

Of the twenty two credited terrorist killings, he had been responsible for nine. He found it hard to believe that in less than one year he had killed nine terrorist bombers, all men.

After the third he was able to control most of his body's reaction to the deaths. By the fifth he was able to control it completely. He still *felt* and experienced each of the *Terrorists Bombers* die. Each time, it was as if *he* died. At first he was traumatized after the killings. Now he understood and controlled the reaction.

Death was no longer an unknown entity to be feared. Damon had died too many times. He knew Death well. It came as a shock to find out that most of the Terrorist Bombers that he had 'Smoked' were just people who had been manipulated by others. Some were good and some were bad.

His inner selves understood the necessity of what he was doing more than he did, and they had helped a lot. Damon Gray now hated what Terrorist Bombers *did* almost as much as he hated them. His hatred for them was now a *cold hate*, one that he could easily control.

He hadn't wanted Mr. Smoke to be a media *hero*, just sensational global news. That is why he sent the graphic pictures to the news media. He had wanted Mr. Smoke to be a *terrorist bombers terror.* It was working but not as fast as he would have liked.

▲ ▲ ▲

Scene Forty Four

He switched to an American channel.

It was early evening there. The channel was at the start of a story.

"... broadcasting live from our satellite remote vehicle and NYKZ's own Linda Lacey. Linda, what is going on? Bring our viewers up to date."

The television screen switched to the stunning, award-winning blonde. She paused because of the transmission delay. Then her signature slight head tilt as she listened.

"Thank you Brian, and welcome to NYKZ's *Satellite Roving Report*. I'm Linda Lacey and we are here in a farmer's field just outside of New York City." The camera, doing a full three sixty, scanned the entire area. The sun was setting and everything stood out in stark relief. The old run down buildings in need of serious repair, the new vehicles in front of the house, and a large vehicle with SWAT written on it hidden in the trees, alongside the Satellite News Van.

"We are here with the New York City Police SWAT Unit and do we have an exclusive for you. Earlier today in New York, we reported that a subway train was derailed and buried, killing twenty passengers and injuring eighteen others when a subway wall suddenly collapsed in one of the tunnels. Because of all the rain we have been experiencing, a water main explosion was thought to be the cause.

Just minutes ago it was confirmed as a bombing. I was at the police station doing some research when a call came in from a man claiming to be a farmer and living at this address."

She leaned into the camera and dropped her voice. "I heard him claim that his best friend had planted a terrorist bomb in the New York subway system for some organization. The farmer couldn't remember the name. His friend told him that, as he was fleeing the scene, he panicked. From what I understood of the conversation, he thought he saw someone trailing him. Thinking it might be Mr. Smoke, he hightailed it to his best friend's farm house and asked his friend to let him hide out here for a while. We arrived on location just moments ahead of the SWAT vehicle.

"They have just called the house and said to the farmer that there has been an accident with one of their family, and could he and his wife please come to hospital immediately.

"What ... oh I'm sorry. I wasn't supposed to tell what they said."

Suddenly Linda's voice raised in pitch and volume.

"Wait! Something is happening! *Turn the camera to the house quick! Quick!!* A man and woman are coming out of the house! *They are coming over to the van!*"

A man and woman came running toward the camera, the woman slightly behind, being pulled by the man.

Linda's voice rose again, "The SWAT Team is now storming the house! They are inside the house!"

Her voice rose higher with excitement, "Keep the camera on the house. We can talk to the couple later.

"There are noises coming from the house. I don't know whether you can hear them. Crashing noises. Wait! The noise has stopped."

Her voice dropped to a whisper.

"The door is opening. Someone is coming out. *They have him! They have the Subway Bomber.*" The last was said loudly and excitedly.

The camera focused on the bomber. The man kept his head turned away from the camera. When they passed the farm couple, the captive tried to break free and attack the man. The suspects face was digitally blurred.

"You were my friend! Why did you do this? You were my friend!" he screamed.

"I still am. That don't mean that I wouldn't turn in a friend who was a scum sucking terrorist bomber." The farmer responded. "If I wasn't your friend I would have *Smoked* you myself, saving Mr. Smoke the trouble. My cousin died in that explosion. His wife called me earlier. *May you rot in hell, asshole!*" The last was said with great passion, though not loudly.

The SWAT team dragged the *suspected* terrorist bomber away kicking and screaming and cursing.

Turning to the couple, Linda asked the woman, "What did it feel like to have a terrorist bomber in your home?"

"I don't know *what the hell* you're talkin' about. All I know is, we get a call that one of our family is in the hospital and we come outside and then my husband drags me over here."

She turned to her husband. "What the hell is goin' on, Henry?"

"I'll tell you later, Martha. It's a long …."

What he was about to say was interrupted when the SWAT team hustled them away.

"Well … I guess New York's *best* don't want anyone or anything to mess up the bust. This is Linda Lacey live, saying you saw it first on NYKZ. Back to you Brian."

"Thank you Linda …."

Scene Forty Five

Click.

Damon turned off the TV. He pushed a button on his watch.

Moments later Hastings entered.

"You rang sir?"

"Yes I did Hastings. Have a seat." Hastings sat in a seat directly across from Damon.

"As you know, Hastings, I have not scheduled any more tours. I have been spelunking the property and doing, well, *other things*. I have to talk to you about the *other things*. The reason for this is that you are the only family that I have left."

He paused for a moment to gather his thoughts as he saw the quickly suppressed, startled look on Hastings face. "Yes Hastings, I consider you as family. My *extended family*. I know that I am not as other people are, and I know that you also know that. You have been with me since I was a young boy. You know what I went through. You stayed with me through it all, even though you did not understand most of it. Because of my father and mother, you have devoted your life to me. I understood and accepted it, *until now*. You are the only one of my family that hasn't died on me. I think that is because we are not blood related. That is the *only reason* I have allowed you to stay. Things have changed with me and I am not as I was. The *other things* that I have been doing have been dangerous. They are going to get *more* dangerous."

He paused to check Hastings reactions. There were none. "I could not handle it, Hastings, if something was to happen to you because of me or my actions, without giving you knowledge to protect yourself, and the choice to stay or go. With your permission, I would like to tell you what is going on, and to *ask* you to keep it to yourself, should you choose to leave. I will not *demand* it, for I feel I have no right to. It is of my doing and you have been no party to any of it. Do I have your permission?"

"You do sir, but before you go on, let me tell you a few things that I know so that you don't have to explain those." He paused and Damon nodded for him to continue.

"Your father and mother told me a lot about you and your abilities when I first started with them. You were a beautiful child, even when you lost your *abilities.* You grew into a fine man, sir. You are the only person I know who doesn't talk badly of others. To me that *was* and *is* your greatest *gift,* and that is a *gift* that you have kept through it all. I also know that you are an EH and that your abilities have come back."

Damon was shocked although he didn't show it. To Hastings the question showed it. "How did you know that my abilities have come back?"

"Because you are not quite as paranoid as you used to be. It was just a feeling. I'm glad, sir. Oh, and whatever you share with me, *stays with me.*"

"Thank you Hastings. I'm not quite sure where to begin. I guess I should start with ……. Oh, what the hell … *I am Mr. Smoke,* Hastings."

"Holy shit! Mr. Smoke? Really? Jesu …." Hastings paused for a moment, took a deep breath and then continued "Excuse my language sir, you took me by surprise. Please continue."

"Before I do, I need to ask you some questions. Do you want to stay on with me or leave? And if you do stay on, do you wish to participate in my quest to eradicate *terrorist bombings* globally? I need to know the answers to these questions before I can give you any more information. It is for *your* protection, more than mine."

"Do you even need to ask, sir?"

"Yes, Hastings. I think I know the answer, but I need to be sure. Maybe you would like some time to think about it? Maybe ..."

Unable to stop himself, Hastings jumped to his feet cutting him off.

"The answer is *yes*, sir. I'd love to help you *Smoke* every terrorist's bombers ass in the world!"

Damon smiled at his childlike enthusiasm.

"Calm down, Hastings. Please sit down. Before we go *Smoking* anybody's *asses*, I need to bring you up to date on what's been going on."

"Yes, *sir*." Hastings sat back down.

Mr. Smoke brought Hastings up to date on *everything*, leaving nothing out.

▲ ▲ ▲

"You say you somehow '*know*' *who the bomber is* and can track him with your *homing sense?*"

"Yes. At first I went *Elseware*, passed out if you like, and when I became *aware* I had full knowledge of the bomber and their current location. Now though, I no longer lose consciousness. When I read about it, or see it on the news, the information suddenly materializes inside my head. At first it felt like my head would explode off my shoulders but I've learned to handle it. I feel, a *something*, like a *click*, and then Switch kicks in. By the way, I can no longer get Switch off my finger. It seems to have become a part of me."

"That is the weirdest story I have ever heard, but I remember thinking to myself when I saw the ring for the first time, that I have never seen anything like it. It is beautiful. You say it is sentient?"

Damon nodded slightly. "Yes, it is."

"You mentioned something else that doesn't sit quite right. You said that the other two *ninjas* in *Eleseware* were supposed to blend into you, but I don't think they have, *totally*. Every once in awhile you say 'we'. You never used to do that."

"I know. You are right, we are *not* one. Almost, but not quite. I have most of their memories but not all. Don't ask me how I know, I just do and I've been thinking about it. Golden said that we were on some kind of time constraint and we may have gone slightly over. I remember the flight attendant touching my shoulder to wake me up before the descent. She may have interrupted the process. It could be that it was a combination of the two. This may be *how it is supposed to be*. If so, I can live with it. I know that I am greater with them than without, and they were pure when we blended. Whatever *we* will become, will be a direct result of our actions. Maybe that is what will finish the blend."

Hastings bent his head and sat in silence for a few moments, digesting what he had just heard. His mind was in turmoil. Finally he raised his head and looked into Damon's eyes.

"You told me some things that, to me, are impossible. If it had been anybody *but you* telling me those things, sir, I would have them committed to a mental institution, *immediately*. I know this sounds as crazy as the things you told me, but, I believe you."

He smiled at his boss. "But you knew that I would, didn't you?"

Damon nodded and returned the smile. Hastings took a deep, steadying breath and continued.

"I think that answers all my questions, for now, except one."

They both said at the same time, "Where do we go from here?"

They both smiled.

Damon answered.

"New York City."

Scene Forty Six

New York City Court House: nine a.m. Court Room 101. Two mornings *after* the New York City *subway bombing.*

"All rise. Order in the court. Order in the court. His Honor, Judge Mortimer Sneddley presiding. You may be seated"

The court room was packed.

Charges were being laid against Hickey Steadman, the man charged with the New York City Subway bombing.

Steadman was charged with multiple counts of murder, acts of terrorism and multiple other crimes. He plead *not guilty.*

A lawyer from one of the top criminal law firms in the country, Diceman, Floyd and Capishaw, appeared on behalf of the defendant and requested that bail be set.

The lawyer argued that only one witness *claimed* that the defendant planted the bomb, and that it was hearsay evidence and not admissible. Bail was denied. The lawyer asked that, because of the publicized footage, nature of the arrest and the national coverage of it, his client have a speedy trial and behind closed doors.

A speedy trial was granted, much to the dismay of the prosecutors' office, but the judge decreed that the trial would be *open* to the press.

There was no way that Judge Sneddley was going to pass up an opportunity like this.

This could be his ticket to fame and fortune.

▲ ▲ ▲

Scene Forty Seven

I t was the last day of the trial of *accused terrorist bomber* Hickey Steadman.

As Paladins company jet was soaring over the ocean towards New York City with its two passengers, Damon looked at Hastings sleeping peacefully. He was relieved to have told someone about himself. Someone that he could trust! He now didn't feel so alone.

He had known Hastings since he was nine years old, almost five full years before he lost his abilities.

He recapped in his mind:

Name: Hastings, first name David (Age - late forties.)

Occupation: Damons Butler & Chauffer

Previous Occupation: Ex-military, US Special Forces. Twice decorated

Physical Description: Tanned olive skin, grimly rugged looking, black eyed, thick salt and pepper hair (skull cap style), with a trimmed, sculpted, short, matching salt and pepper goatee. He was still extremely fit, agile and tough.

▲ ▲ ▲

Damon walked the memory path.

Garret Hastings has been with the family for twenty six going on twenty seven years. A career soldier of eight years, he was trained as a Navy Seal in guerrilla warfare and deep penetration missions. While he was on leave in the US, awaiting re-enlistment, he was injured in a horrific car accident that left him neutered, wheelchair bound and unfit for duty.

Hastings was told that, because it happened when he was *technically* Honorably Discharged, (his signed re-enlistment paperwork got *lost* somewhere, never to be found) the US military would only give him his accrued pension, a ridiculously small amount that would leave him almost destitute.

While visiting a friend in the hospital, Doctor John Gray, Damon's father, was on hand when they first wheeled Hastings into the same room.

Hastings didn't talk much. Overhearing the doctors talking about how Hastings *could* walk again with an operation, but wouldn't be able to because he couldn't afford it, John looked at his chart and got access to Hastings medical records.

The greed and lack of compassion that the doctors displayed *angered* John. (Damon remembered, *vividly,* his father talking about it to his mother.) They had not even given him the minimum service required. It was needless in their esteemed opinion. *He just couldn't afford it.* It was as simple as that!

That very day, Dr. John Gray offered Hastings a job. He also offered, at no charge, to give Hastings back the use of his legs on the condition that he, Dr. John Gray, perform the operation himself. Dr. Gray had seen, first hand, the mistakes that surgeons made in their speed to get to the next operation so they could buy their *next* new mansion, boat, car or horse.

He showed Hastings his credentials. He didn't need to. Hastings agreed without looking at them. He would rather be dead than wheelchair bound, and later told John that he had considered ending his life upon release from the hospital. He had no fear of death and did not think justifiable suicide was wrong.

He believed in fighting to the end, *but he also believed in personal choices.*

Done at John and Mary Gray's residence, the operation gave him back total mobility. This was due to Dr. Gray's skills as a surgeon, with Mary assisting; the unorthodox new procedures he used, *that he had created*; the short time that it was done after the accident, and the exercise regimen that Hastings had to adhere to.

Dr. Gray was unable to reverse the damage to his testicles but with hormone treatment designed specifically for him, consisting of swallowing one small pill a day, Hastings was able to enjoy a normal sex life.

Damon knew that Hastings would gladly have died to protect John and his family. He had put his life on the line for them on more than one occasion. He now was almost as paranoid as Damon and felt obsessive about protecting him.

Hastings was Damon's first unarmed and armed combat weapons trainer. He was a hard, strict trainer who loved the military life and discipline. Even now Garret Hastings was a deadly weapon. Damon had learned well. Damon grew to love all the martial arts and weapons training and soon surpassed Hastings. In Damon's eyes, the Cosmic Source had seen fit to grant him a friend. A friend that now was going into danger with and for him. He now had a team of two for his cause.

Damon Gray, alias *Mister Smoke*, was no longer paranoid about Hastings safety. That vanished when Hastings had agreed to join in the cause. Hastings knew the risks and was willing to take them.

Scene Forty Eight

New York City Court House, Court Room 101, eleven a.m.

The court room was filled to capacity. And then some. The Fire Marshal had turned a blind eye, this once. He knew that he had little choice in the matter.

The room was buzzing, with multiple conversations going at once. Reporters were on their cell phones, booking space on the front page. Spectators and reporters alike were speculating on the impending verdict.

It was the final day of the trial of the New York City Subway Bomber trial.

"All rise. Order in the court. Order in the court. His Honor, Judge Mortimer Sneddley presiding. You may be seated"

The jury had requested an early morning wrap up of the trial and they were there at eight am.

Unusual to say the least, the media reported. The trial itself had only lasted two days.

The closing arguments of the Subway Bombing trial were done and the jury was sent off to deliberate and return a verdict.

At one fifteen pm, the jury returned and found the defendant *not guilty* due to lack of evidence. The news media went crazy.

Questioned afterwards, a number of jurors said that they all agreed that the farmer did not make a credible witness, with his past and current history of alcoholism and criminal record for drunken driving, assault, etc. The defense team did a fabulous job of discrediting him. Although most of the jury thought that he did it, the police could not produce any other proof to convict him.

While all this was going on Steadman was sitting in his seat, smiling. The judge had thanked and dismissed the jury, and told him that he was free to go, or was it the other way around? He couldn't remember. He could never be charged with these crimes again!

He already had book deals pending. Hickey Steadman could now tell his story and why he did it for his organization, the Modred Society. And *then* he could get his revenge on his ex-best friend turned traitor.

As he was sitting in the courtroom gloating, someone leaned over and whispered into his ear. "Who paid for your defense Hickey Steadman?"

He spun around but could not see who had spoken. He turned to Howard Diceman, the head of his defense team. "Did the Modred Society pay for my defense, Howard?"

"No."

'Could it have been James out of his personal account?' Hickey thought, *'Sure, that was who it was'.* His direct superior in the Modred Society.

"Then who paid you to defend me? Was it …" He stopped. No names, that was the rule. "You never did tell me, Howard."

"What? Oh, excuse me, I see someone that I need to see." He turned away from Steadman and started to leave.

Hickey grabbed his arm and whispered hoarsely, "I *fucking* asked you who paid you to defend me. Don't you walk away from me, *asshole!* I know where you live."

Howard Diceman looked around to make sure no one was within earshot, then looked directly into Steadman's eyes and said quietly. "Really? That's nice. Because you asked *that* way, I suppose I have to answer your question. Can't have you going around bombing my house or car, or killing my family and friends like you did in the subway, can I? But no more questions. After I answer this one question, *I really must go.* The person who paid for your defense said he knows where you live also. Small world isn't it?" Diceman smiled. It wasn't a nice smile.

"A Mr. Smoke paid cash for your defense, Steadman. I never did have the pleasure or privilege of meeting him personally, just talked to him on the phone. He is the one that was willing to put up your bail money at the beginning. He said he would get together with you later, for a *smoke.* Whatever in the world he meant by that, I'll never know. I guess that's between the two of you. I didn't know you smoked. And it's *Mr. Diceman* to you, *Deadman,* I mean *Steadman.*" Howard Diceman smiled that hard smile again.

"Have a nice day." With that he pulled his arm away from Steadman's numb, sweating fingers and walked off smiling into the crowd of waiting reporters.

As Diceman was talking to the press, Steadman came out of his shock. Rising in a panic he ran up to Judge Sneddley, who was leaving the courtroom and screamed. "I confess. I planted the bomb. Put me in prison."

"You have been found not guilty. Leave this court room or I'll have you thrown out."

"You can't do that! You don't understand. Mr. Smoke is going to kill me. He paid for my defense. He's out there waiting for me right now. It'd be like committing murder. Put me in the *Witness Protection Program* and I'll tell you everything! My bosses names, their bosses names, everything. Please don't send me out there. Please." He dropped to his knees crying. Then he fell to the floor and hugged his knees.

The news media picked up on what was going on and rushed over. Two had already videoed the whole screaming scene.

"Quick, take him back to my chambers. Let no one near him." Mortimer Sneddley told the officer of the court.

"Contact the District Attorneys Office. They should know what to do. Place armed guards at both doors. We don't want Mr. Smoke getting to him *before* we get our information, do we?"

"No sir, we don't." Reaching down he pulled the subway bomber to his feet.

Ten minutes later, two uniformed police officers, coming in the back way, arrived with warrants, to escort the confessed terrorized terrorist bomber to the DA's office. They left through the back door to avoid the crowd.

They never arrived at the DA's office. One hour later, through an anonymous phone tip, a New York police officer found the New York City Subway Bomber, in a *closed* mens public urinal in a subway station, not far from the courthouse, shot once through the head.

The news media ate it up. They were all over it. They found out that the DA's office had *not* sent anyone over to pick up Steadman right away, because they didn't know what to do with him. They had calls in to the FBI, but the agency had not gotten back to them by the time the news came in that Steadman was dead.

Pictures were again sent to the news media.

The following day, S.T.U.N.T., *(Strategic Tactical Unit Neutralizing Terrorism)* a US agency that didn't officially exist, received a flash drive with Hickey Steadman telling all he knew about his organization. It was obvious that he thought that he was talking to someone in authority with the government. The voice asking the questions had been modified. It could have been a male or female voice.

Scene Forty Nine

Blackstone.

The afternoon following the New York Subway Bombers death, Damon and Hastings were sitting in the main library facing each other.

"Well sir, you have now officially gone double digit."

"Yes I have Hastings, and thank you. I couldn't have done this one so easily, if it wasn't for you."

"I think you could have sir."

"I could have eventually yes, but it would have involved risking the lives of police officers. Because of you, we avoided that. They would never let one officer take custody of Steadman. Everyone thought that Mr. Smoke works alone. This will probably never work again, but it worked this once."

"Yes it did, sir, and you're right. I didn't think of that. It's been a while. I'm glad to know I was of some help."

"Going back to what we talked about last night, have you come up with a code name that I can call you when we are on a Smoke mission or to let you know that I am on a Smoke mission, one that won't give your identity away?"

"I have sir. *Gunman* would be as good as any. I like it. And if you like, *Gunner* when there is immediate trouble, either yours or mine."

"Good. And you can call me Mr. Smoke and just Smoke if there is a problem. We'll work out some code words later. Right now, I want to get a workout in before I get dressed for dinner. Is everything ready?"

"Yes sir. Whitner has everything in order. One of the spare rooms has been prepared to your specifications, for them. And speaking of them, Lord and Lady Brighton will be arriving in three hours."

Smiling at his boss, he continued. "You sure timed it down to the minute sir, the New York *Smoke,* that is. I can scarcely believe we made it there and back in less than twenty four hours. Brilliant sir, if I may say so."

"Yes, timing is everything, isn't it? Thank you, Hastings. I'll call if I need you."

"Very good sir."

▲ ▲ ▲

Scene Fifty

D inner was superb. Whitner and the staff were happy to see Lord and Lady Brighton again. After dinner, Damon showed them what he had done since he had last had them over.

The Brighton's loved what he had done to Blackstone in the six months that he had owned it. The change was staggering, almost overwhelming, to both of them.

It did not look like the same Castle Blackstone that they had sold.

No massive changes were done that they could see, rather it was a multitude of little things, moving and arranging the furniture as well as adding a few pieces, redoing the lighting and a host of other things.

The grounds had been changed slightly, also. Sylvia said that she *felt* that it looked the way it *should*. It was perfect to her. She said it was as if he had taken the rock that they had sold him, and chipped and polished until he had uncovered and polished to perfection, the flawless diamond beneath.

Lord Brighton said from what he had seen, Damon could realize a decent profit, if he was inclined to sell it.

"I shall never sell Blackstone or property." He paused and then said something in a way that stuck in both of their minds. *"Ever."*

"The way he said it was so *final*, like an irrefutable law of the universe." Sylvia said later.

After the tour they retired to the master library, the library where Damon had purchased Blackstone. It had been changed slightly also and more books had been added.

As they drank their favorite wine and Damon drank coffee they visited and caught up on what each other had been doing with themselves.

"Have you heard the latest news about Mr. Smoke?" Sylvia asked Damon.

"I'm afraid not. I've been working on my next musical project. An outdoor six month North American Tour with four hours of new music."

"Oh, it sounds marvelous! Tell me all about it."

"We can talk about that later. It is long and boring. The final product won't be but all the work involved will. Tell me the latest news and gossip about this Mr. Smoke character."

"You tell him, dearheart. I only caught parts of it. It seems that he made fools of the United States legal system." Sylvia looked at her husband.

"No dear, the United States legal system made fools of themselves, as we probably would have also. The man is brilliant, Damon! It now seems that he *does* work for an organization or individual of some kind. There were at least *two* involved this time."

Michael went on to describe what the news media had reported and what he had found out from S.T.U.N.T..

"Two average looking police officers, average height, a little overweight, one tanned skinned and the other they think was of African or East Indian descent. Only one spoke and there was nothing noteworthy about his speech except that he was a native New Yorker. The Judge grew up in the Bronx and recognized the brogue. He said you can't fake that. We got the pictures the same time as the news media."

Refilling his glass Michael continued, "I wanted to bring you up to date on the security systems that you designed for us to sell to the French Surrette, the US S.T.U.N.T., the Canadian C.T.A.C.C., the Russian U.R.S.S., the Israeli S.P.I … well, I won't name them all. You know them; you designed the systems for them. I just want you to know that all of the organizations are very happy with their respective systems."

He paused and smiled at a memory. "I was a little hesitant at first, to demand five million dollars for each one, but they jumped at it. Every one said that it was a bargain if it worked as well as ours. Which, from their response, I'm glad to say, surpassed their wildest expectations."

Michael leaned forward. "They like the fact that we are not the supplier and don't know who it is." He smiled. "I have to tell you, Damon, that I love your payment system. The money was wired into an escrow account and transferred twenty percent to ours and eighty percent to your account, upon the approval activation code they punched in when they had tested it thoroughly. Once the money transferred, you sent their system an activation code that would cancel the automatic shut down after ten days. They loved the added bonus of instantly connecting them directly and *securely* with everyone on our network system. We can talk with each other *twenty four/seven* or email, whichever we prefer. Plus the voices are electronically altered if the communication is verbal. They love your language translator. It works flawlessly. We all have our privacy. "

"Fine, but did the ballistics check out on the American bullet?"

"I knew it! The two hundred million from the sale of his security systems doesn't interest him, but Mr. Smoke does!" Sylvia announced in an *Ah Ha, I told you so,* voice.

"It was *not* two hundred million, darling, but it did come close to paying for Blackstone."

"Really? I was just joking, trying to make a point. Blackstone?" she looked at Damon. He smiled and nodded.

"Well ... *good for you!* But that is *not* the point I was trying to make! The *point*, Mister Doctor Gray, is that you have to get out in the real world, not stuck here making beautiful music and creating a six month outdoor North American Tour."

She looked shocked. "Wait a minute, I'd like to do that!" she shook her head to clear it. "Well never mind how much fun it is, you have to take a break every now and then to stop and smell the roses. When was the last time that you did that?"

"Six months ago when I first came here for the fishing weekend."

"You are joking, right?" Damon just looked at her. "You're not joking. Well Damon Gray, that is about to change. Tomorrow night we are going to the theater and watching the Phantom of the Opera. I've got a friend who knows a friend of a friend who can get us front row tickets. Are you up for it?"

"Only if we all go in costume." Damon smiled.

"Wonderful. Do you have a date that you can bring?"

"My schedule doesn't leave a lot of time for a social life, I'm afraid. Sorry, but it will just have to be the three of us."

He looked at her and said sternly, "And don't try to set me up with a friend of yours either. I am highly allergic to blind dates. I tend to ignore them. Is that acceptable?'

"*Is that acceptable?*" she scowled, mimicking him. Then she smiled, "I guess it will have to be, but you'll never know the *hottie* I had in mind for you! Besides, that just means that I'll have two *half* handsome phantoms escorting me to the play. Hmmm. Does that mean I'll end up with only *one* handsome date?"

Michael burst into laughter.

"Well Michael," Damon asked, "were they able to send you the results of the ballistics?"

"Yes as a matter of fact they did. I pocketed them as I was leaving the office. Take a look." Michael handed him a sheet of paper.

As Damon took the paper he asked casually. "Did your organization get to buy the *Golden Bullet,* or was it some other organization?"

"It was Scotland Yard actually."

"Too bad." Damon said as he started to read the results.

"Not really, old chap. It was a good thing, actually. I think it was a brilliant plan to get the police forces of the world on the same page, so to speak. In a stroke, it worked *to do* what I have been trying *to do* for years. Remember, I mentioned it to you months ago? I said it was impossible? I asked you to work your magic on it?"

"Mmmmm." Damon said absently as he read it. When he finished, he looked up. "It looks to me that they are saying that it is a match. Am I correct?"

"Yes, you are."

"How many does that make, twenty two, twenty five? I don't keep up on it."

"Actually it is only ten, Damon."

"That's not what the news media is saying."

"True, but when has the media *ever* reported the truth, except by accident?"

"True … true. Are you any closer to figuring out who he is?"

"Not he, Damon. They."

"They? Oh that's right. I remember you mentioned that it now looks like he may have an employer or organization backing him. You said that there were at least *two* men on the last *Smoke*?"

"Yes."

He then told Damon all he knew of the incident. "I'm tempted to say that Mr. Smoke may even be a New York City police officer. It doesn't make sense any other way. I am going to send my thoughts to them, on Monday, that they should check their officer's days off against the dates of the Smoke strikes. It might lead to something."

"Do you really think so, Mickey?" Sylvia asked. "Do you really want to catch him that badly?"

"No dear, not really." Michael sighed. "It is just that he is making the police forces and governments of the world look ludicrous. Not good for public morale."

"Are you sure about that?" Damon asked.

"Which part?"

"That it is *not* good for *public* morale. I think it is. I think that it is *not* good for the *governments* of the world morale. They want to catch him because he is making them look incompetent, which any government can be made to look. They have laws that they have to uphold in order to serve the public and be responsible to them. Anyone with half a brain can mock them and make it look plausible. That is why there are secret organizations, such as yours, around the world, that work outside the law to get things done. In my opinion, Mr. Smoke may work for *just such an organization,* one that operates outside of the global government's rules and laws." He looked around fearfully and dropped his voice to a stage whisper. "Maybe even a *secret* government agency."

Sylvia laughed out loud.

Damon smiled at her and then continued seriously.

"I think that they function by their own set of rules and laws. As does Mr. Smoke and his associates within the organization, and I am sure he, or they, will die by and for the *Agency.* As for Mr. Smoke, I also think that he is not sane in the traditional sense. If an organization is employing him, I don't think they are controlling him. He definitely walks to the beat of a different drum. I have to tell you I *do* feel a little safer. According to the news, terrorist bombings have gone down drastically in the last few months and public polls are reporting that people in war torn countries are feeling more secure because of Mr. Smoke."

Sylvia smiled incredulously. "Are you trying to tell me that a *certifiable nut case* is running around out there with a *loaded gun,* killing mad terrorist bombers and maybe anyone trying to protect them, and that I should be feeling safer because he is?"

"Yes I am Sylvia. Your husband is doing things *very similar* to what Mr. Smoke and his Organization are doing. The only difference is that a group of men said the A.T.C.U. should, or could, do it with *impunity* in this country. Am I correct Michael?"

"Well …. The answer is a resounding *yes* Damon! You are one hundred percent correct. I have never thought of it that way before, but yes, you are right. What I am going to tell you now can never be repeated, *agreed*?" Damon and Sylvia nodded their heads.

"We, and by *we*, I mean the A.T.C.U., would love to be doing what Mr. Smoke is doing, but we still need to prove to our superiors that they are guilty beyond a reasonable doubt. Only four of his strikes are confirmed terrorist bombers by our information. Four more were suspected and two we had no idea they even existed. We can't operate like Mr. Smoke, but that doesn't mean that *I* wouldn't like to. That is the problem that all countries organizations like ours are facing in this situation. We don't want him to stop but we are mandated by our superiors *to* stop him. By any means necessary."

He paused for effect. "And I don't mean arresting him. It means that we have carte blanche by every world government to *Smoke* Mr. Smoke, *and* anyone associated with him."

"Well, if he does what you would *like* to do, then I hope they *don't* catch him or them!" declared Sylvia. "And, come to think of it, I do feel safer because *I* have a gun toting, genuine one hundred percent *nut case* married to me."

Michael looked at her surprised. *"Gun toting, genuine one hundred percent nut case?"*

Sylvia smiled sweetly and continued, "Well sweetheart, you do carry a *big* gun and you *did* say that Mr. Smoke is brilliant and you would *love* to do what he does and *you both* agree that he must be a mental or nut case and so for those reasons I feel safer. Not safe but safer."

She put her finger to her chin in thought; then chuckled. "And I have a feeling I will feel safe when my husband and I are tucked into your bed tonight Damon!"

Both men looked at each other and grinned.

"And I know what both of you are thinking. You both think that I say '*and*' a lot and you both think I don't know what you're thinking." Both men smiled.

She stood up. With hands on hips, she stamped her little foot and added, "And I didn't mean *your* bed Damon, I meant your *guest room* bed." This time they all laughed.

She reached for the wine bottle and topped off her husbands and her drink. "More coffee Damon?"

▲ ▲ ▲

Scene Fifty One

It was the beginning of daybreak and the sky was a deep crystal clear blue. Stars could still be seen, but they were fading fast, as the sun chased them away. The kind of morning you only see in movies.

Turning away from the window beside her, ShabNab rose lithely from the bed she had been lying in. The man was still sleeping deeply. She reached into her purse and pulled forth a small bottle. Placing a surgical mask over her nose and mouth she opened the bottle and poured the contents onto a handkerchief. She then placed it over the nose and mouth of the sleeping man. It was so expertly done that he did not awaken.

Padding on bare feet, she silently passed through an open doorway into the central room of the hotel suite. Miles, the sleeping man she had just drugged, liked to have his aide watch as he conquered his women. Thus, the open door to the bedroom.

His aide, Guthrie, was sleeping on the chesterfield couch facing the bedroom door. He had fully enjoyed a full view of the previous night's proceedings. A miniature video device was mounted on a tripod to his left. He had removed it from the bedroom after he thought they had both gone to sleep. ShabNab had watched him viewing the footage and relieving himself.

He was now snoring lightly. She performed the same procedure on him. Again, he did not stir. She smiled to herself, in pride. She removed her mask and gently took the aides head in her slender hands. It lolled limply. With a sudden savage twist, she snapped his neck like a twig. Twisting his head around to face behind him, she bent down and whispered into his ear, "Dear Guthrie, I don't want you to see what I am going to do to your boss. You have had all the enjoyment from me that you will ever have."

She dressed quickly and then left the hotel suite only to return shortly with a suitcase containing ropes and restraints and a large leather case.

She quickly and expertly strapped the naked man spread eagle to the bed. She then moved and set up the video camera with tripod and positioned it back to where Miles had placed it the night before, to a full bed view. Strapping the ball in his mouth, she stripped and sat back to wait for the handsome US Senator Miles Frederick to rouse.

Adjusting the screen slightly for a better view from where she was sitting, she pushed the play button and critically watched her previous night's performance.

ShabNab felt pride that she noticed only a couple of instances where she could improve. When the end came, she erased the memory and set the machine to the *record* mode. She then picked up a ladies fashion magazine and curled up like a cat.

A short time later, he started to stir. Out of the suitcase, she removed and opened a well used leather case containing several medical instruments. She adjusted her tools on the nightstand and sat on the bed beside him, lotus position.

"Good morning Senator." she purred in a soft throaty voice with a slight accent. Senator Miles Frederick eyes popped open. Slowly they came into focus as awareness returned.

"I hope you slept well."

The Senator tried to move and couldn't. His blue eyes were wide with anger and fear. Striving futilely to twist his head, he tried to scream at the door. Only a soft muffled sound came out.

"*Now, now,* my dear Senator, just calm down. Don't rush a good thing. Good for me that is. I don't want you worn out too soon. Your screaming won't bring the cavalry. These penthouse suites are completely sound proofed. Nobody heard my screams of pleasure last night and no one will hear your screams of pain today. Poor Guthrie won't be able to watch this time, I'm afraid," ShabNab paused for effect, "or any other time."

Senator Miles Frederick tried to talk around the ball in his mouth. He couldn't.

"You are probably wondering what is going to happen to you. That depends on what you tell me. I know that you are one of the heads of S.T.U.N.T." He gurgled frantically.

"No, no, dear Miles, don't try to deny it. I know. I know *a lot* of things about you. Would you like to know why? Because I'm *gifted*, Miles. That's right, *gifted.* Some of my gifts are downright scary, even to me. But I love being scared. It makes me feel *alive.* I don't scare as easily as I used to, Miles. I won't bore you with the details of all of them, just a few of the pertinent ones.

"When I touch you," she said running her fingers lightly over his chest and stomach, "I can feel your emotions, your helplessness, your fear, your rage. When I touch you I can feel when you are telling the truth. If you answer my questions truthfully, I will let you live. Not as the man you used to be, but alive. Alive is good."

Her voice dropped to a whisper, "I know. I was dead once and I wasn't big. I was small." She shivered and hugged herself. "Like when I was a child. Helpless. I didn't like it at all."

ShabNab shook her head, hair flying in all directions like a television shampoo commercial. Her shivering stopped as suddenly as it had started. Her voice resumed its normal tone.

"The truth is, I hated and feared *it*. I'm glad I came back. But the fear draws me like a magnet. I now like to experience *death* and *dying* through *others*, trying to understand *it*."

ShabNab suddenly smiled. Miles breath caught in his chest. She was extremely beautiful, of that there was no question. Her innocently unlined face was exotic, of mixed heritage. Her large, pale, ice blue eyes were mesmerizingly beautiful, her minimal makeup enhancing them even more. Miles, at first, thought she wore colored contacts. Her body was that of an artists dream model, flawless. She had large, high and full, well shaped firm breasts with dark upturned, thick, oversized protruding nipples. When aroused, they protruded out a full inch, if not a bit more. She was slender of form and hairless from the neck down, with flawless golden skin and beautifully muscled without seeming masculine. Even her well rounded muscular arms had turned him on. That was the reason he had pursued her last night and brought her to his hotel room. But when her small nose wrinkled slightly and her full lips parted, the smile she just gave him transported her into another category altogether. She looked like an angel from heaven. He blinked several times to dispel the illusion.

"How old do you think I am, Senator?" Miles didn't move, just looked. "Most people think I look anywhere from nineteen to twenty two. I'm thirty five." She placed her hands behind her head and arched her back provocatively. "I'll have you know that I have a daughter that just recently turned seven. Her name is VaShena."

Here she frowned, dispelling the illusion of angelic innocence. "I won't tell you how many men I went through until I found one, *like me,* to impregnate me. Once I found out I was with child, I killed him. He was the best assassin I knew. He was the Blades *Personal Assassin.* Now I am. He should have seen it coming, with his abilities, but he didn't. He was in love with me. That made it easy. That is why I never get too close to anyone. It hampers my abilities. I can't stand it!"

Still frowning she continued, "Where was I? Oh yes, VaShena. It turns out that my bastard child is totaling lacking in any of *my* abilities *or* her fathers. Not only *that*, *none* of my *talents* work on her! She is an enigma to me. I hate her. She is not what I wanted. I wanted someone like me, who would be able to understand me. Someone I could teach. It is just not fair."

She shook her head sadly. "Oh, she is smart and sweet enough. Everyone that knows her, loves her and comments on her quick intelligence. They also say that she is the spitting image of me. That could cause me problems one day."

Her face cleared. "Oh well, I'll take care of that when and if the time comes. Of course she doesn't know of my disappointment and hate. I hide it well. My Superiors were ecstatic when they realized that I was pregnant. Especially the Blade himself. My superior would not hesitate to kill me if she wasn't around, or knew that I didn't love her. You see, he thinks he can control me through her. He thinks I love the little bastard bitch. It makes him feel secure." ShabNab caressed his face lovingly.

"When he first recruited me, he passed me down the line, until all the men had screwed me multiple times. I figured, why not? It had been done to me since I was nine years old at the asylum. Until I turned *ugly* on them, that is. Then they left me alone. I didn't *dare* turn *ugly* with the Blade, Leader and Head of the Sword of Xandu. My beauty was my control over him at first." She smiled proudly into his eyes.

She continued softly. "How did you think I got so good, or did you think it was all you? None of the Sword of Xandu wants to touch me now, not after I sliced and diced Vashena's father. He was *supposed* to be their best terrorist assassin and, except for me, *he was*. Only the best could be the Blades Personal Assassin. The Blade was angered at first, that is what he said, but I could see in his aura that he was afraid of me. I had taken out his best. So he started sending me off on their highest risk missions hoping to get me killed. I succeeded every time. In fact, so many times that he now values me more than all his petty assassin soldiers. He has made a fortune on me. So what, *I* have made a fortune on me."

ShabNab laughed softly and leaned over, her long thick erect dark nipples brushing his chest, and whispered in Miles ear. "The Blade doesn't know of my *abilities* Myles. He just thinks I'm just a beautiful crazy zealot who believes in the Sword of Xandu motto, *Terror for Hire*, which is to supply terrorists to anybody willing to pay."

She shrugged her pretty shoulders. "He is right on both counts. Only the Blade knows that I'm certifiably insane. Committed by the state for killing my parents at age seven, the Sword of Xandu recruited me from an insane asylum, as a child of fourteen. By then I had learned to control most of my abilities. I was taught and mastered six deadly martial arts, by six of the most dangerous psychotics in the world, and mastered every one by the time the Sword of Xandu offered me employment."

She smiled again, but this time he saw through it and it frightened him. "What he doesn't know is that he doesn't need my child as a control over me. I would beg on my hands and knees and do *whatever* he told me, just to keep on doing what I am doing. It gives me purpose. I am a warrior, Senator, a mercenary for *any* cause. The Sword of Xandu supplies the causes. I am the deadliest and best *mercenary, assassin and terrorist artist* there is, but just killing for the sake of killing does not satisfy me. There is no *art* in that. Without them, I don't know what I would do. I would be small again. I couldn't handle that."

ShabNab shivered and hugged herself for a moment, savoring the experience, then arched her back, stretched and continued.

"Between assignments, I take other training to enhance my knowledge, skills and abilities. Although the *trainers* of the Sword of Xandu taught me well, I need to keep expanding. *I will never be small again!*" The last was said with quiet insane passion.

Suddenly she flowed to her feet. Looking down at him she said softly. "Normally I only tell the people I am about to *kill*, my life story. It softens them up. The truth can be scary, can't it? But if you cooperate, I will let you live. Just barely."

Turning away, she covered her long wavy auburn hair totally with a surgical cap and then placed on her mask. She reached into her purse and took out a set of dark brown contact lenses and put them on. Then, still naked, ShabNab crossed over and pushed the video player *record* button.

Miles bit back a scream. He was a smart and brave man, he knew that. He also knew that one day, if he wasn't extremely careful, he could be in a position like this. He cursed himself roundly. What a fool he was. His dick had finally been his undoing. It didn't take rocket science to know that she was going to kill him, no matter what he said. And he was sure that she knew that he knew she was lying. His whole body was slick with sweat.

ShabNab picked a tool from the nightstand. It looked nasty. She walked over and looked down at him.

"United States Senator Miles Frederick, we are going to find out all of your secrets, starting with *our* most pressing one and that would be Mr. Smoke.

"My, what beautiful eyes you have."

The death of United States Senator Miles Frederick shocked the nation. He was a handsome and charismatic leader. The government did not give details except to say that he was on the island to address the Global Tobacco Grower's Annual World Convention and was one of the casualties of the St Bernard Hotel terrorist bombing that killed thirty two and wounded seven.

The Governor of the Island of St. Bernard, one of the world's large tobacco producers and exporters, assured the media that they would have the culprits in custody shortly and that no one was to worry about any future terrorist bombings.

Scene Fifty Two

D amon sat at his computer and read the various reports from the different agencies and organizations, that he now had access to.

He had just finished watching the news of the St. Bernard Hotel bombing.

He knew who and where the bomber was as soon as he saw it on the news channel. It was the same as always, but this time with a few twists.

It was a woman! Switch tingled on his finger and when her face appeared in his mind, her startling ice blue eyes jumped out at him, they were *so* similar to his.

The computer reports confirmed his suspicions. This was not the usual terrorist bombing. The Sword of Xandu claimed responsibility, one of the most secret and fanatical terrorist organizations in the world. *Terror for Hire* was their axiom. No one knew who the heads were, where their headquarters was located, or even in what country.

They claimed the Tobacco Extremists Cult paid them to do it, for their cause. The Tobacco Extremists Cult denied it. They claimed that they could do their own bombings.

The Sword of Xandu had never claimed *any* glory for other organizations in the past. They always stayed in the background, letting whatever person or organization that hired them take all the credit. That was the purpose of their existence. That was what was advertised by word of mouth, and what kept them gainfully employed.

To Damon, it looked like a twofold plan. A diversionary tactic to cover what they had done to United States Senator Miles Frederick and to attract Mr. Smoke's attention to their organization.

In the last part they had succeeded. The bomb was set off in the living room of the Senator's hotel suite to do the most damage to the hotel. What the terrorists didn't know was that a building supporting wall was between the bedroom and the living room. It was one of many improvements and additions that were added in a renovation after a hurricane. None were recorded on any blueprints, as none were used. It bore the brunt of the explosion and helped protect the Senators body.

A fire alarm had been pulled just minutes before the blast, saving almost all of the hotel guests and staff. The news reported that the hotel staff did an admirable job in the evacuation, knocking on doors and assisting the guests that needed it.

A few hotel guests still died. The ones who didn't believe in fire alarms.

The Senator was found buried by rubble but still intact and with the remaining pieces of him still strapped to the bed.

Damon was fascinated. This one went way beyond anything he had previously experienced. The *cold rage* was still there but it seemed somehow diluted by the discovery of the Senators body and all that it entailed.

And the fire alarm. *Why had someone set off the fire alarm?*

Something was wrong with this one. Something didn't seem right. Not that it mattered. He quoted the first of his bakers dozen to himself, *Put first things first.* He was going to *Smoke* ShabNab Mishak. Period. End of story. Then on to the next.

He researched ShabNab. Nothing came up on her full name. It seemed that she was only known as ShabNab. She was more of a ghost than he was. No facts, only rumors.

There was one rumor that she was the concubine of the Sword of Xandu's leader.

Nothing conclusive.

One rumor reported that she was extremely ugly.

Dispelled. He knew that she was not ugly.

One rumor had it that she was between eighteen to twenty two years old. The same rumor had persisted, on and off, for fifteen to twenty years.

Nothing conclusive.

One rumor was that she had been one of many recruited from one of many European insane asylums. *Nothing conclusive* came back on that search also.

But on this rumor, he felt *something*. An imagined squeeze from Switch, an *esper* sense, or *something*.

He put together another type of search, more refined. It would take awhile but he wanted to make sure. He stood up, hit the enter button on his MAC to send off the search, and headed for the gym. He still had time for his workout regimen and shower before he was meeting Michael and Sylvia for dinner.

Scene Fifty Three

Dinner was superb. Michael and Sylvia were as entertaining as usual. They enquired how his last tour had gone. Damon told them what *he knew that they already* knew. From the press releases, it was a smash hit, a *sellout* four week Italian tour.

Waiting around for terrorist bombers to strike, *sucked*. He'd started touring again and had just finished the short one he was discussing with them.

Sylvia said that they would like to buy two sets of center, front row seat tickets, with back stage passes, to his next London concert, if it was at all possible. It seemed that she had been bragging about Damons musical genius to a certain royal couple, (she didn't call them by name) and had impressed them enough to ask if she could secure tickets, for all four of them, to attend one of his London performances.

Because of their advanced age, they didn't travel as much as they used to, Sylvia told Damon. That was why the London location.

"And they are looking forward to a backstage meeting with the Gray Ghost!" Sylvia finished with a flourish.

"I don't have a London concert planned." Damon informed her solemnly.

"Great! That means we can still get tickets." Both men laughed.

"What are you two laughing at?" Looking at Damon expectantly, she continued, "Well, what are you waiting for Damon, plan one immediately. I've done *my* job. I sold *four* tickets for you."

All three laughed.

"There is a one week spot in a month's time that I might be able to book. Let me see what I can do. Please excuse me for a few moments."

Before Michael and Sylvia could respond Damon pulled out his cell, turned his head slightly away from them, and made a call. When Syl started to say something, he held up his hand and spoke softly into the mouthpiece. They couldn't hear what he was saying. He spoke just under the room noise. He then listened for a minute or so, then thanked whoever he had been talking to, and hung up.

"Done. Six, one evening performances, with the London Philharmonic Orchestra, booked one month to the day from now. Happy, Lady Brighton?"

"Are you kidding me, Damon?" Damon *almost smiled* at Sylvia and shook his head slightly.

"Who does something like that," Michael asked almost in jest, "books a mini tour with the London Philharmonic Orchestra, on a whim, for one of his friends. What kind of strange creature are you, Mr. Gray Ghost? Whatever kind you are, thank you for making my wife so happy. This is the first time I can remember seeing her speechless. Close your mouth dear, it doesn't become you."

"What? Oh … you …Was my jaw really hanging open?"

"You will never know darling, you will never know. You might want to thank Damon also."

"Damon …" Sylvia paused again, "Oh hell, I feel like an idiot, *thank you very much* seems so … so … inadequate."

"The way you said it made it more than adequate. You are welcome. Besides, I could use the publicity, from the house of royalty. I don't want to disappoint them. I just hope that I can live up to your claim that I am a musical genius. How are things on the home front?"

From there the conversation wandered around the globe until it got to the St. Bernard Hotel terrorist bombing.

"My chauffer, Hastings, mentioned to me that an ex-military friend of his said it was done by a woman. A ShabNab something or other. Been around for fifteen to twenty years. He didn't know if that was her first or last name. Thought you could use the information." Damon stopped and looked at his friend.

"What's wrong Michael, you look like you've seen a ghost?"

Michael had paused in his eating and his face had gone snow white.

"What did you say that name was, Damon?"

Damon answered casually as he took another bite of his dessert.

"A ShabNab *something*, or a *something* ShabNab, why?"

"Just wanted to make sure that I heard right. ShabNab, right?"

"Right."

Sylvia looked at her husband with concern. "Sweetheart what is it? I've never seen you look or act this way before."

"I'm alright Syl. It just took me by surprise that's all. She ..." Michael stopped.

Sylvia looked at her pale husband strangely.

"Who is this ShabNab darling?"

Flagging their waiter to bring him their guest check, Michael turned to Damon.

"Do you feel up to having us over for a nightcap at Blackstone?" he asked as he signed for the dinner. Damon nodded.

Rising immediately, he said abruptly, "Great! Let's go."

They took separate cars. Michael didn't talk until the three of them were in the main library, where they all liked to be.

Sylvia faced her husband. "Alright Michael, what is going on. What's with all the cloak and dagger *stuff*? You wouldn't talk to me all the way over here. Speak to me, sweetheart. What is it?"

"Sorry Syl, but I couldn't afford to take the chance that someone would overhear what I was about to blurt out there. I will explain it all in just a few moments. Damon, is Hastings around? I'd like to talk to him."

Damon nodded.

"I gave him the night off, but I have an idea that he is around somewhere. He loves Blackstone almost as much as I do. I'll see if I can locate him. Whitner, bring Lord and Lady Brighton their favorite wine. Excuse me, I'll be right back."

Both left the room leaving Michael and Sylvia alone.

Sylvia leaned toward her husband and said softly, conspiratorially,

"Do you think Damon and Hastings ... are ......?"

"No I don't ... and I don't care. Do you?" Michael replied in a normal tone.

Sylvia straightened up and replied in her normal voice.

"No, not really ... Well, yes I do. I mean, *I don't care* but I *am* curious. Aren't you?"

"No."

"Why?"

"Because darling, I had Hastings checked out. Straight as an arrow. A whole quiver full of arrows. Two whole quivers ...."

"I get it, I get it! Why didn't you tell me?"

"I didn't know it was that important to you, to know Hastings *leanings*, if you know what I mean."

"I don't care about *Hastings* ... what you said. I meant, I was curious about *Damon*."

"You said you were curious if they were *an item*. We have no information on the Gray Ghost. Who would you think would be the next person to check?"

She waved her head in a *blond* way. "*ooooo*, you are *sooo* smart, mister smarty pants."

In a more serious tone she continued, "Yes, you are right. My mind wasn't working that way. If he is straight, then why won't he let me hook him up with some of my hot single lady friends?"

"Like?"

"Well, Gloria for instance. She is smoking hot and she's been single for a while."

"Gloria? Isn't she the one that ..."

"Hush, someone's coming! ... and... ok... maybe she was not the *best* first choice. You caught me by surprise, that's all. We'll talk later when I'm more prepared for battle."

"How in the world do you prepare for battle?"

"Pink negligee."

"I surrender."

Whitner entered the room and as he was pouring the drinks, Damon entered.

"I found him in the gym. He said he would freshen up and come as soon as he could. Do you want to wait for him to come, before you explain, or do you want to start now?"

"Let's wait until I talk to Hastings. I just want to talk to him in the hopes I can glean some more information on ShabNab. Let's all sit down, shall we?"

Hastings arrived shortly and repeated what Damon had told them and was not able to add to it. After an obligatory nightcap, Hastings bade them goodnight.

They sat in a triangle and Michael told both of them all that he knew of a woman called ShabNab.

Scene Fifty Four

Fifteen years ago, as a young diplomat *with promise,* on his first diplomatic mission to Israel, Michael was introduced to a young girl named ShabNab at a formal dinner function. One of many that he attended.

ShabNab was on the arm of an Arab Schaeke, he didn't remember his name. Sylvia was surprised at this because he was usually excellent at remembering names and asked why. He admitted that he had been more than a little tipsy. He went on to say that later that evening, he again met her as he was refilling his punch cup. He had stopped drinking earlier, when he felt the effects of drunkenness coming on. He had gone to the mens room and forced himself to vomit the contents of his stomach.

Sylvia smiled skeptically. Michael ignored the smile, though his face flushed slightly, and continued.

She again introduced herself to him and formally shook his hand. She spoke slightly accented English, almost American in style. She asked if he had seen any of the tourist sites since he had been there. He said '*not many*', that his duties had kept him quite busy. She offered to take him to some of the more exotic ones. He accepted. He said that, because he didn't have his agenda with him, they had set up an appointment the next day. A late meeting, at the pool area of the hotel he was staying in, for a quick drink and to finalize a time for the tour.

"I don't understand," Sylvia interjected again, "did you make the suggestion to meet at the pool, or did she?"

Thinking back, he said he was *fairly* sure that it was her suggestion. He started to pass over the meeting, by just saying that they made arrangements to meet the following day.

Sylvia would have none of it. "We need to know everything, as you would say. It might trigger unknown memories."

Michael agreed and described as much of the meeting as he could remember.

When asked by Damon, Michael described her. He said that her most striking feature was her very large, slightly slanted eyes. Eyes of a pale white, ice blue that seemed to swirl with motion and emotion. She was full lipped and had long, white, straight teeth and a dazzlingly beautiful smile. He wasn't sure if they were real.

With long, straight, thick, heavy, dark chestnut hair, ShabNab was taller than normal but not too tall, deep golden skinned, (suggesting mixed heritage) high, firm, full breasts, topped by large, upturned, thick protruding dark nipples, that showed through all the clothing that she wore. She had a tight and extremely flexible, slender, athlete's body.

He said that when she walked, her body didn't jiggle like most girls. No bust bouncing or jiggling. He saw her coming towards him when they met at the pool and he couldn't see her from the waist down. It looked like she was gliding on motorized roller skates with little or no upper body movement. She looked to be in her late teens and his description of her face *exactly* matched the one in Damon's mind.

In his mind, she was clothed, so Michael's description of her body in a skimpy one piece swimsuit he accepted.

What started out as a quick, after work meeting, turned out to be an all night affair. They ended up back in his hotel suite, making out. He admitted to being rather smitten with her looks and at first, he thought they were going to make love.

Shortly into it, he knew they were just having *incredible* sex. She was far and away *too* experienced. It was an experience that he would never forget. He mentioned that she had no body hair from the neck down, making her seem younger than she probably was.

Towards the end, something happened that shocked and scared him. It may have been that someone he didn't hear passed in the hall. Whatever it was, caused a change in ShabNab that he found hard to describe.

One moment they were going at it and the next moment she was crouched on the floor, in an attack position facing the door, his condomed member waving in the air. He knew a ninjitsu stance when he saw one. It was the *'crouching tiger'.*

That shocked him, but when her head spun to encompass the room, her face had changed.

Although it was dark in the room, it seemed as if there were subtle alterations to all her features and her body seemed to have lost its smoothness. Her body had *somehow* become angular, her muscles corded, twisted and sinewy, with thick ropey veins an arteries popping out all over her arms, legs and body. In the shadows of the night, *just for an instant,* she turned *ugly.*

That was the only word that came to his lips. *Ugly.*

Then her face passed from his line of sight and her body resumed its shape, as she rose to a standing position.

When she turned back to him, she was as she had been. Beautiful beyond words. To this day, he wasn't sure if he hadn't imagined it in the heat of passion, or if it was just the shadows, or both.

Before he had a chance to react, the phone on his bedside rang. He jumped, then answered it. It was his Commanding Officer, telling him he was on his way up from the lobby to talk to him.

Before Michael had a chance to respond, the phone went dead.

ShabNab's hearing was very acute. She gave him a radiant smile and grabbed her handbag and matching swimsuit, squeezed his limp member and pulled off his condom, gave him a quick kiss and whispered into his ear, "Thank you for a *wonderful* evening, Michael. We'll finish it tomorrow, after the tour. Bye for now."

With that, she popped the condom into her mouth, ran to the balcony doors, opened one ever so slightly and slid through and closed it, just as the large hand of his Commanding Officer hammered the door.

He quickly wrapped a robe around himself and opened the door. As soon as he opened the door, the Commander stormed into the room.

"Are we alone, son?" Word had it that the general called all of his aide's *son*. His lack of memory for names was legendary.

"Yes, sir." was his reply.

Ignoring him, the general walked straight out onto the balcony, throwing the doors wide and signaled to someone below. He watched for a moment and signaled again.

Turning, he walked back into the room, closing the doors behind him and made a quick tour of the premises.

"Good! She's gone."

"Sir?"

"We know you brought a young lady up here earlier. A consort of one of the Schaeke's, I don't remember which one. You are a smart lad, you're young and your family is well connected. You could have a great career ahead of you. And I like you, so I'm going to give you a word of advice. Be careful son. Schaeke's don't take kindly to someone else dipping *his wick* into *their magic lamp*, if you get my meaning? *Not good for international relations.* Understand?"

"Yes sir."

"Besides, she could be working for any one of the countless terrorist organizations this bloody country has. You are a little young, but your death, by any terrorist group, would still make for headline news. Always keep that in mind, Michael."

"Yes sir." Michael said he never forgot those words, because his commanding officer called him by name.

The General went on to tell him that his mother had been hospitalized, as a result of an accident that placed her life in grave danger. To save her life she had to have an immediate operation. She had an extremely rare blood type. Michael had the same. The General told him to throw on some clothes quickly, that time was of the essence and it was critical that he leave immediately. A military jet was fired up and waiting on the runway, just across the hotel lawn, to take him.

As Michael was leaving, he saw the General attach a secure device on the hotel phone, sit on the bed, and make a call.

He never got to take the tour with ShabNab.

After the transfusion and operation, Michael was informed that he would not be returning to Israel. The hotel he had been staying in had been *terrorist bombed*, completely destroying a reinforced military hotel suite, just shortly after his take off.

The General was the only casualty. The talks had been aborted. Michael's hotel room was the one that had harbored the terrorist bomb! Michael was questioned and exonerated of any blame. An intensive military investigation, by both Israeli and US armed forces, concluded that Michael was the intended target.

He had mentioned ShabNab's name and their date. Her name was placed on a temporary list of possible suspects.

At first he dismissed the idea. She couldn't have planted a bomb. There was no place to put it. All she was wearing was a skimpy one piece swimsuit.

Then he remembered the tiny matching purse, but in his mind it wasn't big enough to harbor a bomb big enough to *totally* destroy a large hotel suite with reinforced walls.

He learned, soon enough, that *very small bombs* can make *very big explosions*.

When an obscure terrorist organization, one that didn't allow women in their elite faction, claimed responsibility and stating their usual dogma *'Death to all Americans'* and *'Death to all who support*

America', ShabNab's name was taken off the temporary suspect list. He wasn't so sure it should have been.

He was placed under protective surveillance for six months. When no more attempts were made, the surveillance was dropped.

Over the years vague rumors about her would pass through his ears but that's all they were.

Vague, *misty* rumors.

After the story and a few more drinks, Damon and the Brighton's parted company. Damon said he would ask Hastings to question his ex-military friend about any additional information on ShabNab.

When they had left Damon reviewed what Michael told him. *'Stranger and stranger.'* he thought to himself. He went and thanked Hastings for backing his story and went to bed.

He dreamt of ShabNab.

Scene Fifty Five

The following morning, after his workout and *breakfast mulch*, as he thought of his energy drink, he headed to the catacombs. Today he was going to check out a small, hidden, very special cave. It was not the smallest cave and *very special* didn't even come close to describing it. On the way down Damon remembered how he found it....

▲ ▲ ▲

He had a trusted qualified builder reinforce and gird all the cave walls and ceilings, even though, with all his and outside expert testing and results, he knew that structurally they didn't need it. The walls and ceiling were of an extremely hard, black rock. He doubted that putting a two hundred storied, earthquake proof, monolithic solid concrete building over them, would cause them to collapse. Even in the event of an earthquake. The building might, but not the catacombs. They had survived since their creation at the birth of the world.

Damon had flown in the *expert appraisers* at night, by a security helicopter that they could not see out of. From the helicopter, they were conveyed to the catacombs by a totally enclosed security van.

They had agreed to be blindfolded from the helicopter to the van and from the van to the catacombs. All the equipment, that they requested, was awaiting them on their arrival, plus some that they hadn't. They used it all.

There were four of them from different parts of the world. Three men and one woman. One was from England.

They had been given a retainer when commissioned and, at the completion of their findings, were paid the balance owed them and flown home. It took them two weeks. They had all signed confidentially contracts. Not that it mattered. Damon had hired them on their auras and a handshake. He *knew* they were trustworthy. They also didn't know *who* had hired them or where it was they were taken.

For reasons of his own, he reinforced the cave walls anyway, with titanium beams custom made to his specifications. They surpassed building regulations by at least thirty times. They were non reflective and complimented the cave and tunnel walls beautifully. Most of the caverns floors he didn't touch. Some, amazingly, were fairly flat and some were not. He loved the look. Of the catacombs twenty seven caves, he only leveled six cavern floors. He did not cover the beams with paneling or walls of any sort. He liked the rock walls and tunnels showing.

He brought in the twenty four hour crew shifts, (three, eight hour crews) the same way he brought in the expert appraisers. The three crews were housed in the top cave of the catacombs, the sleeping quarters sectioned off. Their meals were served there also. They worked seven, eight hour days on and were flown home for seven days off. Another set of twenty four hour crews were flown in for that week.

After almost seven months of twenty four hour construction, it was finished.

▲ ▲ ▲

The day before he went on one of his concert tours, was the day he found *the door* that led to the hidden cave.

It was at the end of a short natural tunnel or room at the lowest level of the catacombs, branching off of the last cave that he had titanium grid reinforced. It was the last cave of the catacomb system, an offshoot. Although it was not the largest, it was the largest one on the lowest level, which is why he saved it till the end. It was also the deepest, being at least one hundred feet below the next deepest one.

Although random, the majority of the caves were grouped fairly close together with multiple access tunnels. Seven were offshoots fanning out in an irregular star pattern. Some you had to go down to the lower levels to gain access to one of the upper offshoot caves. Others, the opposite. There were between five to seven levels, depending on how you grouped them.

As much a maze, as a catacomb, Damon thought.

The cave in discussion was an offshoot on the lowest level. It had been completed just hours previously.

Before he released the crew, he wanted go over the last cave again to make sure that they hadn't missed or skipped anything. A couple of times, when they first started, the crew either under or overdid the girding of a cave and he had them redo it.

The last few were perfect and he was confident that he would be able to release them and pay the builder the balance of the contract. He always had the crew gird around the multitude of little offshoot caves or tunnels, if he felt they were too small or didn't warrant it. Whatever the entrance shape, whether square, circular, oval or rectangular, he had exact measurements made and titanium beams created in the shape of the outline of the offshoot entrance's shape. He felt it added character to the caverns.

The last one was in the shape of a triangle. At a distance it looked like it was a cutout, it was so precise. As he got closer, Damon became aware of natures fingerprint on it, the slight imperfections that made it even more impressive.

As he was passing by the triangular opening Switch pulsed multiple times. Damon stopped.

What was going on? Switch had never pulsed like that before.

He turned and entered. He remembered liking the exactness of the triangular shape of the room, that nature had created and shaped at the beginning of creation. Damon looked closely at the walls and floor. He saw nothing different.

The last time he combed the walls, ceiling and floors he found nothing. He had used every piece of his equipment on this cave, as he had on every other one, including the Dalmenda probe, to double check every inch of the cave for hidden cavities. He did this before he had brought in his crew to install the titanium grid support.

Had he relied too much on his equipment and not enough on his abilities? Switch pulsed once.

"Very funny." Damon said out loud, with a slight smile.

He flipped the light switch and the alcove lit up. He had recessed lighting installed in every nook and cranny of the catacombs.

He combed the walls again. It took him most of the day. Still nothing.

Sighing, he turned away. Switch pulsed again.

'Don't worry' he thought, 'we'll be back'. Switch pulsed once.

He went to talk to the contractor.

Damon signed the release papers and transferred the final payment to the contractors account. He thanked the contractor and the crew, for a job well done, as he saw them off.

After they had gone, Damon Gray went immediately to a washroom and removed his disguise.

As he came out of the washroom, he smiled in relief. He liked disguises but was glad to get it off.

In the beginning, when he had first started wearing disguises, to leave his concerts undetected, he was nervous.

Once he knew that the person or people believed his masquerade, he got a small thrill of pride, for a job well done.

The thrill got less over the years. He had to wear them a lot. When he met his booking agent in a public place. When he met with his advertising team, etc, etc.

He wore specially tinted glasses at all his performances and backstage parties, so that no one could see his unique eye color.

Paparazzi were always hovering, waiting to snap a picture of Damon Gray, the Gray Ghost.

He phoned Hastings and told him he would be in the catacombs for awhile and could be reached on extension 'C27', which stood for cave twenty seven.

The entire catacomb was completely finished to his specifications. When one cave was finished with the reinforcement titanium grid, the other teams came in and finished the cave off to his additional specifications.

It was late. He went immediately down to *cave twenty seven*, grabbing a bite to eat on the way. When he got there and passed the triangle opening Switch pulsed multiple times again. *Just making sure, Switch. Thank you.'* Switch pulsed once.

He walked into the alcove and faced the back wall squarely. His left hand held the remote control. He turned out all the lights in the cave and the entrance leading to it. Total blackness surrounded him. Looking and searching with all his senses … he saw nothing. Ever so slowly he pressed the remote and brought light back into the triangle alcove only, in very small increments.

He was using all his abilities, gifts and senses, when something suddenly clicked inside him when he blinked and, with his *aura vision*, he saw it! A black area on the right side of a black wall. He looked at the spot. It wasn't there! Damon closed his eyes and then looked at it again, using his *aura vision*. He could then see it clearly. Opening his eyes and consciously *not* looking at it with his eyes, he studied it with his aura vision. It was a black triangle. Not black really. More than black, if such a color existed. Blacker than black. It wavered on the wall approximately six feet, six inches from the floor.

'No chance of anyone bumping into *that* by accident.' Damon thought.

He reached up with his right hand and placed it in the middle of the triangle. Nothing.

He pushed lightly. Nothing.

He slapped it sharply. Nothing.

He placed his hand in the middle of the *BTB* Triangle and said "What do I have to do to get you to respond, say '*open* sesam'..." he stopped.

Upon the word *open* the wall silently swung inward, the hidden hinges on the left.

"Stop." The wall stopped immediately. "Close." The door immediately returned to its original position.

Taking his hand off the *BTB* he said, "Open."

Nothing.

Placing his hand partially on its edge and partially he spoke the '*open*' word again.

Nothing.

The *BTB* panel needed a full hand contact. When he again placed his hand on the center if it and spoke the word "Open", the wall swung inward again.

He walked forward and looked in. It was black. He could see nothing. He started to step forward...

The phone rang. He turned up the main cave lights, walked over and answered one of the camouflaged phones, hidden in one of the beams, not once taking his eyes off the triangle open doorway.

"Hello? Yes. (Pause) I'd love to. I'll be right up."

Hanging up the phone, he walked over to the *BTB* and closed the door.

Damon Gray went upstairs to join Hastings for a midnight snack. As they were eating, Damon brought Hastings up to date on the day.

▲ ▲ ▲

Damon was at the *BTB* panel the following morning bright and early. All the lights were on in cave twenty seven and the triangle alcove. He had brought extra lighting, mounted on tripods.

He placed his hand in the middle of the *BTB* Triangle panel. Once it was in place he looked at it directly.

Although he couldn't feel it, no matter how hard he tried, with his aura sight he saw the *BTB* curl slightly around his hand.

After further testing, Damon concluded that it needed full hand contact in order to interpret the speaker's language. Brilliantly simple and effective.

He opened the triangle door and turned on one of the tripod lights. He could not see in very far, it was so black. The very blackness seemed to absorb the light, reflecting none back.

He bent and looked at the floor. It was perfectly smooth and of a non reflective black material. Turning off the lamp he took a flash light from his work station, turned it on and walked into the black room.

As soon as he stepped over the threshold, Damon Gray knew immediately that this was not a creation of nature.

Light appeared in the room, from an unknown source!

The interior was a three sided perfect triangle. Four, if you counted the floor. All were black, floor and walls and it was seamlessly smooth.

Standing just inside the entrance way, he looked around. He had no intention of getting trapped inside with the door snapping closed.

Using his aura sight, as he faced the doorway from within, just around the corner from the other *BTB*, at the same level as the one outside, he located on the left wall a *BTB* Triangle panel the same distance from the door as the outer one.

It did not surprise him. That is where it should have been. He turned off his light.

He then continued on into the triangle room. Once he passed into the safety zone Damon watched as the door closed silently. Once it

247

was sealed you could not see where it was. Without his aura sight he would be hard pressed to find the *BTB*.

He wondered how the builders found it, unless they all had aura sight, which he doubted highly.

But that didn't surprise or excite him as much as what happened instantly after the door finished closing and sealing.

Except for being non reflective also, the walls did not match the black floor. He was facing the door wall, when the door finished closing and was surprised that the wall turned to liquid mercury in color. It seemed to move constantly, sluggishly. He could not see his reflection. He studied it briefly, then turned his head to the right. The right triangle wall was brilliant liquid ruby red. He turned his head to the left. The left triangle wall was a liquid gold. He looked at the floor. It had not changed.

He could not tell where the light originated from. It was bright, without being too intensely so. The three sided pyramid was totally bare of any ornamentation. *'Not that it needed it'*, he thought.

But what was it for? What was its function or use? Why had Switch brought him here?

He studied the entire interior walls. They felt like a soft sand paper, almost velvet in texture, which would help explain their non reflective nature. Why did they look wet?

When he placed his left hand on the BTB and said *"Open"*, nothing happened. When he placed his right hand on it and said *"Open"*, it did. Damon looked at his hand. It seemed that Switch was much more than a switch. Switch pulsed once.

He would pursue this matter at another time. Switch pulsed once.

He went back into *C27* and brought his workstation in, with a portable power source.

After hours of intense study and using every tool he had on hand, he could find no more BTB's or anything else. The walls and floor were of unknown and unclassifiable material. Indestructible, as far as he could ascertain.

Time to use his abilities.

He ran his hand over every inch of the walls and floor.

Nothing.

Frustrated he stood in the middle of the triangle cave and turned around slowly. On a single impulse from Switch, he kept on turning and turning, slowly at first, then spinning faster and faster, keeping his head facing forward at all times.

He was about to quit when he saw a flash out of the corner of one of his eyes. He sped up more. The flash kept repeating.

He braked abruptly facing the ruby wall. He dropped to his knees and grabbed the floor to stop it spinning.

When he got his equilibrium back he stood and looked at the ruby red wall.

Nothing.

'Dammit' he thought, *'its there somewhere'*.

He walked up to the wall. Placing his hand on the wall he felt the texture.

Then keeping his hand on the wall he walked back and forth covering the entire area where he thought he had seen the flash of light.

Still nothing. He swore to himself. He was running late.

He turned away to head back to get ready for the tour when Switch twitched lightly multiple times.

He stopped. *'Dammit again!'* he thought. He had unconsciously been using his *left* hand!

He held up his right hand and looked at the interwoven tricolored ring, with the embedded triangles capturing and reflecting the light. Still as beautiful as always, he instinctively kept her away from abrasive surfaces. He knew, from testing, that nothing could scratch dent or mar her surface, yet he strove to protect her.

When he had first slipped and called Switch *her* instead of *it* he surprised himself. When he tried it again *she* acknowledged him. *It* suited *her*. Not that it mattered that she *was* a she. But, better to be a *she* than an *it*, was the feeling he got.

"Well Switch, what do we have here? Do you think you can find the light?" She squeezed three times lightly. More like a mental squeeze, he thought. That meant maybe.

"Well my lovely, let's give it a try."

With that said, he covered the area of wall again, but with his *right hand* this time. He moved Switch slowly.

When he finished one sweep and started to bring his hand back, Switch started tugging to keep on moving.

Startled and curious because she had never done anything like that before, he allowed it. About eighteen inches from where he had originally stopped, his right hand plunged forward suddenly into the wall.

The wall instantly surrounded his arm as he went deeper. He felt his hand close on something cold and strangely shaped. A perfect black triangular opening appeared around his hand, the instant he touched it.

Instinct kicked in and, still holding the object, he pulled his hand back slightly. It came with it. He withdrew the object.

It was a large, strangely designed, black triangular key of some sort. He glanced at it, turned and left the triangle cave, closing the triangle door behind him.

Putting the key in his pocket, he started running. He had a concert to catch. As he ran, he mentally thanked Switch. She pulsed once. That meant yes. *'Oh well'* he thought *'what can you expect with a limited vocabulary?'* Switch pulsed once. Damon laughed.

▲ ▲ ▲

Scene Fifty Six

The tour was over. It was a smashing success. He was happy with the reviews and had a good time, but he had been looking forward to the end of it from the beginning. That was something that had never happened before. Usually he was consumed with all aspects of his tours. Not this one. He could hardly wait to get home to Blackstone and the *'TC'*.

Now he had the time to continue where he left off.

When he reached C27 and went into the *'triangle cave'*, or *'TC'* as he thought of it while he was on tour, he went directly to the black triangle opening, pulling over his mobile work station full of equipment. On a band around his head was a *remote*, full spectrum, camera lens to record everything he saw and did. He turned on the receiver.

The triangle opening was still there. He slipped the black key back in, without turning it. When his hand exited the opening the black triangle vanished as if it never was.

He was stunned. He ran his left hand over the wall. Ruby hard, with no outline or anything, to show where it was. He tried forcing his left hand through, like his right hand before, but it wouldn't go.

Looking at Switch he asked. "Are you willing to try again, Switch?" One pulse.

"Let's do it." Slamming his hand forward, the wall allowed access and formed around his hand, like it did before, instantly turning into the triangular black opening upon contact with the key.

He removed the key. As it had when he took it the last time, it stayed open, awaiting the key.

He sprinkled some small pebbles inside the black triangle. They were pushed out instantly when his hand exited.

This was some serious *Jhinn,* or *Source Force,* as the old tomes taught. This lock was at least twenty five thousand years old.

While on tour he'd picked up some equipment and tested the key. It was of no substance that he knew of, and he knew all that *today's* modern science knew. While it may not be totally indestructible, it resisted his best efforts. He hadn't tried everything, because he didn't want to damage or destroy it. In a way, it reminded him of Switch. He gave up trying to analyze her also.

He took some sand and sprinkled it in the open triangle. As with the pebbles, it immediately was pushed out, keeping the interior of the triangle opening spotlessly clean.

Damon smiled to himself.

He checked the opening before he reinserted the key. As he suspected, no sand, dust or debris of any kind would be allowed to hamper the keys connection to the insert mechanism.

Scanning the wall, with all of his equipment, showed no room or cavity behind the lock. His main scanning probe, the Dalmenda, could pierce or scan solid matter up to and including one hundred meters.

Nothing except solid rock.

What he saw, as he first flashed a light inside the triangle, stunned and excited him. Blood red, silver and gold interwoven triangles were imbedded in the flawlessly smooth black rock interior of the triangular opening. They seemed to be random in placement. Surrounding the interwoven triangles, brilliant, faceted, translucent, deep royal purple symbols and figurines were also embedded, with writings of a kind that he had never seen before.

He looked closer. No, not *embedded* he decided, *suspended*.

Setting up the lights so that everything within the triangle opening was illuminated, without glare, took a little time.

All the writings and triangles were three dimensional, like they were *suspended* in time and space. The walls didn't reflect any light but seemed to absorb it, but everything else did.

Damon didn't mind. In fact, he was in his element. Not a lot of things excited him anymore, but this did. On the tour, he enjoyed testing the key and speculating on what treasure the key would unlock, or *more importantly*, what it kept locked in, or out.

He touched all the sides of the triangles, to prove to himself that the walls existed.

The back wall was blank, except for the triangular key hole that seemed to be floating in the middle.

When he reached in, with his right hand, to touch the lock on the back wall, it passed right on through. He kept reaching, until he could reach no more. He tried it with his left and his hand hit a wall where the wall should have been. When he went to touch the key hole, his hand passed over it. It seemed to exist slightly beneath the black surface. With his right, he positioned his hand behind it. He could still see it, so it wasn't beyond his reach, looking closer than it actually was.

He hit the back wall with a sharp pick like instrument in his left hand to see if it would bend or shatter. Nothing happened. It was like hitting a diamond hard wall. It dulled the point on the first blow. With it in his right hand, it passed through.

He took the black key and put it inside. He tried to go off to the side. It pulled his hand to the lock. Well, not exactly pulled, he decided after many tries. It was as if it was in an invisible force field funnel, leading only to the lock. Further research confirmed it.

Another mystery occurred. When the key entered the confines of the triangle, brilliant cobalt blue markings appeared on all three sides.

When he put in anything attached to his body, nothing happened, but the moment he let go, the object was immediately propelled out, as the pebbles and sand had been.

Another thing he had noted. Whenever he put his right hand in the Triangle opening, both Switch and the matching wall triangles brightened slightly, and his finger or mind felt a very slight pulsing sensation.

After a week of exhaustive testing and study, Damon stopped.

The following morning he brought Hastings down to the TC, as he had *officially* named the triangle cave.

▲ ▲ ▲

Scene Fifty Seven

"Holy jumping sheep dip, what is it?" Hastings exclaimed when he first saw it.

"It is a doorway or gateway of some kind, to 'Somewhere' or possibly 'Somewhen'."

"Like 'Elseware'?"

"I don't know. I haven't been through it yet."

The doorway they were talking about was a twelve foot high perfect triangle wall of swirling liquid silver, encased by a thin black border, that intersected the ruby and gold walls.

"Watch this." Damon said. He reached inside the black triangle and did something. The new wall turned a liquid swirling blood ruby red, again with a thin black rim surrounding it. He did something again and it turned a shining swirling liquid gold with a slim black border outlining it. He did something again and the wall disappeared.

"Well, you got my attention. Are you going to explain or just leave me here with my mouth hanging open?"

"Did you notice anything?"

"Yes, and it's scaring the *shit* out of me. All three of the colors are in your ring and from what I remember you telling me, your ring brought you here. The triangles in your ring match the triangles in the black key triangle opening. What is going on, Damon?"

"What else did you notice?"

"That the gold, red and silver doorways are outlined in black?"

Damon waited.

"The wall edges of the pyramid have a thin black line or border around them also?"

"Exactly! Excellent, Hastings! Good job."

"Listen Ranger, I'm glad you liked my observations, but I don't know what the hell you're so excited about. I'm still in the dark. Don't have a clue. Baffled. Not comprehending ......?" Hands turned up he smiled, questioningly.

Damon laughed "I see. You observed, but did not understand. I didn't either at first. You see, it ..... Ranger? What brought that on; you've never called me *Ranger* before?"

"Well sir, it just slipped out in my frustration. I'm sorry, I didn't mean to offend. It's what I've sometimes thought of you as. I don't know whether you know it or not, but I have some Native American or Indian in my bloodline." Damon nodded that he knew. "Well, there are two kinds of Indians in my mind. Indian Chiefs and Indian Braves. An Indian Chief I never wanted to be. I function best as a field agent. I am the Indian Brave. The Toronto that helps makes the *Ranger,* the *Lone Ranger.*" He suddenly smiled at his boss. "Coincidently, it is also what I thought of Mr. Smoke *as,* after the golden bullets incident."

Damon smiled and went to say something but Hastings raised his hand. Damon stopped.

Hastings continued. "Sir, please let me finish. I know from what you have told me in the past that you don't feel like a brave man. I disagree. You have proved time and again to me that you do have courage. True courage, not just bravado. When you lost your parents, it must have been ... I don't know the word. I guess *really, really* bad will have to do." Hastings looked hard at Damon, then continued.

"You pulled through and kept on going, sir. I know that when you lost your grandparents, it was almost, if not *as bad*. You continued. I have seen great people forever broken and brought down by less.

256

Good men and women. Strong. Brave. Courageous. Intelligent. You were *alone* sir, as alone as I have ever seen anyone *be*. You *wouldn't* or *couldn't* let anyone get close to you. You were badly hurt, broken and bent, but you straightened out and healed yourself."

Hastings shook his head at the memories. "Nobody else was able to help. Not even me, not *anybody*. You did it *on your own*. I know you don't see it, but I do. Even if I don't say it, I sometimes compare you to the *Lone Ranger*. *Ranger* is the name I always called him, it sounded way cooler to me as a child. And I considered myself your Indian Brave, Toronto."

Damon paused for a long time looking at Hastings.

No, not at him. Through him.

Suddenly Hastings saw something change in Damon's eyes and face. It was subtle but it scared him. Had he hurt Damon with something he said? What Damon said next took away the fear as if it had never been.

"I was only curious. Thank you, Hastings." he said softly.

With that he turned away to the black triangle control switch and explained to him that twelve o'clock was *off*, two o'clock was *red*, six o'clock was *silver* and ten o'clock was *gold*. The key almost pointed to the corresponding color at the two, six and ten marks.

That made it easy to remember, Hastings had said.

Damon told him that he had put his right and left hand through each color with no ill effects.

He asked Hastings if he, after the ShabNab *Smoke*, would assist him in his experiments. He wanted to go through the doorways.

Hastings grinned and said "Absolutely, sir."

Damon smiled.

▲ ▲ ▲

257

Scene Fifty Eight

Later that night as they were having a coffee in the library, Damon looked at Hastings and said,

"Hastings, what you said earlier hit a lot of tender areas inside, which tells me you were right. Inadvertently, you created within me, an epiphany. I suddenly realized that for the past twenty plus years I have been living in constant fear and didn't know it. It was just another part of me. When I regained my abilities, some of the fear went away, largely due to the rage I felt towards the *terrorist bombers*. What you said made me look inside with three sets of eyes."

He saw Hastings eyebrows go up in a question. "Yes, three sets of eyes. *Still*. And I like it. It's like I can relax and one of them can take the *look out* for me. Usually it's Golden. If you recall, he's the *Prime Instinctual*. He loves that kind of thing. What we saw, was what you said. I also found I could make some internal changes. Correction. *We* could make some changes. Without Golden and Garnet, I don't know if I could have done it on my own. One of the main reasons that I agreed to the meld is that, *inside* I knew something was wrong with me, but I couldn't see it."

Damon's eyes lost focus as he smiled at a memory. "When I was young and had my abilities, I couldn't see my own aura. My father said that all aura readers that he knew, and he knew *a lot*, I later found out, could not see their own aura. I told him that one day I would be able to. He laughed and said if anybody could do it, it would be me. Today, in the Triangle Cave, I realized that I could see my own aura!"

He smiled at Hastings. "I saw the fear *within* me Hastings."

"You saw *your own fear* within you, sir? How can you see *fear* inside yourself?" Hastings asked incredulously.

"Correct. I'm not sure I can explain *how* I can see my fear. Suffice to say that I *saw* and *recognized* it, *studied* it, *understood* it and then *controlled* it. It really is a small thing once you understand it.

"Fear is good. It is in our genes to help keep us alive. *A Survival Instinct*. I now have fear as my *ally*, and *not my enemy*. That was what you noticed in my eyes."

Hastings jumped slightly.

"I saw in your aura that you noticed the change in me. I saw *your fear* flare for an instant. I don't try to read your aura, as a rule, Hastings. I try to respect your privacy, but I had my aura sight on high when it happened. My apologies if it upset you. That was not my intention. What I started this conversation out to do, was to tell you that this epiphany paled in comparison with what you told me. I can't believe that for all those years I thought I was *alone*. I don't feel *alone* anymore. *Thank you for that, Hastings.*"

The last Damon said softly. Hastings knew that he was serious and what it meant to him.

Swallowing the lump in his throat he replied, "As they say back in the United States, *No Problem, Kemo Saabee.*"

"*No Problem?*"

Hastings smiled. "What can I say? It's the cool new saying among young people today. I noticed that not many of them say, '*you're welcome*', anymore."

They both laughed and just before they parted, Damon said, "Toronto?" Hastings grinned and shared a memory.

"What can I say, sir? I was a kid learning all the big cities in the US and Canada. Toronto in Canada was the coolest name to a young boy. Instead of Tonto he became Toronto to me. When I got older, *Ranger* became *Danger Ranger* to me. I never thought of you as a *Danger Ranger* before. (pause) Now I could, sir."

▲ ▲ ▲

Two days later Damon met with Hastings.

"I discovered a new element of what the triangle cave is and does. Upon further testing, I found that it helps me *focus and expand my mind or consciousness.* Or should I say *us.* As well as all my abilities. It somehow separates and brings them out. I realized later that it was the triangle cave that helped me *find* my own internal aura sight. Once I found I had internal aura sight, I noticed other abilities that were dormant in me. They probably would have remained undiscovered, had I not gained the ability to see my own aura. The TC helped me to bring them to fruition."

Hastings frowned, "TC?" His face cleared. "Oh, I see. Code for Triangle Cave. Good call. If it slips out, no one will know what we are talking about."

Damon nodded and continued, "It's hard to explain. Time flows differently in the room as well, when the door is closed. It was probably created by a *being* or *beings* in the distant past to replenish and enhance their powers. We may never know."

He smiled with the enthusiasm of a child. "It's like a *Lens.* A *Multidimensional, Intradimensional, Interdimensional Focal Point* that helps *me* focus. A place where I can go and think crystal clearly, as well as a gateway."

Hastings held up his hand palm out.

"Whoa! You totally lost me on the *multi lens gateway thing.* But never mind that. Did I hear you say you had *other* abilities, as in *more*? Are you saying you've got *more* abilities?"

Damon nodded slightly.

"Yes. There was a crossover effect when my parents added to and altered my genetic structure in the womb. The *TC* helped me to see and identify them. It also helped me to understand them and grow them *all* to full maturity. Some are big and some are small." Damon shrugged slightly.

"It's almost impossible for me to describe most of them. I have no words to explain them."

"Don't worry, sir. I probably wouldn't be able to understand what you explained anyway. I only understood every third word you *just* said."

They both laughed at the truth and humor of that statement. Damon continued.

"It also helped me to figure out Golden and Garnet. I think we are as blended as we will ever be, which is fine with us. I can now control Switch totally. She is now a *part* of me." He raised his hand to show no ring. Suddenly it appeared and then was gone in an instant. "I can make her visible or invisible at will."

"That will be a great help to avoid detection." Hastings agreed. "That ring could have been our downfall. It is *way* too noticeable. Bye the way sir, I have everything you asked for, to proceed with the ShabNab Smoke."

"Great! Then let us proceed with it."

Scene Fifty Nine

ShabNab Mishak retired early. It had been a long day.

The meeting with the Sword had gone well. He was happy with the video and the information she got out of United States Senator Miles Frederick. He especially liked the skill she used to prolong his life until he told her everything just for the right to die. He didn't like the fact that the Senator knew nothing about Mr. Smoke.

First and foremost the Blade was a business man. Terrorism was a business like any other. Without good management, it would fail. Many had. The Sword of Xandu didn't. He ranted and raved to ShabNab that Mr. Smoke was impacting his business in a very bad way. Expenses were up and profits were down tremendously from last year because no one wanted to make the bomb drops. No bonuses were being given out this year, at year end, to any of the Arms and their so called terrorist bombers.

"If they won't do what's asked of them, fuck'm! After we took credit for the bombing, they will have to earn their pay when Mr. Smoke comes here, courting you." he smiled to ShabNab. She smiled back at him sweetly. "Not *you*, of course, Mishy. You have earned a big bonus. Let all of my Arms eat their hearts out with jealousy. I can hardly wait to get my hands on him, or should I say, your hands on him, Mishy. You can make *anybody* talk."

He called her Mishy, a nickname of her last name, to let her know that he knew who she really was. It was the pet name the guards of the Gorsier Insane Asylum called her.

She smiled at the memory later. What a farce! She could read from his aura that he was confident in his ability to control her and only a little frightened of her skills, as would any sane person who employed her.

Frightened, not *terrified*, as he would be if he knew of her *abilities*. And she would never let him know. She needed him too much and she could never let him know that. What he didn't know is that she would *kill the world* to keep him alive. He gave her life purpose. She would never let him know that either. Or that she hated him with every fiber of her being. There were a lot of other things that he could *never* know.

If he did, she'd have to kill him very, very, *very* slowly.

▲ ▲ ▲

Scene Sixty

The Blade sat at his desk after ShabNab left his office, pondering. It had been a long day for him also.

ShabNab hadn't changed much, if at all, from when she reached full physical maturity at twenty one. She still looked late teens to early twenties.

Blade had qualms, at first, about recruiting her at age fourteen from the Gorsier Insane Asylum. The Arm, who had multiple talks with her, had convinced him that the timing was right to recruit her. She was extremely deadly and she was still trainable.

The Blade was glad he had taken the Arms advice. Upon meeting ShabNab Mishak for the first time, he knew he had made the right choice.

He recruited a lot of his top assassins from Asylums and Mental Institutions around the world. Being a brilliant businessman, he asked for referrals from everyone he hired. He paid out a huge referral fee, if their referrals were hired.

When first talking to ShabNab, she had quickly referred four inmates to him, of which he initially hired three.

Because one was in for life for multiple murders, he had to kill and revive him, as he had ShabNab. As with all convicted murderers that he recruited from Asylums, Mental Institutions and Prisons, he had all traces of him removed from the system. No one ever noticed.

To the world, they were dead anyway. The remaining two, he paid to have legally declared sane. Later, he hired the fourth.

ShabNab made sure that she asked for her referral fee on the fourth and even though it was two years later, he gladly paid it.

'Only a brain dead moron wouldn't have', Blade thought to himself. She had a great eye for recruiting. Only rarely would she suggest someone. Now he hired them sight unseen. She was *never* wrong.

One had died on his first assignment and she returned the referral fee. The Blade was surprised and refused saying that he did complete his assignment.

ShabNab said that all her referrals came with a two assignment guarantee. He smiled and took the money.

He was thankful that she had not died on any of those initial high risk missions he had sent her on, after she killed his top assassin, his Personal Assassin, Jack Smithers, VaShena's deceased father.

The Blade hadn't known at the time that ShabNab was pregnant by him. Jack had been the Blades *Personal Assassin* longer than anyone else had been.

Two years. A record.

At the time ShabNab didn't know that Jack was the Blades *Personal Assassin*. The Blade knew that she would have killed him another way, had she known. A way not connected to her. He would have, if he had been in her shoes.

The Blade had no doubt that after the Smithers killing, ShabNab thought that the extremely high risk missions assigned her, were to have her sent out to die. That was not the case at all.

After his *Personal Assassin* had been killed, the Blade needed another that could take his place. The Blade always had the best working solely for him.

The high risk assignments were really tests. Three other assassins were also being tested. All three failed miserably.

ShabNab was the only one that seemed to thrive on the ultra dangerous missions and *that* was the *only kind* he would have as his *Personal Assassin*.

They were the ones he gave the toughest assignments to. They were the ones who protected him when he felt he needed it. They usually only lasted a year or two. Even the best have an *off day*. They were also *paid* the best to *be* the best.

No one, except his Arms, knew who his *Personal Assassin* was. Everyone who worked for the Sword of Xandu knew that the reigning Blade always had a *Personal Assassin*, but never knew who. It could be anyone in the ranks except the Arms. The Arms were too valuable at what they did.

Each Arm controlled nine assassins making the number ten, one team leader (the Arm) and three teams of three.

The Blade liked those numbers. If more needed to be added, they were added under the nine to a maximum of nine, making it ten, counting the leader. They were then given the title of *Hand*, then *Fist*. Under that, if more were needed, were the *Thumbs* and then the *Fingers*. Only seven times, in their many centuries of history, had the full ten *Arms, Hands, Fists, Thumbs* and *Fingers* been used.

They had never been defeated. There was a series of arm and hand movements that were used to identify Sword of Xandu members to unknown members.

Absently, the Blade went through the process. First, he crossed his right arm to touch his heart with his thumb straight, touching the skin of the first finger, fingers bent under and back at the first knuckle beyond his thumb, signifying allegiance. Then straighten the arm straight out in front, signifying the *Arm*. Then closing the fingers fully and wrapping the thumb over them, signifying the *Fist* it was made into. Then extending the thumb sideways, signifying the thumb. Then opening the fingers straight forward with the thumb alongside, signifying the Hand. And lastly, spreading all the fingers and thumb to signify the Fingers. When asked rank, no words were spoken, only hand and arm signals.

The Blade smiled when he realized what he was doing. He stopped and looked at his fingers. Thick, powerful, hairy fingers. He clenched them both.

Of average height, he was big boned and muscular. He looked bigger than he was. His body was thick, tubular, with little or no indentation at the waist. His legs and arms looked like tree trunks. His waist had little surplus fat on it. With clothes off, his body resembled that of a black bear, without the fat. And he was quicker. As quick as a startled snake. He had been told that his eyes were his best feature. Set deep beneath the black shaggy brows, they were large and of a soft dark brown color.

Slowly, on his fingers, as if not trusting his mind, he counted the years. Eight years! He could scarcely believe it.

For almost eight years ShabNab had thrived as the Blade's *Personal Assassin.*

Ever since she had killed the father of her child, his *Personal Assassin* before her. It happened a few months after the killing of Jack Smithers with a special meeting called *by* the Arms. It was *after* the Blades secret *Personal Assassin 'testing'* of the four top candidates.

It was originally to suggest that ShabNab be segregated from the rest of the assassins, fired or killed. They were terrified of her, especially the ones who had slept with her, forcibly or otherwise. (Which was all of them who weren't gay.)

They felt they might be *next* on ShabNab's list. No one except the one who had referred her and her recruiter (both had been killed on assignments) knew her real name or history and she never told anyone of her assignments. Only the Arm who assigned them to her knew.

No assassin was supposed to talk of their assignments but many did, bragging and exaggerating them to their buddies. When a serious infraction happened, the Arms took punitive measures. They knew that they couldn't control it totally, but needed the assassins to know that there were limits and they were being monitored.

In a few cases of dangerous information leakage, the Blade had to kill the braggart *personally*. Each had been given at least one verbal warning. The Blade did not like to kill his livelihood. He told his Arms, more than once, that he did not consider his weapons to be as valuable as he considered his Arms and Assassins to be. And it was damn hard to find skilled Assassins and even harder to find *competent* Arms, he would add. He also told them that although he would allow minimal harmless bragging among the ranks, he would tolerate *none* from his Arms.

In his first year of reign as the Blade, he had brutally killed three of them. What ShabNab had done to Smithers was nothing compared to what he had done to his Arms. After the third he had no more problems.

ShabNab was one of the very few, if not the only one, who *never* talked about her assignments.

She had been asked many times, by many, what she did there. All she ever did was smile. One of the many tests the Blade had, that she knew nothing about, or ever would.

The Blade trusted *nobody* totally.

At the meeting, the Blade told his Arms that he knew what was going on in the ranks and had already decided that she would take the place of the one she killed. She would work just for him. None of them had jurisdiction over her any more.

Not knowing of the tests for his *Personal Assassin*, the Arms were stunned at first but none of them argued. It satisfied everyone's concerns. She had been a floater, joining whatever regiment that the Blade felt needed her at the time.

She had never been asked to do a team job. She was too damned weird. No one trusted her.

That was when ShabNab Mishak became the Blades *Personal Assassin.*

▲ ▲ ▲

Scene Sixty One

L ying naked on her bed, ShabNab stretched luxuriously. She
had just finished a workout and a shower.

She never understood the need some people had for a bath.
Why would anyone wash off the filth of their body into the tub they
were sitting in? She had tried a bath once. When she got out and
drained the tub, she had looked closely at the tub after it drained.
If that much dirt and scum was stuck to the tub after the water had
carried whatever dirt it could hold down the drain, what was still on
her body and in her private areas?

She showered immediately. She could visualize the dirt washing
off her body and down the drain. In the Asylum everybody showered.
There was too much chance of disease.

'Damn' she thought, 'Even after all these years I still think of the
Asylum.'

She had just finished a long debriefing session with the Blade, on
the Senator assignment, after a turbulent seventeen hour flight.

The jet landed on the Blade's private runway outside his castle
near Maracaibo, Venezuela, the Sword of Xandu main headquarters.
They had locations in every major country in the world but this was
the headquarters, where the Blade controlled all.

The Castle always impressed her. It looked as if it had been built
in the sixteenth century but it was much newer. It was big enough

to barracks an army of at least five thousand soldiers which, she was told, it had at times.

What they housed now were one hundred terrorists, excluding her. One hundred staff (the German liked the number one hundred, thus did the Blade) and a small nation's net worth of weapons of mass destruction.

The Sword had bought it from the ancient gentleman known only as '*the German*'. A man who knew how to protect himself.

The Sword did not negotiate. He paid the full asking price for it in cash and considered it a bargain, which it was. No one had expressed interest in it up to the time that the Sword had heard of it.

The price had been reduced to the point where the German was about to take it off the market. The German was appreciative, but he knew that the full price offer *also* came with a price.

The Blade told ShabNab that the German graciously spent a full month showing and explaining the entire castle to him. It amazed the *Personal Assassin* that it took that long. It was sold furnished.

The German had a security, policing, monitoring and policy system in place that the Blade considered perfect and he hadn't varied it to this day. Every known electronic surveillance device and equipment had already been installed when the Sword had purchased it twenty years previously.

He told ShabNab that he updated the security systems quarterly. It was the best that money could buy. The Blade said it was a smart investment for the return, and he considered himself a smart man.

Over recent years, he told ShabNab that he had been offered up to twenty times what he paid for it.

ShabNab knew the Blade was a brilliant man. He was one of a very select few whose *intelligence* she respected. It was the *only* thing she *did* respect about him.

He was seventeen when he joined the Sword of Xandu. He was twenty two when he seized power and title and replaced the reigning Blade.

There was a knock at the door.

"Who is it?" she called.

"Room service with the meal you ordered."

"Bring it in." She did something and the door opened. The waiter rolled the serving table in. He almost tripped when he saw ShabNab lying naked on the bed with her legs spread casually, provocatively.

"WWWhere wwould you like to eat?" he stammered not taking his eyes off her.

Gliding to her feet in one beautiful and impossible movement, she smiled at him.

"Right here, young man." She pointed to the table in front of him.

"Where?... Oh yes, how foolish I must look. Excuse me." Blushing, he tore his eyes from her and set the table. "Is there anything else I can get you?"

"No. Come back in forty five minutes to collect the dishes please. You're new, aren't you?"

"Yes miss. Is that all?"

"No, it isn't. I'll give you your tip when you return. As you can see, I don't have anything on me at the moment."

"Yes miss, tthank yyou miss." With that, he fled the room.

ShabNab smiled. He was young and very good looking and he didn't know about her. Tonight could be a very good night.

She sat down and ate her meal.

▲ ▲ ▲

As she ate, she remembered looking at the Blade closely during the debriefing. At forty five the Blade was an incredibly ugly man. As a young man, ShabNab felt that he had a certain rugged charm but as the years went by, his inner nature seemed to manifest itself on his face. Thick pitch black hair covered his head.

As a young man it drew the ladies. She had seen it. At forty five, the denseness of it, mixed with the shaggy eyebrows and his craggy his face, made him look like a primitive Neanderthal. ShabNab knew his looks didn't concern him. He could and did have any woman he wanted. He was a physical and sometimes brutal lover. A few even came back for more.

No one knew his true name. All ShabNab had ever known him as, was the Blade. He had heard of her through an asylum inmate who joined Xandu, after being recruited, then pronounced legally cured and released. He sent one of his ten Arms to talk to her. The Arms were his generals.

After many talks with her, posing as her relative, the Arm recruited her from the asylum when the Blade was twenty four.

Acting on the Sword of Xandu's plan, when she received a certain phone call, ShabNab complained of a severe stomach pain and was taken to the infirmary where she took the pill the Arm had given her. She collapsed, died and was promptly pronounced legally dead by the Coroner, who was *conveniently* on hand.

The Coroner cleared the room immediately and injected her with a stimulant and restarted her heart several minutes after she was dead. Her body was switched with that of a young female prostitute who had very recently died of a drug overdose. The Sword of Xandu provided the body, as always.

The Coroner assured them that makeup would cover the multitude of needle tracks on her arms and body.

Forms were signed for her to be cremated immediately, her death was recorded and witnessed by the recruiting Arm of the Sword of Xandu, money exchanged hands and Arm of the Sword of Xandu injected a mild sedative and removed her body from the Gorsier Insane Asylum.

She awakened in the Blades castle and was a basket case for another twenty four hours, screaming that *Death* was alive inside her.

She was placed in a straight jacket after killing two and maiming four attendants. Finally she calmed down, was cleaned up and brought to see him.

She apologized for the deaths and explained to the Blade that she was highly allergic to narcotics or stimulants of any kind. If she had known they were going to give her a sedative, she would have warned them.

He accepted her apology, talked at length with her and was taken with her beauty and wit. He took her many times over the years and thought nothing of it. She never complained. To him, she seemed to enjoy it. She had turned into his best and finest terrorist assassin, and eight years ago, his *Personal Assassin.*

She would take any job and do it with precision and in whatever style was asked. Special requests were her favorite. Only once had someone recognized her handiwork in twenty years and then only once.

She never made the same mistake twice. That was her selling factor for the Sword of Xandu.

Whenever a particularly dangerous mission came up they sent her. As with all of the previous *Personal Assassins*, she was said to be invincible, her sex and identity kept a secret. For all any outsider knew, the *Personal Assassin* was immortal, used for only the most dangerous of missions.

If any person or organization used the *Personal Assassin,* they paid dearly. Her work did keep her busy. Only the Blade and his ten Arms knew of her.

Dinner was delicious.

Scene Sixty Two

"Did you have a good time shopping?"

"It was wonderful, sir."

"Why are you back so late?"

"I didn't think it was *that* late, sir. Did I miss something? I wasn't told there was a time I had to be back by."

"There wasn't. I was just curious, that's all. Let's get down to business, shall we?"

"Of course, sir."

The Blade paced his office for a moment in deep in thought.

"What is your opinion on the situation?" he asked.

"We can't go after him because we don't know *who* or *where* Mr. Smoke is. I suppose we will just have to wait." ShabNab replied.

Two weeks had gone by since the murder of the US Senator and the bombing of the hotel and still no sign of Mr. Smoke.

ShabNab had just returned from a day long shopping spree in the city with an armed escort of ten. She thought the ten men bodyguard was utterly ridiculous but it was the only way that the Blade would let her leave the premises. She was getting stir crazy and agreed.

They had left bright and early and she had just returned. The Blade had told her to report in as soon as she returned. She had stayed out extra late.

"I almost regret that we took the assignment to go after Mr. Smoke. I don't want to keep you tied up. It could cost the Sword of Xandu a lot of money, if you are taken off the market for an extended period time to find and kill him." He smiled. "After you got all his information, that is."

"You could do another bombing, more spectacular this time."

The Blade walked to the window and looked out at the starlit sky.

"We don't do *Freebies* unless we absolutely have to. I only agreed to take the Mr. Smoke contract because it fit in nicely with our information gathering from the Senator contract. If the Senator hadn't insinuated that he might have information about Mr. Smoke to the press to get reelected, I might have done this differently. I expected him long before now." He gestured at the window. "I'm not sure I want you *out there*, where he can get to you *alone*. Dammit, this is not turning into the cost effective contract I thought it would."

ShabNab stood and looked out the window into the dark.

"Maybe *out there* is where I *need to be*." She said. "No one in their right mind would tackle this place, except maybe me. And even with me, it would take time and I know the place."

The Sword smiled in acknowledgement and satisfaction.

There was a buzz on his desk. He pushed a button. "What is it? I told you not to disturb me."

"Yes sir, I know. The security systems agent has finished installing and updating the system. He has been waiting for five hours to show you the add-ons and updates, and get your signature. He said he has been having intestinal problems all day, which have been vouched for by his security team. They found it amusing even though he didn't," the voice chuckled, "*and he didn't.* He said he has been here since early this morning and would like to go home, if that's alright with you sir.

"I know more about the damned system than that kid knows. I checked it this morning when he brought it in. I'll check the installation myself in a few minutes. Sign the work order for him and send him on his way with thanks. I was made aware of his little problem and frankly, I don't give a shit. If I came out I would probably kick his ass for bothering me. Those pompous little computer geeks get under my skin sometimes. Not old enough to shave and making thousands of bucks an hour. They act as if *their* security system is …. Oh … what the hell, just do what I told you to do."

"Yes sir." Click.

"Safe for another three months are we?" ShabNab smiled.

The Blade laughed suddenly. "With you here we are." He reached over and grabbed her. She slid into his arms. He ripped her blouse off. She didn't have a bra on.

"You didn't like my new blouse?" she pouted. He stopped the pout with a grinding kiss.

▲ ▲ ▲

Later in bed ShabNab reflected back on *why* the Blade had taken her. He hadn't done that in years and years. It must be that all guests had been removed from the castle, so that they would spot a stranger instantly. Even the computer geek had four men watching his every move.

She heard two men laughing and talking on her way to her apartment. She just caught the tail end of it. Something about how the geek had a hard time shitting, surrounded by four assassins and how many times he had wiped his ass afterwards.

The voices stopped as she walked by topless. The red finger marks were still showing on her breasts. He'd lifted her off the floor by her *great tits*, as he called them, and slammed her onto his desk.

They knew that the Blade had just *'taken'* her. That's how the Blade liked to refer to it, he had *'taken'* her, or he *'took'* her, or he was going to *'take'* her.

As one of the Blades many women had said in the powder room one time to her, "God how I loathed those three words used that way." She said *it took away all dignity on the part of the woman or women as the case might be.* Like the woman *'taken'* was *less* than a hooker.

Personally ShabNab didn't give a shit. If you were going to be *taken*, then just shut the hell up, *take it* and *enjoy it*. It was one of her forever changing philosophies.

She rubbed her puffy red sore crotch, smiled and went to sleep.

▲ ▲ ▲

Scene Sixty Three

Mr. Smoke had done his homework on the Sword of Xandu Castle. Castle Florentine was the legal name. Damon had researched the castle and grounds as well as the inhabitants.

It did not surprise him that it was shrouded in mystery, myths and rumors. He could find very little on the internet concerning it. When it was built, no one seemed to know for sure.

The first recorded mention of it was when it was registered to a Count Florentine in the early eighteen hundreds, but writings of the Count hinted that it was older than that. It was located on the top and in the center of a plateau measuring two miles across at its narrowest point. The entire plateau had belonged to all the previous owners since. Not one of them had sold off parcels of land.

It was as it had been when Count Florentine owned it. Of the Castle itself, little was known. It took up about a third of the plateau estate.

Mr. Smoke had detailed satellite surveillance pictures of it from one of his own orbiting satellites. On all the *other* satellites, the castle was *non existent*.

He was very impressed with the Sword of Xandu. Someone sure knew their computer *'stuff'*, probably the Blade. No information was available on him, other than the fact that he owned it.

An out of country corporation owned Castle Florentine. Cutting Edge Inc. was the name of the corporation on the title. The owner was also a legal resident of Venezuela. He went by the single name *Blade*. Everyone called him *Sir* or *Mr. Blade*. He was a registered resident and his twenty five year old picture on file was very blurry. He was not registered as ever having a driver's license or any other form of photo identification.

▲ ▲ ▲

Scene Sixty Four

Mr. Smoke was the security installation geek that had so much trouble with his bowels earlier that day. He knew the security measures to get in would be stringent so he had come prepared.

Initially it had shocked him to find out that one of *his* companies supplied the hardware, *in addition to* the technicians that did the installation and maintenance of the security system. In retrospect, it shouldn't have. His computer companies were the best in the world at what they did.

They *hadn't* done the satellite jamming that kept Castle Florentine off and out of, the world's global satellite's systems. It seemed the Blade did not put all his eggs in one basket. Ordinarily, that would have made it a lot more difficult to get in, but not in this case. The timing couldn't be better. He had to wait a week longer than he wanted, but it turned out okay. ShabNab was still there.

The three month maintenance and upgrade was due and he was to take the technician, Dabnee Gehlhausen's place. Dabnee had done the upgrade twice before. They were close to the same height.

Dabnee had long, muddy brown, lanky hair and sported a patchy, scraggily looking mustache and goatee. He wore an expensive scuffed and tattered baseball cap backwards on his head, advertising the female tattooed rap artist, *SumBitch*.

He wore Buddy Holly glasses tinted bronze to protect his brown eyes from the constant computer screen radiation. He was big and had soft round shoulders. The kind you get from sitting at a computer all day. He was soft bellied also.

He wore expensive, baggy, LowRider jeans under his pot belly and layered two long sleeve and extra long bodied Varian Draney heavy duty tee-shirts, each a different vivid base color. Damon was happy that his teeth were white and extremely even. Dabnee had spent a lot of money in his mouth. Finishing the ensemble was a pair of Rockwell hi-top basketball shoes.

Dabnee Gehlhausen was twenty nine years old and a computer *super* genius. His people skills were non existent. Mr. Smoke had accessed his interview video files, to learn his voice patterns and mannerisms. He had also observed him at various *after hour* clubs, during the previous week and had struck up a few meaningless conversations with him.

It had been easy for Mr. Smoke to break into his apartment in the early morning and sedate him before he woke up. He then poured a special liquid, of his own design, down Dabnee's throat. He placed a plastic sheet on the bed and after arranging Dabnee's naked body to his liking on it, he set about changing himself into Dabnee Gehlhausen.

When he returned from the castle that night, he found that Dabnee, as expected, had voided his bowels and pissed on the bed. Damon cleaned him up and then he dressed Dabnee up in the clothes that matched what he had worn for the day.

He then undressed and peeled off his fat suit, brown contact lenses, flesh colored latex fingerprints, makeup and disguise. Putting them on the plastic sheet that was on the bed, he wrapped up the whole works and put it into a hefty trash bag.

He dressed casually, loaded the computer technician into the car and drove him to a hospital emergency entrance. He stopped the car, transferred the unconscious man to the driver's seat and folded him over the steering wheel so that it wouldn't move, lifted Dabnee's head, took out a sap, measured and then carefully hit him hard on the head. Then he aimed the car at one of the concrete pylons, put the car in gear, took Dabnee's right leg and jammed the foot down on the accelerator, slamming the door shut as it took off. It slammed into the pylon at a speed fast enough to almost knock it over.

Medical staff converged on the car. No identification was on him. He had tucked it under the floor mat to make it look like it had fallen out of his pocket. It would take them awhile to find it. He entered the hospital just long enough to make sure that Dabnee was alright, and then Mr. Smoke vanished like his name.

After safely disposing the hefty bag, he drove the generic tan rental car that he had parked at the hospital to a spot below the plateau. The night sky was covered with heavy cloud. No stars shone. There he switched into his dark grey Mr. Smoke outfit. He crouched below the rim of the plateau closest to the castle and opened a small electronic piece of equipment.

He extended and opened the long, dull, non reflective antennae dish on it and raised it to just below the rim and aimed it at one of his satellites. He made sure to keep it in the tall grass and protected by shrubs. He punched in some codes on the keyboard and hit a button. A red light flashed. He repeated the procedure several times, punching in different codes each time. Each time the light would change, going from dark red to bright red, from dark amber to bright orange and finally from dark green to bright green. When all the connections were finally made, the bright green light stopped pulsing. He then turned off the machine, collapsed it and put it into one of his pockets.

Looking across the plateau he saw, with his special glasses, that the security infrared laser beams were off. That meant that the motion detectors and buried pressure sensors were off as well. Knowing where they were, he stepped around them just to be safe.

Watching for auras, he made his way across the plateau to the castle. At the bottom of the wall he paused and viewed it through a scanning device. The readings agreed with his findings.

It looked impressive at a distance but was easily scaled by any professional rock climber. Running up the wall quicker than a scalded lizard, he dropped down the other side to land feather light onto a building rooftop.

Pausing for a moment, he scanned the area for auras. Testing the castles security equipment and systems earlier that day had given Mr. Smoke full knowledge of the castles design and its electronic defenses. What it *didn't* tell him was the routine of the security patrol. With the intensity they had shown when he was there, he knew that patrols would be a controlled random pattern, leaving nothing to chance. They were waiting for Mr. Smoke, of that he was sure. But the waiting had to have been a drain.

Normally a security sweep is demanding but not intense. They had been running two weeks on *full* intensity. The first few days they would be jumping at shadows. After the first week their efficiency would suffer tremendously.

Each day after would lessen their abilities and effectiveness. By the end of the second week, they would be emotionally exhausted. They went through the motions but their focus was gone. His experience with them earlier had confirmed it. They had only pretended to check him thoroughly when he first arrived. They knew who he was. He had been there twice before.

The bathroom charade was just that, a charade. He had no problem placing the white ceramic adhesive strip to the underside of the toilet bowl lip. Contained within it were the sender and receiver by which he had controlled the castle's mainframe computer.

The mainframe was not connected to any outside source. It could not be hacked or compromised that way. The computer room ceiling was protected from outside penetration surveillance equipment by special tiles. Tiles not sold on the open market.

Normally that would have made it perfectly secure. It had no wireless capability built in, not until Dabnee had installed an invisible one this morning. It was distributed in such a way that it would never be discovered, but his control device needed to be close to the computer to work.

Removing the strip covering the adhesive *activated the adhesive* and within minutes it had bonded seamlessly to the underside of the toilet. Even if you knew where it was you wouldn't be able to see it. Damon checked it on one of his successive visits to make sure. He couldn't feel or see it.

The miniature power supply was long lasting and heat rechargeable, but the range was limited because of its size and the castle walls being so thick.

He had placed it in the location that he did because he had access to one of his special satellites that could reach it through the window opening. The same one that he had used to view the entire castle with. That was how he found it.

Luck did have a little to do with it. He instructed the satellite to continuously monitor and record until otherwise ordered. Someone had opened the window, to air out the bathroom of a smell they didn't want detected. In all likelihood, a drug of some kind. It was after week *one*.

When he viewed the footage, Damon silently thanked that nameless drug addict who couldn't stand the pressure. That one bathroom was his ticket in. He knew before he went in which toilet he was going to use.

Damon had taken a laxative earlier that morning and when it kicked in, he frantically asked to use the nearest bathroom. The ploy worked beautifully. The four guards had to hold back their laughter the first time. By the third they were down to two guards who did not feel like laughing. Damon had eaten some very spicy food the night before. It stunk horribly.

The entire episode was done to protect Dabnee. If Dabnee was ever questioned, he could honestly say that he had no knowledge of the day. The way he set it up, when Dabnee awoke in the hospital, he would be told that he had driven himself to the hospital and passed out as he arrived. When the doctors had examined him, they would discover evidence that he had survived an almost lethal bout of food poisoning.

Knowing doctors, as Doctor Damon Gray did, he knew they would tell him that he was a lucky man to have gotten there when he did. They would tell Mr. Gehlhausen that they had worked frantically to save his life, and they would believe it. His loss of short term memory the doctors would attribute to a combination of two things, the results of the blow to the head from the car wreck and the effects of the food poisoning. No one at the Sword of Xandu would doubt the validity of the claim. They had witnessed it personally.

As Dabnee, Damon had met with the Blade upon his arrival. Just before they first met, he felt ShabNab leaving the premises. He cursed mentally, then shrugged and focused as the Blade walked up to him. *'No distractions'* he told himself as he dropped back into Dabnee's character. He could see the controlled tension in the Blades aura. Physically he didn't show it. He talked easily with Dabnee, at length, about the new system. Damon could see the buried contempt in attitude towards him. That meant that the Blade bought the disguise. He knew, at that moment, that Dabnee was safe.

The Blade would never admit to himself that he could be fooled. Two weeks previously he might not have been. The tension had worked its magic on him as well.

Mr. Smoke estimated that his security team was performing at seventy five percent of peak capability. From his aura, Damon estimated that the Blade was functioning at ninety five plus percent of his usual capacity and that two or three percent reduction was enough to pull off the deception.

The Blade impressed him. The Blade was a man to be reckoned with. Behind his primitive looking face blazed an intellect that Damon recognized as far above genius.

Damon allowed himself a small smile of satisfaction as he remembered. A super genius usually had a super ego and the Blade was no exception.

▲ ▲ ▲

Scene Sixty Five

Dabnee was safe, but Damon wasn't so sure that Mr. Smoke was. He was ready to move on when he saw an aura come around the corner.

The person passed him, then stopped and started to turn around. Damon cursed himself mentally and *instantly* masked his aura as the person completed his turn. He stopped for a moment and then headed back his way slowly.

'*Dammit*', he thought, '*why* wouldn't *some of them have aura sight?*'

He saw the man stop and look toward the area where Damon was crouched. The man was now close enough that, with his natural night vision, Damon could now see him clearly. The man shook his head as if not sure.

Then Damon saw something he had never seen before. The person below him extended his aura upwards, towards Damon's location. Mr. Smoke dropped to his stomach, so as not to be seen and darted noiselessly to the other end of the roof.

The aura did not follow him. After a moment or two the figure shrugged and moved on. Thanks be to the *Source* for his diminished capacity. Two weeks ago, he would not have hesitated to sound the alarm. Now, he passed it off as the jitters.

When the man passed, Damon proceeded to the main building, watching for auras as he went. He paused for a moment at the chosen door and did something to the lock. There was a soft click and Mr. Smoke entered the building.

ShabNab's apartment was on the top floor, at the same end of the hall as one of the staircases. She liked easy access.

Crouching in the stairwell, Mr. Smoke's *aura* sense surveyed the area leading to ShabNab's apartment door. Two auras were standing guard, talking to each other.

He tried to focus and extend his aura sight beyond his body and into the hallway of the guards. It proved to be quite easy. It was similar to *Astral Travel,* but he was still connected to and conscious of his body and its surroundings.

They didn't react when his aura stopped within inches of theirs. He backed up his aura and sent it into the apartment.

An aura was lying on a bed. He could tell by the rhythms that she was sleeping. He went closer to check out her aura. As he approached to within approximately thirty feet of ShabNab, Damon felt a tingle of contact and ShabNab's aura flared brilliantly and seemed to fly out of the bed.

Instinct kicked in and Damon's aura immediately vanished from the apartment. Concealing his aura totally, he looked at the miniature computer screen in front of him and watched, as the camera eye he had placed under the door showed everything in the hall.

Suddenly the door opened and a naked ShabNab appeared holding a small pistol in her hand. She smiled at the two men and then looked up and down the hall. She asked if all was quiet. They smiled and said, yes, everything was quiet, but you could see the tension in their movements.

With his own aura cloaked, Damon was watching with his aura sight when ShabNab did what he had seen the other man do earlier. Pausing after she had looked up and down the hall again, Mr. Smoke saw ShabNab's aura expand and travel up and down the hallway and into the stairwell, then snapped back to her so quick it seemed to vanish. She smiled, said goodnight and the door closed.

Damon experimented as he waited for things to return to normal. He found that he could alter his aura and turn it colorless, which should render it invisible to another with *aura sight.* An hour later he sent his altered aura sight again into the apartment. It wasn't as clear as his full aura sight, but it did the trick. A wonderful and unique experience.

Mr. Smoke smiled. He thought he had discovered *all* the ways to use his new abilities. Now he found out that he could copy others as well.

From her aura, ShabNab was sleeping again. Mr. Smoke's altered aura approached to within a foot of her. There was no reaction or changing of aura in ShabNab. It worked!

Damon retreated and practiced with his colorless aura sight until he could see as clearly as he had with his color aura sight.

The changing of the guards happened at three am. The guards leaving were tired and the ones relieving were also, having just awakened. It was done with no talking. Hand signals only. Damon studied them as they went through their ritual. Obviously they did not know each other.

Once the signals were completed, the early shift left. One by way of elevator and one by way of the stairway by Mr. Smoke. The one taking the stairway never saw Mr. Smoke, even though he thought he looked everywhere. When Damon had changed into his Mr. Smoke outfit, he *became* Mr. Smoke, *terrorist bomber assassin.* Nobody would see him, unless he wanted them to.

The two sentries talked quietly for awhile, then were silent for awhile.

Mr. Smoke deactivated the alarms in ShabNab's apartment, with a miniature device.

One of the Assassins said he would do the coffee run. When he left, the other sentry walked to the end of the hallway and then back, not that there was anything to see. He did it to keep awake. When the other guard came back just minutes later, they sat and enjoyed their coffee.

Mr. Smoke was in ShabNab's room.

When the guard went to stretch his legs, Mr. Smoke was across the hallway and into the room before he was halfway down the hall. Once inside, he reactivated the alarm by her door left handed. In his right was one of his guns cocked and silenced. Once the alarm was reactivated, a matching gun seemed to magically appear in his left hand.

Glancing around the entrance way, with his special Smoke glasses on, confirmed that there were no lasers or motion sensors set up. Hugging the wall he walked quickly to the entrance to the living room and performed the same sweep. All clear. He approached the bedroom.

Just to be safe, as in the entranceway, he skirted all the floor coverings. Lifting them to check for sensors would have set them off just as surely as stepping on them. His altered *clear* aura sight probe told him that his target was still sleeping. He swept the rest of the apartment. There were two bedrooms. He detected no other auras.

ShabNab's bedroom door was open, the other closed. He reholstered his left gun, and slipped through the open doorway as silently as the Gray Ghost he had been named by the media.

He took in the room at a glance. He noticed the open door to the bathroom. No aura. He closed the bedroom door silently, not taking his eyes off the target. No variation in her aura. Mr. Smoke raised his Smoke glasses on their swivel to rest on his face mask's fore head just above his eyebrows.

ShabNab was lying on her back on top of the covers stark naked. Damon was expecting it. He knew she slept that way on purpose. She had a stunningly beautiful body and many would be distracted by it, giving her a split second edge.

He was now glad of the incident earlier that brought her into the hallway. If he had not seen her and came into the room and she was

290

awake, he could now be a dead man, or at least in real trouble. His respect for her increased substantially.

He hesitated when he reached the edge of the bed and placed the gun just inches from the center of her forehead. Her face in repose looked like an angel.

Another tactic he realized as he looked closer. She had freshly applied makeup on. That was not the reason he hesitated.

Mr. Smoke had never killed a woman.

"Are you going to hurt my mommy?" a small voice asked quietly, in Portuguese.

ShabNab's eyes flew open. Damon placed the silenced barrel on her forehead and whispered softly, in perfect Portuguese,

"Move and you are dead ShabNab. Blink once, if you understand."

ShabNab blinked once, not moving a muscle.

Damon looked at her for a moment, to make sure she understood. *"Do not speak."* She blinked once again.

Looking up and to the side, Damon saw the most beautiful girl child he had ever seen, dressed in a white and lavender pajama set, standing in a doorway that lead to a second bedroom. Without a doubt, ShabNab's daughter.

She looked to be between four and five years old. She had lavender eyes. He looked at her hard and said nothing. Inside he was shocked. How could he have missed her?

She looked at him solemnly, not smiling, not frowning - awaiting his answer.

It hit him like a Mack truck. She didn't have an *aura!* No wonder he hadn't seen her. Sending his clear aura probe to her, he realized that she could do what he was doing. Shield her aura!

When his clear aura probe touched her body, he saw the purest aura he had ever seen. Almost pure lavender, the color of her eyes.

Her little face looked shocked for an instant and then her aura vanished again. All this happened in less than a heartbeat. He still had

ShabNab in his line of sight and she knew it. She knew a professional when she saw one. She would patiently await her opportunity.

Damon replaced Mr. Smoke. "What is your name child?" he asked gently.

"VaShena." She said proudly, but not loudly. He could tell that she did not want to startle him into pulling the trigger. Damon made a decision.

"No, VaShena, I am not going to hurt your mother, unless I have to."

VaShena gave Damon the most beautifully radiant smile and whispered, *"Thank you."*

"You are welcome, VaShena." responded Damon.

She then turned and walked back into her bedroom and closed the door silently behind her.

Turning his eyes and full attention to ShabNab again, *Mr. Smoke took over. "If you ever drop another bomb again, ShabNab Mishak, I will come after you and kill you. You can thank your daughter for saving your life."* Mr. Smoke paused at what he saw.

For less than an instant in time he saw pure hatred cross ShabNab's face, then it was serene again. Not that her face changed. It was something Mr. Smoke saw and felt with his *other* abilities and senses.

"I see you hate your daughter." Her body aura twitched in surprise. She didn't move. Mr. Smoke didn't pull the trigger.

"There is not a terrorist bomber alive today that has seen my eyes. Tonight is a night of firsts." Reaching under ShabNab's pillow he removed her pistol. Checking quickly and thoroughly he found two more.

Backing up out of immediate danger range, he produced a set of hand cuffs from one of his pockets. He tossed them to her and told her to put it around one wrist and the other on the bed post.

She looked closely at the handcuffs and said softly. *"No."*

"No? You would rather hurt your daughter by dying?"

"No, but I can't put on these handcuffs. If I do, I will disappoint my daughter by being killed by the Blade. I can't get out of these cuffs. Someone

292

will have to cut them off. The Blade does not tolerate failure. He used my daughter to force me to set you up. That was the first time I have ever planted a terrorist bomb. I didn't know what it was. I thought it was a drug drop. He told me after, so I would be prepared. If he sees me in these, he will have me killed."

She smiled a breathtaking smile at him. No reaction crossed his face. She continued in her soft throaty voice.

"I'll tell you what I'll do, Mr. Smoke. I'll help you escape. Not that you need my help, but I can't afford to have you caught in the castle. It would mean my death, if you talked. You let me invite those two guards in to play and I'll keep them busy for, say an hour? Would that be enough time?"

"You are good. I can't tell if you are lying or telling the truth. It shall be as you say. Close your eyes tightly for ten seconds and then call them in."

She closed her eyes and opened them immediately to say one more thing.

Mr. Smoke had vanished.

"I said close you eyes." A voice whispered. She did.

Ten seconds later she opened them, checked in on her sleeping daughter and then went to the front door and invited in two *very* surprised guards. They were new to her.

Scene Sixty Six

Damon thought about VaShena as his private jet headed back to the United Kingdom. He was going to fly commercial but changed his mind and had Hastings pick him up at an abandoned runway a few hours drive from Castle Florentine. Damon arranged to have the rental car picked up there. As the jet raced above the clouds, Damon reviewed the night's events.

He was at the part when he had disappeared into VaShena's room as he awaited ShabNab to fulfill her end of the bargain. When she checked in on her daughter ShabNab did not see him.

With his altered aura sight he saw her invite the sentries into her bedroom. VaShena lay as if sleeping on her bed. When the time was right and he was about to leave, he heard a whispered, "Thank you, Mr. Smoke" issue from VaShena. It was said in perfect English!

He turned to look and her beautiful lavender eyes were looking at him. She saw his eyes crinkle in the mask and she smiled back. "Just because I'm young doesn't mean I'm dumb. I listen to what's going on around me. You have beautiful eyes too." She looked intently into Damon's eyes for a moment, then smiled. "All six of them. Goodnight." Again in perfect English.

She rolled on her side and closed her eyes. He walked over and looked down at her.

She was smiling.

She was sleeping.
He turned and left.

Scene Sixty Seven

Hastings walked over and sat down opposite Damon Gray. He looked out over the clouds below. He had brought a back up pilot in case Mr. Smoke needed his help in other ways.

"Great night for a pickup. Clouds were so heavy, no one could see us. How did it go? Did you add another notch to your gunbutt?"

"No I didn't, Hastings and I'm glad I didn't. I hesitated when I put the gun to her head. I don't know why. I know I can kill a woman terrorist bomber if I have to, but I'm glad I didn't this time."

"Bring me up to speed, boss."

"Boss?"

"Is it okay? I feel the need to call you something else on a Smoke mission. *Smoke* or *Smokey* doesn't feel right."

Damon smiled and nodded. This was a side of Hastings that he had never seen. Damon liked it.

"I've got more. Wanna hear em?"

"No."

"No!? But …"

"I can handle Sir, Mister or Doctor Gray, Mister Smoke, Damon and Boss, but that is my limit. Yes?"

"Yes sir. Those are my best anyway." They both smiled. Something good had happened to their employer/employee relationship and they both liked it.

Damon brought Hastings up to date.

"Wow, sir! You saw a man who, by example, taught you to narrow, clear and send out your aura sense to other rooms. You met a little girl who can mask her aura like you and who maybe can read minds and you watched her mother going at it, *enthusiastically* is the word you used, with two soldiers as you walked out of the room?" Hasting smiled lecherously. "Now that is something right out of the twilight zone. Whatever pills you are taking, I want some. What a trip!"

Damon laughed.

They continued to talk of other things as their plane raced across the early morning sky to greet the morning sun.

▲ ▲ ▲

Scene Sixty Eight

The sentries had left satisfied.

ShabNab paced her apartment. How had Mr. Smoke reached her without her knowing? How had VaShena known that he was there?

He must be gay, she thought. He didn't react to her beauty at all. If he wasn't gay, why didn't he react? Everybody reacted to her eyes. He didn't.

Why hadn't he shot her? How had he vanished? Why could she see him and not sense him? Who the hell was he? So many questions and no answers.

ShabNab entered VaShena's bedroom via the connecting bathroom. Her daughter was sleeping peacefully. Somehow the little bastard bitch had saved her life. God, how she hated the little bitch.

She sat on the side of the bed and looked down at her daughter. So small. So fragile. So helpless. ShabNab smiled. Somehow, it made her feel better. She knew that someday she would have to kill her daughter. She could not stand to have a less than a perfect offspring. She would keep on searching until she found another with her abilities to mate with and she would not kill *that* one until she was sure that he had given her a perfect son or daughter.

VaShena was suddenly looking at her. ShabNab had not seen her eyes open. What a beautiful set of eyes. She smiled at her daughter.

"Are you alright mommy?"

"Mommy will always be alright, dearest."

Scene Sixty Nine

"Something's wrong." muttered the Blade, tapping his right index finger on his desk. "He should have been here by now."

Suddenly, he surged to his feet and walked around the huge desk and stopped in front of the standing woman facing the desk. The Blade seemed to tower over her

Looking down at ShabNab he stated, "He has already *Smoked* at least one terrorist bomber since you made your drop. I have too many lucrative assignments for you. We are losing millions with you here. You have to make another bomb drop."

"No."

"No?" he said softly, dangerously. "You were ready to earlier, to smoke him out."

"That was then. This is now, sir. He won't come after me if he hasn't by now. He's probably heard the bomb drop was made by the *Personal Assassin* to the Blade of the Sword of Xandu. We need to have someone else do it and I will shadow them and either kill him or capture him, whatever your preference. Personally, I'd like to take him apart to see what makes him tick. It would be fun."

The Blade laughed and relaxed. "For a moment Mishy, I thought you might be scared. Silly of me, wasn't it? Alright, we'll do it your way. It *is* a good idea for many reasons. We don't want him killing our little immortal *Personal Assassin*, now do we? You'd be too hard to replace."

"I'm five foot nine barefoot. I weigh one hundred and forty eight pounds naked, of which only eight pounds is fat and you know where they are located. You've abused them enough, not that I'm complaining. No one, except you, has ever lifted me off the floor by them, carried me across the room by them and thrown me on my back. The last time it took a week for your finger indents to fill in and two weeks for the bruising to fade. I have killed a six hundred pound fighting gorilla bare handed. I'm not your *little* immortal *Personal Assassin*. I am your *deadly* immortal *Personal Assassin*."

"A week you say? We'll try for two weeks next time, *if there is a next time*. I think you're exaggerating on the eight pounds. That's four pounds each. I think it's more like two to three pounds each. Bye the way, I like what you did with the Senator. Do the same to *him*, only with Mr. Smoke, bring me his balls." He smiled. It was not a nice smile.

"I want to dry them out, have them gold plated and make earrings out of them as a gift for you. He will be our crowning achievement. You will wear them at all functions. I know you've had your nipples pierced also. I should, I had them pierced. Maybe I'll have you wear them hanging from them when you are here. Once word gets out that we *Smoked* Mr. Smoke, business should double within six months."

Smiling, ShabNab nodded. "Anything you say, sir. Anyone in particular you want to pick to do the drop?"

"You pick the man you want to drop the bomb. The Black Hand wants us to do one for them. Pick an Irishman. One we can afford to lose. Personally, I find the bombing of innocent civilians repulsive, but business is business. You have to go where the money is."

Snapping his fingers, he said. "Patrick O'Flaherty. Wasn't he one of the *two-some* you had the other night?"

"Yes he was. Not all that good either. Good choice. Want him to be the one?"

"Yes, I do. I'll give him the assignment and inform you of the particulars later. Take off your clothes and put them on the chair over there."

ShabNab disrobed immediately and placed her garments on the chair and returned to stand before him.

"At ease, Assassin." ShabNab put her hands behind her back and spread her legs shoulder width apart. The Blade walked around her slowly.

"Your clothes are a little wrinkled. I will have them pressed and brought to your room shortly."

Quicker than one would have expected from one of his bulk, his hand flashed forward with a resounding slap on the front of her hairless mound between her legs. It turned bright red. He then produced a pair of large golden bell earrings and handed them to her.

"Put them on." She put them through her nipple holes. "That is all. You are dismissed."

As ShabNab turned to go the bells tinkled musically. She made sure they continued to tinkle as she walked to the door.

As she reached the door, the Blade said, "I am angry that we have not killed Mr. Smoke by now. You have disappointed me, Mishy. If anyone looks at your red crotch you are to offer its services to them. Is that understood?"

"Yes."

"Yes what?"

"Yes sir."

"Or your chest."

"Yes sir."

"Fine. Fine. That will satisfy me. You know the rule. Only satisfy the clean ones. Stay clean. Cleanliness is next to godliness. I'll be in touch."

As ShabNab passed into the hall she noticed that it was changing of the guard. Men were everywhere.

ShabNab's crotch was a lot redder by the end of the second day. It had been many years since he had done that to her. But as she told her daughter, it was better to be *red* than *dead*.

Besides, she liked it, she said. She hadn't had a workout like that in years.

▲ ▲ ▲

Scene Seventy

Damon Gray stood alone.

He studied the silver triangle doorway in the TC. He had found out that only one with a ring could reach the key. Once activated, anyone could access the doorway until deactivated. The key could not be removed by anyone without a ring.

Anyone could go *through* the doorways. Both he and Hastings had put their hands through. No mechanical device could transmit or receive from the other side. Damon had tried all frequencies. Damon had learned everything he could from this side of the triangle.

"Can we return, Switch?" One pulse.

"Can we return safely?" Nothing.

"Is it safe on the other side?" Nothing.

"You don't know?" Nothing.

"You're not sure." One pulse.

"Should it be safe?" One pulse.

"Are there dangers that you know about?" One pulse.

"Are there dangers that you don't know about." Nothing.

"You are not sure." One pulse.

"You seem to know a lot about this. Is it over twenty five million years old?"

One pulse. "More than fifty million years?" Two Pulses.

"More than thirty million years?" Two pulses.

"Pulse once when I hit the right number. Twenty six, twenty seven, twenty eight…" pulse.

"Thanks. I'm not sure what that does for the situation. Do you know how old you are?" Two pulses.

"Are you over thirty million earth years old?" One Pulse.

"Over a billion earth years old?" One pulse.

"Holy …. Have the three of you ever been blended before?" Two Pulses.

"Are you from this universe?" Two pulses.

"So, you are from a different universe?" Two pulses.

"A different *realm* or *dimension*?" Two pulses.

"Are you each from different realms or Dimensions?" One Pulse.

"Are Golden and Garnet from your dimension?" Nothing.

"You don't know." One pulse.

"But two of you, the gold and the ruby, were on their fingers." One pulse.

"But you are not part of them?" Nothing.

"You're not sure?" Nothing.

Damon frowned. He wasn't asking the right questions. "You were part of them?" One pulse.

"You still are?" Nothing. The light clicked on in Damons head.

"I get it. They are no longer one. We three are now one. Are the three of you one?" One pulse. Pause. One pulse. Pause. One pulse.

"You are three separate and yet one?" One pulse.

"Can you be separated again?" Nothing.

"You don't know." One pulse.

"I notice that I can no longer seem to take you off. Can I?" Two pulses.

"Is this your doing?" Two pulses.

"Do you know whose doing it is?" Two pulses.

"Did you have to agree individually to it?" One pulse.

"Are you more than a Switch?" One pulse.

"You are now part of us?" Nothing.

"Separate but part of us, like Golden and Garnet are?" One pulse.

"What happens to us happens to you?" One pulse.

"Are you part of us for a reason?" Nothing.

"You don't know?" Nothing.

"Are you allowed to answer?" Nothing.

"Not right now?" Nothing.

"Can you override my will?" Two pulses.

"Are you all totally subservient to my will?" One pulse. Pause One pulse. Pause. One pulse.

"Thank you. All of you. Now let's take a walk through the triangle doorway, shall we? The silver one first?" One pulse.

Damon stepped through the silver triangle doorway.

▲ ▲ ▲

Scene Seventy One

"Dammit! ... Dammit! ...Dammit! That was a damn foolish thing to do, sir! You could have been killed." Hastings glared at his boss. "Did it even occur to you that you could have let me know first? I could have monitored something .... or done something...." He finished lamely.

Damon smiled.

"The rooms were safe, Hastings. Do you want to hear what I found or do you want to continue your tirade?"

"Sorry sir, but ... oh, nothing. What did you find out?" Hastings let out a sigh. "Tell me all about your expedition, sir."

"When I first walked through it shocked my system slightly, like vertigo, but not quite. It was a unique feeling. On the other side was a matching triangular room with no visible exit, except the one I came through. It was all silver, with a black floor and the walls were outlined in black. Like the one here. But this room wasn't empty. It was loaded with every kind of silver colored precious metal you could think of and more. There was art of a kind I have never seen before. There were goblets of every kind. The room was filled with a worlds worth of treasure. When I touched them with my left hand they felt real. When I touched them with my right hand they felt ... I guess the word is *'wrong'* somehow. *Real* but *'wrong'*."

Damon held up his right hand. Switch appeared, then disappeared.

"Switch was telling me something. I went to bring a goblet back through to test it when Switch pulsed rapidly. I didn't bring it through. It is probably a good thing. As I was walking back through the room, I *felt* something pull me. A *glowing* is as close as I can come to describing it. I headed towards it climbing over mounds of treasure to get to it. As I got closer the *glowing* feeling shrunk and intensified. When I reached it, it was nothing more than a plain mirror framed in a simple white gold or silver frame. To my eyes it didn't glow but to my other senses, it was almost blinding. When I touched it, the *glow* vanished! It was just a plain and simple mirror. When I looked into it I could see myself. When I looked at the treasure behind me in it, it wasn't there! I turned and looked. The treasure *was* there. The mirror just didn't show it." Damon smiled. Hastings was biting his tongue to keep from speaking. Damon continued.

"I looked again in the mirror and turned it to view the entire treasure. The room was not *entirely* empty! It did show *something*, Hastings. Floating off to one side was what looked to be an oval silver headband or necklace. Walking sideways and backwards, sometimes around and sometimes over the treasure, I finally located it. I had to dig down into the treasure to uncover it. It *was* an oval headband, crafted of a silver metal I could not immediately identify and with a large *pale milky, almost silver in color,* triangular stone set in it. The stone was dull and unremarkable looking."

Damon paused for a moment, lost in the memory.

"The plainness of it should have tweaked something in me. Nothing in the place was plain and simple *except* the mirror and headband. One thing I did notice. They both felt the same in both hands. Holding it with one hand I looked in the mirror as I set the band around my head. As I brought it down towards the head the band flipped over and settled on my forehead with the stone triangle point down. I had been holding the headband with my right hand. I knew Switch would warn me if it wasn't safe. It fit perfectly. There were no seams anywhere in it, even where the milky silver stone was. It seemed to be a part of it. I didn't realize it, until just now, but the metal or whatever it was, didn't feel cold on my skin. It was the same temperature as my brow. I looked at it in the mirror. It sat just over the eyebrow line, in my indent. The band was slightly wider than the silver gem stone, flaring around it flawlessly. As I looked in the mirror I saw the dull smoky silver stone change to a perfectly clear, brilliant diamond like stone. I looked into it through the mirror and could see no bottom to it and yet it was flawlessly clear. It was very freaky, Hastings. It was as if my skull was not behind it. It seemed like nothing was behind it. A clear universe of nothing." Damon paused again.

"I carefully put the mirror down to take off the headband. The moment my hand left it, the mirror vanished. Needless to say, I was astounded. The treasure was the *guard* of the headband. The mirror was the key to finding it. It would reflect nothing but the headband. Once found and placed on my brow properly it was no longer needed and vanished. Needless to say I was a little disgruntled. I reached up to take the headband off and view it, but it wasn't there either."

Hastings couldn't restrain himself. "Did you ever find it again?"

Damon smiled.

"Patience, my dear friend, patience. The quality of a story is in the telling."

Hastings laughed and visibly forced himself to relax.

"Continue, sir. I'll *try* to keep quiet."

"As you wish. Even though the mirror had shown nothing else in the room, I searched the room thoroughly anyway, just to be sure. I then came back and searched the other two rooms. They were identical except for the items. In the Gold Room all the treasure was in gold or encased in gold. The *finder* was a plain magnifying glass encircled in a plain gold casing that, again, showed nothing of the treasure but did show a wide *gold* colored bracelet with an embedded dull red colored triangle stone or metal. I retrieved it and went to put it on my left wrist but it wouldn't go. I then tried it over my right and it went over easily and shrunk to fit, just over my wrist bone perfectly, triangle point facing towards the elbow. I studied it under the magnifying glass. Again it matched the temperature of my body. The dull stone looked like it was part of the bracelet band. Somehow it didn't look metallic but *stonish*. I could see vague veins in it. As I was studying it I saw it change, as had the one over my eyes. It turned into a flawless, crystal clear ruby red in color. It then sunk under my skin and vanished. Holding the magnifying glass I walked through the *gateway* back, hoping *it* wouldn't vanish. No such luck. The magnifying glass vanished as I stepped through the *gate*. The Red Room had a wide *ruby red bracelet* that I found with a *ruby encased 'compass'* is the closest I can come to describing the instrument. The ruby bracelet was very similar to the other one. It was embedded with a golden colored stone. Again, as with the other two, it was not cold to the touch. As with the gold one, when it shrunk to fit just over my left wrist bone, the stone went a crystal clear golden color and vanished or sunk into my wrist. It faced the same way as the other. I had tried to put it on the other way but it wouldn't go." He paused for a moment to take a sip of his coffee.

"When I came back from the Red room I opened the Silver Door to double check things. As I approached the door, I saw my reflection with only the silver headband and clear *diamond like* stone on my brow. As you know we have never seen our reflections in the doorway before. I was stunned. I went back and did the same with the other doors. With the Red Door I saw my reflection with only the red bracelet on. The Gold Door showed me wearing only the golden wristband." Damon paused again, had a sip of his coffee and looked intently at Hastings.

"Then some weird things happened."

"What in the *hell* do you call *weird?* You don't think what you just told me is weird? If *that's* not weird ..." he saw the look in Damon's eyes. Sighing, he said softly, "Continue with the weird stuff, sir."

"If you remember, on the top of the triangle key handle there is a raised triangle set into it to let you know where the top is."

"Yes, I remember it."

"Well, I was a little freaked out and decided to shut the gateway down until I could sort it out in my mind. When I turned the key to the off position, my thumb pressed on the raised triangle. Whether it was an accident or not, I don't know. I *feel* it was *not* an accident. I think it ..." Damon saw the look in Hastings eyes.

"Sorry, I got a little off track, didn't I? When I pressed the stud, the key pulled down and the triangle turned black. *BTB* Hastings, blacker than black. As I approached the doorway, I saw myself with the ring, headband and wristbands.

It was weird to see myself floating in a sea of black. I reached up with both hands to see if the headband was really there. It was, but only for a moment. I touched and felt it with both hands. When my two hands touched it, I saw all three bands run together and sink into my flesh. I could feel it. Not restricting, sinking and blending. Quickly I tried to grab the headband, but I was too late. All that I could see in the *BTB* mirror doorway was the three triangles. One clear triangle on my forehead, one golden yellow on my left wrist and one ruby red on my right wrist. I walked up very close, arms still up and triangles facing the black doorway and used my *close-up vision* on the one on my forehead. The three looked identical in size. I wasn't sure I wanted to leave to get any instruments. The three triangles looked different in the BTB doorway. I could see them clearer. They each gave off a glow. As I looked closely I saw a smaller matching colored triangle inside each one and a smaller one inside of it. It went on endlessly. They were each turned so that their corners were in the middle of the bigger triangles wall line. It almost looks like an eye. A triangular eye. Even the clear one. It didn't look *empty* anymore." He refilled his coffee cup and continued.

"Remember I said identical?"

Hastings nodded.

"In size, you said."

"Correct. At the center of the *clear* triangle, in the middle of my forehead, is a *silvery* triangle pinpoint of light. In the middle of the *red* triangle, on the back and behind my right wrist, is a *ruby* triangle pinpoint of light, and in center of the *golden yellow* triangle, on the back and behind my the left wrist, a *golden* triangle pinpoint of light. *Brilliant* is the closest word that comes to mind that really describes them. *Dazzling* doesn't come close. It is like they are miniature triangular suns."

"Can you see them without the *BTB* doorway? Can I?" blurted Hastings?

Damon laughed at the outburst. He knew that Hastings was bursting with questions and was trying to hold them in till the end of the story.

"Patience, my friend. Patience for just a bit longer. The tale is almost ended." He paused again to gather his thoughts.

"Where was I? Oh yes, I walked through the *BTB* doorway."

Hastings went white!

"You what? *Again?* Without testing it? Without having me there to *help*? Without …" Hastings was beside himself with anger. Speechless for a moment.

Damon was silent as his friend pulled himself together. He had *never* seen Hastings so upset before. He knew that Hastings was obsessive about protecting him.

"Oh … *fuck it.*" Hastings looked shocked at his own outburst. "Sorry sir, please continue with the story."

Damon could not help it. He erupted with laughter. Hastings turned red, then seeing the humor in it, started laughing also. When they calmed down, Damon continued.

"Relax, Hastings. I knew that Switch would warn me if there was danger. If she doesn't know, she will pulse a danger signal to me. When I stepped through, I entered into *Elseware*."

Hastings forgot his anger and embarrassment.

"Holy …... *Elseware?*"

Damon nodded.

"Does that mean that anyone can go to it? Could I?"

"I don't know, Hastings. I *think* you can on your own, after the first time, but if not, I can always take you. It seems that anything directly attached to me will go through the gates or doorways."

"Great! When can we go, sir?"

"*After* I finish my story, Hastings!" Damon said gently.

Hastings smiled.

"Yes, sir. I know sir. Knowledge is power. Sorry, sir. Please continue."

"After many months of study, I found out the BTB doorway can take an *Adept* to any*where* or any*when* they want to go, but it seems that they must have been there before. I was either *thinking* of *Elseware*, or it *popped into my mind,* as I stepped through the first time. I rather think it was the latter. It can't take the *Adept* where they've never been or can't visualize perfectly. I found that I am an *Adept*."

Hastings nodded his understanding.

Damon paused.

"Let me backtrack and side track a bit. In *Elseware* I didn't need to eat or sleep. The months of study were really years and years. I had *mental* or psychic *voices* come to me and teach me. They are like Switch, Golden and Garnet. Older than time itself. They spoke telepathically, yet in distinctly different languages. I understood them and conversed in their language. A unique experience. My mathematical *ability* allows me to learn languages at phenomenal speed, but this was instantaneous. I thought I was very gifted. *I'm not,* compared to what is out there. When my parents manipulated my genetic structure, they created something that had not been created before Hastings. I guess I created something of a Dimensional, Interdimensional, Intradimensional *shock wave.* The voices were interested in me. I'm *different.* They taught me a lot. They took me to the *next level.*" Damon paused for a moment and smiled.

Hastings looked startled.

"Time flows differently there, Hastings. I know I was only gone a couple of days here, but many, many months passed in *Elseware.* I had a heck of a time resetting my personal computer watch when I got back. It did not want to believe me. I finally had to hook it up to Mac. Only then did it believe and allow the changes. My next watch is going to be much more adaptable and flexible."

"How can you make a watch more flexible? Isn't that like military intelligence … impossible?"

Damon Gray laughed. So did Hastings. The joke was not that funny, but it broke the tension between the two of them.

When the laughter died, Hastings spoke.

He explained to Damon that the reason that he had been so upset and reacted the way he did, was that he had been almost physically ill when Damon told him what he had done. He didn't care if Damon got into trouble in *this* world. He could *find* him. He could *help* him. He took his oath to himself to protect the Gray family to the *nth* *degree*. But he couldn't help Damon Gray, if he couldn't find him. And he couldn't, if Damon was in another world or dimension.

In the simple words of a soldier, Hastings shared this with Damon.

Damon was shocked at the revelation. He had no idea that Hastings had sworn that oath to himself, after his father had saved his life. He told Hastings that he was freed from that obligation.

"I'm sorry sir, but I really don't have a choice in the matter. I didn't make the oath to you or your family and the person I made it to will hold me to it, until my dying breath." He smiled. "Now…. on with the story, sir."

▲ ▲ ▲

Scene Seventy Two

D amon continued.

"I was told that a creation *like mine* was predicted, or foretold. These beings, Golden and Garnet, that now are a part of me, could not live *or even exist* anywhere else. Just think, Hastings, they and the triangles have been waiting for someone or something *like me* for at least *twenty eight million years!* And that is just on *this* world's time. Who knows how long they have been there. Other worlds have had access to the Triangle Rooms for much, much longer. None of the voices seem to know what my destiny is, or even if I have one, which is good. That means I can choose my own."

Hastings looked at Damon hard. Suddenly he smiled.

"Are you joking, sir?"

"About what?"

"Oh hell, I don't know! Any of it? *None* of this seems real or possible." Hastings shrugged helplessly. "My mind and body's in shock."

Damon held up his arms, the top of his wrists facing Hastings.

Hastings was still smiling when both of Damon's eyes widened slightly. The right eye turned a swirling bottomless blood red orb with no pupil. His left eye became a slow moving liquid gold cat's eye. The clear triangle between his eyes seemed to be devouring him as did the golden and red triangles on his wrists.

Only Switch seemed non-threatening.

"Okay, okay, I believe you. Turn it off for god's sake. *You are scaring me, Damon!*" The last was said as a warning.

Damon instantly returned to normal.

"I'm sorry Hastings. I thought a demonstration would validate my statements. It was thoughtless. I did not foresee your reaction."

Hastings breathed a sigh of relief.

"I'm alright, sir. I know....I know... you told me. You warned me." He took a deep calming breath.

"Okay, do it again."

Damon did.

Hastings leaned forward and looked closely at the triangles. He then turned his attention to the red and gold eyes. After a few minutes he sat back and nodded.

"Hello Golden. Hello Garnet."

"Hello Hastings." Replied two distinct and separate voices out of Damon's mouth. They were each Damons voice, but with slight variations.

Each eye looked at him, blinked separately, alternately, like the separate beings they were, and then returned to their normal silver color.

"That was awesome, sir! You can't blame me for thinking that you were joking or exaggerating, can you?"

"Of course not, Hastings. If you were to tell me, I wouldn't believe you. Logic dictates that what I just told you and showed you, *can't exist*. I am not going to tell you what I can now do. It would blow your mind. What I would like you to remember is that I am still Damon Gray and your friend."

"I have never doubted that sir. For a moment, though, I thought you might have been *possessed* by them, if you know what I mean. When I saw you weren't, I was fine. If there is any more you want to tell me, now is the time. Right now, I think I'll believe anything you tell me."

Smiling, Damon said, "That is all I wanted to tell you, *for now.*"

"For now?"

"For now."

"Well, if that's the case, where do we go from here, sir?"

"Back to work, soldier."

Hastings smiled. *This* he understood. A *Smoke Mission*.

▲ ▲ ▲

Scene Seventy Three

"Michael, where is my white garter belt? You were wearing it last."

"I was *what?*" called Michael from the bathroom.

"Around your head, remember? Where is it? It's my favorite."

"Oh, that one! I put it in your lingerie drawer. The right one, if I'm not mistaken."

"I found it. Thank you, sweetheart." Sylvia called out from the bedroom.

▲ ▲ ▲

"That's the one you don't wear panties with, isn't it?" Michael asked later, as they were waiting for Damon to arrive for dinner at Coutances.

"Silly!" she smiled at him, giving him a kiss, "I haven't worn panties since we got married."

"I knew that!" he said quickly. Too quickly.

"Sure you did, sweetheart." She stood in her white formfitting evening minidress and custom made, totally clear, high heeled sandals.

"I'm glad you had this designed and made for me. I love how the lace trim at the top and hem snap on and off. I can't wear it out, but I'm dying to see what kind of reaction Mr. Smoke will have."

"Mr. Smoke?" Michael asked puzzled.

"I meant Mr. Gray. I mean, Dr. Gray. Sorry. I've been reading and listening to the latest on Mr. Smoke to bring Damon up to date."

"Who said you couldn't wear that dress out? Do you have any idea what I paid to have that dress made to your exact measurements and my specifications? I'm supposed to be an ex-playboy, remember? No one knows I'm the head of A.T.C.U. Can't have people saying I'm married to a prude can we?"

"Really?"

"Really, darling. The more daring the better, as far as I'm concerned. I want every red blooded man in the world lusting after my wife."

"I hear and obey, oh mighty master. Gee, being married to you is going to be a lot more entertaining than I expected. Oh, don't look at me that way. I meant that I would be *thrilled* to play that part. Just remember, you gave your approval and encouragement. I'll be right back, don't go away." Sylvia smiled and left the room.

When she returned, the two inch lace hem was missing off the top and bottom of her minidress. The top of her dress now just barely covered her nipples, the hem *just* covering her private area. Her curled, thick golden blond hair had been let down to drape over her bare shoulders and down her back. Her large full lips had been outlined subtly to make them pop out.

Michael whistled. Or tried to.

"Wow!" was all he could say.

"Why, thank you, kind sir. I call it my micro-mini, man manager, look."

"It works for me. There's the doorbell. Damon is here. Let's see his reaction."

▲ ▲ ▲

Damon loved the *Coutances*. Michael and Sylvia gave him a tour after dinner.

Damon asked question after question about the place. He said he liked it almost as well as Blackstone and if he had seen it first, he would have had a hard time making a choice between the two. Sylvia laughed and said that he probably would *just* have purchased *both of them.*

Damon said very matter of factly that, *yes,* he probably would have. Sylvia looked shocked. Damon then laughed. Sylvia and Michael laughed also, but Sylvia didn't know for sure what she was laughing about.

In bed, later that night she asked Michael. "Do you really think he would have bought both of them?"

"I don't know, darling. I really don't. Nothing that man does is normal."

"He's gay! He's *got* to be!"

"What makes you say that?"

"When he first came in, he took my hand and complimented me on my good triceps and calf development since we saw him last."

"What am I missing here? Don't you work out so that people will notice your great physique?"

"Of course I do, as do you, but that is *not* the point. Whether you realized it or not, I had removed every piece of jewelry except for my wedding rings. I was wearing an almost see through, skin tight, white dress that showed off every curve of my body. You had the dress designed specifically for my body. You had it designed specifically to *accentuate,*" Sylvia giggled as she tried to imitate Michael saying '*accentuate*' in a British accent, "remember, sweetheart, that's the word you used. You said you wanted the dress to *accentuate, not* crush, my nipples because they are so large, thick and stick out so far. I made sure that my nipples were erect and engorged. I removed my garter belt and nylons so there would be no lines distracting his eye. I made sure I stood in front of a lamp when he first came in so that he could see that I had no underwear on. That's just *a few* of the things I did, when I left and took off the lace trim, and then he had the *nerve* to compliment me on my calf and triceps development! You walked

320

around with a boner all evening. With him, nothing! He *has* to be gay."

"A *boner?* Where *do* you Americans come up with your words? And thank you for noticing, darling. I agree with you on everything except the last. I'm not convinced."

"How can you lay there and say that?"

"He never looked at my *boner* once. And he didn't compliment me on it either. Besides, he might be under endowed. He might have had a *boner* and you couldn't see it. Or, you didn't turn him on." He finished innocently.

"You are impossible! Sometimes I can tell when you are joking and sometimes I can't. Maybe you're right though. He should have complimented your *boner.* It *was* impressive. Even the maids noticed. Did I ever tell you that you're the only one to ever totally fill me?" Syl smiled at her husband and continued smugly.

"I bet that's the *only* reason you married me. I was the *only* one who could take all of you easily. Right?"

Lord Brighton laughed and kissed his wife. She kissed him back.

"Well?" she prompted.

"Well what?"

"Am I right?"

"Well, I must say that it *really, really is* the *only* reason I married you." he responded solemnly.

Sylvia laughed delightedly,

"Though you are not the only one. There was one other."

Sylvia sobered.

"Really? I thought I was huge in that department. Who was it?"

"ShabNab. She took me easily and with room to spare."

"Really?"

"M'hm" Michael agreed as he kissed her neck.

"Was she as good as me?" She asked innocently.

"No one is as good as you, Syllie." He told her honestly.

She smiled her beautiful smile.

"And you call *me* Syllie. You know what I meant. Getting back to Damon, he didn't seem to notice my outfit or comment on it."

"The staff hardly noticed your new outfit, darling. Are *they* gay?" he teased.

"No. That's because I *always* walk around naked when you are not around. The French are *much* more sophisticated that way *and* passionate." She teased back, loftily.

"Maybe you should do it when I'm around also." He kissed her again.

"Maybe I will. But don't be surprised if the staff looks nervous at first, knowing you're watching them look at me."

He touched her. She arched her back, thrusting up her chest to him.

"Poppycock. I'll be too busy watching you myself." They both laughed and kissed.

"Aren't you going to close the bedroom door?" she whispered.

"Do you want to me to continue or do you want me to stop and go close it?" he continued to touch and kiss her.

"Ohh....... Hush and kiss my lips."

▲ ▲ ▲

Scene Seventy Four

Daylight found Damon working out in their gym when Lord and Lady Brighton joined him.

Afterwards they showered, dressed up and went into the city for an early lunch.

It was a little out of the way place that Sylvia had heard about. They were seated in the back, by a fireplace, enjoying a French coffee after their meal, when three men walked into the place.

You could tell at a glance from their faces that they were not there for the food. Sylvia, Michael and Damon were the only patrons at the time. The lunch hour rush had not started yet. The men said something to the owner and then headed back to their table.

Seeing them approach, Damon excused himself and rose to go to the *men's room*. He didn't have time. The three men produced silenced automatic weapons and, in French, told them to empty their pockets.

The owner looked sick. He went to put his hands under the counter when one of the three, who had been watching him out of the corner of his eye, shot him quickly three times through the chest. He then turned his weapon back to the three.

"I said, empty your pockets." He said again, this time in heavily accented English.

They did as requested. The leader, the one who had shot the owner, looked at their identification and turned to Damon.

"One of you owns the Coutances. The owner told us." He motioned toward the dead man. "Are you the one that owns the Coutances?"

"*No.*" Damon replied in French.

Turning to Michael, he asked the same question. Michael didn't hesitate.

"Yes, I am."

"Sign this and you will die quick. Do not and we will rape and kill your beautiful blond wife and do the same to you and your friend, only much slower." The leader placed a document on the table.

Michael's head automatically bent to read the piece of paper and the leader started to hit him with the barrel of his gun.

The gun never made it to Michael's head. All three gunmen fell to the ground as if pole axed. Without a sound.

Michael and Sylvia could only stare as Damon bent down and removed his star cufflinks and belt buckle from the bandit's throats. He wiped them off quickly and expertly and replaced them. He then searched the corpses clothing and removed everything of value they had, identification, money etc. Without pausing, he quickly and thoroughly wiped off all the cutlery and dishes that they had touched and picked up all the documents on the table and tucked the dead bandit's documents into his inside jacket pocket. He handed Michael and Sylvia their personal belongings back.

All in the space of less than a minute.

He then turned and said to the two of them calmly.

"I think it is time to go. Don't run. Walk normally."

As they passed the owner, Damon reached down to confirm that the man was really dead and then took their slip, containing their food order, out of his apron pocket.

In its place, he put the money that he had taken from the bandits, which was a thick wad. He then picked up the phone with a napkin, placed it on the counter and dialed the emergency police number.

Calmly they left the building.

▲ ▲ ▲

Back at the Coutances, the Brighton's and Damon were sitting by the pool, sun tanning.

Nobody had talked on the way home. Damon drove. When they arrived, Michael suggested that they change and meet in thirty minutes at the pool.

Damon asked for fifteen more to finish cleaning his cufflinks and belt buckle.

Forty five minutes later they were all at the pool.

"I had a life insurance policy placed on the café owner's life for a million dollars through one of my companies and back dated it two years. His family will not do without." Damon said by way of opening the conversation. "Last year he was diagnosed with cancer and couldn't get insurance. I was informed that he only had months to live."

Sylvia looked hard at Damon.

Damon smiled back at her.

"What happened back there, Damon?"

Damon placed the document that Michael was ordered to sign, on the table.

"It seems that there is a person who was not happy that a *foreigner* bought this property. He lives just down the street, from the name and address on this bill of sale. A Monsieur Rameau Balenvenue. An older man in his forties. Not in the best of health."

"Forty is not old!" Sylvia exclaimed.

"When your health is poor, it is." Damon replied.

▲ ▲ ▲

Scene Seventy Five

An hour later the door bell rang. Damon excused himself and went inside.

A few minutes later, a man in a dull brown suit followed the butler to the pool.

"I said you were entertaining sir, and that you have been home all day, but Inspector Noirvouis insisted on interrupting you. Something about an accident down the street. A Monsieur Balenvenue, I think he said."

"That is fine Napoleon. Thank you."

"Should I bring him a drink, Monsieur Brighton?"

"Of course, Napoleon. Inspector, what would you like to drink? Please have a seat."

"A brandy would be nice. No ice, no water." The Inspector spoke in excellent English.

"Right away, sir." Napoleon answered in English. He left and was back within seconds with the drink.

The Inspector sniffed it appreciatively and took a small sip.

"Ahhh, that is a fine brandy. Thank you Lord and Lady Brighton." They both smiled and nodded.

"You speak excellent French, *Monsieur Brighton.*"

"Thank you Inspector. So does my wife."

"What in the world is going on?" Asked a shocked nasally American voice. "Did I hear correctly? Did I hear him say there was an accident concerning one of the neighbors? Inspector Noirvouis?"

The inspector turned and watched a balding middle aged man approach. He had a bit of a paunch and a terrible overbite and walked splayed footed. Pushing his sunglasses up, he tightened the beach robe around himself self consciously as if embarrassed by his physique beside Michael and Sylvia.

"Yes there was. And what, may I ask, is *your* name, monsieur?"

"Franklin Stone. Most folks just call me Franklin. You can too, if you want. I've been trying all day to get these nice folks to sell my employer this place, but they're not having any of it. Maybe they should. Was he robbed? Mugged? Raped? What a neighborhood. I might have to suggest to my employer to lower the offering price."

"No, no, monsieur Stone. The man died trying to fix his roof. He apparently was very frugal and fell to his death. Nobody saw it and I wondered if any of you had been out recently."

"How recently?" enquired Franklin Stone.

"Within the last two hours or so?"

"Well, I'm afraid that lets us out. We've been here all day. I can vouch for them if you need me to. Swear on a bible, sign a paper or whatever you want. This is exciting!"

"No, no, that will not be necessary." Finishing off his drink, he stood. Lord and Lady Brighton rose also. The inspectors eyes popped when Sylvia arched her back slightly, thrusting out her huge chest at him and reached out her hand to him. He took it in his. Sweat appeared on his face. He smiled and kissed her hand.

"It is *so* nice to meet the local law enforcement." She cooed. "I hope we meet again under better circumstances."

"I look forward to it!" He announced. Turning to Michael, he gave a small bow and said it was a pleasure to meet him, and that he was sorry to have disturbed them.

As he was leaving, he stopped, turned and said that they *shouldn't* sell the Coutances. He said it was a wonderful neighborhood. He looked at Sylvia when he said that.

Michael assured him that he wouldn't. As the Inspector was leaving, he could hear the annoying American trying to change their mind.

'Nice couple.' He thought, *'I hope we get more like them to move in around here.'*

▲ ▲ ▲

When the inspector had left the property, Napoleon came and informed them.

When the butler had gone, Damon excused himself and returned moments later as himself.

Michael and Sylvia watched him as he approached. He moved like a hunting beast, graceful and perfectly poised.

"Well, that was fun. What shall we do next?" Damon said brightly. Then he smiled.

Sylvia smiled back. A brilliant smile. So did Michael.

"Well, that was fun. What shall we do next?" Sylvia mimicked him and started to laugh. Soon they were all laughing.

When they had calmed down, Michael said to Damon, "Thank you for saving our lives. I shouldn't have looked down. It was a normal reflex and I couldn't control it in time. Thank you."

"Yes Damon, thank you." said his wife, "And you handled that Inspector beautifully. I was sure sweating there for awhile. I was worried that he could smell it which is why I arched away from him when I gave him my hand. Well, I'm going skinny dipping to get rid of the stink and I'm not going to ruin my white bathing suit with the chlorine water. Anyone care to race me across the pool?"

Without waiting for a reply, she pulled her long thick golden blond hair back and slipped a rubber band around it, shed her swimsuit and dove into the pool in one fluid movement. She surfaced to see both men joining her.

Damon still failed to react to her.

▲ ▲ ▲

Scene Seventy Six

"You just had to find out, didn't you?" Michael teased his wife, later that night, after their love making.

"Well, you did lie to me! I had to check him out." She snuggled his neck and nibbled his earlobe.

"What do you mean I lied to you? About what?"

"He's not what you said. He's much smaller than preadolescent. How does he pee out of it, without spraying everything? He couldn't possibly get it out far enough to *not* pee his pants. He must squat to pee. *I'm* bigger down there than he is. And I couldn't see any testicles or sack. And he's as bald down there as I am."

Michael grinned. "I don't know whether he squats to pee, but I do agree with you on the rest. *This* time I *was* looking."

He pulled a small digital camera from under the pillow.

"Now I've told you more than once, you've got ten years to stop taking pictures of my naked body!" Sylvia announced indignantly.

"Just documenting our marriage memories, darling. Pictures to show our grandchildren."

"Grandchildren?"

"Absolutely. I *definitely* don't want *children*."

"Oh, well that's different. *Fifteen* years then." Sylvia said as she smiled and posed.

▲ ▲ ▲

Afterwards, Sylvia went serious.

"That wasn't the first time he's killed, was it?" she asked softly, lying cuddled in his arms.

"No, it wasn't. He's a pro. It didn't faze him a bit. He rose when he saw them approaching and stood in a position to do what he did. He calmed us down, cleaned everything and walked us out of the restaurant in record time. I'm pleasantly surprised that you didn't react to those three hitmen's killing."

Sylvia snuggled closer. "I've seen a lot of violent death." she said quietly. "As you know, my parents died when I was twelve, in a white water rafting accident. I was with them. My aunts were killed by a drunk driver, when they were driving home after celebrating my twenty first birthday with me. They were the wild and crazy partying spinsters that took me in and raised me, after my parent's death. They were the last of my family. I told you I worked on a ranch, during school breaks, when I was younger. Remember?" Michael nodded. She was silent for a moment, remembering.

"I've seen cowboys break their necks, trying to ride horses or bulls. I've helped with the castrating, killing and butchering of the steers and cows. I've even survived two bank hold ups, one where people got shot. For some reason, death has never affected me much. Even when friends died, I just accepted it. It is just a part of life. Those three hitmen were just *meat* to me. I know I'm different that way. I don't like innocent young children hurt though. That upsets me. I *was* happy for the café owner though."

Lord Brighton looked at her, startled. "Happy?"

"Yes. I was happy when Damon told us that he had him insured. And the money in the apron. Those were wonderful things he did …. but," she paused, then continued in a softer tone, "he killed our neighbor, Balenvenue, didn't he Mickey?"

"Yes Syl, he did. He made it look like an accident, but he did it. I have a file on Monsieur Rameau Balenvenue. He is, excuse me, *was* forty two and in superb physical condition. A black belt in many arts. Fancied himself as a bad man. Loaded with daddy's money. His parents died under mysterious and suspicious circumstances. He was the *only* heir. He was the main suspect, but nothing was ever proven. He was never married. He'd been arrested several times, on assault charges. Some on women. No convictions. I make it a policy to know who our neighbors are. The reports infer a whole lot more, but no proof. I don't know *how* Damon found out his address so fast. I think he really must be a wizard."

Sylvia started to say something, but Michael raised his hand and continued, "One moment dear. In my professional opinion, to protect our lives, Damon entered Balenvenue's house, broke his neck, carried him up to the roof and threw him off. I checked with Napoleon and he was not seen leaving the building or returning. I think he ran all the way over there and back. The car mileage hasn't changed."

"But isn't the house three miles away?"

"Almost exactly, why? Oh, I see. You are wondering if he could have exited unseen, run three miles, kill a man, carry him to the roof and throw him off, then climb down and run three miles back, enter unseen, change and meet us at the pool, all within forty five minutes. The answer is, *I couldn't do it*, but somehow Damon did. You saw him swim. That man puts Olympic swimmers to shame."

"Should we ask him?"

"Is there any need to? He saved our lives. We both know it. He knows it. I don't want him to have to lie to us, do you?"

"I see what you mean. No, no I don't." She said quietly. "I loved his disguise with the inspector. I almost laughed it was so real." Michael nodded in agreement.

Kissing her husband softly, she rolled over and said, "Goodnight, my love. Pleasant dreams."

"Goodnight, Syllie."

"You know Michael, I'm glad Damon Gray is our friend. I know we can't thank him for what he did down the street, but I'd sure like to. My god, think for a minute! If we *had* called the police, there would have been an investigation, and Balenvenue would have had us killed, or at least tried to, by the time the trial took place. Damon cleaned up the situation completely." Rolling back over to face him, she asked, "Would you have done the same for him?"

"I'd like to think so Syl, but I'm not sure. I might have turned it over to the local authorities to handle. My position might have dictated those actions. I owe him more than I can say. Not only did he save our lives, he protected my position as Head of A.T.C.U.. What he did was so final. I love it. I wish the A.T.C.U. could do that. Only the Gray Ghost and Mr. Smoke can get away with what he did."

He looked over at her. She was already falling asleep. Michael ran his fingers through her sun streaked golden locks. "Pleasant dreams to you also. I love you, my wonderful, Syllie wife." he whispered. He picked up his camera.

"Mmmm," she was asleep.

'Click.' He took a picture of her face.

▲ ▲ ▲

Michael was having breakfast with Damon when Sylvia walked into the room. She walked over and kissed both men lightly on the cheek.

"Good morning. My, I slept like a baby last night. Must have been the swim. Why didn't you wake me when you got up, darling?"

"I was going to, but you looked so peaceful, I couldn't. Breakfast is ready if you are."

"You are wonderful. I am ravenous. Bring it on."

▲ ▲ ▲

They spent the day touring the antique shops in the area. That evening, after dinner, Damon left to fly back to Blackstone.

After they had made their goodbyes and Damon was turning to walk towards Hastings, who was waiting in the car, Sylvia leaned forward and said softly, "Thank you for taking care of Monsieur Rameau Balenvenue, Mister Smoke."

Damon continued his turn and walked to the car, as if he hadn't heard. When he reached the vehicle he turned, smiled and waved and got into the car.

As it disappeared into the night, Michael turned to his wife and enquired incredulously, "Mr. Smoke? You meant Gray Ghost didn't you? That's twice you've done that. It's a good thing he didn't hear, it could have proved embarrassing if he took you seriously."

She gave her husband a kiss on the cheek. "Yes, dearest." She smiled.

They turned and walked back inside.

▲ ▲ ▲

Scene Seventy Seven

As they raced through the night traffic, Damon chuckled in the back seat.

Hastings glanced at his boss in the rear view mirror.

"What is so funny, sir?"

"She knows Hastings. I don't know how, but she knows."

Hastings was navigating the streets to the private landing site, after leaving the Brighton residence.

"There is absolutely *no way* she could know, sir. I'd say she was just teasing, or maybe just testing a theory." Hastings replied.

Damon shook his head slightly.

"No, she said it softly, *surely*, Hastings. I saw that Michael reacted slightly to it. I think, he thought she meant the *Gray Ghost*."

He smiled slightly at the memory and continued.

"I'm glad I didn't react and pretended not to hear. That will make her wonder. *Did I hear or didn't I?* If I didn't, it didn't matter. If I did and didn't react, I might have thought she meant the Gray Ghost. Or it could mean that I am *Mr. Smoke*, the *professional terrorist assassin* that she thinks I am. One thing is for sure. She doesn't mind if I *am* Mr. Smoke. I don't scare Sylvia, or Michael, for that matter."

Hastings navigated a few more hairpin turns at breakneck speed before he said anything more. When he hit a straight stretch, he turned and looked back at Damon.

"Does that mean we *won't* have to kill them to protect your secret identity, sir?"

Damon said nothing.

Hastings head returned to face the traffic.

"Well never mind that, fill me in on the skinny dipping race. The whole staff was talking about it."

"I won." Damon said dryly.

Hastings looked in frustration at Damon in the rearview mirror.

"Thanks," he muttered, "now I know the whole story. I feel so much better. Thanks for keeping me in *the loop*, sir."

"You're welcome, Hastings. Anytime. Just ask."

They both laughed and Damon brought him up to date.

▲ ▲ ▲

Scene Seventy Eight

The prostitute had just left. She hadn't satisfied him. No one had, since ShabNab.

Sitting alone in his penthouse suite overlooking downtown Calgary, Alberta, Canada, Patrick O'Flaherty did not feel right. All his senses and instincts were screaming. A good assassin has a sixth sense and trusts it implicitly. It is what keeps him alive in dangerous situations. Patrick O'Flaherty was a good assassin. Not the best, but good. His sixth sense was top notch though. It had saved his life on many occasions where better and more talented assassins had perished.

Patrick had not wanted to take the assignment to make the bomb drop with all the media hoopla about Mr. Smoke, but he had. Greed and professional pride got the best of him. He hadn't been given a job for awhile and he felt that the offer was just too good to pass up. He also wanted to prove, to the Blade, that he was still a force to be reckoned with. As with all the Sword of Xandu assassins, O'Flaherty was in top physical form.

The drop had gone off without a hitch. He had managed a coup. He had planted the bomb in the Royal Palace, in England, through a series of visits, disguised as different people. Each time through, he brought with him a different piece of the bomb. It had killed a tour group and a number of palace guards.

337

The Blade congratulated him personally. He said that the Black Hand was ecstatic. They even gave the Sword of Xandu a bonus for the job, which he passed on to Patrick. The Blade said Patrick got the whole bonus because he deserved it. Patrick believed it. He had never been paid so much money for a job. He told the Blade that he was retiring.

Patrick O'Flaherty was forty four years old. He had been putting money away for years and this was the nest egg he had been waiting for. The Blade praised Patrick heartily and wished him well. He told him to tell all his colleagues about his bonus, which he agreed to and did. The Blade finished by telling him that he was always welcome to come back and that good men were hard to find, but it didn't feel right to O'Flaherty. Some piece of the puzzle didn't fit.

For one thing, the Blade didn't praise people heartily. Also, it had been too easy for him to retire. He knew that the Blade always let his assassins quit whenever they wanted and always welcomed them back, but usually he tried to talk them out of it. Many times he had succeeded. Word spread that he tried to keep everyone and, if not, would always welcome them back.

Many years before, shortly after the current Blade had first assumed the title and taken power, one of his retirees talked when he shouldn't have. It was said that the Blade had paid handsomely to be alone with the man that a certain government agency had locked away in a safe house. They thought he just wanted to scare him. The results were publicized around the world. He had reporters there within minutes of leaving the building. He had agreed to go in without weapons. With his bare hands, he had literally torn the man apart, limb from limb.

You could retire from the Sword of Xandu, but you couldn't talk. Nobody had since.

Patrick O'Flaherty rechecked the penthouse security system. He checked every room. His building was on a high hill just minutes from the downtown core. It was a circular building thirty stories high. His was the top floor. Three quarters of his suite was enclosed.

One quarter, the balcony, was exposed to the elements but could be enclosed with the touch of a button. There was also a ten foot wide balcony or walkway around the building. They were on each floor, serving as balconies for the apartment condos below. He did his runs every morning around the building on his balcony. As he ran he would look at the panoramic view. On a clear day, the mountains to the west looked so close he could walk to them in ten minutes, even though he knew that they were eighty or so kilometers away.

His elevator was in the center of his suite. The floor plan was an open concept. He'd designed it himself. He didn't want anyone coming upon him unawares. He returned to the fireplace and sat before the fire.

"She didn't satisfy you, did she?" asked a soft, husky feminine voice behind him.

Patrick O'Flaherty rolled out of the couch, spinning as he did so, a gun almost magically appearing in his hand.

There was nobody there. He spun around quickly taking in the whole room. Nobody.

"Put your gun away lover. I'm not going to show myself while your finger is on that hair trigger."

"ShabNab?"

"Who else, Patty Cakes?"

He slowly lowered the gun and took his finger off the trigger. ShabNab walked around the elevator and into the room. She was dressed in a virgin white, form fitting dress that came to her knees. She wore white high heeled shoes and an oversized matching purse. The dress had designs of every type cut out of it, showing bare flesh beneath. He knew she was wearing makeup but he couldn't see it. Whatever she had done with it was spectacular. He thought that she was beautiful before. This took her to a whole new realm. Patrick O'Flaherty's breath caught in his throat. It took him a moment to recover.

"I take it I pass inspection?"

"How the hell did you get in here? My security system is supposed to be foolproof."

"Surely you knew that I was an assassin also, didn't you?"

"I thought you were, but I wasn't sure. I have only heard of *one* of your exploits. I had heard that you killed the father of your daughter and that he was supposed to be pretty good. Again that was many years ago. I thought, until the other night, that you were the Blades woman. There has been talk about you, but all of it has been questions. No answers. No one seems to know anything about you."

Seeing that she was not going to tell him how she got in, he kept his finger close to the trigger. He forced a smile.

"Is this a business or pleasure visit?"

"If it was business, do you think I would be dressed like this?" She spread her arms and did a slow pirouette. This time he smiled for real and put his gun away.

▲ ▲ ▲

Patrick O'Flaherty awoke naked and alone to find himself tied spread eagle on his own bed. He tested his bonds but only managed to tighten the knots slightly.

He stopped trying and lay remembering the previous evening.

It went beyond his wildest dreams. He had never been so satisfied. ShabNab had done things to him that he had never heard of, much less experienced. She had completely drained him, to the point of complete exhaustion. He had almost passed out. Afterward, they had shared a nightcap and he had gone to sleep.

She must have spiked his drink.

It didn't make sense. If she was going to kill him, she had plenty of opportunity. What else could it be?

"You are my bait for Mr. Smoke."

Patrick jumped as if stung. ShabNab appeared in the doorway.

"Excuse me? Can you read my thoughts?"

"No. I would wonder what I was doing tied up and not dead also. Man, you slept most of the day away, you must have been tired. Did I satisfy you completely last night, Patty Cakes?"

"You *know* you did!"

ShabNab smiled radiantly. "Good! Now, as we await the arrival of Mr. Smoke, you are going to satisfy *me*."

▲ ▲ ▲

Scene Seventy Nine

It was four in the morning.

Silenced guns in hands, at the ready, Mr. Smoke sat cross legged on the floor and surveyed the doorway leading to Patrick O'Flaherty's bedroom. He had been in that position for three hours, waiting.

There were two auras in the room. One was Patrick. The other was ShabNab!

That came as a shock. The auras were not together. O'Flaherty's was spread eagle on a bed and ShabNab's was seated close by. Most people's auras were similar, with minor variations. ShabNab's was distinctly different.

ShabNab's aura rose out of the chair and cautiously entered the room where Mr. Smoke was waiting in his TAONA state. She did not see him at first. He blended into the shadows of the room. When she did, she froze. She was wearing the white dress and shoes.

"Good morning Mr. Smoke. I have someone waiting for you in the next room. Please come this way."

Turning slowly she entered the room. She walked directly to her chair, turned and sat. Mr. Smoke was already on the other side of the bed, eye visor raised. Patrick was sleeping. He tapped him lightly with the gun barrel.

Patrick O'Flaherty awoke to see Mr. Smoke standing over him, liquid silver swirling eyes penetrating his brain. Realization hit him. Then he saw the flash from the silencer.

ShabNab watched as it happened. Mr. Smoke then took pictures one handed with ShabNab always in his line of sight.

When he was done, he backed towards the door to leave.

"Don't go! Please don't go!" ShabNab said quickly as he started to exit the room. "They have my daughter. Please help her!" Tears sprung to her eyes and she stood up, took a step towards him and dropped to the floor, arms hugging herself, silent sobs wracking her body.

Her face reminded him of Garnet's face. It was a face that did not know how to cry. Her face did not scrunch up as most peoples do. It would have almost looked serene except for the panic in her ice blue eyes. And the panic showing in her aura.

Mr. Smoke came back into the room.

Scene Eighty

ShabNab seemed to pull herself together and her sobs subsided. Her mind was working frantically. What Mr. Smoke took for panic, was really *rage*. ShabNab hadn't felt that way in a *long time*. She could not lose him now. She couldn't fail!

If he vanished, she was doomed. She would have failed her mission! The *Personal Assassin* to the Blade was not allowed to fail! Ever! To do so, meant *death*. No matter how good she was, one or more of the Blades men would search her out and kill her. She couldn't die again. She would not be small, *ever again*. More than the prospect of death was the fact that the Blade gave her a reason to exist. Random killing held no fascination for her. He gave *her*, ShabNab Mishak, a *purpose* in life. A *reason* to exist. She needed *that* more than *life*. Life, without purpose, for her, would be meaningless. Without him and his Terror for Hire organization, ShabNab would be lost.

She brought her rage down to anger and hate. Those she could control. She noticed that he stood just out of striking distance. *Her striking distance*. He stood oddly. It was not a defensive or offensive stance, but she somehow knew it was both.

ShabNab felt a new sensation. She filed it away for future study.

His strange eyes never left her. She felt that he was reading her mind.

"Will you help her?" she asked in a soft voice.

"Where is she being held?"

"I don't know. At the castle, I think."

"The police have been contacted and will be here in ten minutes. I won't advertise this one. Bring my bullet from the mattress, unless you want it known that Mr. Smoke *Smoked* him. Be at the Sugar Shack Coffee House on the Eighth Avenue Mall downtown at eleven thirty am today. Wear that outfit. Do you know where that is?"

ShabNab nodded.

"Tell me a number that I can reach you at." ShabNab told him.

"Write it down."

She did. When she finished and went to hand it to him, she was handing it to thin air.

Mr. Smoke had vanished like his name.

▲ ▲ ▲

Scene Eighty One

"Well sir, what are you going to do? Are you going to meet her? Are you going to help her? Do you think you can trust her?" Hastings asked, as he drove silently away from the penthouse.

He had been waiting in the dark, two blocks over. No one saw them leave. He did not turn on the headlights until much further away.

Damon had brought Hastings up to date on what had transpired in the bedroom.

Damon did not answer right away. He contemplated the question as seriously as he did all Hastings inquiries.

"I have to meet her, Hastings. ShabNab did not ask me to help her."

"Sure she did. Unless I heard wrong, you told me she asked for help."

Damon smiled and nodded.

"She did, but not for her. She said 'Will you help *her?*' meaning VaShena. She asked for my help twice and both times it was for her daughter. As to whether I can trust her, absolutely not. I don't trust her as much as I do trust you."

Hastings looked confused.

"And that means, totally."

Hastings smiled in understanding.

"Do you think it's a trap, sir?"

"We'll find out, won't we?"

"I'm involved in this one? Great! I finally get to see ShabNab Mishak."

▲ ▲ ▲

Scene Eighty Two

This meeting was absolutely *vital* to her.

ShabNab looked at herself critically, in the hotel full length mirror, as she stepped from the shower. No change. She could *still* detect no signs of aging on her face or body.

Satisfied, she slipped her white dress over her head and proceeded to put on her makeup. As she worked, she thought back over the events at the penthouse and analyzed them.

Reminding her to bring the bullet was a stroke of brilliance on his part.

ShabNab had taken time, before the arrival of Mr. Smoke, to clean and remove any evidence of *her* on Patrick's body. Before she left, she took Patrick's gun and re-shot him in the forehead. She then shot off his private parts, emptying the gun. She left the gun on his chest. That would make it look like a crime of passion, like she had shot off his privates and *then* shot him in the head.

The police would investigate and assume it was either the hooker that did it or one of his girlfriends. Especially with him tied spread eagle to the bed. He was living under an assumed name, so it would take awhile for the Sword of Xandu to become aware of his death. If the Blade found out, he would suspect, but without proof he *might* let her live. After all, she was his *Personal Assassin*. She had not placed *him* in danger.

As it turned out, she had rented the Queen Anne suite, at a hotel in downtown Calgary, just minutes from her rendezvous point at eleven thirty.

Why had he told her to wear her evening party dress to a business coffee shop during lunch hour traffic? Only three reasons came to mind. Of those three only two made sense. One was that he was a voyeur. He definitely did not strike ShabNab as that. The other two made sense to her. She would assume both were correct. One was to make her identifiable to one, or more, of his associates. The other was to take focus off him. The dress was almost illegal looking. Nobody would remember him.

She felt that feeling again. This time she studied it. What she discovered, astounded her. She re-studied it and reached the same conclusion.

She sat down. *'So this is what* genuine respect *for someone feels like'* she thought to herself.

In her entire life, ShabNab Mishak had never felt respect for anyone, except herself. That was how she figured out what it was. To feel that way about someone else, other than herself, made her feel strange and *not* in a good way.

She shook her head and put it away again. Time to deal with that later.

ShabNab tousled her hair artfully, looked at the finished product in the mirror and smiled at the result. Let Mr. Smoke *not* react to her this time.

▲ ▲ ▲

At eleven thirty *exactly*, ShabNab walked into the Sugar Shack Coffee House. It was *the* place in downtown Calgary to meet with friends and business people.

Their food and coffee were award winning. The pleasing atmosphere was that of controlled chaos.

That activity stopped as she walked in and took a recently vacated table in the middle of the room. Almost a minute went by before activity resumed. Shortly after, she watched as a large black man, wearing a yellow suit and gold sunglasses, lumbered in and looked for a place to sit. She could almost feel the ground tremble.

Not finding one he approached ShabNab. A deep bass rumble issued from his chest.

"Mind if I join you, miss? I'm on a time constraint and need to fill the engine."

"I'm expecting someone," she said softly, "I'm sorry." She looked beyond him.

Lowering his sunglasses, he rumbled, "Lucky someone."

A few people sitting close, laughed. She smiled and looked up at him again. Liquid silver eyes stared down at her. Then he pushed the sunglasses up and started to turn away.

"What the heck, *she* is probably going to stand me up again anyhow. Join me, please."

Mr. Smoke took a seat opposite her. The waitress came over and ShabNab ordered. She then looked him over, from head to foot, as he ordered from the waitress. His rumbling bass voice made everyone smile. ShabNab could see no flaw in his disguise.

"You are one dangerous son of a bitch." She said softly. "Thank you for coming."

She went to reach for her purse.

"Touch that purse and you are dead." came a whispered voice out of his slightly parted non moving lips. She stopped immediately. She placed her hands on the table, in full view.

She could not see where his eyes were looking, behind the tinted lenses.

"Don't turn. There is a man behind you and off to your right. He was outside Patrick's building last night, when I entered *and* when I left. I will describe him. Pretend to ignore me."

As she ignored him and drank her coffee, ShabNab listened as Mr. Smokes voice whispered out of still lips, describing in detail what the man looked like.

"Do you know him?"

"I sure do." she mimicked through slightly parted, still lips. "His name doesn't matter, because it isn't real. He is known as Number Two, the Second top Assassin in the Sword of Xandu. The First, or Number One, is the *Personal Assassin* to the Blade, leader of the Sword of Xandu. Nobody knows who that is. This one takes the *Personal Assassin's* place, should he or she die."

'Damn the Blade to the hottest corner of hell' she thought. He didn't trust her and had sent backup. How much did the Second know? Lips not moving, ShabNab spoke softly, just under the Sugar Shack's conversation noise level.

"We have to take him out, Mister Smoke. If he knows what happened at Patrick's, we have to stop him from relaying the message to the Blade. All top assassins work alone. If any grunts *are* working for him, they do not know who or what the Sword of Xandu is. That way, the assassins are more highly prized and command the choicest assignments. Also, the most dangerous."

"Did you hear that gunner? ... Good, take him out on my cue ... ShabNab, when I leave, meet me in twenty minutes in the hotel room written on the napkin under your coffee. The door is unlocked, just push."

Suddenly, Mr. Smoke rose and stretched his fleshy arms. To ShabNab's amazement he went through the *ritual signs* of Assassins and Members of the Blade of Xandu, as he pretended to stretch. She turned her head slightly and saw the Seconds eyes widen slightly and then nod.

"Thanks for the company, little lady. My treat for letting me join you." The deep voice rumbled.

"Where is the mens room?" he thundered to a passing waiter. The waiter hastily pointed to the appropriate door and hurried on. "Best damn coffee in town!"

Out of the corner of her eye, ShabNab noticed that, as soon as Mr. Smoke mentioned the mens room, the Second got up and went into it. To ShabNab's amazement, instead of heading to the mens room, Mr. Smoke thundered to the front of the Sugar Shack, paid the bill and left.

A motion caught her eye. Her head spun around. Someone was coming out of the mens room. He stopped and yelled "Someone call an ambulance! There is a man lying on the floor unconscious."

People crowded around.

ShabNab immediately rose, picked up her napkin from under her coffee and made her way through the crowd to the mens room door. The Second was lying chest down, with his head twisted around and his face looking up, his neck twisted to an impossible angle.

The man who had hollered was nowhere to be seen. She remembered that he looked dark skinned also and had a short black beard. Because there was no one beside him, it was hard to guess his height He was wearing a dress hat and sunglasses and a nondescript, long businessman's raincoat.

ShabNab turned and left the Sugar Shack. At the entrance she saw the overcoat being picked up off the street, by a homeless person halfway down the block. He or she had vanished into the crowd. Of the hat or sunglasses, she saw no sign.

Scene Eighty Three

Twenty minutes later, the telephone rang in the hotel room that ShabNab was waiting in. She answered. She was told to go to another room in the hotel immediately. She did.

When she entered, she heard the phone ringing. She ran into the other room to get it, only to find Mr. Smoke sitting in the living room waiting for her, with a gun in one hand and an open cell phone in the other.

Mr. Smoke closed his cell phone. The ringing stopped.

"Drop your bag."

She did.

He was back in his dark grey assassin outfit. He tossed ShabNab the cell phone. "This, along with all identifying documents, was taken off the Second after he met with his unfortunate accident. See if any of the numbers are familiar."

She caught the phone and sat on the bed facing him, legs slightly spread. She opened it and looked at the *Seconds* recent calls.

She could feel her heart skip a beat when she saw the Blades personal number come up twice. Then she noted the times.

She looked up at the *terrorist assassin* dressed in grey.

"He made two outgoing calls and had one incoming. One was a two minute call at three in the morning, before Patrick's death. The second was a twenty four second call at eleven thirty in the morning.

It was over or stopped as I was walking into the Sugar Shack. I guess my outfit worked as it should have. The Blade has call waiting with an answering machine. He may have been on the other line and told the Second he would get back to him. I checked the answered and missed calls. He had one at eleven thirty four am. He didn't answer it."

She shifted slightly on the bed to a more comfortable position and her legs spread a little further apart. ShabNab smiled her best smile.

"What do *you* think?" She asked.

"We don't like to take chances. We always like to plan for the worst and hope for the best. The rest we just put in a bubble and blow it away. We must assume that VaShena is in trouble. We must assume that *you* are in trouble. We must act quickly."

"*We?* Who the hell are *we?*" asked ShabNab.

"My employers and I. Do you not agree with us?"

"Yes, I do."

"Then the *we* also includes you. Welcome into the web, ShabNab Mishak."

"Thank you, Mr. Smoke. Is there another name I could call you, instead of Mr. Smoke? It sounds so formal."

"Some call me, *sir*."

ShabNab laughed. She leaned forward showing her ample cleavage, spread her legs further apart and whispered,

"Alright, *sir*. Where do we go from here?"

Reaching behind him he pulled a bag forward and tossed it to her.

"Put these on please." Mr. Smoke indicated the bathroom.

She reached in and pulled out a beautifully tailored flight attendants outfit and a platinum blond wig.

She stripped in front of the grey terrorist assassin and held the clothes out in front of her and posed brazenly as she looked at them. She looked at him and then at the open bedroom door.

Mr. Smoke gave no reaction. ShabNab put the outfit on slowly, starting with the nylons. She then went to the mirror, put on the wig and adjusted it. She inserted the dark brown contact lenses and stepped back to view herself. She admired his handiwork. She looked like a different person. She could walk back into the Sugar Shack and nobody would recognize her as the same woman who was in earlier.

She held up the last item and looked puzzled. Mr. Smoke took the small piece of paper from her, peeled the small mole off it and placed it carefully on her left cheek, just under the curve.

The outfit fit her perfectly, downplaying her figure with subtle padding around the waist and hip areas. The shoes felt like they were made for her.

"There is a taxi waiting, to take you to the airport. I will contact you when you land. I have your phone number. Here are your documents and your cell phone."

He handed her an almost new purse. Inside were all her new travel documents, proclaiming her as Mildred Wilson, flight attendant. Her picture was on all the documents. ShabNab studied them closely. They were genuine. She smiled and went to shake his hand. Instead, he bowed slightly. She smiled and curtsied back. She smiled at the open bedroom door, turned and left.

Scene Eighty Four

"How in the world did she know I was there, Smoke?" Hastings asked.

"She's an EH and doesn't know it." Damon replied. "No one has taught her how to control or use her abilities. I assume that it is all self-taught and instinctual, which makes her unpredictable and doubly dangerous. I was trained and learned to use my abilities from birth on. I was connected with my parents. They taught me how to use them and grow them. After we died and I lost my abilities, I still practiced as if I had them. That allowed them to mature, otherwise they would have atrophied. I practiced with them in *Elseware* with Golden and Garnet also. Some of the early memories are still missing."

Damon remembered and shared what his parents and grandparents had taught him. "I know that male EH's mature slower than *Normal's* and reach full mental maturity at thirty five. That is probably why I was able to regain my abilities. I had just turned thirty five when *it* happened. My guess is that all of ShabNab's abilities were never fully realized by her conscious mind. From what Michael told me, she must be thirty five or older. Women mature earlier than men. They fully mature at age twenty eight. She has reached full maturity. I don't know if she can expand her abilities more than she has. There *is* something wrong with her, that I can't put my finger on. She is probably functionally insane."

Damon removed his hood and sat on the bed. Sweat glistened on his brow.

"I hope it didn't show, but when she came on to me, it made me sweat. I have never experienced anything like it. I have never reacted to, or felt the sexual urge. I should have started maturing at age fourteen and hit puberty at twenty one, reaching full sexual maturity at twenty eight. I didn't. When my parents were killed at age fourteen and I lost my abilities, something inside me died. I stopped maturing in certain areas as well."

Damon paused in retrospect, trying to put the pieces together in a way that Hastings could understand. He looked at his bodyguard/chauffeur/pilot.

Hastings nodded in understanding or encouragement.

Damon smiled inside and continued.

"Because I would not let anyone close to me, I never felt the physical sexual urge, therefore no mental or physical sexual growth. The rest of my body matured because I forced it to, through exercise, meditation and a host of other things. My body produces massive testosterone through my prostate and a multitude of *other* glands situated throughout my body. A crossover effect from the enhancements my parents made before I was born. That testosterone overload is the reason my body is in the shape it's in.

"Instead of sexual, my body uses the testosterone to build muscle. I have tested myself and found that I am infertile. I felt that I was, but I had to be certain. No part of my body produces live sperm. In fact, it produces no sperm at all. Again, a crossover effect."

Hastings face showed no expression.

"ShabNab's *sexuality* is a part of her *abilities*. A colossal part it seems. Every EH has different *abilities*, as do *Normals*. Her survival instinct must have *overgrown* her *sexual arousal ability instinct* to compensate, protect and adapt to the environment

357

she was raised in. Just as I have reached full mental and physical maturity, so has she. I think that whatever *abilities* she has, will not grow much. She can fine tune them with outside help, but that's about it."

Hastings nodded in understanding and agreement.

"I agree. I could feel the sexuality radiating off her in the next room. I couldn't help it, I got a raging erection from thirty five or forty feet away. Like you, sir, I have never felt anything like it."

Damon chuckled. "That is *when, how and where* she knew you were. I had you far enough away so that she wouldn't feel your aura. ShabNab's *sexual arousal instinct ability* must be closely connected to her aura sense and have subconsciously picked up the sexual spike in you aura. That is what I meant, when I said she is dangerous. I feel that her *aura sense* is highly developed. She has been using it all her life. Right now it is instinctual, controlled to a certain extent, yet still wild and untamed."

"Might I ask a question, sir?"

"Of course Hastings, what is it?"

"I know it doesn't *socially*, you never let anyone close, but does your lack of sexual equipment cause any problems mentally?"

Damon laughed again, in genuine good humor.

"Not at all. I feel no need to procreate. I feel all urges *but that*. I believe we are remembered and live on by what we do, what we create and sometimes, what we think. Not by creating offspring. Who was Hitler's father?"

"I have no idea."

"Exactly my point."

"How do you know that you have stopped developing in the sexual department? You *did* say EH's age slower and differently than *Normals*. With your parents enhancements it might yet happen?"

Damon shook his head.

358

"Golden and Garnet told me when we blended. They brought all my abilities to full maturity. They did to me what I could never do. Without them I would still be stunted in some areas. It seems my testicles atrophied when my abilities shut down and my body absorbed them shortly after, hence no body hair. We are content with it."

"What if you got strip searched at an airport? After that, you would be easily identifiable."

"I have a realistic set of normal sized genitals that I created, complete with testicles, that I can wear when circumstances dictate. I can even urinate out of it."

Hastings leaned back, put up his arms in a blocking mode, laughed and bellowed "Information overload! Information overload! That is more than I need to know."

Damon looked puzzled and then started laughing also.

When they had calmed down, Hastings continued, "All joking aside sir, you do seem to have all the bases covered. Let's go meet ShabNab in Venezuela."

On the way down in the elevator, Hastings looked at Damon and said with a straight face, "I have another question, sir. Do you squeeze the balls to pump up a full erection?"

Damon just looked at him as Hastings howled with laughter as they exited into main lobby.

"I'm terribly sorry, sir, but I just *couldn't* seem to resist. I know it was in bad taste. I won't bring it up again."

Hastings said in the car later. "I should be long past that sort of thing, wouldn't you think? Must be that sexual blast she sent out." He muttered to himself.

Hastings then shook his head as if trying to clear it.

Damon looked at him with a straight face for a moment, then laughed.

"I'm glad you enjoyed it Hastings. It *was* funny. Since you are not going to bring it up again, pardon the pun, I won't be able to answer your question."

"What? You mean …..? Awww, dammit…. Me and my big mouth."

They both laughed in genuine good humor

▲ ▲ ▲

Scene Eighty Five

When ShabNab arrived in Maracaibo, Venezuela, a short black limo driver was waiting for her. He carried her bag to the waiting trunk and ushered her into the back seat. As they walked through the airport she saw a few fellow assassins that she knew who looked at her and passed on by. They hadn't recognized her!

She accepted Mr. Smokes disguise and identification because she had to. She didn't realize how effective it was, until that moment. Something, as little as a mole, drew your attention away from the face. She realized that sometimes, *less* is *more*. She had used many disguises in the past but always overdid it, to take away from her beauty. She seldom turned *ugly*. She preferred to save that skill for when she really needed it.

Her respect for Mr. Smoke rose again. It would be fun to learn all his secrets, she thought. It would be a long process but she was sure she could make him live long enough to tell all. She knew that he *had* reacted to her, when she had turned on all her charm. She saw him start to sweat slightly.

That was why he didn't shake her hand, she realized suddenly!

It made her feel good to know that he was human.

She was also surprised to find a hidden watcher in the other room. Mr. Smoke knew her too well it seemed.

That pissed her off!

She hadn't let on that it bothered her. Smiling into the other room, as she was leaving, gave her some satisfaction.

She had a lot of time to think on the flight. She had come to the decision that she had to kill the Blade and his Arms *before* they killed her. She knew that Number two had texted a message, *prior* to his last phone call, that he had deleted afterwards. Standard procedure.

She had made a few phone calls, and called in a few favors. She found out that the night Mr. Smoke visited her in the castle, an assassin had caught a brief glimpse of a human aura on the roof of a building where no one should have been. The aura vanished and the assassin thought that he was tired and just seeing things. When he awoke the following morning, his survival instinct kicked in and this time he heeded it. He reported the incident to his superior, who in turn reported it to the Blade. That was how the Blade found out about her romp with the two sentries outside her door. It made him very suspicious.

That was why he had told ShabNab that he was disappointed in her.

He had given her one more chance to redeem herself with Patrick. But he no longer trusted her. He had sent Number Two to monitor and oversee the operation. ShabNab knew that his orders were to kill her, if she failed.

She was lucky that the Smoke organization was there to bail her out.

The Blade *knew* that she had failed. He also knew that Number Two was dead. He knew that she knew, that there was a contract out on her, to bring her back alive for interrogation. He had already put out an order to give her a message to have her return. The message was: *he had her daughter.*

ShabNab laughed. *'Talk about speaking your future into existence'* she thought. At least now, if the Smoke organization were able to check, her story would check out.

The Blade wanted her back to interrogate and kill her. She had been privy to much of his sensitive information over the years. Too much, to allow her to live.

The Blade couldn't allow that.

ShabNab couldn't allow that!

Alone her chances were slim, so she would have to use Mr. Smoke and his superiors' organization to help her. Afterwards she would capture Mr. Smoke, drain all his knowledge and then kill him, after he begged her to.

As she had done with the Blade when she killed VaShena's father and became his *Personal Assassin*, she would offer Mr. Smoke's superiors or employers, to take over as *Mr. Smoke*. She didn't care who she killed for, as long as they could keep her plying her trade. She needed a cause. A reason to exist. Killing terrorist bombers was as good as anything else.

She frowned. Unless there was more than *one* Mr. Smoke, like the immortal *Personal Assassin* to the Blade. Then she would have to work something else out.

She suddenly smiled and arched and stretched like a cat in the back seat. It would be almost as much fun *not* killing and torturing Mr. Smoke, as it would be to let him live and never have her. It was something to think about.

Right now, she needed to focus on destroying the Blade and the *Arms* of the Sword of Xandu. Without them, the organization would cease to exist.

She would then be free to work for another organization. Like Mr. Smokes.

▲ ▲ ▲

Scene Eighty Six

The limo pulled up to a large estate gate. The chauffer punched in a code and the gate opened. He drove through and drove up to the main entrance. He got out and opened her door.

Without looking at her, he said in Portuguese, *"Go right on in. He will be along shortly, if he isn't already here."* He then got back into the limousine and drove off.

ShabNab pushed on the front door and it opened. She entered.

Mr. Smoke was standing there waiting as she walked through the doorway. ShabNab was surprised. She walked towards him and stopped just outside of striking distance, when he raised his arm.

He couldn't have gotten here quicker than her! They had lift off immediately upon her boarding the jet. She looked at him closely. He was wearing dark grey, non reflective, sunglasses. He gave the slight bow. She returned his bow, instead of her previous curtsy. She didn't proffer her hand.

"Follow me, and keep the same distance away, please." issued the voice of Mr. Smoke. Because of the hooded face mask she could not see the mouth move. Was it a recording? Her instincts said no, but she couldn't be sure. These thoughts, and more, raced through her head as she followed him to a large gymnasium. It was a complete martial arts dojo.

In the middle of the room stood another Mr. Smoke.

The Mr. Smoke leading her, stopped just inside the door, bent and retrieved a package on the floor. Turning, he tossed it to her. She caught it deftly and looked at it. It looked like another Mr. Smoke outfit. She was right! There *was* more than *one* Mr. Smoke. She wouldn't be able to kill him, or them, until she had more knowledge. She was very patient. She could wait.

"Put those on. You can strip now and we can enjoy watching you again or you can use that room over there." He said pointing to a doorway.

She went into the room. The first thing she did was remove the wig, mole and contact lenses. She quickly braided her hair.

A few minutes later she returned dressed as they were. The non reflective, wraparound sunglasses, brought everything sharply into focus. A swivel ear cover attached to the ear wires secured it. There was no chance of losing the glasses in combat or vigorous movement. The nose pad was of a blow absorbing rubber that molded to the shape of her nose. It was incredibly light, flexible and comfortable. The lens coating *somehow* enhanced her eyesight. The padded gloves fit like their name and were open at the first knuckle to allow for touch. The shoes also fit perfectly, with just the right amount of grip. The outfit was a perfect fit.

She had tried a few moves and stretches in it, to loosen up before coming out, and there was no restriction at all. She looked at the seams, as she put it on. All the seams were tear-away Velcro. If someone grabbed her and she pulled away, all they would have would be fabric. There were a lot of other features and benefits as well. In her opinion, it was the perfect personal combat outfit.

The Mr. Smoke that brought her in was still standing there. She walked to the same distance away and stood at ease, poised for defense or attack. The other was still in the center of the room.

"Are you prepared for a test of your skills?" asked Mr. Smoke number one. "If we are to agree to help rescue VaShena, we need to know what level your combat skills are. Is that acceptable?"

"It is acceptable. Will it be full contact?" she asked.

"Why would we want to damage ourselves before we go into combat?"

ShabNab smiled under the mask. "Silly question. Sorry."

"No question is silly that is asked honestly. Are you ready? Do you need to warm up?"

"I am ready." She said.

"Please go to the center of the room where your opponent awaits. When I clap once you will commence. When I clap twice you will stop. Is that understood?"

"It is."

"Then teach us what you know. Let the teacher become the student."

Number One gave the slight bow again. ShabNab returned it and walked over to face her opponent.

▲ ▲ ▲

The testing lasted only twenty minutes. It was obvious to ShabNab that Number Two was a pro. He did not attack her once. All he did was block. It was incredible to her that in the twenty minute match, she was only able to breach his defense once! A few times, at the beginning, she had purposely left herself open to attack.

When she realized that he would only defend, she went all out.

As she stood in front of Number One, she felt her respect rising to another level. She would *like* to work for this organization. She *would* work for this organization!

"Thank you for your effort. It was enlightening. You are truly a worthy opponent." said Number One. ShabNab felt a flush of pride at the recognition.

Suddenly a maid, dressed in grey and starched white, appeared with a suitcase in her hand and handed it to her.

"Your clothes are in there, with some others as well. Please feel free to use the adjoining swimming pool. When you have repaired yourself, please change into an outfit of your choice and Miss Valens here will bring you to the meeting room in one hour. Does that give you enough time?"

"It does. Thank you."

"Until then." Number One bowed slightly. ShabNab returned it. She turned to bow to her opponent.

Number Two had vanished.

She turned back to Number One.

He had also vanished like his name.

Damn, she hated that!

▲ ▲ ▲

Scene Eighty Seven

"Do you think she was holding back?" Damon asked Hastings, who was soaking in a tub of ice water.

Damon had just done a *laying of the hands* on him, to stop the swelling.

Hastings rose out of the tub and toweled himself dry, and started to get dressed.

"I don't think so, boss. If that was light contact, she would have killed me in full contact mode. Good thing I was wearing padding. As it was, if you hadn't done your magic *hand healing thing*, I wouldn't be in any shape to help you with the infiltration. That is one strong woman. I would not hesitate to say that she is much stronger than me."

"She doesn't know that though. She doesn't know how strong you are, or what your fighting style is. I noticed toward the end she was getting reckless, trying to breach your defenses. It looked to me like she had gone full out, but I wasn't you. Thanks for your observations and comments."

Hastings paused as he was putting on a sock.

"I'm curious, sir. Why did you want me to intentionally let her breach my defenses once? She almost breached them a dozen times."

"But she doesn't know that, only you and I do. If she hadn't breached you at least once, she would be uncontrollable in the field, trying to prove to herself, over and over again, that she still had it. For our safety, we needed to preserve her self image. It was a perfect bout. I learned most, if not all, of her fighting styles and she has a lot. The important thing is that we earned her respect. Shortly, she will forget that it was a sparring bout and remember only that she was able to breach your defenses once. That makes her controllable."

"If you say so." muttered Hastings good naturedly.

He finished dressing and they went their separate ways, Hastings to finalize the night's arrangements and Mr. Smoke to the meeting room, to meet ShabNab Mishak.

Scene Eighty Eight

When ShabNab entered the meeting room she saw Mr. Smoke sitting behind a large round table. On his right was a balding bespectacled man dressed in a wrinkled, ill fitting suit, with a pen and writing pad in front of him. He was scrunched over, writing on it.

He finished and looked up at her. He had a severe curvature of the spine. His jaw dropped open when he saw her, displaying slightly crooked, nicotine stained teeth. She was wearing her white *cutout* outfit. She smiled at him. All he could do was stare.

ShabNab turned her attention to Mr. Smoke. She walked up to the front of the desk and stood there.

"Please, have a seat."

"Thank you." She sat.

"Mr. Smith, meet Ms. Wilson." They both nodded to each other. "We have never done an operation of this type, size or magnitude. Mister Smith is a military genius and assassin expert, whose vital input could make the difference between life and death, should we decide to go forward. Ours. He is here at my highly paid request. I have used him before and his information and input, in the past, has proven to be both vital and trustworthy."

He bent his head slightly for a moment, as if thinking, then raised it.

"Why did you ask for our help?"

"Whether she knows it or not, my daughter is being held hostage by the Blade of Xandu." ShabNab crossed her legs. Mr. Smith started perspiring, dropped his head and started writing.

"I need help to get her out. To survive, I also need to kill the Blade and his ten Arms or Generals. They are the only ones who know *who* I am and where I can be found."

Mr. Smoke was silent for a moment, then said, "Our employer contracts us to *Smoke* terrorist assassins. That is it. No innocents are to be harmed, if at all possible. So far none have. I guess my next question is, *why* should we help you?"

"You are not helping *me*. You are helping my *daughter, Vashena*. She is an innocent. I can make it worth your while." ShabNab uncrossed her legs slowly.

The grey garbed figure sat silent for another moment.

"That dress is distracting. Take it off, please." The voice spoke quietly.

ShabNab was surprised. Rising immediately she pulled it over her head, folded it and put it on the floor beside her as she resumed her seat. She smiled.

"You're good, Mr. Smoke. You knew that dress was one of my weapons didn't you?"

"Yes I did. Now, we can continue. How can you make it worth our while? You are going to pay us?"

"No. You are going to pay me." She looked at him and smiled her breathtaking smile.

"And why would we do that? If you are inferring sex, nobody is that good in bed, no matter how good they are."

ShabNab looked startled. Then she laughed.

"Don't be so sure of that, Mister. Wars have been started over sex *way beneath my level*, but that is *not* what I was inferring. What I meant was I want to join your organization."

His hands were clasped in front of him, resting on the table. He contemplated his fingertips.

"And what would make you want to do that?" his voice had a smile in it.

"I *need* to do, *what I do*. I am an assassin. Probably the best there is, no offense intended. I can no longer do it for the Sword of Xandu. When they first recruited me, I told them I would do anything they told me to do. I also told them I would be as faithful to them as they were to me. I would trust them as they trusted me. I have kept my pact in that contract. I am willing to offer you the same contract and more." Mr. Smoke's head bent as if looking down at his fingernails.

"You say you are the best. There is very little data to back you in that department, Ms. Wilson. You could be as you say. You could also be a small cog in the international Sword of Xandu organization. Your performance earlier leads me to believe that the former is true. If it is, we would consider your proposal. I take it that they have broken their contract with you, by taking VaShena?"

"Yes."

"Who or what were you, in their organization?"

ShabNab hesitated. She stared long and hard at the grey figure in front of her.

"Who runs this organization, *Mister?*" she asked abruptly.

Now it was Mr. Smokes turn to hesitate. Making the decision, he spoke.

"Will you excuse us for a few moments, Mr. Smith?"

"But of course. Send for me when you need me." He stood, bowed to the two of them and scurried from the room.

After he left, a green light blinked on the desk.

Mr. Smoke then said to ShabNab,

"I do."

ShabNab cursed softly under her breath.

"I guessed as much." She said louder. Her eyes never once left his. She seemed to see through his glasses. She was absolutely still for a few minutes.

Neither of them moved.

"Can I trust you, Mr. Smoke?" she asked softly. Dangerously. Her eyes took on a sleepy look. Gone was her sexy pose. What Mr. Smoke *now* saw in front of him, was ShabNab the Assassin.

"Whether my organization takes you on or not, your information is safe with us."

"That is *not* good enough, *Mister.* These are my terms. I only take orders from you, *Mr. Smoke.* As I was with the Blade, leader of the Sword of Xandu, I will be your *Personal Assassin.*" She waited for a response. Mr. Smoke said nothing.

She smiled at him and continued.

"You are the one I hold responsible for the contract, not the organization. I will be faithful and true to your cause only. I will not work for others. With my life, I will protect you to the best of my abilities. I do not ask the same, because of my profession. The more dangerous the assignment, the better I like it. I will be as faithful to you, as you are to me. I will do my best to never harm an innocent, while on a job. I will do anything you tell me to do. I will trust you, as you trust me. I will not break the contract first. I will not lie to you. I demand the same. You command me. I do not command you. You need not answer my questions, but if you do, it has to be truthful and honest. There must be honesty and truthfulness *only,* between us. Price is not an issue, just pay me well. I require an answer to this immediately. As you mentioned earlier, VaShena's life is at risk every minute we delay."

Silence, then "Continue."

"Continue nothing! Do we have a contract?"

"With one condition."

"What condition is that?"

"I want full custody of VaShena to do with as I choose. Think carefully before you answer."

ShabNab was quiet for a moment, thinking.

"Done! I can't stand the little bitch anyway, you know that. As I asked before, do we have a contract?"

"We do. Now let us continue."

373

ShabNab visibly relaxed. She no longer looked *as* dangerous.

"How many years were you with the Sword of Xandu?"

"Twenty one."

"You were the Blades *Personal Assassin* for how long?"

"Over eight years."

"Eight years? Really? What *exactly* are your *skills, abilities* and *areas of expertise*?"

"How do you know of my *abilities*?"

"I *know*." was all he said.

It was enough for her. ShabNab told him.

When she had finished, Mr. Smoke spoke quietly.

"I am *impressed* and I do not impress easily. Welcome to the *Smoke* organization ShabNab Mishak. You have spoken the truth. Your *aura* and the lie detector you are sitting on, confirm it."

"That is why you had me strip?"

"One of them. The instrument works much better on bare flesh. It is a design of my own."

ShabNab laughed.

"May I get dressed now?"

"No."

She laughed again.

"Too distracting?"

"Correct."

Mr. Smith was called back in.

▲ ▲ ▲

Scene Eighty Nine

Mr. Smith had plans already drawn up, so it was just a matter of fine tuning it with ShabNab's input. When they had finalized their battle plans, Mr. Smith rose and left the room, to inform Gunner of the refinements.

When the green light blinked, Mr. Smoke stood and walked around the table to stand before ShabNab. He removed his gloves and took off his glasses. His eyes bored into hers.

ShabNab was startled. *'His eyes are a lot like mine'*, she thought. *'Why didn't I notice that before?'* She filed the thought away for future reference.

"Please stand and place both your hands in mine." She did.

"When I am touching you, I can tell if there is any deceit in what you say. If you answer me deceitfully, I will have to kill you."

"I have the same *ability*."

"Then you do understand that I am speaking the truth?"

"Yes." She smiled a sleepy smile.

"Ahh, I see you doubt my *ability* to best you. Good. I want nothing less from you."

ShabNab's hand twitched. "Ahh, I see that you believe in my *ability* now. Let us confirm the terms of our contract. Yes?"

"Yes."

"You will do and perform all as you promised earlier?"

"Yes."

"No jobs unless I assign them."

"Yes."

"You only report to me, unless I instruct you otherwise."

"Yes."

"You will do anything I ask."

"No."

"No?"

"No. I will do anything you *tell me to do*. Asking allows me a choice."

"You will do anything I *tell* or *order* you to do."

"Yes."

"You will protect me with your life, while under contract."

"Yes. If you die, so do my assignments. *I will not allow that.*"

Mr. Smoke dropped his hands and backed up. She had spoken true. That truly surprised him. ShabNab *was* certifiably insane, beyond insane, he could feel that in her touch, but she was *his* to do with as he chose. Time to test a theory. A word had come into his mind as he touched her. Crossing his arms over his chest, he spoke.

"Turn *ugly*."

ShabNab went into shock. Her face showed it.

"Pardon?"

"I said, turn *ugly*."

"How did you know about that? Nobody knows!"

"I do. Do it now!"

ShabNab turned *ugly*.

She stood there as Mr. Smoke walked slowly around her, studying everything.

After five minutes of touching and probing every part of her body, he stopped and stepped back.

"Can I change back now?"

"In a moment." Reaching behind his head, he took his hood and face mask off.

"Oh, my god. You're Damon Gray, the Gray Ghost. The Grey Ghost is Mr. Smoke! Holy shit! I am a *huge fan* of yours, have been for years."

"Can you teach me how to do what you do? It is incredible. It is the most fantastic thing I have ever seen. I love it!"

"You *love* how I look? Like this?"

"I hate to disappoint you ShabNab, but yes I do. Can you teach me to do that? I know that you are *different*, look *different*, but *that* is the *magic* and *beauty* of it. There are no massive changes, just little ones creating a mutant, feline, primeval, predatory look. Almost all would consider it ugly. Scary." He smiled. "To me, *it is Magic.*"

"You're crazier than me, I felt that when I touched you. *Now I know for sure.* I can try, but I don't think it will work with you."

"Can you change back slowly so I can watch?"

"I can try."

After many hours and many more changes, he said he had enough information. She returned to her ShabNab body.

"Can you change to other looks?" he asked.

"No. I've tried, but this is the only one I have ever been able to do. I always thought of it as *ugly* because of the way people looked at me. I think *feline, primeval,* and *predatory* are the correct words. They *feel right.* I like it. My body goes *feline primeval* naturally sometimes, when I feel threatened."

"You seem very comfortable in your *altered* body. I also prefer the words *feline primeval.* I take it that you used it quite a bit, at some point in your life."

"Many years." ShabNab shrugged her beautiful shoulders. "It was just a part of my life."

Right then, Damon's cell phone rang. He answered it, listened and said into the phone "Great, Gunner. Put everything in the gyrocopter and we will meet you there in twenty two minutes."

Looking at ShabNab he said "We will talk of this later. Has VaShena seen you *primeval?*"

"She has. She reacted like you. She thought I was cute. She said I looked like a hairless cat that one of the Blades chefs owned, with hair on my head. She called me *Kitty Face*, her *Girlie Transformer*."

"Has the Blade seen your *primeval* body?"

"No, I couldn't do that. He couldn't stand it. He would have had me killed in an instant. He has done work for some sort of secret mutant hater society. I heard him talking to someone about EH's, whatever that means. Why do you ask?"

"We are going in *tonight*. I want you to go in *primeval*, so you are not recognized if caught and unmasked. Are you okay with that? Can you function effectively in that form?"

"I'm many times stronger and deadlier *primeval*, than *normal*, in combat situations. I'm fine with that."

"I want the Blade saved till last. If we try to take him first, VaShena may be killed…."

"We've already been through that, sir."

"I hadn't finished. When we get VaShena, I want you to take the Blade and use your considerable skills to find out everything you can on his assignments with the EH group and any other information on terrorist bombers in the Sword of Xandu, *excluding you*."

"Really?" ShabNab asked excitedly. "The Blade?"

"Yes. The Blade."

ShabNab leaned in slowly and kissed Damon on the cheek. "Thank you, thank you, thank you. I won't charge for him. Can we go now please?"

"Put your combat outfit on. Don't turn *primeval* until I tell you to."

"Does anyone else know my secret?"

"No. Not for sure."

"*Primeval* is our secret, right?"

"I would like to tell one other person. The one you sparred with."

"No. Just you."

"He *is* part of the team."

"I cannot command you. I can only ask. It is important to me. Are there not some things about yourself you don't want revealed?"

Mr. Smoke paused.

"Agreed. Just me."

"Thank you, Commander."

"Commander?... Why not? Commander it is."

"What is my code name?"

Damon thought for a moment.

"How about Misty?"

"I like it. Mister and Misty Smoke."

"Welcome to the team Misty." Damon smiled and put forth his hand.

ShabNab hesitated. Deep inside her, she somehow knew what a true handshake meant to him, what it *cost* him. She also knew what it would *cost* her. She smiled and reached out and took it. She needed it. She would pay the cost gladly.

As she turned to leave, Damon said quietly.

"I know you didn't turn to us easily, ShabNab. The Blade really gave you no choice. I checked on VaShena. She *is* being held, to bring you back to die. The Blade is a *fool*. He may be brilliant, but a *fool* nonetheless. Anyone can make an honest mistake. I take it that I was your target?"

Misty jerked slightly. She nodded, wordless. Damon took her hands in his again.

"I do *not* hold that against you, nor do I hold you accountable for that. What I *do* hold you accountable for, is your words to me, and my words to you. Those I hold *sacred* from this moment on. I do not demand the *truth* from you. To me it doesn't exist. It is only someone's opinion. I demand *honesty and trust*. Your words. My words. Do I make myself clear?

"Yes, Commander."

He released her hands.

"Good! Now let's go kick some Sword of Xandu butt."

▲ ▲ ▲

Scene Ninety

Introductions had been made. Real names were used. Permanent code names were assigned.

"Commander it is, Commander. No more *Smoke*. It suits you." said Hastings with a smile. "A pleasure to meet you, Misty. Your skills are impressive. I look forward to a long and healthy business relationship."

"So are yours, Gunner."

They shook hands, politely.

"My, don't we make a nice deadly triangle." Misty commented. Both Damon and Hastings looked at each other at the same time.

"What?" Misty, as she now considered herself, asked, catching the look.

"We've been running into a lot of triangles recently. It just seemed strange when you said it." Hastings said.

"Is that a *good* thing?"

"It has been."

"Good, because a triangle has always been one of my weapons of choice." She displayed a number of razor edged triangles of black steel in various sizes.

▲ ▲ ▲

Hastings landed the gyrocopter on silent mode close to where Mr. Smoke had parked his SUV on his last penetration there. It was three am.

All three of them were in Smoke combat fatigues, hoods and glasses on. They exited with their equipment and set up where Damon had on his previous visit.

"You know what to do, Gunner. Be ready, on my signal, to cancel the alarm system. Monitor all security cameras and keep us informed." Mr. Smoke said.

"Yes, Commander."

"Misty, you know the plan. You are to take the north wing and work your way to the Blades apartment."

"Yes, Commander."

Mr. Smoke continued.

"From the information you provided, you should be able to take out five Arms and security assassins on your way. Synchronize. It is now three oh seven.... mark! I will take the south wing and meet you outside the Blades room at four eighteen exactly. That should give us *both* enough time. It's a good thing that you have keys to all the rooms in the castle and marked them. You know what to do when you reach the wall."

Misty nodded.

"Ready Gunner? Good. Let's go!"

Mr. Smoke and Misty raced across the field to the wall. Once they reached it, Mr. Smoke saw Misty's body alter slightly within the combat outfit.

It was the *Primeval* that flowed up the wall, like a great predatory cat.

Scene Ninety One

At four eighteen am, Mr. Smoke and *Primeval* met outside the door of the Blade, leader of the Sword of Xandu's apartment.

"Any trouble, *Primeval*?" he asked in a low voice.

Primeval shrugged. "As a matter fact, twice I came close to blowing it. Those Arms were great. I can see why the Blade chose them. Don't worry though, they are all sleeping the long sleep." She produced a set of keys and inserted them into the correct locks. She did not turn them.

"I take it *you* had no problems?" she asked. Mr. Smoke nodded.

"I checked my apartment. VaShena is not there. Let us hope she is in here."

"You know the drill. Are you sure you want to take out the Blade by yourself? You told me he is the deadliest man in here."

"He is. As you may have noticed, I am not a man."

Subtle changes occurred under the outfit filling it out more.

"You are going to take him as Misty." he stated. It was not a question.

"Oh, I will show him *Primeval* when I am questioning him. That will help to speed the process. He is afraid of mutants. Let him think I am one."

She paused for a moment. "Maybe I am, but I don't need *Primeval* to take care of him. Thank you for letting me have him, Commander. I have dreamt about this for years. You have made my dream a reality."

"You are welcome." He produced some documents, a pen and an ink pad. He handed them to Misty.

"Get him to sign these documents and put his right thumb print on all documents. Try not to get any blood on them. They are dated a week ago and registered with all the appropriate authorities. One is a bill of sale for Castle Florentine, contents included, and the others are the transfer documents to one of my Companies."

"Mhmm," Misty purred, taking the documents. "You sure do know how to turn a girl on, Commander. This just gets better and better. I owe you big time for this."

"I'm glad that it makes you happy, Misty." She could hear the smile in his voice.

"You are sure he still has his hidden little soundproof questioning chamber off his bedroom?"

"Yes Commander, and stocked with all the tools I need to extract the information you need. He likes to take his work home with him. I'll meet you back at the Dojo when I have the information. It may take awhile."

"Fine. Let's do it!"

▲ ▲ ▲

Scene Ninety Two

Back at the Dojo, VaShena was sleeping peacefully in one of the bedrooms. Damon Gray was looking down at her. She truly was an innocent.

When he and Misty had entered the apartment, Misty went immediately to the Blades bedroom. There was a gurgling sound and a soft crash, then silence. Misty appeared in the doorway and gave the thumbs up.

Mr. Smoke made a sweep of the apartment. VaShena was in the third bedroom.

When he had walked through the bedroom doorway in the Blades apartment, VaShena was sitting on the bed, fully dressed, long dark hair combed and tied clumsily with a pink ribbon in a ponytail. With her bags packed.

She gave him her prettiest smile and said, "Hi, Mister Gray. I knew you would come for me. I'm ready to go now." She held out her little arms towards him.

He scooped her, and her two small bags, into his arms and left the Castle. She asked no questions.

When he arrived at Gunners location, he gave the thumbs up. Gunner pressed the switch on one of his machines.

As ShabNab told him later, it reverberated throughout Castle Florentine. The voice was electronically altered to induce fear and panic. It said that the Blade, leader of the Sword of Xandu was dead as were all his Arms. All persons were to leave immediately. Armed government troops were on their way, to kill all within. The monitors showed military aircraft in the air. The panicking voice said that *aircraft bombers* were on their way. The castle was to be leveled. There would be no prisoners. Alarm bells were going off, red lights were flashing, sirens were blaring and voices were screaming.

None of the Security Systems worked. The massive steel doors to the armory were locked and bolted. They were inaccessible. The only personal guns allowed in the Castle were with the security assassins and Mr. Smoke and Misty had removed them from their unconscious forms while on their way to take out the Arms. *Nobody* in the castle had weapons.

None of the computers worked, thanks to the programs that Mr. Smoke had installed on his previous visit.

Castle Florentine was totally vacated in less than ten minutes.

One hour later, forty military vehicles pulled up and four hundred military personnel stormed into the empty castle and took up residence. They were actually civilians, cleaners, computer techs, cooks, bottle washers, etc. A few were hired mercenaries that Hastings knew, who disposed of what was left of the ten Arms.

Some of the retreating soldiers had their vengeance on the dead bodies of the Arms for real or imagined slights.

Castle Florentine was his.

Scene Ninety Three

Four nights later ShabNab appeared at the Dojo. Damon, Hastings and VaShena had just finished eating supper and were relaxing in the library. She was still in her combat outfit and it was spotless. She looked stunningly beautiful.

Hastings rose silently, nodded to her and exited the room. ShabNab smiled her breathtaking smile and returned the nod.

VaShena, who had been playing with her dolls, looked up and saw her mother standing there. She stood and said quietly, "Hello mommy."

ShabNab walked over and squatted down and patted her daughters head.

"Hello VaShena. It's good that you are safe." She looked seriously at her daughter. "Don't call me mommy anymore. Call me .... What is my new name Commander?" she looked at Damon.

"Catherine. Cat for short." Damon said without thinking.

"As you order." She returned to VaShena.

"Call me Cat or Catherine. I am no longer your mother. I have given you to this man here. *Forever.*" She pointed to Damon.

Her daughter looked at Damon questioningly. He nodded.

And then back to her mother.

"Really?" she asked.

"Really."

VaShena jumped up and threw her arms around her mother.

"Oh, thank you Catherine. Thank you. This is the *best gift* you have ever given me. Thank you."

She then turned to Damon and said, "I'll be good. You'll see." She smiled and sat back down with her dolls. "Did you hear?" she whispered to them. "You did? Good. What?" She frowned. She stood up. She looked at Damon, ignoring her mother.

"If Catherine gets a new name, don't I deserve one too?"

Damon looked at Catherine. She just smiled. He turned back toward VaShena.

"Of course." he said.

VaShena smiled. "*Now you take your time*, Commander Gray, and find a *good one*. Can my last name be Gray too?"

"Absolutely." VaShena looked puzzled. "That means yes."

She smiled and her lavender eyes shone. She bent down, picked up her dolls and said, "I'm going to bed. I'm tired. Is it okay to come see you in the morning, Commander Gray, to see if you've found my new name?" Damon smiled and nodded.

VaShena headed for the door. At the door she turned, *smiled her mothers smile*, and said to her mother. "You won't be able to wear *him* out Cat. He's *Mr. Smoke!*"

She left the room.

Damon laughed. "What was all that about?"

"I have a voracious sexual appetite." Cat smiled. She reached into her garment and produced the signed documents he had ordered her to bring to him and more. He looked at them closely. There were no blood stains on the paper.

"Very good, *Catherine*.......?"

"*You* tell *me*. You chose my first name."

"Nipp."

"Very good. Cat Nipp. I like it. Catherine Nipp it will be, Commander, if that is alright with you. ShabNab Mishak is no more."

"I'll have your documents made first thing in the morning. Bring me up to date."

Cat disrobed and put her clothes in the corner. She walked over and sat, lotus style, at his feet in front of the chair.

Damon smiled.

Cat smiled.

"I know," Mr. Smoke said "No distractions, right?"

Cat smiled mischievously. "Right, Commander."

"Maybe I should talk with the *Primeval*?"

"I don't think so sir. She turns you on too much. You don't want to be distracted, do you?"

"You are right, Catherine. Bring me up to date. Just the headlines. I can listen to the recorded version later."

She did. In her left hand was a large capacity flash drive with all the information that she had gathered from the Blade. She handed it to him.

"I only erased the screams. As you ordered, none of our dialog is missing. You are going to learn some interesting things *about me* from him. They are all true. There is all his information on there. All his bank accounts and access codes. All his property around the world. Everything he owned. He was more than happy to sign everything over to you in the end. I kept his right hand functioning. He died penniless." She smiled her beautiful smile.

"Thank you for that, Commander. I can't tell you *how good* that makes me feel." She spread her legs slightly, unconsciously. Damon noticed that her mound was glistening.

She followed his gaze and smiled.

"That's why Cat is such a good name for me. I'm always insatiably curious and ready for action. I hope VaShena is right."

Damon ignored her. "Those are unique earrings you are wearing, Catherine. They look new. I haven't seen you wear jewelry before."

"I just had them made. This is the first time I've worn them. I will probably wear them till I tire of them. Then I'll put them with the rest of my special jewelry collection. Do you like them?" She arched her back and turned her head back and forth so he could view them. He looked at them closely.

"Yes I do. I have never seen anything quite like them. Each of them is slightly different in size and shape."

"Thank you." She smiled, again mischievously, cat like. "You know, I thought the Blade would have put up more of a fight. Only minutes into our talk he knew he didn't have the balls to stand up to me. He caved in shortly after. I had him beg me for a day to end his misery. I'm glad I didn't. At the end, he gave me the names of every terrorist bomber he had ever used and their computer access codes. He had a phenomenal memory. It'll keep me busy for a long, long time."

Damon bent forward and looked at the earrings closely again. Then he smiled.

"Very creative, Cat."

"Thank you."

"Does our contract have hours?"

"No, you own me twenty four seven."

"*Own* you?"

"That's right. You *own* me twenty four hours a day, seven days a week for the length of our contract. I thought you knew that."

"I just wanted it clarified." Damon stood up.

Catherine Nipp rose and leaned into him. Her body musk smelled delicious. Her eyes, when she looked at him, were heavy with desire.

"Take me any way you want." She whispered in his ear.

"No."

"No?" she said startled. "Are you gay?"

"No."

"Would you, if I turned into the *primeval*?"

She turned into Primeval.

Damon Gray looked into her dilated pupils and smiled.

"No." he said softly, firmly. Ignoring him she continued.

"I've never made love in this form so I may be too small for you." Primeval said.

Damon laughed and led her into the bedroom and sat her on the bed.

"No." he said again.

"I don't understand…. *You* don't understand! I need you at least once. I need you in me. It is a compulsion I have. I don't know why. The Blade trained me. I cannot control it. Please, just once. Any way you want it… Please!"

"No! Stop! It is not that I don't find you beautiful, Primeval." He said gently. He pulled down his pants and stood exposed before her. "This is why it can't happen."

"What happened?" she asked wide eyed, flicking his member with her little finger. She kept flicking it as he told his story.

When he finished she smiled. "At least let me try to get that in me."

He sighed and agreed. She had no success. She was the right size for him, but Damon could not get hard.

Primeval was getting frantic. She kept rubbing herself against him.

Damon told her about his family jewels.

Her eyes lit up. "Get them. Hurry." she said frantically rubbing herself all the while. He got it and attached it to himself. She calmed a little.

"Wow! It's beautiful. It looks and feels so real. How does it work?" He showed her.

"Have you ever used it before?"

"No."

"So, you're a virgin right?"

"Right."

"Great! Let me show you how to please me. It's too big for me. Can I change back?"

Damon nodded.

She changed back to Catherine.

▲ ▲ ▲

Primeval woke up in Damon's arms feeling refreshed. She was shocked. She had never fallen asleep in anyone's arms. Never! And she had never slept as Primeval.

Damon was looking down at her.

"Satisfied?"

"Yes. I can't believe you satisfied both of my forms. I am totally satisfied. For a virgin you sure know *how* and *where* to kiss me. I am now okay inside. You don't have to do it to me again and I will still be okay, because I know that you were not play acting. We were touching. I have the same *ability* as you. I felt you want me. I felt you need me. I felt you satisfy me in a way I've never been satisfied before. You have your demons, Commander, as I have mine."

"You are right. I do have my demons. Would you like to meet two of them?"

Primeval laughed, "Absolutely."

She stopped laughing. Her face betrayed her shock when Golden looked at her out of the left eye and Garnet looked at her out of the right eye. She studied them.

"Hello Primeval. Hello Cat." Two voices issued out of Damon's mouth at the same time.

"When you screw me again, can they join in?"

"Absolutely." They all laughed.

After Primeval had a shower, she came back naked to the bed and said, "What now, Commander?"

"Well, I won't tell you to do this, but I will ask you. Hastings can't function well with you around. Could you please go *satisfy* him?"

"If I do, will you have sex with me when I want it?"

"No."

"Once a Month?"

"How about, as often as you can convince me to, but in whatever form of yours I choose."

"Done. Ha! Just so you know for future reference. I will please anybody you ask or tell me to. I love sex. I don't think I want to as Primeval though. I'm not sure anybody but you is going to want this body for sex. I'm too small down there for one thing. You are almost too big for me. We both lost our virginity with this body. Oh, what the hell, I've got to stretch it some time. There is no time like the present. I'll start on it right away if you want me to. So if circumstances dictate, I will happily do what you tell me, Commander."

"No, not for now. You shared with me. Allow me to share with you. I climaxed when you did. I experienced my first orgasm with you."

"Really? You came? I didn't feel you." Her eyes went *dangerous.* Insanity lurked behind them. "You can't orgasm. We said *truth* only, remember."

Damon reached over and touched her hand.

"Don't doubt my words." He spoke earnestly. "I touch you so you will know I speak true. I experienced your orgasm *with you* Cat! Don't you understand? I can experience my partner's orgasm as if it is mine! I didn't know my body could do that. I would like to experience it again with you. I will not command you in this. I won't."

Her eyes lost their madness, as if it was never there.

He paused for a moment and let go of her hand. It lay limp. "As far as asking you to have sex with others, from now on I'll just tell you, Primeval. It's more time efficient."

Primeval smiled happily.

"Can I change back now?"

"Do you want to?"

She touched his hand. "I am touching you also, so you will know that I speak true." She continued seriously. "I only do what you tell me to do. That is what I do. I'm glad that you like to share me with others. That is a very special gift to me. You don't get jealous. You don't do it out of cruelness or contempt. You do it because you know I need it and you supply my wants. Sometimes when I want to change and you say *'No'*, I orgasm. I think you know it and do

393

it unconsciously to control me, but it *is* a total turn on. It works. When you are near, I will not change without you commanding me to. On an lone assignment, it is my choice. That is part of the contract. Please just command me and don't ask if *I want to do anything*. I always want to do everything. I have no conscience or morals. I am free of those, if I ever had them. You are my guide." She removed her hand.

"Change. Go please Hastings and come back to me and change back to yourself."

"Are you saying that Primeval is my true form?"

"To me it is. And isn't that what counts?"

"Yes, oh mighty master." Primeval bowed and scraped to the door, changed to Cat, smiled her smile and said "Anytime you want to, Commander. And as often and long as you can take it." Laughing, she ran naked down the hall to Hastings room.

▲ ▲ ▲

"Thanks for sending her down to me, Commander. She walked through the door, naked, smiled her smile and said that you sent her down to satisfy me in any way I wanted. I took her at her word. I'm okay for a month now. I have never had anybody like that. And she seemed to love it. I could never do that on an ongoing basis."

"Should I send her to you once a month, Hastings?"

"Whoa, hold on. A month may not be long enough. I'll let you know, if that's okay."

"Certainly."

Damon produced a large flash drive, from one of his pockets and handed it to Hastings.

"Listen to this recording and give me your input. I edited out certain personal information about Catherine Nipp, ShabNab's new name. ShabNab Mishak died in the Castle."

Hastings nodded in understanding.

"I've listened and I think I've got all that I could out of it. You have more life experience in this department than I do. Get back to me as soon as you can."

"Yes, Commander. I'll get on it right away."

▲ ▲ ▲

Scene Ninety Four

It was morning.

Primeval was sleeping beside Damon. They were both lying on top of the covers. There was a small knock on the door. She was naked. He had on shorts.

"Who is it?" asked Damon.

"Gary, sir. I was wondering if you would like breakfast in bed sir."

"Come in, Gary."

Gary entered. He looked surprised to see a naked woman in bed with Damon.

He walked up to the bed and looked long and hard at Primeval's body.

"Do you like what you see, Gary?"

"Is she as good a lay as she looks, sir?"

"How good would that be?"

"The best, sir!"

"She's even better, Gary."

▲ ▲ ▲

Primeval woke up with a start. What a dream! She laid back, smiled and stretched spread eagled on the bed.

She was lying on top of the covers and so was Damon. As in the *dream* he had on shorts and she was naked. That was how he liked her.

There was a small knock at the door. Damon's eyes flashed open. He sat up.

"Who is it?" Damon asked.

"My last name is Gray. I don't know what my first name is yet!" Piped a little voice in the hall. "May I come in?"

He looked at Primeval. She nodded. He smiled at her. She smiled back. He bent over and kissed her lightly on the lips. Until Damon, Primeval had never been kissed by anybody. He tasted delicious.

"Yes, you can."

The door opened and VaShena walked in.

"Good morning Commander Gray." She said politely. She saw who was with him.

"Hi Kitty Face!" she smiled. Then she stopped smiling. "Are you still Kitty Face or do you have a new name also?" she asked, very seriously.

"No. I will always be Kitty Face to you, when I am like this."

"Good. Too many names can be confusing." she turned back to Damon, stood very straight and said.

"Have you found my new name yet?"

"I have."

"You have? You *really* have?" she whispered in amazement. "Already? You must have stayed up *all night* looking!" she looked nervous. "Do you want to wait to tell me, so you can try it out and make sure you found the right one?"

"No, it is your name. No one else's. Yours only. Do you want me to say it out loud or whisper it to you?" Damon's voice dropped to a whisper at the end.

"Maybe you should whisper it to me, so we don't scare it away." She whispered back. She leaned forward and so did Damon. He whispered into her ear. She stood up. She mouthed the word silently a few times, looked at Damon and smiled.

"It fits my tongue." She said proudly. "Thank you."

"You are welcome. Would you like to go out and come in again?" asked Damon.

"Why would I want to do that? I'm already in."

"But we don't know who came in. It could have been anybody." Damon said solemnly.

"You're right!" she ran out and closed the door carefully.

Knock, Knock.

"Who's there?" asked Damon.

"Natasha Gray. May I come in?" piped the little voice again.

"Natasha, is that you?" asked Damon excitedly.

"Yes it is, Commander Gray."

"Well what are you waiting for Natasha? Come on in."

The door opened and Damon touched her with his clear aura sight. He saw the brightest and purest aura that he had ever seen walk through the door. She was not shielding herself from him this time. He couldn't see her face, it was so bright. He didn't need to. The aura matched her eyes. Pure untainted lavender.

Primeval felt *something* but saw no aura. All she saw was a happy little girl.

▲ ▲ ▲

Scene Ninety Five

"Meet me in the Dojo in one hour, dressed in Smoke fatigues."

"Yes, Commander." responded Cat.

One hour later they faced each other, at opposite ends of the Dojo, in full battle gear.

Mr. Smoke spoke.

"Change to Primeval." Cat did.

"We are going to fight, Primeval. No sparring. Not to the death, but to total defeat. Do you understand or have any questions before we start?"

"Yes Commander. *Why* are we fighting and *why* Primeval?"

"When you sparred with Hastings, I watched and evaluated. You are, by far, the best hand to hand combat fighter I have ever seen. I feel that has made you overconfident in your abilities. You think you can take me as Cat. I felt that in you. It is good to have that confidence, but you have never seen me fight. Never judge what you don't know. The reason for *Primeval* is," he paused, "I want to take away *any* excuses on either of our parts as to a just outcome. *Primeval* is the strongest and fastest of you. Are you ready?"

"I am."

He clapped his hands once.

Primeval was across the thirty foot room in two bounds. She landed purposely to the side to leave no opening to be hit before she landed. Mr. Smoke had not moved. She moved in cautiously, unsure of his tactics.

She went for the quick victory. She missed! She spun away quickly before he could strike. He did not strike! She flew at him again. She could not touch him!

No matter what she did, she could not touch him! For ten minutes this went on. She was sweating profusely. She jumped back across the room and said.

"Okay, I can't seem to touch you, but can you beat *me*?"

"Come find out, but be warned. I *am* going to hurt you. Please understand that."

With an unconscious feline snarl, she was back across the room and on the attack.

Within seconds she was on her back, on the floor, dazed. *What the hell had happened?* Mr. Smoke was walking lightly towards her. She rolled to her feet and threw a kick at his knees. He swayed ever so slightly and his elbow came down on her upper leg muscle. She collapsed on the floor in pain and rolled. Quickly, she overcame the pain and reflexively kicked him in the crotch. He smiled. She cursed. He didn't respond to that blow. It was as if he allowed her a mistake.

Within another ten minutes she was unconscious on the floor.

▲ ▲ ▲

Primeval awoke with Damon's hands on her body. She laid still and felt his hands.

She had heard of healers who used the *laying of the hands*, but this was the first time she had experienced it.

Every pain he touched receded and vanished within seconds.

She watched his face as he worked. Sweat drenched his blank face. He was not seeing through his eyes. He was seeing through something else.

When he finished, his eyes came back into focus.

"You are *one tough mother* of a fighter." He said wearily. "I have never taken that long to take someone out! Ten minutes, fifteen seconds. Before this, my longest bout lasted three minutes, two seconds." He saw her looking at his hands. He shrugged and smiled.

"Don't ask me to do this often. My healing ability is designed only for me. It drains me terribly to heal others. I have only done it to Hastings once and now to you. Your injuries were much more severe. You never gave up. I had to knock you unconscious. No permanent damage has been done. I have repaired you."

"What do you mean, *no permanent damage?* You broke both my arms and legs! I remember distinctly."

"Try to move."

She did. Her arms and legs were fine. Her legs felt stronger. She flexed them.

"I *'transferred'*, is the best word to describe it, some muscle tissue from your stomach to your calves. It should give you greater balance, power and agility. If you are not satisfied I can transfer it back. It will take a little time though, and I have to rest for awhile."

His face *did* look ashen with fatigue. She checked out her calves. They looked great! She stood. Her center of balance had changed. She tried a few moves.

"These new legs are great! Thank you. Will they transfer over to Cats form?"

"I don't know. They should. Change and find out."

"I just needed you to tell me." She changed. It transferred over. The effect was spectacular on a form with body fat.

"Wow!" was all she could say when she looked in the full length mirror.

"I agree." said Damon.

"I would say that this makes up for you breaking and bruising every muscle and bone in my body."

"Technically........"

"You know what I meant. I really don't hold you responsible. I went into it with both eyes open. I needed to be broken as I was, to know that it was not a lucky blow on your part. I accept defeat, but I don't feel angry. Why is that?" She looked at him, with lost eyes.

"How would I know? I'm emotionally crippled, with a hundred and fifty year old man's knowledge, in a thirty five year old body that is as fit as a twenty one year olds in perfect physical condition. A lot like yours. My face looks older though. It's the silver mixed in with the blond. Maybe it's because you now *trust* me? And you know I *can* kill you, as I said I could."

Cat laughed. "I understood *'How would I know?'* The rest was confusing. I didn't understand what you meant. It doesn't matter. I think it's because I met a better fighter." She smiled her smile. "Can you teach me your fighting skills?"

"If you teach me yours."

"Agreed."

"I'm taking Natasha to a movie and hot dogs after. I will see you tomorrow at noon in Castle Florentine. I will be in the Blades vacated office."

"As you order, Commander. I'm going to test these new legs on some of the men in the city. Bye for now." With that she ran towards the door on her new legs.

When she reached the door, she turned and looked back at Damon, who still hadn't moved from where he was sitting.

Cat spoke softly, but her voice carried to the farthest corner of the room. "I accepted defeat, and didn't feel angry, not only because I had met a better fighter, Commander. A large part of it is…" she paused for a moment, struggling to find the words. At last, she said the words, like it was an epiphany. "A large part of it is because I respect *you* and who you are … and what you do, Commander. Holy shit!" With that, she fled the room.

▲ ▲ ▲

Scene Ninety Six

It was Saturday morning, at Arrow Wood Estates, their in England. Michael and Sylvia had given the staff the weekend off. It was a rainy, dreary day. They had just finished breakfast.

"Michael," Sylvia called from the living room. "did you send any of my photos to the magazines?"

"What?"

"I said... oh, never mind." She muttered as she continued to read the tabloid, sitting in the nude, lotus style.

"What is that you said darling?" Michael said, walking into the room.

"Did you send any of my pictures into the tabloids?"

"No, why?"

"Someone did and it's *ruining* my reputation, that's why!"

"What in the world are you talking about?"

"They have this innocent little picture of me sleeping. They say I look like Grace Kelly. We have to stop this! I've worked hard to get the sexy, beach bunny, bride look for you and they are ruining it. We have to do something. Think of something."

Her husband laughed when he saw the picture.

"I took that one Syl, one night. You looked so beautiful. I had it on my desk when I gave that reporter an interview on the life of a retired playboy. I bet he copied or stole it. What should we do?" He leaned forward and kissed her lightly.

"I want you to send my best, nasty nudie shots, to a porn magazine anonymously! You've got some good ones."

"Which pictures should I send?"

"I don't know. Let's take some new ones! Pictures of you making love to me."

"We'll have to have someone else take the pictures."

"Someone else?"

"I can't make love to you and take the pictures at the same time." He paused for a moment in thought.

"Wait, I've got another idea. What would really make the tabloids go crazy?"

"The only thing I can think of, is infidelity." Sylvia responded.

"Right! How about a love marathon, with you satisfying multiple men at once?"

"Oh Mickey, I couldn't …….. Could I?" she asked innocently, teasingly.

"They would all be at least my size or bigger. I know of three guys that make me look like Damon Gray. We've been chums since I hit puberty." He gave his wife a lecherous smile. He leaned forward and continued softly.

"Did I ever tell you, all the young men had a measuring contest in Military College and seven of us won. Out of twenty five hundred boys I was second. Only the Donkey beat me. Needless to say, it made our reputations with the ladies. We were known as the Magnificent Seven. I won't bore you with the details of our conquests. Suffice to say that being fabulously rich allowed us many kinky, downright bizarre and wonderful sexual adventures. We've all been friends since. They are the poker group I play with once a month. You know them all."

"Really? Your poker group? Wow! Have you done anything with them since you and I got together?"

He looked at his wife. She smiled.

"I told you there would never be a problem if you had sex with other women. Your job might require it. I will only have a problem if you *make love* to anyone else."

"No, darling." He smiled. "You are more than I can handle and I love it. I will tell you all about it *if* it ever happens."

"That' fine, now tell me more about your poker group."

"Just think, darling. Six well endowed men, one bigger than me."

"Now that's a statement to bring wet dreams!"

"The Donkey can't always come to the monthly game. He's kept busy."

"Isn't he a porn star? He seemed so nice when I met him."

"Yes, he's huge. Has to have special condoms made. No woman on film has ever taken all of him. I think you could."

"Really, sweetheart?"

He leaned forward and took her hand in his.

"Frankly, Scarlet, I *do* think you'd do a *damn* fine job." He said in his British accent version of Clark Gable. She giggled.

"I'm getting excited just thinking about it."

"Shall I arrange it?"

She paused and looked at her husband hard. He smiled. Sylvia looked startled. Then she smiled back hesitantly.

"I thought you were just joking …. Are you really serious Michael?"

"I am. It did start out as a joke, but I could see it turned you on as much as me." What he said was true. She looked deep into his eyes, not smiling.

"I don't think I could do it, though, sweetheart. I don't want to risk losing what we have. Yes, the fantasy is exciting, but I've found the *fantasy* to usually be far and away more fun than the *reality*."

"Oh, but this fantasy will be better than the reality. I have no intention of using the Six of The Magnificent Seven. They can be pigs that way. Nice pigs, but pigs none the less. I'm talking about three men that you will have as much fun with as me, if not more."

"I have *never* had better sex, than I've had with you."

"If, when you meet them, you don't want to continue, that's fine. I'll be surprised and disappointed, but I'll get over it."

Sylvia looked at her husband suspiciously. "You'll be surprised and disappointed if I don't want to continue? Okay, what *aren't* you telling me, Mickey?"

"Just trust me on this. Meet them and then make your decision, alright?"

"Who are they and what are their names?"

"I know them all very well. Intimately, as a matter of fact. One is German. His stage name is *Handle*. One is Scottish and his stage name is Angus the *Bull*. The last is Spanish and his stage name is *Donald Juan, Don for short*. You will love them all."

Sylvia laughed. "All right husband. Bring them on." Then she asked seriously. "Do you think things will change between us, you know, sexually, afterwards?"

"If you mean, would it get better, absolutely. Imagine. We will have our own porn movies to watch and turn us on when we get older. And our Grandchildren."

"Grandchildren?"

"Absolutely. And we should have a lot. I heard that grandchildren are better than children, which is perfect, because I don't want any children!"

Sylvia laughed. "You've already used that one, but it's still cute. You know that I don't want any children either. But, no more teasing, *please!* Would you *really* like me to do this, sweetheart?"

"Absolutely. Give me a few minutes to make some phone calls." she nodded and he left the room. "They might want to wear masks!" she called after him.

He returned twenty minutes later.

"What took you so long? How did it go?" She asked nervously.

"They are on there way."

"Now? But I thought …"

"They didn't want to wait. They thought you might change your mind. So did I. We have the place to ourselves till Monday morning. I decided I couldn't do the shoot justice on my own. I figured if we're in for a penny, we might as well be in for a pound and do it right, so I arranged to have delivered over, three photographers cameras, as well. I called in some favors and got six world class movie cameras and a professional videographer also to arrange the set for us and he is very well connected to the media. He swears the equipment is the finest that money can buy. They're the best of the best, fully automated. He will do the lighting as well. Every frame will be crystal clear. If there's a great shot, the camera's will get it. The equipment will all be here in one hour. The three men shortly after."

"Oh my gosh, this is really happening! I look a mess. What'll I wear?"

"Just your smile dear. I'm kidding. Here, let me help you." He took her up to the bedroom and helped her pick out an outfit.

"Bye the bye. One of the demands I had to bow to, to make this happen is that I agreed, on your behalf, to let all parties experience you multiple times." he looked at her innocently.

His wife laughed impishly. "We'll see after I meet them. I thought that this was to be a one time deal. Are we going to do this again?"

"I don't know. That's up to you. You might get *addicted.*"

▲ ▲ ▲

Sunday night at twelve o'clock midnight, the house was empty of men and photography equipment, except for Michael and Sylvia. The last had disappeared an hour previously.

Sylvia came out of the shower wrapped in a towel and stopped to look at her face in the mirror. Her face didn't have eyebrows. It made her whole face look different, in a good way. She decided she liked her face without eyebrows, even without makeup. It made

407

her big eyes look bigger. She had waxed them off at the last minute when they wouldn't shape right. Her eyebrows were pale, fine and thin anyway. She had applied her makeup theatrical style for the shoot.

Everybody had loved it. Michael, the Bull, Andy and Don.

She turned and jumped on the bed facing her husband.

Her whole body was pink and glowing. Her full lips were swollen slightly.

"Wow, I sure didn't think it would take two *whole* days, pardon the pun. And the things they made me do! You were right, it could be *addicting*. That was a cute play on words, *a dick thing*. Are we really going to show everybody everything we did?"

"Yes, we are."

"Good! I was just checking. I would hate to do all that work and not get recognized. How do you think it went? How did I do?" she asked shyly, smiling nervously.

"I'm not sure. We may have to do it again." He said seriously. Sylvia looked shocked.

"Again? Are you serious?" She smiled uncertainly.

"Yes."

"Okay. When and with whom?"

"Whom?"

"You taught me well." She smiled impishly.

"Now and with me, if you are up to it."

Sylvia smiled, pulled off her towel and stood in front of him. Looking down at herself and then back up to her husband, she said.

"Am I up to it? If you will notice I couldn't be any more up to it than I am right now. My whole body is swollen with desire. You know that what you just said would do it, didn't you?"

Michael smiled a smug, self satisfied smile and nodded, not speaking.

"Yes, my Lord. I thought you'd never ask."

A few minutes later, she giggled and said. "My god, are you ever *small compared to your friends.*"

"Hush and kiss me with your beautiful, swollen lips." he laughed. She did.

▲ ▲ ▲

Scene Ninety Seven

The entertainment world was buzzing. Sylvia was the talk of the town. Pictures of her were rampant on the internet. Soon the videos followed.

She was named, the Internet Porn Queen ,by the news media.

"And here is the Internet Porn Queen, Sylvia. Sylvia can we ask......."

Reporters descended on the couple in droves.

To all the questions, Michael professed anger and indignation, along with, "No comment."

Sylvia just flashed her radiant smile and said "No comment."

She continued to wear her makeup theatrical style. She continued to no longer sport any eyebrows. Her facial lips had remained slightly swollen or enlarged.

People asked her if she had injections. Where did she get it done? Women around the world wanted their lips to look exactly like hers. Millions of women waxed off their eyebrows.

No matter how rude the question, Sylvia just smiled and said "No comment."

Michael's parents were mortified. Michael calmed them down by saying that it was a good thing that the news media had not gotten wind of any of *his* younger exploits. He said hers paled in comparison.

What she *wouldn't* answer, were answered by the media. They had a field day.

Sylvia also answered, when asked by the media if it would happen again, "No comment."

Michael asked her if she would like that. She said "Yes, but no more cameras or videos unless it gets really, really kinky and different."

Michael laughed and said, "If that's the case, we'll need to get more memory cards."

"You know me too well, husband." She laughed naughtily.

▲ ▲ ▲

Scene Ninety Eight

The Board of the A.T.C.U. were very upset at first. They didn't know how to react to the media frenzy.

They requested a formal hearing at the parliament building at their *secret room*. The Prime Minister was there.

Michael chose not to bring representation.

He faced the members of the board alone.

It took all of them by surprise.

When confronted with it, Michael supplied all with a complete video collection and pictures of the exploits of his wife. He told them he didn't want to hold anything back. They didn't know what to do. Everybody took them home to view them. Nobody brought them back.

It turned out that there was really nothing that they *could* do to Michael. He had done nothing that he could be held accountable for. Neither he, nor Sylvia posed any threat to the government or his organization, by what his wife had done.

Later it proved to be beneficial to the A.T.C.U. Michael and Sylvia were invited to places and parties they had never been before. Places where Michael gained important information on *terrorism*. Information that allowed many to be arrested and imprisoned.

At one such gathering, Lord and Lady Brighton were invited and taken to an illegal arms warehouse, where Sylvia posed in front of the weapons with and for the six horny terrorist arms dealer's cameras.

When they went to prison, they bragged that they all knew her. No one argued. The pictures were used to help convict them. They had copies sent to all their friends. They, in fact, helped convict themselves.

Any suspicions anybody had on Michael's involvement with A.T.C.U. were dispelled.

They were in demand everywhere.

They were the talk of the town.

When further exploits of his wife surfaced, they turned a blind eye. Copies were, of course, requested. And supplied.

No more formal hearings were requested.

Many, if not all, on the Board, invited them to all of their social events as well.

No party or event was complete without them.

Michael and Sylvia rode the media wave and enjoyed every minute of it.

Scene Ninety Nine

"Lord and Lady Brighton, sir." Whitner announced to Damon Gray.

"Thank you Whitner. Please bring their wine."

"Damon!" exclaimed Sylvia. "How are you? It's been forever." She ran up and gave him a big hug.

"It has been awhile hasn't it?" Damon said. He gave Michael a handshake.

They sat and enjoyed the fireplace in the library, Damon's favorite room.

"I hear you picked up a castle in Venezuela. How is it?" Michael asked.

"You *are good* Michael. How in the world did you find out?" Damon looked shocked!

"You sent us an email offering to sell the arms that came with it. Remember?"

"Oh, that's right." They both laughed.

"Thanks for helping me to find that buyer." Damon added.

"You are welcome. They were happy with the deal. They thanked us for putting you in touch with them."

"Oh, enough shop talk. Tell me about yourself." Sylvia demanded.

As if on cue, Whitner entered the room.

"Miss Natasha Gray." He announced formally.

A little girl, who looked about four or five, in a light silver dress with lavender trim, walked in. Her long, dark chestnut hair was curled and lavender ribbons were tied in simple bows and placed randomly throughout her hair.

"Thank you Whitner. That will be all." her little voice piped.

"Yes, miss."

She watched him leave. When he was out of earshot, she turned to Damon.

"How was that?" She bent forward slightly and spoke lowly, so Whitner wouldn't hear. "Did I do alright?"

"You did great Natasha." Damon smiled. "Just like a princess would."

Natasha beamed. Then went serious. "Thank you, Commander. And who are you?" she asked, turning to the Brighton's.

"I am Michael and this is my wife Sylvia. We are good friends of Damon Gray."

"Oh good, then I can tell you." She looked around slowly, to make sure none of the staff were around.

"Be on your best behavior. We have a Lord and Lady coming over for dinner. Be polite and try to be interested in what they are saying, even if they are *'stuffed shirts'*, whatever that is."

She turned to Damon. "It was okay for me to warn them, wasn't it? Or did you already do it?"

"No, I didn't warn them. Thank you Natasha. Who told you those things?"

"Gertrude did. She said they used to own Blackstone before you did, but almost never came here. I wonder why. It is so beautiful. Like you, Sylvia." She said looking up at Sylvia. "Mysterious and wonderful and beautiful. If you are a friend of the Commander, then you *have* to be wonderful, like Blackstone. Don't you love it? I love your eyes. Will you teach me how to look as beautiful as you, someday? It doesn't have to be right now. I can wait. Nice to meet you, Sylvia." She held out her hand and smiled up at Sylvia.

Sylvia was silent for a moment. She looked at Damon, then back at Natasha.

"Natasha, it is nice to meet you." She reached down and shook the child's hand.

After she released it, Natasha said, "Now, I *know* you're wonderful."

"Why thank you Natasha. That is the best compliment I have ever had. You have beautiful eyes also. I have never met anyone with pure lavender eyes before. And I also agree with you on Blackstone, it is beautiful and mysterious and wonderful. But it wasn't this way until Damon … ah, the Commander, bought it and worked his magic on it."

"You must be a very good friend if you know he can work *magic*. We are going to be best friends, you and me. I mean *I*."

She looked at Michael.

"I haven't forgotten you, Michael. Sylvia can be my best *girl* friend and you can be my best *boy* friend!" she stuck out her little hand. Michael shook it.

"You are like the Commander a little bit, but not the same. He is way, way, way *more dangerous*. You are wonderful too. Can you play music like him?"

Damon, Michael and Sylvia laughed.

"No." Michael responded. "Nobody can play music like Damon Gray."

Natasha looked at Damon and said "Commander, may I go and play with my dolls until supper or the Lord and Lady arrive, please?"

"Yes you may, princess."

"Thank you, sir." She turned and dashed for the door. At the door she stopped, turned and laughed,

"I'm not a princess! Sylvia is. See you all at supper." With that said, she turned and fled.

"Where in the world did she come from? She is precious beyond words." Sylvia said to Damon.

"It is a long story, Sylvia. I rescued her from a pirate stronghold where she was being held captive. She was waiting for me to. That is her short version." Damon laughed.

"Why did you invite us tonight, Damon? Not that I'm complaining. We'd love to see more of you. I felt when you called that it was something more. Was I right?"

"Yes, Michael you were. You are the first *real friends* I have made since my parents died. I have decided that I would like to bring you closer into my circle if you would like."

"Why would you want to do that, Damon?" Sylvia asked. "Are you sure you can trust us?"

"You already know some of what happens in my inner circle, like the restaurant incident, Sylvia. I appreciate your silence, both of you. And yes Michael, I ran both ways and broke his neck. I didn't drop him off the roof though; I just positioned him to look like it and *then* climbed onto the roof and made the appropriate marks."

"Were you eves dropping on us?" Sylvia said with mock surprise.

"Would you really like to know?"

Michael and Sylvia looked at each other. Something passed between them. Michael answered for both of them.

"You hold our lives in your hand, Damon. One word from you would have every terrorist in the world hunting us and our family. You have saved our lives on at least two occasions. If you are asking for our silence on anything you tell us … you have it. Unconditionally." Michael paused. "The answer is *yes*."

"Why didn't you just say so? I know I can trust you two....The answer is, No, I just have extremely sensitive hearing." All three laughed.

"You can tell Michael *now*, if you like Syl." Damon added.

"Tell him what?............You mean I was right? You *are* Mr. Smoke?"

"What? Mr. Smoke? What a joke Syl...................." Michael stopped.

417

"Holy... *Fucking*.....Shit! *Are* you Mr. Smoke, Damon?"

"Yes I am. And none of those three words make any sense to me, Michael. Does it have something to do with angels and animals?"

Both Michael and Sylvia broke into uncontrollable laughter.

When they had calmed down a bit, Damon said, "I didn't think it was *that* funny!"

That started another bout of laughter. Damon looked puzzled. Finally Sylvia gasped out, "It's not *what* you said Damon, it's *how* you said it!" She looked at him closely. *"And you knew it!* You *do* continue to amaze me."

Damon smiled.

Wiping his eyes, Michael said seriously, "I should have known. The night of the café incident, I told my wife that only *you and Mr. Smoke* could get away with that. You both operate outside the law. Happy to meet you *Mr. Smoke*." He stuck out his hand. "This is my ravishingly beautiful wife, Sylvia."

Damon shook both their hands.

"I'm Princess Sylvia, didn't you hear Natasha?" Sylvia said with a twinkle in her eye.

"You've been promoted. It's Queen Sylvia, isn't that what the media calls you?" Damon responded. Again they all laughed.

"Oh, I will be having someone joining us for dinner. My Personal Assistant. She knows that I am Mr. Smoke. You will meet her shortly."

"*Her?* You've invited a woman to dine with us? Who is she Damon?" Sylvia asked excitedly.

Just then Whitner walked in and announced, "Miss Catherine Nipp."

He turned and left.

Catherine walked directly to Damon and she gave a slight bow. She was wearing high heeled shoes and a two piece version of her signature white cutout dress in a miniskirt style. The skirt sat extremely low on her hips and was scandalously cut down in the front like the top of a heart. The top hung straight down and stopped just below her bust line, showing glimpses of the bottom of her breasts as she moved. The top was connected to the skirt by a series of strings of pearls.

"Good evening, Commander."

"Good evening Catherine. Allow me to introduce you to my friends. Michael, Sylvia, I would like to introduce you to my Personal Assistant, Catherine Nipp. Catherine, Lord and Lady Brighton. I have informed them of my Mr. Smoke status."

Michael was stunned. It was *ShabNab Mishak* who walked up to them. She hadn't changed at all in fifteen years, except for her abs and legs. They were beyond exquisite, he thought. That was the only difference he could see in her, as she turned and held out her hand to him.

"Hello Michael. It's wonderful to see you again." She said as he took her hand in his.

She then held out her hand to Sylvia. "You are even more beautiful in person than on the screen Sylvia. It is a true pleasure to meet you."

"Thank you." Sylvia placed her hand in Cats.

"Again?" Sylvia asked. "You two have met before?"

"Many, many years ago." Catherine said with her smile. Her ice blue eyes gleamed, catching the light.

Sylvia's eyes widened. She smiled back.

"You're *ShabNab!* Why, you don't look more than twenty years old. Why did you try to kill Michael?" she asked curiously, with no anger.

"*ShabNab* is no more." Cat said softly. "My name is Catherine Nipp. And I didn't try to kill Michael, Sylvia. I never *try*. I *do*. I made sure his plane was in the air before I took out the general. He was my target." She smiled again. "But enough shop talk. Can I get your autograph on my Video discs?"

"Of course. If you would like, I'll have complete copies made from our masters, so there is nothing missing."

"I'd love it, thank you." Their hands parted.

Whitner appeared, "Dinner is served."

▲ ▲ ▲

Scene One Hundred

After dinner, the four retired to the Library, again. Natasha had been put to bed by one of the nannies. She had hugged Lord and Lady Brighton and said she hoped that she would see them again. She said that she wasn't sorry that the *'stuffed shirts'* hadn't come, that they were *much* more fun!

Michael and Damon were talking to each other, and Sylvia and Catherine were talking to each other. Michael and Damon were talking shop. Sylvia and Catherine were talking of other things.

At one point later on, Sylvia said, "I absolutely love your calf development. Can you give me your routine and can I borrow your abs tomorrow night? We have a function to go to."

Catherine laughed. "Thank you for the compliment, Sylvia. It is appreciated. For both you'll have to talk to the Commander about that. I got both of them from him."

"Really?" She turned her head. "Damon?"

"Yes, Sylvia?" Damon answered, cutting off his sentence to Michael.

"Catherine said I had to ask you about getting her abs and calf muscles. She said she got them from you. When can we start? I'll do whatever you tell me."

"Is it alright with you, Michael?" Damon asked his friend.

"Of course. Why wouldn't it be?"

"Alright Sylvia. Please stand and take off all your clothes."

"Excuse me?" Sylvia said in surprise.

"You heard me. Stand up and take off all your clothes."

"You heard the man, dear. Do as he says. He must want to evaluate your body."

"Yes dear." Sylvia laughed. She stood and disrobed.

"I'm going to have to knock you unconscious. Is that all right?" Damon asked.

"What in the hell are you talking about, Damon?" Sylvia demanded exasperated.

Damon laughed and explained the process. He finished by saying, "Awake your body resists the changes. I can heal when a person is awake, but not make integral changes to their anatomy. It takes a lot out of me but if you are willing to put your body in my hands, I think I can improve it slightly. Your body is in phenomenal shape. Like Cat's, I don't have to do a lot. The choice is yours. If you would like something special, I can try to oblige. Well, Sylvia?"

Sylvia just looked at him. She started to laugh and stopped. She looked at Catherine. "Cat, is Damon speaking the truth or is he just pulling my leg. No one can do that, can they?"

"No, *they* can't, Syl." Cat said. Sylvia started to smile. "But *he* can. The Commander did it to me while I was unconscious, after we fought to *defeat* and he beat me senseless, breaking both my arms and legs in the process. I'm the second best hand to hand combat trained killer in the world. Mr. Smoke has agreed to train me to match him. In return, I will teach him all I know. The only thing that will give him the edge when he has finished training me will be his superior size and strength." she finished with a quiet pride.

Sylvia was astounded by the things Cat was saying. There were so many things about Damon Gray that she didn't know. She would pursue this later.

"I'd love to do it, Damon. What do *you* think, sweetheart?"

"Is it reversible, Damon?" Michael asked.

"Yes it is Michael. I can change it again. I'll probably never get it back *exactly* the way it was before, but I will get close. About ninety nine point eight percent. It is an instinctual process for me. I will do Sylvia no harm. I will only do what feels right for her body."

"I'm okay with that, are you, darling?" Michael asked his wife.

"I don't know … Only ninety nine point eight percent, if I don't like it?"

Damon nodded seriously. Sylvia burst into spontaneous laughter causing Michael and Cat to as well.

"Of course I am. I'm ready. Before you punch my lights out, does anybody have any suggestions that they think will improve me?"

Catherine spoke.

"To highlight your abs, you might want him to move some of your waist and hip fat up and increase your bust size a couple of cups sizes and to strengthen and tighten up your skin. Make your skin more elastic, is what I was trying to say. You look great now, but with increased bust size, gravity works on them. He strengthened my skins elasticity. I don't know whether he knew it or not."

"I did Cat. Thanks for noticing."

Michael spoke. "This may sound silly, but could you increase her butt size and lift it slightly? I think it would look more exotic."

"I agree." Cat said.

"It all sounds good to me. Can you do all that, Damon?"

"I am yours to command, my queen." Damon laughed. They all joined in.

"Anything else, your majesty?" Damon asked dryly.

"Oh, and could you make sure my facial lips stay as they are. I used a lip enhancing gel on them and they swelled to this size and haven't gone down. I love them this way."

"Lay down please." was all he said.

Damon touched a nerve and put her under.

▲　▲　▲

When Sylvia awoke, she didn't feel a whole lot different.

"Am I done?" she asked.

Everybody was looking at her.

She sat up. She felt the added weight on her chest. Looking down she said, "Holy cow!"

Everybody laughed, including her, as soon as the words popped out of her mouth.

"I didn't mean it *that* way!"

She stood. Someone had brought a full length three sided mirror in. She looked at herself from every angle. Damon had made some dramatic changes in her body. All improvements, as far as she was concerned.

She ran to Damon, chest swaying and hugged and kissed him. Damon swayed on his feet and then sat down in a chair.

"Thank you. Everything you did, you did perfect!" she said. Turning to her husband, she posed.

"What do you all think?"

"Just look at my pants." Michael said. The pants answered the question.

Sylvia turned to Catherine and looked at her questioningly. "Your honest opinion, please."

"The truth is, I have never envied another woman's body in my life. I do now. The Commander will have to do some more work on me, if he will?" she looked at Damon.

"Yes, Cat, but not for awhile, alright?" Cat nodded, satisfied.

"I must now go to bed for awhile. Cat, please show them out. How about we all go out two weeks from now for dinner and a play? Make a weekend of it. You might want to wear that blue green spandex dress that accents your unique turquoise eye color, Sylvia. It should still fit you."

"You're right. It's one of my favorites." She acknowledged.

Everyone agreed.

"Make the arrangements, Catherine. After you show them out please come back and help me up to bed." Looking at Sylvia's concerned face, he smiled.

"You've worn me out my queen, but only temporarily. I'll be fine tomorrow. Goodnight."

After the Brighton's had gone, Catherine helped carry, strip and put Damon to bed. He was very, very weak. He looked emaciated.

She was about to leave after she had laid the covers over him, when he spoke.

"I am not commanding Cat. I am asking you to strip and lay on me. I need some of your strength. It will make you weak for a little while only. Will you let me have it?"

"Why do you ask me these questions?" Cat suddenly stormed, her eyes blazing with madness. "You are weak! I could do as I want with you. You are not a threat to me right now. Why do you not command me?" She was shaking with passion.

"Because I need to know the answer." he said simply.

Shaking uncontrollable Catherine Nipp approached the bed and looked down at Damon. He could see and feel the insane madness showing in her eyes. Then clumsily she climbed on the bed, pulled back the covers and lowered herself on top of him.

"Do you want me or Primeval?"

"You, Cat. You are just as important and beautiful to me as Primeval. Don't you know that?"

Afterwards as they were lying together, he whispered into her sleeping ear. "Thank you, Kitty Face." Damon wasn't sure, but she seemed to purr for a moment.

▲ ▲ ▲

Scene One Hundred One

Seven days later, Damon finished working on Cat's and Primeval's body. He worked on Cats body first and then had her turn Primeval to see the effects on that body. Then he finished in reverse, working with Primeval's body first then Cats. It took him a week to complete. It had taken him only one full day to completely recover from Sylvia's transformation, thanks to the energy he absorbed from Cat. It would have taken another two days without it. She was fine the next morning, following the drain.

After he had finished with her transformation, she did not look like ShabNab any longer. No one would recognize her except for her eyes. She looked older, but not much. She gained a slightly more mature look in her face. Between twenty five to thirty years old.

Her new face and body was all Cat's and Primeval's visions. Damon just followed her wishes. It didn't matter to him at all what she looked like. It was her body.

He did make some minor improvements, though. He quickened her reflexes tremendously. When he saw how well it turned out, he performed the same changes on himself, unbeknownst to Cat.

He found a way to increase her stamina twofold. He again performed the same changes to himself, but his was exponentially greater because of his two, fully functioning, hearts. She never knew he wasn't that way already. He also substantially increased her flexibility and his as well.

When he had finished with her makeover, he could have done Sylvia's without breaking a sweat. He had increased the density of his entire body.

He got that trick from Primeval. Because of it, like Primeval, his body fat decreased dramatically to the point of nonexistence and his muscles stood out in high relief, even relaxed. He looked like a human anatomy model thinly covered with golden flesh. Because of the lack of body fat, he toughened his skin by increasing its density. He then had to thicken it so that if someone touched or pinched it, it would feel normal. It looked the same, although it felt smoother. He tested it. It was extremely hard to cut or puncture. He could heal quicker also, with no scarring. He had to increase the nerve endings in his skin to compensate.

He also did these same modifications with Cat. She actually had him overdo her sensitivity. He observed her and readjusted his to match hers. It made him much more aware of things. As he told her later. "I learned as much from you, as I gave you. Thank you."

Cat didn't understand and didn't want to. She had a new toy to play with. Herself.

In forty eight hours earth time, with the help of the three triangles, Switch, Garnet and Golden, Damon went *Elseware* and forced his body to gain thirty pounds of muscle to bring his body dimensions close to his pre-dense body, to be able to fit his clothes properly.

His clothes still didn't fit after the weight gain. His proportions were different. They were still large around the waist and extremely tight in the shoulders. He stood nude on his rotating body analyzer and the light beams created a three dimensional computer image of him. He designed and ordered a new wardrobe to fit. He emailed the patterns to Giovanni Bruno. He had three outfits made immediately and flown in and delivered in three days. They fit to his satisfaction.

He had Whitner take all the clothing that didn't fit to one of the local charity stores. He told Cat to replace her complete wardrobe as well. None of her clothes fit her properly either.

She said, "As you order, Commander." and ran out the door with her new company credit card to comply.

She was back four days later with a small number of extra large suitcases.

Damon was surprised.

When questioned, Cat just said that a few extraordinarily beautiful clothes were better than a closet full of beautiful ones. Also less confusing.

She had her signature cutout dresses made to her new measurements, in three colors and in three lengths. Micro-mini, mini and to mid knee. She bought no underwear. She knew that Damon didn't like them. It was distracting to him.

When he was out, Cat walked around Blackstone dressed, but when the Commander was in she walked around nude. The staff quickly acclimated. They had seen her nude so much that they didn't react to her unclothed body at all.

Catherine, in her designer clothing, affected them *very* much.

▲ ▲ ▲

Hastings returned to Blackstone. He had been gone three weeks to finalize the sale and delivery of one company jet and to oversee the completion of the new one.

The new one was designed by Damon. The computer system they put in was done according to the blueprints. Nobody knew what they were, much less how to use them. That was Hastings department. Everything tested out fine.

When he arrived at Blackstone, he didn't recognize Catherine at first. She happened to be wearing only sunglasses and high heels when she came around a corner, almost walking into him. His eyes popped.

She smiled her smile and said "Hello, Hastings. How was your trip?"

"Cat? Is that you?"

"Yes it is. I can see you like my new body. I think you better have the Commander send me to you again. He's in the gym." She walked away.

"My trip was good." He called after her. She turned her head, lowered her sunglasses and smiled right into his eyes.

"Shit!" he said to himself, under his breath.

He found his boss working out. He walked up to his bent over back and said.

"Commander, what happened to Cats body?"

Damon lowered the weight slowly, put it down gently, straightened and turned around, undoing the band that held his hair in a pony tail to keep it out of his eyes..

"Holy….. never mind Cat! What has happened to *your* body?"

"Hello Hastings. Nice to see you also. Yes, the weather *has* been good, hasn't it? And how was your trip?"

"What …… *What are you talking about?* I've been gone a little over three weeks and I come back to……." He stopped himself and took a deep breath.

"I shouldn't be surprised." He said shaking his head. He started to chuckle, then laugh.

"I'm sorry Commander, but it was a bit of a jolt. I walk through the door and see the sexiest naked woman on the face of the planet ask me how my trip was. It wasn't until she smiled that I recognized her. She is perfect in every way, Commander. She is every man's *Wet Dream Woman*. She told me to have you send her to me. Then as she was walking away, she hit me with a sexual blast that made me wet my pants. Honest to god, I came in my pants."

"Done. And I'll tell her not to use that weapon on you again."

"Thanks. For both. The one plane is sold and delivered and I flew the new one back. Sweeeeet! I love it. There is nothing like it in the world and the feeling I get flying her matches it. Now tell me, what the hell has been going on while I've been gone, sir. Your face looks thinner, harder. Older by a few years. I take it you've been *Elseware* for a long time, judging from the length of your hair. Your new body looks positively scary sir, intimidating. You are close to the same size you used to be. You seem slightly smaller in the chest, but it may be just an illusion caused by the thicker and broader arms and shoulders. The way everything is put together seems, uh, different."

He studied Damon's body intently for a moment. "Harder somehow, ropey looking. Your muscles look like interwoven, braided steel cables. You have no body fat. I can see every one of your muscle fibers. "You look like you're getting ready to go to war, Commander."

He squeezed Damons arm. "I knew it! It feels the same as it looks. You look like you could lift a fully armored tank and throw it across the room."

"Don't be ridiculous. A fully armored tank? Come on, Hastings. Maybe a stripped tank but not a fully armored one." They both laughed.

▲ ▲ ▲

Damon brought Hastings up to date on all that had transpired since he had gone, *minus Primeval.*

"I heard on the news about Queen Sylvia." Hastings said later. "The media is all over it. They are claiming that she has had major plastic or reconstructive surgery done to every part of her body. I guess she has, in a way. Anyway, it seems that she is now being deluged with movie offers from all the major studios. What a blast it has to be for her. It couldn't happen to a nicer person."

"I agree. Cat and I are going out with Michael and Sylvia this weekend. Do you think you could take Natasha to Disneyland?"

"I would be delighted. I have to tell you Commander, I love that little girl. There is just something about her ......oh, forget it. I don't know how to explain it. Can we take the new jet?"

"I wouldn't have it any other way. Have the copilot sit in the back for awhile and have Natasha fly it for a bit if you like. You can drop us off at the *Coutances* on your way and pick us up on the way back. By the way, I can modify your body a little, if you would like?"

"No thanks, Commander. Not right now. I'm happy with the way I am, thanks to your father. I will tell you when, and if, I decide to take you up on that. I *will* accept healing though when I need it."

"Done. Send Cat down and I'll send her to you."

"I'll come to you as soon as I can get out of bed tomorrow." He smiled. "For a healing."

▲ ▲ ▲

Scene One Hundred Two

Damon now wore his family jewels constantly. After Damon had perfected the family jewels, he'd custom designed a unique adhesive mixed with his own DNA to attach it to his body. The adhesive he used was breathable, allowing it to bond and become part of his body indefinitely. It would not come off unless he used a special adhesive remover. It bonded and blended with his body seamlessly creating a perfectly natural look. Catherine agreed to teach him the art of pleasing a woman sexually. She made him use it on her multiple times to make sure it felt right and to teach him new moves and techniques. He could make it grow to a multitude of different lengths, sizes and hardness's. Located in the testicles, the tiny powerful rechargeable batteries were powered by the heat of his body. At its smallest setting he was able to have sex with *Primeval*.

The first time was an experience they both would never forget. He had to use his healing powers to repair the skin on his back, chest and arms. After she had sexually trained him, Damon now had sex with Cat and Primeval only rarely, though he enjoyed it on those occasions immensely.

Cat knew he did. She still maintained her plethora of lovers. Hastings had tired of her quickly and was off with his other women. He said that she was just too *physical* for him.

▲ ▲ ▲

Damon and Cat arrived at the Coutances early Friday afternoon.

The weekend with the Brighton's was eventful. Michael and Sylvia loved Cat's transformed body. Sylvia teased Michael that the bulge in his pants was caused by it. He didn't deny it.

The two women took center stage everywhere they went. They both wore dramatic stage makeup. The paparazzi went crazy.

Cat wore a long soft platinum blond wig, her white micro-mini, two piece, cutout dress and gold contact lenses. She carried no purse and wore no jewelry. White stiletto heels showcased her legs to perfection. She had Sylvia lightly oil and wipe her body and it shone like polished gold under the night lights.

Sylvia wore the stunningly short blue green metallic dress that Damon had suggested. It complimented her glowing ivory skin and made her turquoise eye color jump out. When she turned a certain way it became almost transparent for a fraction of a second. As with Cat, she also wore nothing under it, skin glistening. Cat had lightly oiled and wiped her body also. Silver purse and stiletto heels, matching Cat's in height, finished her wardrobe.

They were both the same height, but as Cat was broad shouldered, seemingly slender and full busted, Sylvia was fuller figured with a huge chest. One with pale flawless skin, the other a deep, glowing, golden skinned.

The two of them together were an overpowering combination.

Crowds parted for them. Cameras flashed.

Michael was casual elegance at its finest, dressed in a soft smoky taupe Armani outfit.

Damon was in disguise. He wore a casual black suit and a soft black, high neckband, collarless shirt, with his black button cover and matching cufflinks and belt buckle. His soft black shoes had a soft sole. He sported a simple goatee and long sideburns. He wore his long silvery golden hair relaxed like a lion's mane. Tinted glasses and a black cane completed his disguise.

Late Saturday evening found them back at the Coutances sitting around the pool relaxing and having a nightcap.

Sylvia suggested they all go skinny dipping again, stripped in seconds and jumped into the pool. All three followed her in order of the amount of clothes they had to take off. Michael was the last. Afterwards they sat in the nude and finished their drinks.

Michael said to Damon, "You have done a lot of work on your body. You still look slim in clothes, but my god man, you look absolutely *massive* in the nude. Freaky almost, verging on alien. I have never seen anything like it. Can you coach me to get me to look like that?"

"I'm afraid not Michael. I went through a special process that I may never be able to repeat. I now think I had some help creating this body. When I altered Cat's body and your wife's, I altered mine as well, to what you see now. I find I can't remember exactly how I altered mine. I know *what* I did, just not *how* I did it. That is not normal for me. I have a photoneumonic memory. I should be able to remember *everything exactly* when I try. Sorry, Michael. I would be able to enhance you like I did with your wife, if you like."

"That's alright Damon. I may take you up on that at a later date, if that's alright with you?"

"Of course it is Michael."

Michael and Sylvia said nothing, at first, about the *jewels*, but they looked.

Damon ignored their looks. Sylvia finally said "Uh, Damon what is that?"

"What is *what*?"

"You know." She nodded at his crotch.

"Oh, you mean my *family jewels*?"

"Your what?" She looked startled.

Damon laughed and gave them the highlights about it.

"Can I touch it?" Sylvia asked excitedly.

Damon looked at Michael. Michael laughed.

"You've seen her video?"

Damon nodded. "You did a great acting job and makeup, Michael. Brilliant work."

Michael looked stunned. "How did you know it was me? Do you think anyone else will notice?" he asked anxiously.

"Not a chance. It was perfect. You changed everything about yourself beautifully, subtly. And your video editing skills are truly amazing. A masterpiece. Congratulations."

Cat looked startled. "You played all three parts *yourself?*" Michael nodded. Cat laughed. "That is absolutely priceless . A true work of genius."

"Thank you Cat. Please keep it to yourself?"

She nodded with a smile. "My lips are sealed. *Perfection.* Absolute *perfection.*" she said to herself.

Michael continued, "I don't mind anything she does Damon. I am a bit of a voyeur that way."

Damon nodded to Sylvia.

"Why, it's warm!" she exclaimed, "and it feels so real. How big can it get?"

"Really big!" Cat said, "He was a virgin before me. Let me show you how it works."

With that she proceeded to show Sylvia how to make it different sizes.

After a few minutes Damon said, "Alright girls. That's enough. You don't want to wear the batteries out do you?"

"Don't listen to him." Cat told Sylvia. "They are rechargeable. His body heat recharges them. And besides, I haven't been able to wear them out."

Damon and Michael laughed.

"Damon?"

"Yes Michael?"

"All of my wife's private parts seem to be standing at full attention. Had you noticed?"

"Yes, I had. I think it's time you took her to the guest bedroom." Damon advised seriously.

Michael and the girls laughed.

435

"I noticed that Cat has been looking at your rock hard member, sweetheart." Sylvia observed standing and closing in on her husband.

"Well, I was remembering that the last time he used that on me, when we were interrupted, the one we didn't finish, remember Michael?" said Catherine turning to Michael.

"Yes I do, Catherine. Vividly!"

Sylvia said to Cat, "You are the *only* one he's ever bragged about, Cat."

"Really? He bragged about me?"

Sylvia nodded.

"I love *your* enhancements, Cat." Michael said. "They are breathtaking."

"Thank you. I used your wife's augmentations as a model."

Sylvia turned to Damon as she put her hand around her husband.

"Damon, I like your *crown jewels*! They look so real. I'm glad that you can experience a woman now.

"*Crown Jewels?*" asked Damon.

"You *know* what I meant, *Mr. Smoke!*" Her voice was teasing to cover her error.

"Yes I do. You meant that they just got *promoted!*

Everybody laughed.

Scene One Hundred Three

"You will do all Smoke killings as Primeval. Change as you see fit."

"As you order, Commander." She was carrying the Smoke combat outfit, complete with new silver contact lenses.

It was a cloudless Monday night. They had returned that morning from the Coutances. Damon had watched the news on the flight back to Blackstone. There had been another terrorist bombing.

"You have the location coordinates and pictures of the target memorized?"

"Yes, Commander."

"Good. These are for you. Make sure you bring them back in the same condition."

Damon handed Cat a small leather case. She opened it. Inside were two safety razors. They were equal in length. One had a regular double blade and one had a smaller, shorter single blade. They were custom made with beautiful chrome engraved handles that had seen much use. Cat picked each of them up.

"They are very beautiful."

"My father made them." Damon replied. "If you are asked at customs, they were your poor deceased fathers. You use them both for different areas of your body."

She looked at them again, unscrewed the bottom handle cap off one and looked in. There was nothing inside the tube. She screwed the cap back on again.

"I don't understand, Commander."

"What you have in your hands, are two gun barrels with *identically rifled barrels*. Those are the barrels I put into the guns that I have secreted all over the world. When you have done the *smoke*, you will clean the guns thoroughly, replace the unused barrels and put them back where you got them, for the next time they are needed."

"Genius, pure unadulterated genius! So that is how the magic Smoke guns were transported. Or should I say gun. Everybody thinks it is just one gun because of the identical rifling. I will bring them back spotless, Commander."

"Bring back *all shells*. Each firing pin is like a fingerprint, also."

"Yes, Commander."

He pressed the intercom. "Are you ready Gunner?"

"Yes, Commander."

Turning back to her, he asked, "Any questions?"

"No, Commander."

"Then, good hunting, Misty Smoke."

Misty nodded.

"Call if you need me." He teased.

"In your dreams, Commander." She laughed.

▲ ▲ ▲

Scene One Hundred Four

"Cat doesn't know I have her powers. I hide them from her. I know she doesn't love me. She says she hates me, but she doesn't. She just hates that I'm not like her." Natasha told Damon as they ate hot dogs and drank soda pop. They were at a playground in the park and she was taking a break and sitting on the park bench.

"How can you see them Commander? Can anybody else?" She suddenly looked nervous, looking around.

"No, I don't think anybody can see them. You hide them well. Too well, I think. Like your aura. We'll have to work on your control, so you can show *just a little* and appear normal. What do you think of that?"

Natasha laughed delightedly.

"Why are you laughing? Did I say something funny?"

Natasha went very serious. She looked right into Damon's eyes.

"No Commander. I'm just happy. Everybody tells me what to do. You are the first grownup to ask me my opinion on something *important!* I think it would be a good idea. When should we start? Now?"

"No, you're having too much fun with your new friends. We'll start later. Go play."

"See!" she said, giggling as she jumped off the seat. "You didn't ask me. You *told* me." Skipping and running, she joined her waiting new friends.

▲ ▲ ▲

Later that night, as he tucked her into bed after telling her a Princess Natasha story, she said "Commander, when are we going to the other world?"

"That was just a story, Natasha. You know that don't you?"

"I'm not talking about the *Princess Natasha story.*"

"Then I don't understand the question. What other world?"

"The one in the triangle room."

There was silence for a moment. Damon was shocked.

"How do you know about the triangle room?" he asked softly.

"I just do."

"What else do you know? Will you tell me?"

"Of course I will, Commander. I'm not afraid to tell you *anything!*" She lowered her voice to a whisper. "You are the *only one* I trust *completely.*"

"Thank you." he whispered back, seriously.

"You're welcome."

"What else do you know?" he reminded her. She giggled.

"I'm sorry! ...... Well, I know you have to get two more things before we can go. I can see them even now. One is a *really black*, eye necklace. The other has three globes, one gold, one red and one silver, connected by a braided leather cord, a bolos like one of the men at the castle used to carry. They will help you find the doorway to where we are going. Oh, and you can't carry anything to find them. " She smiled up at him.

"Do you know where these things are?"

She nodded her little head vigorously. "One is behind the triangle lock. The other is hidden in the gold triangle cave somewhere. Only touching it will reveal it."

"Is that all?" he smiled back.

"I can't see them until I get real close to you, but I see your ring and your three triangle eyes. And sometimes, your *other two*. You're almost all blended together. That's all…. oh, no it isn't! I know two other things." She giggled.

"And what are those?"

"I know that all three of you love me. You don't have to tell me, I just know it."

"And the last thing?"

"Silly, you know."

"I do?"

"You don't?"

"No. I'm sorry, I don't."

Natasha sighed. "Then, I'll just have to tell you. I know *that I love you too*."

"Oh….. Yes, I should have known. I'm glad you know we love you. The reason that we haven't told you….."

"I know. It's for my protection. I told you, you didn't have to tell me." She turned to her doll, "Sometimes grownups, just, don't, listen." She whispered.

"Goodnight Natasha. Pleasant dreams."

"Goodnight Commander. If I don't tell you I love you, it is ……."

"For my protection. I know." He bent and gave her a kiss.

As he was leaving the room, he heard her whisper to her doll, "I'm going to marry him when I grow up. All three of him."

Damon smiled and closed the door.

▲ ▲ ▲

Scene One Hundred Five

A week later, Damon was standing at the lock in the triangle room. He had been there hours and still no luck. On a hunch he stripped. Nothing. He then went and got the adhesive remover and removed the crown jewels.

Bingo! When he placed his right hand in the middle of the opening holding the key and put his left in, he could reach behind the lock! He felt something round. He pulled. It took every ounce of his strength and over an hour to get it out. Once out, the resistance stopped immediately. He was not expecting it. He fell to the floor.

In his hand was a black ball about the size of a large marble. He estimated it was a little over an inch thick. Attached to it was a clear necklace. His right hand moved and Switch pulsed. He allowed Switch to take it from his left hand and place it over his head. The cord shrunk until the ball nestled in the hollow of his neck.

Damon walked back into the other cave and looked into the mirror. The black ball was gone. He reached up with his hand and felt the area. He could feel it, just under the skin.

He shrugged and proceeded nude to the gold triangle room. He sectioned off the room and proceeded to inspect everything with both hands.

On the third day he found it. He was about to call it quits for the day, when he had just finished inspecting a set of rattles and threw them aside. They bounced and he heard two distinctly different sounds as they rattled. He picked them back up. When he shook them separately they sounded identical. He knew. He had perfect pitch. He threw them separately on the pile where he had before and they sounded identical.

Finally he tapped them against each other. There was a difference. He smashed one on the ground. Nothing. He tried the other. Same results. He smashed them together mightily and they exploded into dust that vanished.

On the ground lay two miniatures bolos, each connected by a braided leather cord. Each had a small gold, silver and red ball attached.

He went to pick one up in each hand when Switch pulsed frantically. Instantly he jerked his hands away. He bent down and studied them closely. They looked identical.

'Well Switch, do you think you can pick the right one?' No answer.

He held Switch over one. He held it there for awhile and then she pulsed rapidly. He performed the same procedure with the second one. After a few moments she pulsed rapidly. He moved his hand away.

'How about now?' One pulse.

'Go for it girl.' Relaxing his hand he let it drift down. Switch reached for the one on the left.

His *black eye*, as Natasha called it, suddenly flashed a black beam on the two bolos.

The right one glowed in the black beam. Switch moved over quickly and picked up the right one by the silver stone. The left one disappeared as if it never was.

He held it up to his eyes and examined it closely. When he had finished he felt Switch tug. He let her take over. Slowly Switch started to move the bolos to his groin area.

She placed it at the base of his member where it joined his body, the ruby red ball hanging over one side and the gold hanging over the other. Switch laid the silver ball on the end of his member. The braided cord was just the right length. When he released the ball, he watched intently as it was absorbed quickly into his member. The red and gold balls were absorbed into his groin area where his testicle sack should have been.

He awaited further change. Nothing happened. He felt the area. Nothing. Mentally he shrugged, turned and left the room.

He got dressed, tucked the crown jewels into one of his jacket pockets and went to have dinner with Natasha and Hastings. He hadn't seen them in three days. They had been on a camping trip with one of Natasha's new friends. Hastings had accompanied her.

He had been gone a week himself, on business. Some corporate meetings he had to attend. That was why he was so long getting to *the items*.

When he entered the dining room, Natasha said immediately. "It looks pretty. Oh, it's gone now."

As he bent over to kiss her on the cheek, she exclaimed. "Oh good, I can still see it up close."

"How many new ones can you see, Natasha?"

"Just one on your neck. The black eye. Why, did you find the other?"

"Yes I did. It disappeared like magic. I'm not worried though. I'm sure it'll pop up eventually."

"Oh, that's okay. My dolly said I *probly* wouldn't be able to see that one till I hit *purity*, whatever that is. I don't think I want to hit *purity*. My dolly says it gets bloody once you hit it."

Damon burst into laughter. Natasha just looked at him.

"What is she talking about, Commander." asked Hastings.

Damon explained the two new items. He said he didn't want to say anything until he had them both.

Hastings couldn't see, but could feel the one in his neck.

He didn't ask to see the other area. "I believe you. I believe you." They both laughed.

▲ ▲ ▲

Damon cleaned off the crown jewels and was going to set it on the nightstand when he felt Switch tug at his hand. Again he allowed it. She went to put the crown jewels in place. Damon was going to pull his hand back and apply adhesive when he felt his pubic area bulge forward and stick to the jewels.

He automatically went to pull it off but it stuck as if he had used adhesive.

He looked closely. Damon could *not* see where the jewels left off and skin started. He concentrated on it coming off and pulled again. It popped off easily.

He placed it close again and it bulged forward to stick to it. He practiced a few more times and then went to bed wearing it. It obviously wanted it there.

In the morning Damon noticed that the jewels were substantially bigger. He went to pull off the jewels to wash it. He jumped as he touched it. He could feel it! He concentrated and pulled. It came off easily.

Once off, it went numb immediately. He slipped it back on. Immediate feeling with *extreme* sensitivity. With practice, he found that he could mentally control the length, thickness and hardness. He found he could still not orgasm or climax, but the sensation was pleasant.

He pulled it off and did some tests on the jewels. The entire molecular structure had been changed. It was much denser, thus heavier. The batteries in the testicles were gone, vanished. The testicle bulbs were still inside and felt real, but they were of an unknown molecular substance also. The inside was designed in a pattern that was alien to Damon. It seemed to collapse in on itself while maintaining its integrity.

The small samples he took evaporated within ten minutes of removal from the jewel. After he cut anything off the *jewels* to study, the *jewels* sealed and grew the piece removed *immediately*, with no scarring. He found that the *jewels* could feel pain also, but had a built in breaker switch when it got to a certain point.

In other words, if he was kicked in the crotch, he could still function at *peak*. He also found that it could get a lot smaller and shorter, or bigger and thicker, than the original. He could shrink it smaller than the limp size, down to his size without the jewels on. That was good. He could still satisfy Primeval.

He didn't try to find its peak. He found it unnecessary. If he took it off enlarged or shrunk, it immediately returned to its original size.

Damon put on the crown jewels and went down for supper. He had spent the entire day experimenting with and examining it.

▲ ▲ ▲

Scene One Hundred Six

Damon sat quietly, in the Blackstone library, after Cat had made her report and left to go out on the town to celebrate her entrance into the teens. Thirteen to be exact.

She had just finished her thirteenth Misty Smoke assignment. She had built quite a dossier on the EHE for Damon as well. He took quite an active part in gathering information on them, also, and combined it with her information, using 'Mac'.

In the six months that Cat had taken over as Misty Smoke, the news media were in their glory. Rumor had spread that many of the terrorist bombers had been brutally tortured by Mr. Smoke, before they were shot. Pictures of the terrorist assassins were sent to the news media, by Misty. The pictures now were usually of the face and upper body. Sometimes the head was turned, so that only half the face showed.

Police agencies around the world agreed that some of the bodies recovered had been tortured and mutilated. They did not confirm or deny that Mr. Smoke was the one responsible.

Terrorist bombings were at a record low. Terrorist organizations globally were in turmoil. Every one of them thought they had a mole in their midst. Blood flowed like a raging red river, trying to find him, or them.

The guards that Mr. and Misty Smoke had disarmed, when the two of them took over the castle, spread the rumor that Mr. Smoke single handedly had destroyed their organization.

Knowing that all their personal information was in the castle's computers, many assassins had retired and lived in terror under assumed names in various countries.

The balance of the Sword of Xandu assassins had been picked up by other organizations. Terrorist work was scarce, with their sudden influx into the open market place. Prices dropped drastically and wars were started between terrorist organizations.

Damon fed all terrorist information, not directly related to bombings, to Michael at A.T.C.U. Michael looked like a hero. He was their golden haired boy. Arrests and convictions from Damon's information mixed with theirs were at ninety nine percent. A few got off in the beginning, due to human error. That was corrected *fast*.

The A.T.C.U. became the global nucleus that other government agencies came to *quietly*, to ask for help on *their* fight against terrorism.

Damon roused from his reverie and called Michael on a secure line. He had more information to pass on. Not all information was passed electronically between the two of them. The sensitive and important information was passed directly, either by phone or in person.

They made a special effort to get together at least once a month. It was sometimes twice. Damon smiled as he placed the call. Michael and Sylvia were as close to him as Hastings and Natasha were. They had become part of his bizarre extended family, and he, theirs.

He remembered their get together, the next morning after the poolside Crown Jewel incident. The breakfast, the inane conversations about nothing. The comfortable closeness of true friendship. He smiled at the memory.

Damon pondered the situation. What should have been a strange relationship, *wasn't*. It felt normal. Maybe he was as crazy as

Catherine claimed he was. He mentally shrugged. What difference did it make? None.

He stopped pondering.

Life was too short to worry about the *good* things in life.

Michael answered the phone and they set up a time to get together.

They decided to meet at a restaurant in Paris, for dinner.

One of their favorites.

▲ ▲ ▲

Scene One Hundred Seven

I t was a rain shower night in Paris, France. There was a slight chill in the air.

The restaurant was the *Paris François*. Dinner was delicious, as usual. Cat was able to be there. Both Michael and Sylvia were happy to see her. She was always invited to their meetings, whether business or not, but she had only been able to make it a few times because of her schedule.

The women were the center of attention as usual. Sylvia was dressed in a pale pink outfit. Cat was Platinum haired and dressed in a black copy of her white cutout mini-dress.

Damon and Michael were always amazed at how well the two women got along. There was no rivalry between them at all.

Michael joked and said that it was because they were each a Goddess.

Sylvia was the Goddess of Love and Cat was the Goddess of Sex.

After dinner, Damon left to get their coats and Cat took that opportunity to go to the Ladies Room.

Almost immediately, a well dressed white couple walked into the room wearing unbuttoned, high fashion long raincoats and stylish rain hats. Both were dark haired and wearing heavy rimmed, tinted designer glasses. The man's open coat showed an expensive suit underneath and tasteful soft soled shoes. The woman wore a short dress with matching flat soled coordinating shoes.

They walked towards Michael and Sylvia's table laughing and talking to each other.

Ten feet away their hands darted into their overcoats and a sawed off pump action shotgun appeared in each of their hands. They fired six shots each into Michael and Sylvia within two seconds, then turned and fled the building.

Damon rushed back into the room to see the shooters across the room running out the doorway. His eyes took the scene in at a glance. Cat appeared almost at he same time.

Running to his friends, Damon called to Cat, "Get them, *but don't kill them.*"

Without answering Cat kicked off her shoes and ran after them.

Damon ran to the table before anyone had a chance to react. The top of Michaels head was missing and his body was riddled with gaping holes. Damon felt no pulse.

Sylvia had a weak pulse. He dropped to his knees, closed his eyes and laid his hands on her wounds to stop the bleeding.

As he was concentrating, he heard,

"Damon. Stop! Don't!" He opened his eyes to see Sylvia staring at him. She had rolled her head over to look at him and he saw that part of her face was missing.

She looked at him out of her one remaining eye.

"Relax, Syl." Damon said softly, "I will save you."

"Don't save me. Please don't! I couldn't bear to live this way. *Look at me* Damon."

He did. The damage was massive. Along with the destroyed left side of her face, her left arm was missing below the shoulder, along with the left breast and part of her left ribcage. Her right hip was mangled also.

"Damon." she said, calling his eyes back to her ruined face, "You need to let me go. I need to be with Michael. He is waiting for me. He ..."

A spasm of pain crossed her face. Damon quickly touched her neck and Sylvia's face cleared. He cradled her in his arms.

"As you wish, my queen." He answered quietly.

His eyes widened as her unblemished astral face replaced her damaged one.

Her two turquoise eyes glowed as she smiled her beautiful smile up at him.

"Thank you, pureheart. Michael is standing right beside you. He said to tell you he loves you like the brother he never had. I love you too. I know you know that. Carry our love with you forever ...."

Whatever else she was going to say, remained unsaid. Her face faded to be replaced with her ruined one.

She was gone.

Damon looked up and for a moment saw the two of them, standing whole in front of him, holding hands and smiling down at him. They waved and faded as they turned and walked away.

How long he sat there, he didn't know. The hysteria, screaming and hollering of the patrons faded into the background.

Damon felt a hand touch his shoulder. He looked up. The police and paramedics were there.

"Monsieur? Monsieur? Are you alright? Can you understand me?" a policeman said in French.

Damon rose smoothly to his feet. *"I am fine."* He answered in perfect French.

He answered their questions. He couldn't tell them much. He told them what he had seen. He produced his identification as Bernie Hoggins, American businessman.

When questioned about the Platinum haired Cat, he said that Michael and Sylvia had arranged the date for the evening. Her name was Felix, he had been told. She was a friend of theirs. He assumed that she either fled in terror or ran to get the killers vehicle license number. Because she hadn't returned, he told them that it was probably the former.

As they were questioning him, his identification was being checked out. It did. A married international pharmaceutical rep on a business trip. He told the inspector that he and Sylvia were an item in college and they had maintained the friendship ever since.

Satisfied, he was asked to sign their statement. If there were any further questions they would contact him.

As the four of them had come in the Brighton's car, Damon accepted a lift in a police car to his car at the Coutances, after he had gone to the bathroom and washed off the majority of the blood on his clothes.

As he was leaving the building, he reached down and scooped up Cats black shoes.

When they arrived at Coutances, the police officer offered to let him inform the staff. He accepted. The police officer sat in the police car as Damon approached and knocked on the door. He left immediately after he saw that Napoleon recognized Mr. Hoggins, smiled and allowed him to enter.

Damon was the one that explained to Napoleon what had happened. Napoleon went into shock and fainted. Damon caught him and carried Napoleon to his bedroom. He placed his hands on him and put Napoleon into a healing sleep.

He then went directly to his room. Cat was sitting on his bed naked, lotus position. Gone was her wig and contacts. Tossing her shoes on top of her folded dress on the end of the bed, Damon walked over to the wooden valet and started to unbutton and remove his clothes and hang them on it.

As he stripped down to his shorts, he said to Cat in a soft voice, "Report."

"I reverted to Primeval as soon as I left the restaurant, Commander. I followed the fleeing couple, a young man and woman, to a parking garage. When I saw the car they were about to get into, I attacked. I stuffed them into the trunk and took them to a safe place I know and secured them. I await your orders on what to do with them."

"Find out everything you can." He paused in what he was doing and looked into her eyes.

Cat shivered slightly as she looked into them. She was looking into the eyes of one insane, the eyes of chaos and madness. One eye was a swirling blood red. The other was a liquid Golden swirling Cats eye. They changed in random patterns, back and forth with his soul chilling liquid silver eyes.

She was mesmerized.

He looked away.

He continued undressing, and in short chilling sentences, enunciating every word, finished with, "Who they are. Who they work for. Why they did what they did. And anything else that you think will be of importance. Take your time, Misty. Get all the information you can. Record everything. Delete nothing. Report back to me at Blackstone. Hastings will pick you up, whenever and wherever you want."

"As you order, Commander." Catherine arose in one fluid motion and slipped on her dress and shoes.

He laid on the bed and stared at the ceiling as she silently left the room. She noted in passing that all his muscles were twisting and writhing like snakes on his body. Tears tainted with blood coursed a brilliant scarlet down the sides of his head. His calm face seemed unaware of any of it.

When the door closed, Cat, with her increased sensitivity, heard and felt the bed shake as Damon convulsed silently in agony and blood red tears.

She stood for a moment listening. Shaking her head in wonder, she turned and walked to her room to change.

'What kind of man or demon am I working for?' she thought to herself, not understanding.

She mentally shrugged. *'What the hell, why should I give a shit? He's just a whole lot crazier than I am, that's all! And I knew that when I first touched him!'*

Satisfied with her answer, she showered, changed into her work clothes and Misty Smoke left the Coutances unobserved.

▲ ▲ ▲

Scene One Hundred Eight

Primeval had returned to Blackstone one week after the death of Michael and Sylvia. She had complete information on all the questions Damon had asked and more.

Leroy and Caitlin Housteader were a wealth of information. It was to be Leroy's first and last job before he took over the reins of power from his aged uncle, William Housteader, head of the EHE organization.

It was a *Trial by Fire*, a ritual that had been perpetuated since its inception, long lost in the forgotten past. Every Head and spouse of the EHE had to have killed at least one EH before they could achieve the Head position. Leroy and Caitlin had not. Everything had been planned down to the tiniest detail, to ensure a successful mission and transfer of leadership.

After the extermination of the target EH and her spouse, Leroy and his wife were to leave the parking lot and drive left for five blocks where a white van was parked with ramp down to take their car inside and whisk them off to safety.

Cat had turned right and made an immediate left and vanished before any of the EHE observers could react. They must have thought she was Caitlin.

They couldn't see what happened in the enclosed parking lot and didn't see *Primeval* enter the building, render them unconscious, strip off and put on Caitlin's coat, glasses and hat and stuff Leroy and Caitlin into the trunk.

Cat's natural hair color was similar to Caitlin's. She had pulled off her Platinum wig when she left the restaurant and stuffed it in Caitlin's coat pocket before she stuffed them into the trunk and left the parking lot. She had spotted the lookouts.

A little luck and her instinct had sent her right instead of left.

One long unbearable week had passed for the unlucky couple. They had been broken by the second day and by the end of the week were begging and whispering for the final release. They could no longer scream.

Cat had done her job to perfection. Damon reviewed the recordings and could find no fault with them. She had done a better job than he could have. He told her that. She enjoyed and appreciated the compliment.

He found out that Sylvia was a confirmed EH, by the EHE (Enhanced Human Exterminators). Her parents were confirmed EH's also.

The boating accident that killed her parents, and almost her, was not an accident. It was orchestrated by the EHE. Through an error in the small town newspaper reporting that all were killed, Sylvia was presumed dead also.

The retraction a week later was never noted. She came to their notice after her sex scandal and notoriety. Upon investigation she was discovered to be the daughter thought drowned so many years previously.

The newspaper retraction was found. Sylvia and her husband Michael, were to be Leroy's and Caitlin's *Rite of Passage* into the leadership position as the Head of EHE. The EHE, upon further investigation concluded that she was not known in the EH community and would pose no serious threat to exterminate.

Her husband was a rich ex-playboy, Lord of the Realm, who did nothing of value in the world. He would not be missed either.

They could not have foreseen the intervention of Damon and Cat in their calculations. After the disappearance of Leroy and his wife, their sources came up cold on the couple accompanying them at dinner. They didn't exist!

The police reports were missing and their names were not on any record anywhere. Even the Reporting Officer's report book was found to be missing the pages of the incident.

▲ ▲ ▲

Damon now had every name of every member of the famous EHE *Two Hundred*. He told Cat that, much as he would like to, he would not go against any of them. Like the terrorist bombers, he would only kill the killers, that killed in the future.

He instructed Cat to bag up the various parts of Leroy and Caitlin into two hundred and one baggies.

He had them packaged and hand delivered to William Housteader and the Two Hundred at their homes, with their full names and addresses written on them. Inside was a note as to *who* and *what* was in the baggie and that if any one of the *Two Hundred* ordered or killed one more EH, they, along with all their families would be exterminated by the *highly secret EH Ghost Assassins Guild*.

All the names of their immediate families were included along with their addresses. They were told their families would die first and the Two Hundred last. The note finished by telling them to disband at their next meeting.

The note also had a *p.s.* that some of *them* were *EH!*

He signed them,

Ghost Assassin

▲ ▲ ▲

Scene One Hundred Nine

William Housteader sat on his throne as Head of Operations for the EHE.

All the Two Hundred were there.

There was absolute silence in the room.

William spoke. "As you are all aware, the parcel you got, was a part of my nephew and his wife."

His powerful voice carried to the back of the room. Time had not been kind to the Head of the EHE Organization. The price of power had extracted its payment in full.

William's body was ravaged by age, but his voice still maintained its power. The sound system enhanced it.

"Last night I received a visitor. The *Ghost Assassin* himself!" he paused dramatically.

There was a collective gasp and a murmur swelled in the room. It was instantly quelled by his voice.

"Yes, the *Ghost Assassin*. He somehow managed to walk through the finest security system in the world and into my bedroom and wake me out of a sound sleep." He laughed heartily.

"And God Damn It, it pissed me off. At my age, I need all the rest I can get!"

A few of the Two Hundred chuckled with him.

"Then the skinny little twerp had the gall to tell me that *EH's* are the same as you and I. He said that they were *through* being hunted and killed, for being born *gifted*." He spat the word *gifted*. He paused and glared out at the Two Hundred. They sat spellbound.

"*Now that really pissed me off!* I told him that they weren't being *killed*, they were being *exterminated* for the good of humanity. I told him that he and all EH's were soulless devils from the deepest darkest corners of hell and that he couldn't scare me...."

"I was wrong!" He paused again for effect. The Two hundred were hanging on every word.

"I am a God fearing man, you all know that! I thought that nothing could scare me anymore." Nodding his head he repeated softly. "I .. was .. wrong. When I told him that he and all EH's were soulless devils from the deepest darkest corners of Hell, the son of a bitch had the nerve to say, '*No, not all. Just me, maybe.*' Then he proceeded to confirm my statement. He took off his ninja glasses and two inhuman eyes stared down at me. One was a blood red swirling orb and the other was a liquid golden cat's eye." William shook his ancient head at the memory.

"I have to admit that it scared the hell out of me. Literally. I messed the bed!"

Again a few laughed.

"It wasn't funny!" William thundered. An awkward silence descended. He continued after a moment.

"Anyway, I rallied and said that he had just proven my point. I won't go into the whole discussion. I will just say that he restated the note that he had sent all of us. I told him to *shove it up his ass*. He couldn't hurt me any more than he had already done when he killed my nephew and his wife. They were the last surviving members of my family. Leroy was to succeed me as Head of Operations. You *Top Ten* know that. You voted your approval on it. Thank you for that. My wife died two years ago. I told the *Ghost Assassin* that he could not scare or hurt me any more. The little prick had the nerve to *laugh* and then *told* me to tell you what happened. *He ordered me!" The last he roared* as he glared out over the *Two Hundred.*

Then his head sunk in memory of his shame.

"The little prick," he muttered again, "I told him that I would. I told him it wouldn't cause the Two Hundred to turn tail and run away, scared. We have been an institution since before recorded history. The EHE Organization is *eternal.* He could kill a few of us but we would get him and his organization eventually. We are survivors!" His voice rose in volume.

"We are *eternal!*" He voice rose again,

"We are the EHE! *We are Human!*" the last was a scream, like the screeching voice of an insane woman.

His voice had failed him at the last. Silence permeated the room.

He cleared his throat and looked out at the Two Hundred. He had expected a different reaction. He chuckled. His voice was back.

"I invited him here to say the same thing to you tonight, but I guess he couldn't make it." That caused a reaction.

"What the *hell* did you do that for, William?" asked a voice in the front row.

The Head of Operations looked down and saw the speaker.

"Because, *Eric,* he can't get in here. We not only have the most sophisticated security system in the world, I also took the liberty of staffing the place with the world's finest professional Assassins. The best that money can buy. We don't bow down to threats, Eric. We never have."

"Yes, that's true William." Eric Truant responded, standing up. "In the *past* we never have. In the *past* we were *invincible.* And you also know *why.* In the *past* we were *invisible.* Nobody knew who we were! Oh, a few were known and were killed, but they didn't know the whole Two Hundred. None of us do, but you William, and your Top Ten. We only know our Head, which is you, William, and our immediate cell leader. That is the way it has always been. *Now,* we are *all* known. Every goddamned one of us and our families! We are not invincible or invisible any longer William. If one of us *kills* or orders an EH *murdered*, all of our families will be brutally murdered. You've already killed off your son and wife and your nephew and wife are dead. You really have nothing to lose William except your life, and you've lived a long *rich* one. Not so with a lot of us. I for one am walking away."

"They were not *killed or murdered*. They were *hunted* down and *exterminated!* Like insects. Like an infection. We keep our race pure!" he roared. He stopped and looked down at Eric.

"You know the penalty for leaving the Brotherhood, don't you Eric?" William finished softly, his eyes glittering with the insanity of a fanatic.

"Yes I do, William. I've thought about it, a lot, since I got the package. To leave is death. I can accept that. I knew that when I took the Oath of Allegiance. What I *can't* accept is my *whole family's death*. *EH's* have a lot of valid reasons to wipe out every one of us and our entire family. I don't blame theme them. I would, if I were in their shoes. I researched EH's in history. You *do know* what I found out, don't you, William? Except for the Spanish Inquisition, which *was* a sick, historical *joke*, mostly written by confirmed liars and murderers, I couldn't find anything against them. Don't you find that a little odd, William?"

The Two Hundred murmured approvingly.

"That's because of us!" William Housteader thundered. "We have been the cleansing sword and spear! We have kept the balance. The race pure!"

Eric shook his head sadly. "This is not the sixteenth century William. We all have computers. We are intelligent people. Don't try to feed us that line of *horseshit!*

"God damn it, William, you make me sick to my stomach! Hell, *I make myself sick to my stomach,* when I realize what we have done! What *I* have done. I and everyone else in this room joined the EHE Organization because it is one of the richest and most powerful organizations in the world. Our forefathers started it. We have all become stinking rich. That's why we joined. If we had to *kill or murder*, not *exterminate* William, *kill and murder* the occasional *gifted* innocent and their families, so be it. We would swallow the *racial purity bullshit* and smile. We were invisible. We were invincible! We are not *invisible* anymore! And we sure the *fuck* aren't *invincible* anymore either, as these body parts in baggies affirm. *Fuck you and fuck this fucking EHE Organization. I quit!*"

The Two Hundred all started talking at once.

"Arrest that man!" William shouted over the roar. Two Sergeants at Arms walked up and grabbed Eric Truant.

He did not struggle.

▲ ▲ ▲

"Could I have your attention please? Everyone please stay seated." A deep, melodious ghostly voice said over the intercom.

"Will the two gentlemen holding Eric Truant, please let him go. You have to the count of three. One...."

"It's him!" screamed William. "I know that voice. It's the Ghost Assassin!"

"Two."

"Hold that man. Somebody find him and kill him!"

"Three."

The two Sergeants at Arms heads snapped back and they fell to the floor, blood and brains leaking from their foreheads.

"Everyone stay seated!" the voice commanded sharply . "Whoever stands, dies immediately!"

Nobody stood. "Please have a seat Eric."

Eric sat.

"Ninjas," screamed William, "find him! Kill him!" No answer.

"I'm sorry William, but all twelve of your *worlds finest Assassins* are sleeping. The *final sleep*, that is."

There was a pause for effect. It worked. Silence reigned supreme.

"What William Housteader said about my visit last night was true. I was human once. I am not anymore. Anyone who wants to leave the organization, may leave now. Anyone who wants to stay can stay. The ones that go will be free of our wrath, unless they start hunting us again. The ones who stay will be killed, and all their family will be killed. I have EH's at all of your houses and hideaways, right now. Once I give the word they will be killed. And just to let you know that I am serious I will mention some. Someone in the middle stand up."

A man in the center of the room stood.

"Your family is at a small farm in Bolivia, in the mountains. It is a five bedroom ranch style home. Am I correct?"

"Yes." The quivering voice acknowledged.

"Sit down. Anybody else want to test me?"

Another man rose. A big man. An angry man. He was glaring all around.

"Your Mistress Brigitte is in Bordeaux, France, with her cousin Fernando. One oh five Frothier. Your wife Danielle and your two children Frankie junior and Isabelle are in North Dakota, in the Blue Moon Hotel under the name Swenson. Shall I mention where your two brothers and four sisters are?"

The big angry man was not angry any more. He was a big scared man. He sat down without being told.

"Anybody else? Good. I would like to start with the first row." the eerie voice continued.

"I want everyone who wants to leave, to stand one at a time, speak loudly and clearly, so all can hear and renounce their Pledge of Allegiance to William Housteader, Head of Operations *and the EHE* and leave quickly. No visiting or speaking. The penalty is *death*."

One by one they rose and renounced their Allegiance and left.

At last only William Housteader was left. He sat stunned.

"What is *your* choice, *bedshitter*?" came the ghostly voice.

William's face flushed. He pulled out two automatic guns that he had been hiding under his robes looking around wildly and waiving them.

"May the Almighty God *damn you to the hottest corner of hell*, Demon. Come out and fight me like a man dammit!" he roared.

"Why should I? Did you ever give a *gifted* person a fair chance?"

"You're a coward, Demon. All hell spawn are. I will rebuild the Two Hundred even bigger and stronger and more loyal. Men with vision. My vision. To keep the human race pure! Maintain the racial purity!"

William stopped surprised. Both of his guns tore out of his hands and hit the floor all bent and twisted. He realized that they had been shot out of his hands. He was exposed!

A *calm* settled over him. He sat very still and waited for the bullet. Instead he saw a puff of smoke in the middle of the room and the Ghost Assassin emerged and walked towards him.

Housteader watched mesmerized as he approached the blood red dais. The Ghost Assassin vaulted from the floor to stand in front of him.

William knew that no human could do that.

"So, you've come to face me, have you Demon? Do you feel brave, killing an unarmed old man?"

Damon chuckled. William frowned. His calm was cracking.

The Ghost Assassin answered. "Would *you*, William? I think you have. I guess I could, if you'd like me to. Would you like me to feel brave, William Housteader?"

"Go back to hell, Demon. You'll get no begging from me."

"Really?" The Ghost said "We'll see. And I am not a demon. I am a Damon!" With that he pulled his hood off.

"Damon Gray to be precise. You knew my parents and grandparents."

William's eyes bulged. "You are EH? Nooooo!" he closed his eyes and moaned.

Opening them, his eyes had the look of insane madness. His voices hissed, "I killed my *only son and his wife* because he killed your parents and grandparents without proof of EH status."

He started screaming and jumped at Damon.

"You made me kill my only son!" he raged as he tried to attack Damon. "My wife never talked to me after that! *She never spoke to me again!*"

Mr. Smoke *took over* and held the old man captive. William froze as Garnet and Golden appeared in his eyes.

"So …." Mr. Smoke said, laughing very softly. William wet his pants at the laugh. "I *was* right. Your people *did* kill all of my family."

Turning his head he called out, "Misty, I have a job for you."

Another puff of Smoke and Misty appeared beside him.

"You called, Commander?"

"Take him and find out all his information. Take your time. William said we couldn't make him beg. Oh, I forgot to make the introductions. Misty Smoke, meet William Housteader, former Head of Operations for EHE."

Misty took off her hood and smiled at William. She then bound him securely.

Damon replaced his hood and walked away.

"Come back and kill me you coward!" William screamed in fear. Misty Smoke scared him far more that Damon.

Misty Smoke. Where had he heard that name?

▲ ▲ ▲

Scene One Hundred Ten

Four months had gone by since the highly publicized deaths of Michael and Sylvia Brighton. The news media had finally let them rest in peace.

The killers had never been apprehended. Bernie Hoggins, American businessman was unreachable and unavailable for comment, sans the blonde *mystery friend* of Sylvia's also.

Without them, the stories withered and died.

Michael and Sylvia's bodies were flown in secretly and it was a closed caskets funeral.

Damon, Cat, Natasha and Hastings attended. No cameras or media were allowed. Only close personal friends and family were invited and admitted.

Michael's parents respected Damon's wishes that they remain anonymous and off all guest lists. Michael's mother was admitted to a sanitarium shortly after the funeral. She suffered a complete nervous breakdown.

She was released after a few months.

In their wills, if they died separately, the surviving spouse would inherit all. Michael and Sylvia had left all their property and personal belongings to the Brighton estate, namely Michael's parents, with the exception of the Coutances and contents. It was to be quietly offered, by the family's barrister and executor of their estate, to Damon Gray for the same price as they had paid for it.

To avoid contest in the matter, it was stipulated in the wills that *if* the sale was publicized or contested in any way, the terms of the will would change and all of Michael and Sylvia's possessions would be auctioned off and the money divided evenly and given to the stipulated charities of their choice.

Damon purchased it. The money was wired into Michael Brighton's parents coffers within hours of the sale. Michael's father contacted Damon after the sale and said that their son and his wife did not have to put those conditions in the will. He and his wife would gladly have acquiesced to their wishes with no hesitation or argument.

Damon said he was unaware of the conditions and thanked him for the call. He offered to pay a current appraisal price, but Michael's father said that they would have none of it, that they cared nothing for the estate. It was Michael and Sylvia's love nest, not theirs. He also thanked Damon for purchasing it. It saved him a lot of headaches. No matter what the appraisal price, they would have taken any offer to get rid of it. It would not be an easy property to market, as Michael had told them when his mother asked when and if they might sell it. She was nervous about them living in another country, even part time, and prophetically so, it proved to be.

He finished by saying that Damon was welcome anytime.

Napoleon and staff were delighted that Damon had purchased the Coutances.

Damon went there often, as it reminded him of Michael and Sylvia. He would walk for hours throughout the estate soaking in their presence.

Natasha loved it also. It was her magical kingdom.

▲ ▲ ▲

Scene One Hundred Eleven

"That was a *great* Princess Natasha story, Commander. Thank you very much. My dollies and I really liked it."

"You're welcome Princess Natasha. I'm really glad you liked it. Now, if it's alright with you, I'd like to talk to you about some things." Damon replied.

"Absolutely!" the Princess piped. Damon smiled at the big word she used. He sat on the edge of Natasha's bed for a few minutes, lost in thought. Finally he looked at Natasha and put his right hand over hers. Natasha looked at Damon very seriously and started playing idly with Switch, even though Switch was under his skin.

"I have to tell you and ask you some things and I'm not sure where to start. I guess the first place to start is with Michael and Sylvia. I know that you liked them a lot, didn't you?"

"Yes I did and I still do." Natasha said very seriously. "I know that they are very happy together. I talked to them at the funeral. They asked me not to tell you, until now."

Damon looked at her questioningly. "Until now?"

"Yes Commander. They are in the room now. Sylvia laughed really hard at your Princess Natasha story. She said you should write children's books."

"Why can't I see or hear them, Natasha?" Damon asked seriously.

"Michael said it may be because you are not naturally gifted that way. I am. I see *lots* of spirits. You saw them together when Sylvia passed over, didn't you? At least that's what Sylvia said. She said *she thought* she saw you see them."

"Yes I did. But then they turned and faded away."

"Michael says that *you* didn't see them, Golden did. They can see the three of you now. At first they were afraid for you, but I explained Golden and Garnet to them. Michael said to try to see them through Golden's eyes. Can you try that Commander?"

"Yes I can, Natasha." Damon was bringing forth Golden even as he spoke. He smiled as he looked at Michael and Sylvia through liquid golden cat eyes."

"Why are you wearing different clothes Sylvia?" Damon asked.

Sylvia's lips moved.

"I can't hear you Sylvia."

Sylvia smiled and nodded.

Both Sylvia and Michael reached out and touched Damon at the same time. He could feel their touch! Light feather weight touches. Something passed between the three of them. Switch pulsed softly.

Sylvia spoke again.

"Just because I'm a ghost doesn't mean I can't look good, does it? Do you like it, Damon?" Sylvia said turning and modeling her iridescent white micro mini skirt.

"You look beautiful Sylvia. Why haven't you two passed on?"

"I think it had something to do with your trying to heal Sylvia, old chum." said Michael. "It seemed to create a bond between us. Not that we're complaining. We are in no rush to go to the great beyond. It will always be there. We're not sure how long we will be here, but we are going to enjoy it while we can. Right darling?"

"Right, as always, my love." Sylvia acknowledged. She turned to Damon. "I had a dream about you Damon. It turns out it was right. Wasn't it, dear?" she looked at Michael.

"Yes it was darling. Yes it was."

"I didn't know that spirits could dream." Damon said.

"When I was *alive*, silly." Sylvia said as if it was *obvious* what she meant. All four laughed.

When the laughter had died down, Damon looked at the three of them. Michael, Sylvia and Natasha. His face took on a serious look. All three voices came out of his mouth at the same time.

"We have some things to discuss and it *now* concerns *all of us* ......"

▲ ▲ ▲

Scene One Hundred Twelve

Damon Gray looked down at the naked golden body lying beside him. Cat was sleeping peacefully. Her body aura glowed with peaceful satisfaction. She was happy. She had just returned from a Smoke mission. After the debriefing, they had wild sex and fell asleep together. It had been a long time since Damon had been with her. He had been awake for awhile, going over things in his minds.

Damon noticed a change in Catherine.

Her breathing remained the same but her aura changed slightly. Damon knew she was awake. Cat opened her eyes and looked at him. She smiled. He smiled back. She touched him. She stopped smiling.

"When are you going?"

"Today." He said quietly.

"You found the right Gateway?"

"I found it a week ago."

"Then why wait till now?" she asked puzzled.

He just looked at her.

"Well?" she asked again.

Nothing.

"Shit, is it a secret or something?" Cat asked exasperatedly.

Damon finally spoke, "You *really* don't know, Catherine?"

"Shit, shit, shit! Either answer the question or tell me you won't. *Shit!*"

"I'm sorry, Cat. I really thought you knew. I didn't go because you hadn't gotten back from your current Misty Smoke assignment."

Cat looked stunned. "What the hell does that mean, Commander? I've got a ton of Misty Smoke assignments to do. You could be gone for years before you'd need to come back and give me some more. What am I missing here?"

"Natasha and I have talked. She asked me once, when were we going to the other world? I told her yesterday that it would have to be when she grew up. She is too young to go now. She knew I was telling her with honesty. I told her that I was bringing in special teachers for her. EH teachers that can teach her to use and bring her *talents, abilities and gifts* to their fullest potential. She doesn't mind at all. As a matter of fact she is very excited about it. She can still see her new friends at the park, both at Blackstone and Coutances. She will be alternating between the two of them, for security purposes. I also told her that I would be back and forth and that I would see her a lot. She was okay with that also. She said that it was how it was *meant to be*. How it *should be*. She said that *time* flows differently where I'm going. *One* of her abilities, I *feel*, is that she has the gift of *far seeing*."

Cat's eyes opened wider.

"She's like me?" she whispered.

"No, Cat, not like you. No one is like you. You are unique. She is very different from you."

Cat touched him. He was being truthful. She sighed and smiled. "At least she's gifted. I don't hate her anymore. That's good." She frowned.

"That's the reason you didn't go? You wanted to tell me about Natasha?"

"No, Cat. I *was* going to leave Hastings to run the empire while I'm gone. He would have none of it. He still feels he has to protect me, even though he says I feel like a steel statue when I stand still. When I mentioned the Gray Global business empire, he mentioned a woman that is running a number of my Corporations. A woman he says he trusts, even though he thinks she likes women, instead of men. He's right. But it also means she feels she has a lot to prove. I've seen her aura. It is a good one. I trust her.

"Hastings says she could protect my business empire until I return. I agree. I know she will. I have it all set up. Hastings had me make some improvements to his body. I did as he asked. He is happy with them."

Cat just looked at him in frustration, still not understanding.

"Speak clearly, Commander. Assume nothing."

"I waited till you came back to see if you wanted to go to the other world, Cat. With me. With Hastings and I. Do you want to?"

"I will not go *anywhere* with Hastings! You are asking if I want to go to a strange world that I have no knowledge of, to face dangers that I don't know anything about, to risk my life for no reason? With you?"

"Yes."

Her eyes got that wild crazy look in them.

"Why do you ask me? Why do ….." she changed to Primeval.

"Cat and Primeval, you *will* come with *me* to the new world."

The fire died in her eyes. She changed back.

"As you order, Commander."

Then Cat smiled at him. "Maybe Primeval will be the beautiful one there. Do I have time to pick up some new makeup before we go, Commander? Will the Crown Jewels function there?"

Damon laughed. "You *do* think about covering all your basic needs don't you?"

▲ ▲ ▲

The End for Now!
Thank you for reading it.
I hope you had as much fun reading it, as I had writing it.
(r.p.w.)

A Sneak Preview of

Gotcha

by Robert Preston Walker

"**D**ammit!"

"Daddy!" Piped up his shocked seven year old daughter from the back seat of their Landrover. "You shouldn't say that word. Mommy gave me heck when I said it. Remember mommy?" Her mother smiled and nodded.

"Sorry Angel. We're running *late* and daddy *almost* forgot some important papers in my office that I *have* to take to the College *today*," apologized Brandon Thomas, Angels father. Turning to his wife, he added, "Char, why don't you back the car out of the garage while I run in and get the files that I need. We're late enough as it is. I'll lock up and meet you out in front, okay?"

"Sure thing, darling. Scurry away." Charlene smiled with love at her husband and waved her slender hand at him as if she was shooing him away. He smiled and threw her a kiss as he darted away. She knew how compulsive he was about being on time. And they were late for an important meeting. A meeting with Q, and *they* didn't tolerate or react well to tardiness either. She finished seat belting their daughter and then got in the driver's side and punched the remote to open the garage door. Once it was fully opened she turned the key to start the car.

▲ ▲ ▲

Brandon was in his home office, located behind the laundry room which was directly behind the Garage. He was behind his steel desk picking up his brief case with the papers that he needed so desperately. They were his students test results. They needed to be in today for them to get their passing grade. He was bent over the open case to make sure that the papers were there. He closed the case.

At that instant his wife turned the key in the ignition.

The car bomb attached to the Landrover exploded.

The garage acted as a gun barrel, shooting the twisted Landrover out to land in the middle of the street. The blast vaporized the walls connecting the laundry room and the office, driving the washer and dryer into the metal desk and into Brandon.

▲ ▲ ▲

Brandon awoke to find himself coughing, with white everywhere. It got into his eyes. He blinked. It was the dust and drywall dust from the explosion from the blast. He must have been knocked senseless for a few moments. He staggered to his feet and stood stunned at the sight of the front of his house blown away. He saw his vehicle in the middle of the street. An agonized groan escaped from him as he staggered over the rubble and ran to the twisted wreckage. No one had come out of their homes. They were either at work or terrified. He looked into the front seat. Parts of his wife were splattered everywhere, but miraculously, her head and face were untouched. Her head and neck looked at him from the passenger seat with an innocent surprised look. She looked like she was going to speak to him. He waited. Then he shook his head and looked with dread in the back seat.

His daughter, Angelina Thomas, was limp in her car seat. She was covered in blood. Whether her mothers or hers or both, Brandon could not tell. She did not look to be breathing.

Brandon heard a soft whistle in the background. He turned around. Four Police cars and two ambulances had arrived with lights flashing and sirens blaring. He felt a tap on his shoulder. He turned to find a paramedic talking to him. He shook his head violently. His hearing returned. The noise was deafening. He covered his ears with both hands.

"Turn off those bloody sirens!" somebody ordered. He allowed himself to be lead away by the paramedic to a waiting medical vehicle. The sirens were turned off. Silence reigned as the paramedics checked him out.

"You are in bad shape Mr. Thomas" Said the young man that had brought him to be checked. "We need to get you to a hospital immediately. Please get in the ambulance."

"What is your name, son?" Brandon asked.

"Al, sir." Came the surprised respectful response.

"Well, *Al*, we are not going anywhere until I find out about my daughter." Brandon stood up and walked over to the vehicle just as the medical emergency unit personnel removed the child from the back shattered window and placed her limp form on a stretcher. They gently strapped her down and proceeded to put her in the nearest ambulance.

Brandon touched his Angels arm. It was still warm. He could see her little chest rising and falling slowly, almost imperceptibly.

One of the rescuers smiled at him. A young woman. She touched his arm and spoke.

"She is *alive* sir, but only *just*. We have no time to spare. We need to get her to surgery stat!" Brandon nodded. Two paramedics lifted rolled the stretcher into the ambulance.

A police officer stepped up to Brandon. "We need to get a statement from you sir."

Ignoring him, Brandon stepped forward and said to the paramedic. "I'm going with her."

The police officer said politely yet firmly. "I'm sorry sir but we need to get a statement from you now. You can follow in the other ambulance shortly. There is nothing you can do now anyway."

Continuing to ignore him, Brandon stepped toward the ambulance. The police officer grabbed his arm.

Brandon looked down at the hand on his arm and then up at the young police officer. "Let go of my arm, youngster. I'm going with my daughter. You can take my statement at the hospital."

"I don't think so, *Mister Thomas*." said the *youngster* grimly. "I need help over here!" he called to his fellow officers. Three other officers that were close by came running over to lend a hand. The one holding Brandon produced a set of handcuffs. The four converged on Brandon. Within two seconds all four officers were unconscious on the ground. The one who had been holding him was handcuffed with his hands behind his back.

Brandon Thomas looked out at the remaining four police officers. "I am going with my daughter. I will give you a statement at the hospital. Is that understood?"

"Yes sir!" said all four officers at the same time. None of them reached for their guns. They saw the look in Brandon's eyes. Contrary to popular fiction, these were *not* stupid policemen. Not one of them was going to mess with a deranged father who could render four veteran police officers unconscious in less than two seconds.

Brandon stepped into the ambulance and closed the doors behind himself. The ambulance raced off, sirens again blaring.

Brandon sat beside his terribly injured daughter, holding her hand. For a long time he just stared at her, then he squeezed her hand lightly and closed his eyes.

"Hang on in there Angelina." he whispered to her, putting all his love in his plea. He opened his eyes and looked down at the peaceful face of his daughter. Suddenly his breath caught in his chest.

Angel opened her eyes and smiled up at her father through the clear plastic oxygen mask. "Mommy says to tell you she has always loved *only you* since she first met you. She said she would be around as long as you needed her."

"I love you, Angel." He leaned forward and whispered.

"I know, Dadd..." She closed her dark blue eyes. Brandon wiped her black curly hair off her pale alabaster child's face.

4

"Please don't leave me, my little Angel. I couldn't bear to lose both of you." Brandon whispered to his unconscious daughter. "I really couldn't." Angel didn't respond.

The two paramedics looked at each other. (That was the strangest conversation that they had ever witnessed. They talked about it later. The little girl shouldn't have been able to talk at all, with all the damage to her chest and lungs.)

Brandon sat holding his daughters hand while the ambulance raced through the streets and had flashback after flashback.

▲ ▲ ▲

Printed in the United States
131487LV00003B/16-57/P